BELFAST SONG

Belfast Song

Mary Marken

Copyright © 2024 Mary Marken

The moral right of the author has been asserted.

Apart from any fair dealing for the purposes of research or private study, or criticism or review, as permitted under the Copyright, Designs and Patents Act 1988, this publication may only be reproduced, stored or transmitted, in any form or by any means, with the prior permission in writing of the publishers, or in the case of reprographic reproduction in accordance with the terms of licences issued by the Copyright Licensing Agency. Enquiries concerning reproduction outside those terms should be sent to the publishers.

This is a work of fiction. Names, characters, businesses, places, events and incidents are either the products of the author's imagination or used in a fictitious manner. Any resemblance to actual persons, living or dead, or actual events is purely coincidental.

Troubador Publishing Ltd
Unit E2 Airfield Business Park,
Harrison Road, Market Harborough,
Leicestershire LE16 7UL
Tel: 0116 279 2299
Email: books@troubador.co.uk
Web: www.troubador.co.uk

ISBN 978 1 80514 502 8

British Library Cataloguing in Publication Data.
A catalogue record for this book is available from the British Library.

Printed and bound by CPI Group (UK) Ltd, Croydon, CR0 4YY
Typeset in 12pt Garamond Pro by Troubador Publishing Ltd, Leicester, UK

For Annie Murphy 1894-1970

With special thanks to Denis

One

BELFAST

Tuesday, April 18th 1911

'If I could have your attention ladies.'

Campbell, the foreman, was standing on the wooden step he used when making his rare announcements. He had his back to the first line of spinning frames and was facing the doorway so that the sight of him stuttered us in our tracks as soon as we came through it onto the spinning hall floor.

'If I could have your attention ladies.' He had a way of saying it – 'la-aidies' – that made it sound like an insult. He stood there, hat pushed back on his head, bell in hand and with a thin smile on his face as he watched us pile into one another in the scrap of space between him and the door. I knew that bad news was on the way. Some of the other women near the front read the situation the same, for I could see ones on either side of me stop talking and fold their arms tightly in front of them.

We watched Campbell, who didn't budge an inch until he heard the clang of the mill gates. At that he puffed himself up and gripped the lapel of his jacket with his right hand. There was a kerfuffle as the last of the women shuffled and shoved their way through the doors and onto the spinning hall floor.

'I want to inform you that a new rule is to be brought in.' A low groan echoed round the crowd followed by a wave of muttering. He rang his bell.

'If there was less chatter, we'd get things done quicker round here,' says he. 'And the new rule will make sure of that. As of tomorrow morning, there will be no laughing, singing or talking during working hours. If I find anyone doing so, I am instructed to fine them a farthing a time.' His smile widened at the thought.

Well, at that, there was a clamour like a field of starlings taking off all of a sudden. Clang, clang, clang went the bell again. In the silence, a hoarse voice shouted out from the back.

'Sure, all that's doing is to sicken the wee bit of happiness we have.' There was no mistaking Bella Dwyer's voice.

We all turned to look in her direction even as another woman piped up.

'Aye, and us just back in after Easter Monday. That's knocked the shine off that.'

I recognised Mrs Hegarty's sing-song, for she lived at the end of our street and was better known for her laughter than her scolds.

'You should be grateful for a day's grace to practise buttoning your lips. I'd make the most of that if I were you. Otherwise, you'll find yourselves out of pocket at the end of the week. Now la-aidies, to work.'

If looks could kill, he'd have been dead before he stepped to the ground.

As it was, after the loudest silence I'd ever heard, the older women began to move to their spinning frames. I looked round at Bridie. She slipped her hand over mine and squeezed. Bridie lived round the corner from us and since we'd started school, you were more likely to find us in each other's company than apart. When we were coming up for twelve, our Maggie'd spoken up for both of us at the mill and we were taken on together as half-timers about two years back. We were proper millies now though. These last two months since we'd been made full-time, we were bringing home a full wage of six shillings and sixpence a week.

We took our cue from the older women. We folded our arms tight against our waists and dragged our feet as if there was a sack of potatoes tied on each leg. Campbell was well out of sight and out of earshot by the time we got to our places. Peggy Arthurs was already at her frame, but she turned round to us, her face wrinkled in disgust.

'May that Campbell fella roast in hell, with all the other divils like him,' says she.

You could have cut the atmosphere with a knife that morning. Every so often a song burst out defiantly and then as quickly trailed off, losing its way. In the dinner break, those of us who'd brought our piece with us sat in the sun in pairs or threesomes. Snatches of talk circled round and up, like the smoke from Father's pipe.

'They'd squeeze the life out of ye to get an extra yard of yarn.'

'They think we're just like machines to be switched on and off as they fancy.'

'Ha! If they could manage that, they wouldn't be bothered to give us as much as a crust of bread.'

It was Thursday before anyone on our section got fined. Mrs Smith was a granny with a kind word for everyone. Apparently, she'd turned to speak to a new half-timer who'd just fumbled her bobbin and was in tears with fear as it went clattering across the floor.

Says she later, when she was outside, 'All I said was "Just say a prayer, Daughter and you'll be alright." I'd hardly got the words out of my mouth, when Campbell was at me elbow. "I'm putting you down in my book, Mrs Smith," says he. And do you know what? I opened my mouth, and for the first time in my life the words died on my tongue.'

Well, by Saturday at 12 o'clock, when we finished for the week, there was many a one had been fined. A couple of those that were cursed with a gob stood to lose a good quarter of their money when their wages were reckoned and paid out at the end of the week ahead. But what was worse was that we were all fed up to the gills after three and a half days where every hour hung heavy on us. Previously, underneath the clatter and din of machinery, there'd have been a ripple of banter going up and down the line of us millies as we waited for the doffing mistress's whistle that sent us racing over to one or other of the two frames we each looked after. We'd change the bobbin and return to hunker down in our place until the next shrill beep, picking up the craic where we'd left off. More often than not, somebody'd be singing one of our skipping rhymes. Towards the end of the working day, the favourite was *My Aunt Jane,* for by that time we'd be dying for a cup of tea and a bite to eat.

> *My Aunt Jane she called me in.*
> *She gave me tea out of her wee tin.*
> *Half a bap with sugar on the top*
> *And three black lumps out of her wee shop.*

As Bridie and I walked through the gates that Saturday, we saw a crowd gathered round Bella Dwyer. I could see her, head and shoulders above everyone else, her thick black bun of hair nodding up and down so furiously that I thought it would fall loose at any second. Bella was a woman that you'd want on your side in any fight. Many's the time I'd watched as her banter wilted grown men like boiled cabbage.

'We can't let them get away with this. Sure, our lives aren't worth living if we can't have a bit of laughter as we work. And if we don't fight them on this, God only knows what they'll be up to next.'

'That's a true word you've spoken there, Bella. But sure, what can we do about it? Who's gonna pay attention to us?' A murmur of agreement greeted the voice from the crowd.

'We can organise. That's what we can do,' hollered Bella so that more women crowded round to see what was going on. 'I'm for going to see James Connolly this afternoon and I'd like a bit of company. Two or three of you going with me would make a difference.'

'Who's James Connolly?'

'Yer man that's organising the Deep Sea Dockers.'

'Sure, he wouldn't have time for the likes of us.'

'We could get in more trouble if the bosses found out.'

Bella didn't need a bell. Her voice boomed out. 'Will yous forever give over quacking like ducks and listen? Mr Connolly's a neighbour. He lives round the corner from us. I've spoken to his wife, and she told me to come back this afternoon. He's glad to help any working body.'

There was a silence. I looked at Bridie and out of the corner of my eye saw other women exchange glances or look down at their feet, their lips pressed tight. A couple of women started to drift away.

'I'll go with ye, Bella.' It was our Maggie. My jaw dropped. Maggie was never one to put herself forward. Mind you, since January, when she and Charles married, it was like she'd turned from a sapling into a tree. I looked over to where she stood, her head clear of those round her. Her brown hair was pulled tight off her face into a plait coiled and pinned at the back of her head. As she eased her way through the other women towards Bella, I could see the firm set of her jaw, just like Father when he'd made up his mind. And then didn't Bridie pipe up, clear as a blackbird.

'We'll go too, me and Nan Rose.'

I elbowed her in the side. 'Whhsst, will ye! Mammy'll have a fit if she hears both of her daughters are off rabble-rousing.'

Bella looked over, trying to see who had spoken. Women made way and so Bridie pushed herself to the front, dragging me by the hand after her.

'You've a good spirit, Daughter,' says Bella, 'but we need older heads for this.' Bridie bit her lip and I could see the red spread across her cheeks as she tried to sink back into the crowd. Bella noticed as well.

'Don't worry, Daughter. There'll be plenty of opportunity to put that spirit to work if we organise ourselves. And look, you've shamed some of these 'uns into stepping up. So you've done your bit for the day.'

Bridie's face broke into a smile.

I didn't see Maggie again until the next morning. When I came back into the house after ten o'clock Mass, she was standing, arms wrapped round herself, staring into the embers of the fire. She wound her hair into a loose knot at the nape of her neck so that it hung down over her right shoulder. The low glow of the fire caught and glinted its chestnut hue. Before I could say a word, there was a clanging of pots and banging of cupboard doors from the scullery. Mammy was clearly fit to be tied.

Maggie turned round, rolling her eyes. She beckoned me closer.

'Mrs Pick's been giving Mammy chapter and verse about who did what on Saturday.' She hissed into my ear. 'I swear I don't know when that woman finds time to do a daecent day's work for she's gossiping day and night.'

Right then, Mammy strode through the doorway from the scullery, a frying pan in one hand and a knife in the other. She pointed the knife in my direction.

'And here's Nan Rose,' says she, 'playing good as gold but so sleeked that she couldn't say a word to me yesterday about what was going on at the mill.' Her clog tapped a furious rhythm on the flagstones. 'Well, what have you to say for yourself?'

'There wasn't anything to tell you,' I said. 'You already knew about how we were all feeling about the new rules. And...'

'So, yer big sister going off with that Bella Dwyer to stir up things with James Connolly is something that happens every day?'

'Mammy, It's not Nan Rose you're upset about. It's me. And I'd have told you myself this morning, but Mrs Pick set the cat among the pigeons before I got here. Now do you want to hear it from me or not?'

I looked at Maggie. Her cheeks were flushed, but she held herself tall, so she looked as if she'd grown two inches. This was our Maggie who wouldn't say boo to a goose, who was the peacemaker in the family, and here she was, like a rock in the face of Mammy's storming.

Mammy too had noticed the difference. She collapsed onto the rocker and let out a wail. 'I wisht to God you'd never spoken up for your sister and wee Bridie Corr to get them a place at Cupar Street, for otherwise they'd be safe and sound with me at Brown's Mill, instead of caught up with all of this.'

'Maybe so, Mammy, but you know as well as I do, that if one of the bosses finds a way of squeezing more out of us, then the others follow sooner or later.' She laughed. 'You could even say that if we win, we'll have saved yous 'uns at Brown's having to come out.'

I bit my lip to swallow a giggle at Maggie's cheek and it's as well I did, for Mammy wasn't amused.

'Maggie, haven't you a titter of wit? It's not even two years since we were all out on strike and having to go back with our tails between our legs after weeks of living on air and scraps.'

'No, Mammy, I haven't forgotten. But what you've forgotten is that the weavers who struck first had their claim settled before the rest of us came out. It was us Johnny-come-latelys who didn't fare well. Anyway, this isn't a strike about money. What we're asking for won't cost them a halfpenny. We're just asking not to have the life squeezed out of us.'

Mammy had stopped her wail. She looked at Maggie as if wondering who this stranger was. Maggie went over and knelt on one knee beside her.

'Mammy, if we don't fight for this, what hope have we for the wee'uns when their time comes?'

I took my chance and slipped upstairs for I needed to get my brain showered after all the commotion. I sat down on my bed, leaning back against the bed end, but the ironwork was too cold and hard for comfort. I scrunched up my shawl to make a cushion for my back and just sat there, gazing out the window.

For longer than I could remember, I'd gone to sleep and wakened every morning to the smell of Maggie, sometimes sweet with her freshly washed hair lying loose over the mattress and sometimes, when it was coming up to bath night, sour and earthy with the smells of the peat fire, of cooking and above all, of the mill.

Many's the night when I was a wee 'un, I'd lie there, curled up against her, my head cradled in the crook of her right arm, while Michael tucked himself in at her left side. She'd a habit of caressing the crown of my head, rubbing her finger back and forth over the tiny dip at the centre. I'd lie there all peaceful, feeling the softness of her skin against my cheek. As my eyelids grew heavy, I'd watch her grey-blue eyes gazing at me in that dreamy way she had where she seemed to be both right beside me and, at the same time, somewhere far off. I'd twist her hair in my fist like a rope to lead me back out of dreams.

That time was long gone. Michael had been sleeping on a pallet downstairs the last seven years. 'Since I was coming up to nine,' he'd remind me every so often when he wanted to play the big brother card. You'd have thought by the talk of him that he'd become a man then and there. He liked the company of Bandit, our wee fox terrier, as they both bedded down by the warmth of the fire of an evening, but he didn't like having Father rouse him as soon as he came down in the morning. Left to himself, he'd be inclined to get to work by the skin of his teeth.

The murmur of talk drifted up through the floorboards, soft not agitated. I eased myself further against my shawl, remembering the night of Mr Reilly's wake, the February before last. That was the night when life changed for Maggie.

She'd gone round to the wake in the early evening, her shawl wrapped tight around her against the bitter night. The wind rattled the windowpanes as it snuck in round the newspaper shoved in the gaps and stuck over cracks. The rest of us had gone to bed, but I couldn't sleep. Even with a sheet of flannelette wrapped round me, the damp of the blankets had chilled me to the bones. I flounced this way and that, feeling every lump in our thin mattress. What was taking her so long?

It wasn't only the cold that was keeping me from sleep. I was dying to know what had gone on. Anything could have happened there, for the line between the living and the dead is a fine one and no more so than when the soul is still passing over.

So I lay there in the dark, listening to Father's snores from the back room and the sounds of the street until I heard Maggie at the front door. I could hear Terence Duffy's voice and another that I didn't recognise – a man bidding good night slowly and softly. I heard the front door open and shut as the men's voices and footsteps died away. I counted the creak of each stair as Maggie tiptoed up. She threw herself on the bed without undressing.

'Nan, are you awake? Oh, be a wee dote and wake up. You'll never guess what happened tonight.'

I propped myself up on one elbow, full of anticipation. My vigil hadn't been in vain.

'Oh Nan Rose, I've met a man.'

I stared at the dark shape of her lying beside me and then flung myself back on the mattress. Was that it? Sure, at any wake there's a crowd of men in the scullery supping whatever's going.

'I've met the man I'm going to marry. His name's Charles.'

The next morning, she was up and singing like a bird. And she was still singing as she came back from the mill. I could see Mammy giving her a long look every so often, but the days went by, and she made no comment. I kept waiting for her to speak, for Mammy was very pass remarkable.

In the end it was Father who raised the matter. It was near bedtime about a fortnight after the wake and he'd been sitting by the fire, one leg stretched out on his stool, his fingers busy with his pipe, tapping and lighting, tapping and lighting. I swear he spent more time playing with that pipe than smoking it. I'd tiptoed up behind him and put my arms round his neck. I was standing there, breathing in the sweet smell of his baccy while Michael played yet another game of solitaire at the table. Mammy was sitting opposite, studying the death columns of the Irish News. Every so often, Father'd manage to pick up a copy as it did the rounds in the warehouse where he worked. This one was a week old and was well and truly thumbed over. I watched her trace each word with her finger. Every so often she'd pause and remark about someone or other that only she knew. The death columns were to Mammy what the pipe was to Father – a way of sitting back and taking it easy for a while. Maggie was in the scullery washing out her other blouse and skirt and singing *My Lagan Love* to herself.

'I hear tell that there's a fella from the Markets that's been paying you some attention these last couple of weeks, Maggie.' Father had waited for a pause between verses. Mammy put down her paper and looked at him, a little smile playing on her lips. I straightened up, letting go of Father and looked towards the door to the scullery. Michael stopped dealing out his cards. Maggie hadn't answered but all sound of washing had ceased. The tick of the clock was all that broke the silence.

'I'd wondered how long it would take for word to get back.' Maggie stood in the doorway, drying her hands on her apron. Father returned her gaze.

'Well, Daughter, I didn't need anyone to tell me what was going on, for ever since the night you came back from Mr Reilly's wake, you've been as bright and light as a lark. I was just wondering how long it would take for somebody to tell me who the lucky fella was.'

At that moment, I was jolted out of my reminiscing about how Maggie met Charles by Maggie's voice from the foot of the stairs. She was calling that the kettle was boiled so I went down to see how the land lay.

'Mr Connolly's a good man, Mammy,' says Maggie as the three of us sat in the quiet of the kitchen, cradling our cups of tea. 'And his wife's got a warm heart. She'd made us all at home before he came in, insisting we sat down. "For yous've come straight from the mill," says she. And when he came in, he listened. He just listened. To have a powerful man sit quiet while we spoke, for him not to interrupt, nor talk us down, nor tell us that he knew what was best before we'd even opened our mouths – that was a tonic in itself.'

At that moment, Father and Michael came in.

'I hear you and Bella Dwyer are leading a strike, Maggie. I suppose the next thing we'll see is you on a soapbox shouting for votes for women.' Michael's big grin faded in the silence that greeted his mischief. Father looked round the room, coming to a halt at Mammy's tight expression.

'Is there a cup of tea in that pot, for I'm dying of thirst? That young priest certainly liked the sound of his own voice. By the end of his sermon, you could hardly hear his words for the shuffling of feet at the back of the church.'

Maggie rose from the table. 'Sit down here Father, for I'll need to be getting home to sort dinner. Charles will be back from Mass by now.' She turned to Michael, but her words were for all of us.

'Just so yous know. There's no strike planned. The first step is a meeting on Wednesday night for us women to decide what we want to say to the powers that be.'

Two

Wednesday, April 26th

Well, by our midday break on Wednesday, those of us eating our pieces outside in the sunshine were buzzing like a swarm of bees. Who was going to the meeting? Who'd support a strike, if it came to it? Although everyone kept their voices low, you could hear the fierceness of the arguments in the hissed whispers. I could feel my heart thumping at the thought of standing up for ourselves, because despite Mammy's gloom and doom, in my heart I was with Maggie. 'If we don't stand up and fight, they'll squeeze the life out of us.'

Later, as Bridie and I made our way home at the end of the shift, she was hopping with excitement. 'I'll call for you, so we get there early,' says she. 'I want to make sure we're in the front row.'

'No, I'll call for you,' says I, 'for I don't want Mammy starting off. That'd put the dampers on it.'

As it was, when we clambered up the steps to the first-floor room above McAvoy's Grocery and Public House, the only ones that were there before us were the organising committee and James Connolly. He was smaller than I expected. He was standing at a deal table with our Maggie and Ellen Kavanagh, who lived round the corner from us. The last of the day's sun, filtering through the only window, cast a glow round the three of them. Even from the door I could see Ellen's cheeks blush as she smiled and nodded at every word he said. Another woman that I only knew by sight was putting out the last of a row of benches. Bella Dwyer was lighting the gaslights. Seeing us, she bustled across the floor, her steps raising puffs of dust from the bare floorboards.

'My wee sparrows, yous are as keen as ever. Do you like my flowers?' She pointed at a jar of daffodils on the table. 'I'd a walk up the Glen on Sunday and picked them, for I thought their wee faces were a sight for sore eyes.'

James Connolly turned as more women started to arrive. He smiled and nodded over at us. Bridie told me afterwards that she could feel her cheeks tingling for the rest of the evening. The room filled up quickly and I thought the windows would crack with the chitter and chatter as we squashed in together. Bridie and I nearly twisted our necks off, turning round to see who all were arriving. In the end, she couldn't contain herself and stood up to get a good look round the room. My shoulder was right and sore before we even started, for she elbowed me every time she recognised someone, bending over to hiss their names into my ear.

'Would ye believe it? There's Eileen and Imelda Dobbin. I had them down as right scaredy cats and here they are.'

And still more women squeezed in until the crowd was spilling out onto the landing. There was a flurry at the front of the hall as Bella, Maggie, Ellen Kavanagh and the other committee women took their seats in a row to the right of the table behind which James Connolly was seated. Bella was sitting next to him with our Maggie beside her. Bella was on the edge of her seat and looked to be counting heads. Maggie, on the other hand, was that at ease, she could have been sitting in her own home talking to a neighbour. She gazed out over the room with a nod and smile as she caught the eye of someone or other that she knew.

Bella rose from her chair and stood square to face us. She paused just long enough for the chatter to quieten before hollering out like a foghorn.

'I thank ye all for coming. It's great to see so many brave souls here. I know we've all had a long day and yous are bone tired. So, all I need to say is that this is Mr James Connolly who's willing to help us organise.' Bella sat down and he stood up. You could have heard a pin drop as he walked to the front of the table.

'Working women of Belfast on whose labour the prosperity of this fine city has been built.' Loud claps and cheers interrupted. 'I'm proud to be asked to help you in your fight to be treated like decent human beings and not like the pieces of machinery that you work so skilfully.' I didn't hear what else he said. Those first words hit me like a fresh wind, swirled round and in me. It was people like us who had built this city. It was. I found myself sitting tall, my feet more solid on the ground. People like us – and now, we were being denied even our laughter and our singing. I found myself stamping on the floor, like a young horse, freshly shod. Before I knew it, Bella's voice was booming.

'Now, we're agreed that tomorrow we hand over this letter demanding that they lift the new rules?' Cheering, applause, a show of hands. Bridie and I shot up our hands.

'And are we agreed that if they don't give us what we ask, that we'll strike?' Less cheering and applause. Hands raised more slowly. But still all our hands went up.

'That's the spirit, Sisters. Now can we have a few more women to go with the four of us that organised this meeting? The more we show strength at the beginning, the better.'

This time, Bridie remembered what Bella had said. 'Let the older ones go in front.' I saw Mrs Hegarty's hand go up, followed by Peggy Arthurs'. Two more hands went up from right at the back of the hall. There was a final round of clapping, a call from Ellen Kavanagh for help in putting away the benches and then there was a mingling and chittering as we headed for the door. I did wonder if I should wait for Maggie, but when I looked back, the eight committee ones were huddled round the table intent on every word Mr Connolly was saying.

The rest of us spilled out through the bar and onto the street – to be greeted with shouts and claps from the men drinking at tables or standing in the doorway. My head was spinning. Bridie and I linked arms and tripped home, singing along with some of the other ones our age. But I couldn't help noticing that some of the older women walked as after a funeral, their shawls pulled tight across their chests, their faces solemn. Out of the corner of my eye, I saw Mrs Smith shake her head as we greeted her in singsong. I hugged Bridie's arm tighter. Nothing was going to dampen my spirits that evening.

On Thursday lunchtime, as everyone else filed outside to eat their piece or scurry home and back before the gates closed again, Maggie, Bella and the others gathered on the landing at the bottom of the steps. The office of Mr Frazer, the manager, was on the fourth floor so they'd a right climb ahead of them. Our calls of encouragement circled them as we passed.

'Keep your chin up, Daughter.'
'We're all behind you, Sister.'
'Give yer man Frazer what for, Bella.'

They still hadn't re-appeared as the horn sounded. I dallied as long as I dared in the shadows at the bottom of the stairwell, for I was beginning to worry about what had happened. They couldn't be sacked for handing in a letter, could they? I was about to give up when I heard their voices echoing down.

'You'd have thought he'd have the daecency to see us right away instead of keeping us waiting until five minutes before the horn.' I recognised Ellen Kavanagh's voice for even in a whisper she shrilled.

'Aye, and when he took our paper from you, Bella, he fingered it so pernickety, you'd have thought he'd been handed a piece of filth from the gutter.'

I didn't know the voice nor the next.

'And what are they paying him to manage this place for, when he can't take a decision himself but has to go running to the owners. You're never important to the high and mighty until you try to stand up for yourselves.'

I saw Bella step onto the landing and then turn back to wait for the others. 'You've got to remember what Mr Connolly said – they'll do everything to put you off your stride. Playing games is second nature to them.'

As they came to the bottom of the stairs, Maggie was at the rear. 'Never a truer word was said,' says she. 'Just as we were walking out his door, he calls over to me, all soft and polite. "I'm surprised at you, Mrs Rice, and you a doffing mistress." Says I, "I am that and looking after my charges like I've been asked to." For I wouldn't give him the satisfaction of the last word.'

I'd never heard her sound so harsh. I stepped out of the shadows and seeing me, she linked my arm, steering me towards and through the door into the spinning hall. As I walked back to my end, the last of the bubbles that had been fizzing through me since our meeting with Mr Connolly popped. I suddenly felt that heavy, you'd have thought someone had lowered me into a grave.

'*Níl an darna suí sa bhuili ann.*' I heard Father's voice as clear as if he'd been standing beside me. And I was back to the time just before I started at the mill. I was on the road to Clough with him, on our way to visit Granny who was ailing.

We were sat on the verge the other side of Ballynahinch with my wee basket of food for our journey between us. I'd unpacked the two hard-boiled eggs, a half can of buttermilk and two farls of soda bread that I'd made the night before. Now that the clop and trundle of the borrowed pony and cart had stopped, the quiet wrapped itself round us like a soft blanket. In my mind's ear, I could still hear the jingle of Cloudy's harness as she bent down to nose and chew the grass. I could see again the fat robin perched on a stile opposite, his breast gleaming red as an apple in the midday sun. I'd flung a few crumbs in his direction and he cocked his head at me, the bead of his eye bright and bold.

'This reminds me of the morning I left home,' says Father. I was immediately all ears.

'I was twelve, the same age as yourself. Me mother'd made me a right piece that morning – two slaps of wheaten bread with stewed rhubarb slathered between them. And a flask of buttermilk, just like this one. That was the first meal I had after leaving home and me sitting on my wee stool at the side of the road, looking back and looking forward.'

'The wee stool that's by our fireplace? That's a funny thing to have taken when you'd to carry it all these miles.'

'It's what I sat on all the time growing up, for I was the youngest. Our mother had an expression. *Níl an darna suí sa bhuili ann.* There's no second stool in the milking shed.'

I was still puzzled. 'Why not?'

'It means, "We've no other choice. There's only one thing to be done." And I wanted something to remind me of that, as well as where I'd come from.' He smiled at me. 'I'd only the clothes I stood up in, the baccy tin that our Seamus gave me and a couple of shillings me mother had saved.'

'And did your father not give you any shillings?'

'He'd died when I was ten. Too much drink and too little food.'

I glanced up at the Pioneer pin on the lapel of his jacket. So now I knowd. That was why Father had pledged never to take alcohol.

The doffing mistress's whistle shrilled, and I was back on the mill floor and scarpering across to the frame to tie up my end. But as I haunched back down in my place, I was back there again on the road to Clough. Father had brought the pony and cart to a halt at the crest of a hill and was pointing straight ahead. I stood up, the better to see. In the distance, the green of the fields gave way to glittering silver-grey water that stretched until it met the sky.

'The sea!' I stood there like a statue, jaw dropped. 'The sea!' I turned my head slowly from left to right, taking in the enormity of it. 'It looks like it goes on forever.'

'Aye, it does that. Growing up with it, I've no sense of the wonder of the first time I saw it, more's the pity.'

He touched my shoulder, and I sat down. He flicked the reins and the pony picked up its amble. I stared straight ahead and as I looked, I could feel my soul dance on that shimmering line where sea and sky became one. It must have been still dancing as we descended the hill and the sea disappeared, for I noticed as if they'd just appeared, the gorse smattering the hillside with yellow and the green stalks of daffodils promising to burst into flower if the sun would only stay and play for a week or two.

A fortnight after our journey, I started at the mill. That first evening after work, my head had felt so heavy all I'd wanted to do was rest it on the table. The fizz and fluster of the day had left me bone tired. Later, when I'd shut my eyes in bed, the noise of the mill had returned, only worse, for the more I'd drifted off, the more the bobbins brattled along the frames, and the dust swirled. I'd eventually sunk into a black exhausted sleep.

The next morning, I'd wakened to the sound of Father calling up the stairs. Maggie was up already, and I hadn't heard any of it. I clumped downstairs and sat in Father's chair, my arms pulling my bent legs close to my chest. I must have looked pitiful, for one and all of them were soft with me. Michael even gave me the remains of a bag of clove rock. I looked up at one point, and Father was gazing at me.

'Ach, Nan, Daughter, work's hard, I know. But there's no second stool in the milking shed, for if there was, sure wouldn't we take it?'

I'd looked up at him then and for an instant, I wasn't gazing at my father. I saw that lad, a bit older than me, trudging the road that was taking him away from his home with every step.

Even as I scarpered again to the whistle, I realised I'd now set out on my own road.

It wasn't until Saturday, right at the end of our shift that Campbell lifted his step down from the hook on the wall beside the spinning hall doors and thumped it down on the floor, barring our way out. He stepped up on it, ringing his bell as if it was Christmas morning, the aul divil. Although he kept a poker face, his eyes glinted malice.

'La-aidies, I am instructed to inform you that the owners in their wisdom have deemed that there will be no change to the recently introduced rules. It will be business as usual on Monday morning.'

Anything else he said was lost in the ruction as our tight-lipped silence that had been gathering since Thursday lunchtime burst like a river through a dam. Above it all, a voice shouted from the back.

'Yer an aul arse-licker, Campbell and ye'll get what's coming to you one of these days!'

At that, we all roared and surged forward a few steps. I could see him shaking his bell furiously, but he might as well not have bothered for you couldn't hear it in the din. For a second, I thought we'd lay hands on him then and there. Bella must have thought so too, for she pushed her way up beside him. Campbell jumped down from his perch and shuffled closer to her. There was another roar, this time of laughter, at the sight of Campbell cowering at Bella's skirts.

She ascended that step like a queen to her throne and stood there, hands on hips, willing us into silence. Our voices trailed away.

'They're like cats playing us as mice,' she thundered. 'But they'll find out to their cost, we're no mice, squeaking and scurrying in fear. We agreed to strike, Sisters. And on strike we are.'

With that, she stepped down, pushed the step out of the way and sailed out through the hall doors, trailing all of us on the floor in her wake. Once outside the gates, she beckoned over the committee ones into a huddle. I'd wanted us to walk back with Maggie, but I had to make do with just a smile and a nod from her as Bridie and I passed by. We linked arms with a couple of the others our age. I walked with my head high and a fire in my belly, for I wasn't only a working girl. I was one of them that was willing to strike and not every working body could claim that.

As each one of our little chain peeled off on reaching their street, Bridie and I closed in together and we walked the last stretch to the end of my street by ourselves. Even though we'd see each other later, I felt like I was losing half of me as we unlinked and she walked on, with a backward glance. I stood at the corner, looking up at our front door. Now that I was alone, the thought of breaking the news to Mammy came to me, like being drenched with a bucket of cold water. I stood, fingering my wage packet in my pocket.

Just as well ye collected yer money after ye signed in on a Saturday morning.

I knew I couldn't stand there, like a young buck with nothing better to do. For the first time, I wondered how it was that Michael could kick his heels at the corner if he wanted but that if I did, some aul biddy or other would feel entitled to tell me off or pass a remark to Mammy with a nod and a 'she'll need to watch herself' look. I was beside myself with excitement and nerves, like a twig bobbing along in a rushing stream.

I turned to cross the road and what did I see but Mrs Pick's big tabby pad round the corner straight into the line of sight of the black tomcat that had taken to parading himself down our street as part of his daily constitutional. They were about three doors apart. They each stopped stock-still, backs arched, tails curled up into question marks. The tomcat inched his way forward, one clawed paw at a time. The tabby arched her back even higher, her legs growing longer as she stood on the tips of her claws. As the tomcat came within leaping distance of her, I got ready to give him a swipe with my shawl for I wasn't going to have him chase her out of her own street. I needn't have worried. There was a hissing and a screeching as each cat eyed the other and readied for the attack. Just when it looked as if all hell would break loose, the tomcat shifted his direction an inch, so that he circled out and past the tabby. She swivelled slowly round on her claws to watch him go.

All of that – and not a mark on either of them. I decided I didn't need any more time. I just needed to go home and stand my ground.

Mammy was already at the table, peeling potatoes. She put the knife down and looked me straight in the eye. 'You may pray to God and His Holy Mother that yous are not out for long.'

I nodded, even as I was wondering if James Connolly prayed. Apart from priests and the odd Holy Joe, men didn't seem to put as much store as women on help from above. I scooped my wage packet out of my pocket and put it on the table. Mammy slowly peeled open the flap of the wee buff envelope and counted out each of the coins until the full six shillings and sixpence stood in neat columns on the table. She counted off two farthings and nudged them over to me.

'I wasn't expectin' to keep any this week,' says I, quietly like, for I didn't want her to be changing her mind.

'Well, they may be the last you'll see in a while,' says she. 'So, look after them.' She put her hand on mine and looked up at me, her face softening.

'What's done is done,' says she. 'But we'll get by. We always have.' She took her hand away and went back to her peeling.

'Make no mistake, though,' says she, looking up again.

'You'll be making up for what you're not bringing in by doin' what needs to be done around the house.'

On Sunday morning, Maggie and Charles called in after eleven o'clock Mass. I hadn't seen him in his Sunday best since he and Maggie married, and I remembered what Mammy had said the first time he'd come to the house to meet us all. Maggie and Charles had gone on to a dance and Michael had taken himself off for a game of cards with his mates. Father and Mammy must have forgotten that I was there. She'd pulled herself out of the chair and had started to gather the cups from the table.

'He's a fine clothes horse of a man,' says she.

'Ach, Agnes, give him more credit than that,' says Father. 'I thought he bore up well enough under interrogation. He's a deep 'un for sure.'

'If you mean he doesn't give too much away, you're right there.'

'Well, that's not a bad thing in a man. You wouldn't want him to be an aul blether.'

I still didn't quite know what Mammy had been intimating, but there was something about how Charles carried himself that meant he stood out that little bit in any group. I watched as he, Father and Michael argued about who was going to win the Antrim Down hurling match the following Sunday. Although Charles was as able as the others to put over his point of view, it was as if it didn't matter to him. He was simply passing himself, whereas Michael was talking as if his life depended on Antrim winning.

It struck me, looking at the three of them who were well matched in build, that if anyone was drawing the scene, they'd have to use a finer pencil to draw Charles. And even though I knew that he could wield a shovel or heave a sack as good as any man, he didn't seem as if he was cut out for that in a way that Father and Michael were.

Maggie came in from the scullery and set cups and a plate of soda bread on the table. Charles glanced round and caught her eye. There it was again, just like that first evening – that second where he and Maggie looked at and through each other and it was as if nobody else existed. It affected me as much as that first time. I caught my breath. I'd never seen two people look at each other like that. Something in the pit of my stomach stirred.

Charles returned to the men's talk, Maggie returned to the scullery, but I stopped still. Was this what love did? Made you look at someone like nobody else mattered? But if so, how come I'd never seen any other couple look at each other like that? Mammy might give Father a knowing look and smile, or he might gaze softly at her as she moved round the house, humming. More often than not, they just seemed to be putting up with each other.

I must have been staring so hard at Charles's back that he felt it, for he suddenly glanced over in my direction.

'A penny for them, Nan Rose.'

I blushed and looked away.

But, as I stirred myself to do something useful, it hit me that something had changed in me. That first afternoon we'd met Charles, I wanted what he had – Maggie's attention. Now I wanted what Maggie had.

Three

Monday 1st May

On the Monday morning after they'd all gone off, I had the house to myself. But I was that agitated, I couldn't enjoy it. I decided I'd be better off working up a lather with some chores. So, I rolled up my sleeves and set to. I stripped the two beds. I blattered and turned the mattresses and Michael's pallet. I shook out our few sheets and blankets till my arms ached and I brushed the floor till the dust danced rings round me. I got down on my hands and knees at the front doorstep and I scrubbed backwards from there, over the wee square of our hall at the bottom of the stairs, through the front room and the scullery to the back door.

By then the sweat was dripping off me. I opened the back door and lifted my bucket, Father's wee stool and my clogs that I'd put by the door before I started. I went out to the back entry, emptied the bucket and sat myself down on the stool. Bandit was lying in the upturned three-sided crate where she spent the day, her nose and front paws juking out. I'd no sooner settled myself than she padded over, trailing the rope that tied her to the nail on our back wall behind her. She rested her muzzle on my knees, her eyes intent on my face. Michael'd named her well. She was as white as a goose, bar two long patches of black hair that ran from a couple of inches above her nose to up and over her ears, leaving only a ribbon of white hair between them. I bent over, scratching behind her ears while I told her about what I'd been up to. She turned her head this way and that, all the better to have it scratched. The sun was up and the entry quiet, for it would've only been about half ten. After a wee while, I leaned back against the wall, wiped my face with the end of my skirt, closed my eyes and let the sun play on my face and arms. Bandit took her cue from me and lay at my feet, her head resting on my left clog.

I must have dozed off, for when I next opened my eyes, the sun was past its height. I jumped up with a start, for Mammy'd told me that while I was on strike, she was coming home at the one o'clock break.

'It'll break up the day for ye,' says she. But she and I both knew it was to make sure I wasn't gallivanting about the place like Lady Muck. I grabbed the stool and went inside. If I was quick, I could have her a piece on the table so that she could just sit down and rest her feet.

As she came in, I could see her glance at the floor and then at the table where I'd poured her a cup of buttermilk and laid her out the last two slices of soda bread on which I'd mashed the hard boiled egg left over from the day before. She nodded to herself as she took off her shawl.

'Sit down, Mammy and rest yourself,' says I. She looked up and gave me a half smile.

'You've earned your keep this morning,' says she as she sat down. Maybe it was because I wasn't so tired myself, but I couldn't help noticing how she slumped in the chair, and the pouce dust gathered in the lines round her lips and eyes. I fought back the notion to go over, put my arms round her from behind and kiss the top of her head, for Mammy wasn't like Father. She was as likely to shrug me off roughly as look up and smile.

She'd hardly sat down than she had to be up and away again, for a half an hour doesn't give you much time to walk home and back, let alone eat.

'Mammy, you don't have to be rushing home on account of me. You can trust me to do whatever's needed. You'd be better off just takin' your time over your piece at the mill.'

She smiled then and put her hand to my cheek. I felt her skin rough on mine. 'You're right, Daughter. You're right. I've got to stop thinking of you as a child.'

Her saying that put me in two minds. I'd been planning to call round for Bridie in the afternoon but that now seemed a childish thing to be doing. Women got on with whatever job needed done round the house and could always find something that required their attention. Men, now, they seemed to work on different rules.

I spent the afternoon being the woman of the house. I cleared out the grate and laid the makings of a fire. I peeled potatoes and carrots for the evening meal and then I set about clearing the darning basket, stacking up the items by the side of it, as evidence of my labour – a handful of odd socks, Michael's other jumper with the elbow out of it and Mammy's other shawl that she'd snagged on a piece of wire, all darned. By then I'd had it with being the woman of the house. I decided I'd call round to Bridie's in the evening as soon as we'd all eaten.

She was sitting on the doorstep and came towards me as soon as she saw me.

'I thought you were goin' to call round for me this morning,' says she, standing, arms folded, in front of me.

'I've been doin' jobs round the house all day,' says I, folding my arms in turn. 'You don't know you're living, Bridie. Mammy has a list, the length of my arm, of jobs that need doing.'

'Don't give me that,' says she. 'I've been ironing and folding all morning. Mammy had a pile of sewing that had to be delivered to that shop in King Street. I thought we'd have been able to walk down together. As it was, I'd to go by myself. It's not the same.'

'Well, don't look at me as if it's my fault. I didn't know, did I?'

At that, her bottom lip wobbled, and she turned away. I linked my arm into hers, squeezing it until she softened her grip. She dropped her head to my shoulder, and we walked slowly towards her front door.

'I don't like being at home when it feels like everyone round you is at work. I thought it'd be a laugh being out on strike, that we'd all be together like we were at the meetings.'

I nodded, for I knew what she meant.

'And you may think I've got it easy but at least you've got the house to yourself. Whereas I've got Mammy and Granny there all the time. Granny doesn't say anything to my face but she's a way of sighing. And I can tell you, there's been a lot of sighing all weekend. Not to mention Aunt Imelda offering up the rosary every night for those struggling to make ends meet.'

The aunt was Bridie's father's older sister. He'd died when Bridie was a wee 'un, leaving Mrs Corr and Bridie with his sister and mother. The four of them had moved from the Oldpark to Townsend Street, for rents were cheaper our way. The aunt fancied herself as head of the family.

She must have knowd we were thinking about her for she suddenly appeared on the doorstep.

'So there you are Bridie, and with your fellow striker, Nan Rose.' She said that last bit, slow and heavy, and with an arch of her eyebrow for good measure. At the best of times, there was something suffocating about the air around her that made me catch my breath. I unlinked my arm from Bridie's, set on escape.

'Well, you may both come in. We're about to say the rosary.' It wasn't so much an invitation as a command.

Bridie and I glanced at each other and then shuffled in, like prisoners to the cell. The granny was sitting at the fire, rosary beads in hand. Mrs Corr was wiping down the table. She looked up as we came in, her face crinkling into a smile, her eyes almost disappearing into the creases above her cheeks. I liked that she always seemed glad to see me. She reminded me of a small bird with her chirping and her quick neat movements. Bridie took after her. The granny and the aunt were tall, long-faced, big-boned women although the granny was stooped with age.

We knelt down, taking up positions against a chair or the table. Aunt Imelda knelt, back as straight as if she'd shoved a brush handle up the back of her blouse. She led every decade – nobody else could get a look in. And she'd a way of praying that sounded less like she was beseeching than demanding. I suddenly imagined God jumping off his throne and scurrying around Heaven to meet her every order. I'd no sooner thought it than I realised I'd committed blasphemy and that agitated me so much, I dropped the rosary beads.

The aunt turned round and fixed me with her bloodhound stare even as she led the Our Father. She'd big lips that she could twist into a bud at the centre of her mouth or pull down at the right-hand corner. When she spoke, she seemed to be eating her bottom lip. I couldn't take my eyes off her mouth, for I kept expecting a chunk of it to be chewed away. So, there we were, her glaring at me and me staring at her. She wouldn't look away and I couldn't.

Bridie's elbow in my ribs broke the spell. She handed me my rosary beads. Out of the corner of my eye, I could see she was biting her lip hard, and her cheek was sucked in. Well, knowing that Bridie was fighting down a fit of giggles nearly finished me off. I prayed the rest of that rosary begging Our

Lady to not let me guffaw. The two of us nearly fell over each other to get out the front door as soon as the last Amen was muttered. We held on to each other as we staggered to the corner, where we collapsed into laughter, the tears tripping us.

'It could be worse, Bridie. Yer Aunt Imelda could work from home like yer mammy. At least she's out at Sinclair's all day.'

'Ach Nan Rose don't be sayin' that. You'll put the jinx on us. I'm tellin' you this. If Aunt Imelda ever stops working, I'll be beggin' to move in with yous.'

By Friday, there was still no word from the bosses. But if they knew how to play the game to fray your nerves, James Connolly and the committee had a trick or two up their sleeves. They booked a hall round the back of St Mary's for Saturday morning at eleven o'clock for any of us who wanted to come for a wee meeting with tea and slices of wheaten farl. That way, we weren't standing about the streets or at home by ourselves when each and every other mill worker was coming home at the end of the working week with their pay packets tucked in their pockets. The wheaten slices satisfied our stomachs and the banter gave us a laugh. We even belted out a couple of songs before we left.

That, and both Michael and Father slipping me a farthing each, got me through the weekend in good spirits. I bought a farthing's poke of clove rock to share with Bridie and I offered the other farthing to Maggie. She gave me a hug but said Mammy'd got there before me.

'She brought half a loaf of bread, a wee pat of butter and a jug of buttermilk round on Saturday afternoon. And credit to her,' says Maggie, 'for she didn't bad-mouth the strike. All she said was "Yous'll be feelin' the pinch with only Charles's money coming in."'

By Monday, the novelty of playing house had worn off. As soon as the others left, I slumped down in Father's chair and wondered what would become of me. I imagined day after day of working in the mill without being able to have a wee bit of craic. I imagined being sacked, with no other job and being stuck at home with sympathy wearing thin. I couldn't decide which was worse. I don't know how low I'd have sunk but Maggie walked in at that moment. She was breathless and wasn't for lingering.

'Bella spoke to James Connolly this morning. We've had a statement from the mill owners. They'll hold our positions until the end of this week. After that we'll be locked out.' I stifled a cry and Maggie continued.

'We're calling a meeting for Wednesday night – back at McAvoy's pub. Can you and Bridie help spread the word? I'm away round to Bella's for she's called a meeting of the committee at her house this morning.' I roused myself right and quick, for it's a lot easier to deal with something that's actually happening rather than being dreamed.

There were no daffodils on the table at this meeting and no bustling about with cheery greetings. Everyone came in quietly, some with their eyes low and some of the older ones fingering rosary beads. Everyone seemed lost in their own thoughts. Even Bridie was out of spirits. I suggested we sit at the back, the better to see what was going on without having to keep twisting round or standing up.

I'd have thought most of us would have known what the bosses had said, for I'd passed many a group of women as Bridie and I spread the word and the snatches of talk were all on the same question: What do we do now? I'd even heard a few, them as like to blame others for their predicament, muttering that they should never have let themselves get talked into a strike. But even so, when Bella stood to speak, we all turned towards her, as if she might say something different. When she read the statement from the mill, a wave of groans greeted the news.

Then James Connolly got up and the room quietened again. The bosses' response seemed like water off a duck's back to him, for he looked as calm as before. It was only when he mopped his forehead before he spoke that I thought maybe he was as human as the rest of us.

'First of all, I want to honour the courage of each and every one of you in choosing to strike. I want to celebrate your determination to fight for better conditions for yourselves and for those who come after you. Your menfolk and families are blessed indeed with women like yous.

'Our struggle as workers for the respect and conditions that we are entitled to by virtue of our labour is a long one. It will not be won overnight, but each generation, each one of us who stands up to be counted, contributes to that struggle and builds the ground on which others after us can stand.'

Bridie and me and a couple of others started clapping and a ripple of applause spread round the room. Mr Connolly nodded before continuing.

'Now, you have been on strike for over a week, and I know the hardship even a week without pay can bring. We also know the strike has not been widespread enough to change the bosses' minds and we need to make sure that you hold on to your positions. In any campaign there is the need to be tactical in seizing what advantage there is to be gained. The question is: 'How do you go back and yet remain undefeated?'

We were all holding our breath and I'd my fingers crossed that he knew the answer.

'My advice to you women is to *march* back on Friday morning all together, with your heads held high, with your arms linking with one another and with singing, laughter and chatter; for you may find that your strike has put a shot across the bows of the owners. They may not be so keen to enforce these new rules, even if they cannot lose face by rescinding them.' He paused. 'And remember. There is no defeat as long as we continue to work in solidarity with each other.'

The applause was subdued, uncertain maybe, until Bella stood up and hollered.

'Solidarity, Sisters! For isn't that how we survive? Isn't that what we do best, faced with all that life throws at us?'

That rallied our spirits, and we tripped down the stairs and out with a bit more spring in our steps.

On Friday morning we met, as agreed, at the corner of Dover Street and the Falls. We linked up into threes or more. Bridie and I were arm and arm with Maggie and Bella Dwyer, and we marched up to those gates like we were going to flatten them. Right at the gates, my voice faltered, and I fancied I could hear others doing the same, but Bella Dwyer and Maggie, more power to them, never wavered and we rallied.

We strode like an army into the yard, through the doors and up the steps to the spinning floor, singing like our lives depended on it. Our voices echoed round the stairwell, bolstering me up even more. We sailed past aul Campbell and yer man Frazer, standing dour faced at the hall doors. If they'd been inclined to speak, we never gave them a chance but carried on to the frames and settled to our business as if there'd never been a change of rule.

As I haunched down waiting for the first whistle from the doffing mistress, I could hear the murmur of women's voices and the giggles along our line of millies. I tried to keep an eye on what Campbell was up to and I could see others doing the same, looking out of the corners of their eyes along their aisle. He was nearly on top of me before I heard the thud of his boot on the flagstones. My mouth went dry. But I did what we'd agreed. I kept my mind on my job but I also made a point of talking to Bridie on one side of me and Imelda Peoples on the other, as if we'd never been interrupted. My hair was literally standing on end, expecting him to pounce on one or all of us. He stalked slowly past, hat pulled down tight on his head and his hands clasped behind him. I could see his right hand curl and uncurl, jangling the keys he was fidgeting with. He reached the end of our line, without stopping once. I held my breath. He turned the corner. I still held my breath. And then I was elbowing and being elbowed, and we were looking at each other in disbelief and delight. Mr Connolly'd been right.

I felt fit to burst with pride.

Four

13th January 1912

It was Saturday and we should've both been home, but when we finished work at midday, Bridie had cajoled me to walk down into the city centre. Our strike was nearly a year gone and with it that feeling of being one with everyone else. It had hit us in different ways. Whereas I felt like I'd been washed up on the shore with the tide out, Bridie seemed to think there was something out there for the seizing and was itching to find it.

We were perched on the balustrade at the base of one of two grand lamps that flanked either side of the Custom House steps. We had lapped the bottom of our shawls into folds to pad us from the cold stone, for the big bright January sun could hardly take the edge off the bitter wind coming up and off the Lagan River. We had a grand view, as we were slightly above and at the edge of the crowd that had gathered.

'Ach Nan Rose, look at those shoes! Leather like lace, and such a dainty wee heel. Wouldn't ye love to be walkin' down the street with those on ye?'

As she spoke, Bridie tightened the braid at the end of her plait of black hair, before throwing it back to hang down below her shoulders. I didn't begrudge her its thickness and length, for it was a palaver to wash and dry – but the colour was another matter. Even though we were both due our weekly wash, her plait gleamed in the sunshine, whereas my 'dirty fair' hair, looked like rats' tails coiled at the nape of my neck. I straightened my legs and glared at my splattered clogs and my socks that I'd need to darn again. 'Walking down the street in any pair of shoes'd be an experience.'

The small flute and drum band that had led the procession up the steps were standing to one side at the base of the lamp opposite us. The half dozen men and boys huddled together, for all the world trying to look as if they had nothing really to do with the business of the meeting, despite the purple and green sashes over their black jackets. One of the younger lads had opened the top three brass buttons of his jacket and was twisting his neck from side to side as if the high collar chafed him. He suddenly looked up and caught my gaze. I looked away and across to the party of women that had followed the band on to the top step.

They were a grand sight, with their velvet trimmed coats and fine wool jackets and their lace-trimmed linen blouses. And the hats they had on them! One woman must have had the plumage of a rooster pinned on the side. Another, big and bulging from her long black coat, looked as if she'd black lace frothing from her head. They all wore a purple and green sash or rosette.

'Those flowers on the brim of her hat! Do ye think they're real?' Bridie elbowed me so I turned to look again at the girl that she was eyeing up and down. She was standing on the end of the front row. She was maybe a year or two older than us and dressed in a sage wool jacket and skirt, with velvet collar and lapels. Her linen blouse was high necked with a row of buttons to the right of her chin. The brim of her black hat was decked with a cluster of cream flowers. I thought of our daily sweat and toil to produce fine garments for women who looked as if they'd never felt a bead of sweat in their lives. It was just as well there was a Heaven, for it'd be hard to endure the unfairness of life otherwise.

The girl looked up, returned our gaze, and smiled, bright as the sun, before turning away to look straight ahead. The woman with the black lace frothing from her head had started to speak. I found I couldn't hear her words, the way I heard Bella Dwyer, for the sound of her voice was like bone china and carried me off to pictures I'd seen of homes where linen was spread as tablecloths, as sideboard runners, as head and arm rests on chairs, as embroidered doilies under plant pots and bottles of scent. I looked at the line of them and everything I saw and imagined carried me further away so that only a few words stayed with me. 'Votes for women.' 'Rights for women.' But what did women like them know about women like me? And what could I trust in women like them? By this time another one was speaking.

There was a thin round of applause, mainly from women in the crowd, although I noticed one or two men clapping determinedly. Couples that had paused to hear what was going on drifted away. I fancied I saw more than one man steer his companion firmly by the elbow. I noticed a small crowd of younger men gathered at the back. They stood, feet wide, hands in pockets, chests puffed up like bantam cocks.

'Go away home for yous'll need to be getting the dinner on for yer menfolk!' one of them shouted and the others jeered.

Bridie cupped her hands round her mouth, so her voice carried loud and clear to the hallions. 'If you haven't anything sensible to say, you'd be better shuttin' your faces for you might learn something!'

'I wasn't talkin' to you for you're nothin' but an aul millie and couldn't even get a fella.'

At that, Bridie was on her feet, steadying herself with one arm on the lamp post.

'And you're nothin' but a big mouth, standing there brayin' like a donkey! Go away off and give us all peace!'

The sideshow had taken over from the main event. The woman with the black lace summoned the band to strike up a tune. Two men in suits who'd been in the crowd moved over to the younger men at the back and after a few words, the boyos went off to find some other sport. The line of women on the front step began to move among the crowd, giving out leaflets.

'C'mon Bridie. Let's go, for I need to be gettin' back. I want to call round to Maggie's later and I've chores to do before that.' I might as well have been talkin' to the wall, for Bridie was intent on the women handing out the leaflets. She clambered down and walked towards the girl, who, seeing her, came in our direction.

'You've a strong voice and a fierce spirit,' she said, smiling. 'What's your name?'

'Bridie Corr. And this is my friend Nan Rose Murphy.'

'My name is Lizzie Balfour. I'm pleased to make your acquaintance.' She handed Bridie a leaflet. Bridie took it and looked at it. There was lots of writing on it. Lizzie Balfour watched for a minute.

'It's about our next meeting. Wednesday fortnight, in the upstairs of The Linen Hall Library, so we will be able to keep rabble-rousers out.' As she said this she looked over to where the boyos had stood. 'We are having a speaker from Manchester, who will be talking about her work with women and girls in the Lancashire cotton mills.'

'That'll be quare and interesting,' says Bridie. 'I wonder what it'd be like working in a cotton mill in England. It couldn't be any harder I'm sure than working in the mills here.'

'Oh, is that what you do?' She gave us a long look, as if admiring something we were wearing. I would never have expected to get a look like that from a girl like her. 'And so, you have come straight from the mill this morning to attend our meeting? That is so impressive.'

Even Bridie didn't know what to say to that. We just nodded and after another smile at us, she carried on into the crowd. We headed off back home. We were barely out of earshot when Bridie linked my arm and started gushing.

'Such a wee angel of a face on her, too. And did ye see how she treated us like we were ladies instead of millies.'

I didn't want Bridie getting carried away, so I hid my grudging regard for Lizzie Balfour and shook my head. 'I don't know Bridie! You put more store by a civil word from a slip of a girl who's never had to lift a finger to earn a farthing when here are we, earning our keep and helpin' keep our families. We don't need a kind word from her to feel we're worth something. Just remember what James Connolly said.'

Bridie pulled to a halt, turned round and stuck her tongue out at me.

'Ach Nan Rose, can ye not keep going on about us being the salt of the earth? I'm fed up being the salt of the earth. I wouldn't mind being the icing on the cake for a while.'

Well, every day after that, Bridie pestered and prodded me about goin' with her to the meeting. I couldn't understand her enthusiasm and she couldn't understand my lack of it.

'Bridie, I don't know why you're so set on carrying on with women who wouldn't give you the time of day if you passed them on the street.'

'And I don't understand why you're so set agin them. You make them out as wrong and they haven't done anything.'

When the prodding didn't work, she took to wheedling.

'C'mon Nan Rose. It'll be a geg. We can see all the style. I bet yer woman from Manchester'll be even grander than any of the ones we've seen so far. And they'll probably have another band. I'll even buy us a wee bag of bullseyes to suck while we're listenin' to it all.'

When that didn't work, she resorted to making me feel bad. 'You know I'd do anything for you. You know I'd go anywhere you asked me to.'

'I've never asked you to go anywhere. Just leave me be.'

In the end, it was her threat to ask Gemma Locke to go that did it. I wasn't fussed about Gemma, and I didn't want her getting in with Bridie, for I could see the two of them off like hares and me left behind. So I agreed.

Two women stood inside the doors of the library, showing the way to the meeting room. I saw the uncertainty in their glance at the two of us. I wasn't surprised, for we stuck out like sore thumbs in the crowd of women milling around downstairs. We were the only ones in shawls and without hats. I was even hoping that'd put an end to the whole shenanigans, for my point would be well made if they wouldn't let us in the door. At that moment, Lizzie Balfour came striding across the entrance hall.

'Bridie and Nan Rose! You've come. How delightful!' There is nothing like hearing your name called in a glass tinkle to lift you up a few inches. Lizzie turned to the other women. 'Emma and Jane, these ladies were at our Custom House public meeting. Isn't it wonderful that they've decided they would like to hear more?' They each cracked a smile even as Lizzie ushered us up the stairs.

'If you can stay a little after the meeting, I want to introduce you to our speaker. I know she will be extremely interested in your experience as mill workers here.' She was leading us up the side aisle to seats a few rows from the top. I was beginning to feel like a prime heifer at market, a good specimen of meat. I didn't fancy being prodded the better to see what I was made of.

'Bridie, we're both up early for the mill in the morning. I wanna get home and have a bit of time to do a few things before bed,' says I.

Bridie's eyes were on the speaker, who was sitting at a small table to the side of the stage, alongside the woman with the black lace frothing out of her head. 'Imagine someone like her wanting to talk to us about being millies. Yer Mammy'll understand if you tell her where we've been.'

'If Mammy didn't take to the likes of James Connolly, she's not going to have time for an Englishwoman even if she does know something about mills.'

By the cut of her, the speaker from Manchester was going to live up to Bridie's expectations. Her hat was black and wide brimmed, with a swirl of black ribbon and dusky pink roses round the bonnet. She wore a fine wool jacket in the same shade of pink. But Lizzie Balfour still had the edge when it came to the shoes. From what we could see, the speaker's were simply sturdy.

While we waited for the meeting to begin, I took a good look round the room. I could see that not all of the women were dressed so fine. The woman right in front of me, for instance, wore a coat that was shiny with wear in places. And the two beside her had the prim, tired look of schoolteachers. Not all of them lived in grand homes then. I wondered what brought them all here, for I imagined they had better things they could be doing of an evening. I began to notice the odd man or two dotted through the audience, and turning round to get a proper look at the crowd I could see that one side of the back row was nearly all men. What is it about men? At Mass, there's the priest and the altar boys right up front and then rows of men perched on the back pews or propping up the back wall, having come in at the last moment or later, and ready as greyhounds to get out the door as soon as the communion's over.

I got no further in my pondering, for at that point, the froth-hatted woman stood up to introduce the speaker. There was a round of applause and yer woman from England stepped to the centre of the stage. She spoke in even grander chandelier tones. I wondered how Bella Dwyer would fare up on the stage with this lot. I wasn't sure how she'd go down, but I reckoned the fire from her belly would set any glass chimes shivering and tinkling. Mind you, yer woman could speak. You could see she minded about the hardships of women in the mills of Lancashire. She praised their hard work and condemned their poor wages and conditions. So, there were women like us across the water. I'd never thought of that before.

As the meeting closed, Lizzie Balfour was at the end of our row before I'd a chance to drag Bridie out. She ushered us up to the bottom of the steps leading to the platform and chatted lightly and brightly while we waited for the speaker. For a girl that had only met us once before, she introduced us like we were prize gems that had been in the family for decades.

When Bridie mentioned our strike, yer speaker woman leaned forward and listened as if her life depended on catching every word. She laughed approvingly when Bridie spoke of us walking back, singing.

'My dear ladies, your experience is very valuable. Very valuable indeed. Might you be able to spare another hour tomorrow evening to talk in more depth, for I leave for Dublin the following day?'

Bridie didn't hesitate, didn't remember for a second what I'd said to her about Maggie and me going to the Women's Novena at Clonard Monastery the next night and had committed both of us before I could open my mouth.

But on the way home, in between her skipping and jigging with excitement, I made it clear that she'd have to go alone. What I couldn't say, given Bridie's high mood, was that Maggie was fretting about no sign of childer as yet. She hadn't said as much right out to my face, but between her and Mammy, there were enough hints of what was bothering her. Knowing Maggie, I reckoned she must be desperate if she was pinning her hopes on prayer. And to tell you the truth, I was more comfortable going to the novena than to another one of these meetings. I'd maybe have more of a chance to talk with Maggie, I'd have a bit of craic with our own sort walking to and from the monastery and I could sing. I loved singing and a church full of song could lift my spirits no matter how low I was.

As it was, despite Bridie's chitter over the next couple of days about yer woman and Lizzie Balfour, the talk at home on Saturday afternoon put all them suffragettes out of my head. It started off quiet enough. Father was stopping up the cracks and gaps in the front window frame with fresh newspaper. Mammy was in the scullery chopping up potatoes and onions to add to a lamb bone for a white stew that would see us through til Monday, and I was hunched up as close as I could to the bit of fire, darning socks. Michael came in, banging the front door hard behind him. I looked up and could see he'd a face like thunder.

'I don't know what's eatin' you, Michael,' says Father, keeping his eyes and hands on the crack he was filling. 'But I'd thank ye not to take the door of its hinges. I've enough on my hands keeping up with what has to be done, without you adding to it.'

Michael opened his mouth to say something and thought better of it. He hung up his cap and jacket and stomped, as loudly as he dared, across to the fireplace, where he stood glowering.

'And, if you've nothin' better to be doing than stompin'

round the place,' calls Mammy, from the scullery, 'you can go out to the back tap and fill the kettle so as there's some hot water for bathing later. And let the dog in while you're at it.'

I could see Michael was seething, but he did as he was told. He'd barely hung the kettle over the fire, when Father, who'd finished with the window, came over to stand beside him. Bandit took up position at my feet, but, like me, all her attention was on the two of them.

'So, what ails ye, Son? It's not like you to be raging around like a bull.'

With that, Michael pulled a scrunched-up sheet of paper out of his pocket and shoved it into Father's hand. Father smoothed it while Michael's right shoe tapped the floor in agitation.

'Ah! The meeting at Celtic Park on Thursday about Home Rule. I thought you were goin' to that?'

Michael shoved his hands into his pockets and stamped hard with both heels.

'I wanted to go to it. I still want to go to it. But with a shilling a ticket, the only way I could go was to see if I could get taken on as a steward. Jim McAnearney said he'd put in a word for me. I was to see him at the Hibernians on my way home from the Yard today, but he didn't show up. And the word is they've got all the stewards they need.' Michael shook his head. 'A shilling a ticket! How do they expect a working man to find that?'

Father rubbed his chin. 'It's not like Jim to let a body down like that. I'd have thought he would turn up to tell ye, one way or the other.'

Jim and Maggie were at school together, although he was a few years older than her. He was a big fella with a widow's stoop and a foot that he had to drag everywhere. As it was, he made up for what he couldn't do with his body, by using his head. Maggie always said he was a great reader and writer. That stood him in good stead for he had got a job in the office of The Belfast Ropeworks when he left school. He'd kept the book learning up and was teaching others Irish history of an evening.

I fingered the two farthings in my pocket. Would they be any good to Michael? I supposed I could do without the red ribbon I'd set my heart on for another week or two and Mrs Dwyer would give me tick for a week for a wee bag of bullseyes. I was spared the decision, for there was a tap-tap at the window. Jim McAnearney must have knowd we were talking about him for there he was. Bandit growled softly while Michael leapt for the front door. Father gave me one of his 'What did I say?' looks and put a finger to his lips.

'I hope you weren't cursing me too hard, Michael.' Jim's voice carried loud and clear into the room. 'I couldn't see the right fella about the stewarding until this morning. You're on for Thursday.' Michael's whoop of delight startled Bandit into a fit of barking. By the time Father had reached over and lifted her off her feet by the scruff of the neck to shut her up, Jim had gone, and Michael was standing in front of us, waving a white armband and grinning as if all his Christmases had come at once.

'Well, more power to ye, Son,' says Father. 'And more power to John Redmond and the Irish Parliamentary Party, for getting this far this time with Home Rule. Whether they'll get any further is another matter, but sure, what can they do but keep trying.'

'And why wouldn't they take it the whole way?' Michael puffed himself up. 'If it wasn't for the support of Redmond and the Parliamentary Party, the English Liberals wouldn't even be in government, never mind changin' the law in the summer to clip the House of Lords' wings. If they can do that between them, why not Home Rule?' With that, he tossed the armband up in the air, caught it and pocketed it, before reaching for his coat and cap.

'I won't be long,' says he. 'I just need to call in at the Hibernians again to let the lads know that I'm on for Thursday.'

As the door closed after him, Father looked over at me, shaking his head, more in amusement than annoyance.

'We all have to learn the hard way,' says he.

'There's many a one in work thinks the same,' says I. 'Peggy Arthurs' brother delivers leaflets for Redmond's lot. She was just saying over break today, that he's been cock-a-hoop these last months, for he thinks we'll have Home Rule by this time next year.'

Father sat down and reached for his pipe. He began to scrape out the bowl, tapping it every so often on the hearth.

'Young fellas! Aren't they always rushin' to think something's over before it's even started?' He opened his baccy tin and began to fill his pipe, tamping each big pinchful down before putting in the next. He seemed to be talking more to himself than me. I was about to pick up my darning again, when he lit a taper from the fire, puffed at his pipe to get it going and sank back into his chair.

'Clipping the wings of the Lords with that Parliament Act in the summer is one thing. Home Rule's another. If it was all over, yer man, Lord Carson wouldn't have accepted the leadership of the Ulster Unionists this very same summer just gone. They're readying to fight this all the way.'

'Nan Rose, is that darnin' not done yet?' I turned round to see Mammy standing in the scullery doorway, hands on hips.

'These are the last few stitches in this elbow now,' says I.

'Just as well,' says she, coming over to check the kettle, 'for we all need a bath before supper.'

She couldn't say anything to Father for sitting down, but

she could make her point by getting at me. I'd wanted to ask him more about Carson and Home Rule, but then again, I didn't want to show my ignorance. I decided I'd be better listening in on the talk of some of the ones at work than having Bridie bend my ear about them suffragettes.

Five

February 7th 1912

I'd never have credited the effect on Michael of being chosen as a steward. His voice deepened overnight. He carried himself tall. He commanded rather than cajoled Bandit. Over the next couple of evenings at supper, he announced every new snippet of information or gossip about the meeting, as if he was Moses bringing back the Ten Commandments. The meeting was to be held in a grand marquee being set up that very week in Celtic Park. The police were to be there in force.

'Not a bad day if you're in the Royal Irish Constabulary,' says Michael on Wednesday, as we sat round the table, finishing our champ. 'Many a one of them is getting overtime tomorrow, whereas us stewards are having to take the time off work.'

Mammy let out a sigh and opened her mouth to speak but Father juked in before her.

'Well Michael,' says he, leaning forward on his elbows, 'as you said yourself, at least you're not having to pay to go.' He looked round at Mammy. 'And with that many police on, all the stewards will be well protected.'

I was smiling inside at how Father had managed to stop Mammy in her tracks before she started yet again on her litany of fears.

'Michael would lose a day's pay.'
'There'd be trouble at the meeting.'
'He'd be injured and then laid off work.'
'He could lose his job.'

Michael had been able to reassure her on Monday that Edmund Boyle who ran the timber yard was more than alright with giving him the day off. 'He says that way, he can hear all about what happens, straight from one of the horses' mouths.'

Now, she pulled herself up from the chair, leaning heavily on her outstretched hands. She sighed long and loud, while the three of us held our tongues. Then, clattering the plates towards her, she bustled into the scullery, her every step sounding out her disapproval.

Michael arrived home around half-six on the Thursday, just as I was ladling out barley broth. He was flushed, and as he sat down, I caught the reek of tobacco off his shirt and waistcoat, along with that sour smell of a crowd of men packed together.

'That was some meeting if you're only back now,' says Father, giving him a long look.

'It was four o'clock before it finished and another hour after that before the last of the crowd left and we could start to set the place to rights.' Michael spooned a mouthful of the broth into him. 'We didn't get started until near two o'clock because yer English Home Secretary fella, Churchill, got held up.' He leaned forward on his elbows and looked up and round at us.

'Accordin' to Jim, who had it from a sergeant he knows in the Constabulary, Churchill's car was stopped and jostled by a crowd of the ones from the shipyard and their like. Seems they were heaving that hard, the car was weaving from side to side. And all the time hollering "Home Rule means

Rome Rule. No Surrender."' He choked on a laugh. 'At least it gave him a taste of what we're up against here with them unionists. We can only hope he gives chapter and verse to Lloyd George and the rest of Cabinet.'

Bandit who was under the table started growling before we heard the knock on the door. Michael, who was nearest, stepped to open it.

'That'll be Bridie for me,' says I. 'We said we'd call round to Imelda Dobbin for an hour or so, for she's going to teach us a couple more set dances.' I looked up at the clock on the mantelpiece. 'She's early for once.'

'Come in out of the cold, Bridie.' Michael stood back to let her pass him.

'Sit yourself down by the hearth and warm up, Daughter,' says Father. 'Michael was just telling us about the meeting at Celtic Park.'

Bridie smiled at Father and then turned to Mammy.

'Mammy was asking after yous all.'

'And tell her we were asking after her. Is old Mrs Corr mended? The last time I saw her, she was coughing right and hard.'

'She's grand now, Mrs Murphy.' Bridie sat herself down and looked over to Michael who was back down at the table.

'Was it a big meeting, Michael?' She spoke in the shy voice I'd only heard her use when she had talked to the speaker from Manchester or sometimes when she was talking about Lizzie Balfour. She looked at Michael as if she was praying to a holy statue. He must've noticed the change in Bridie, for he straightened himself up and turned to face her.

'It was indeed. The biggest crowd I've ever seen. Any time they cheered, I thought the marquee was going to lift from its moorings.'

'So, there were some things worth cheering?' says Father. Michael bristled, not noticing the devilment in Father's eyes. 'Sure, who could listen to John Redmond in his stride, without wanting to call and clap?'

'Well, for myself, it would depend on what he was saying.' Father smiled. 'And what about the other two?'

'Once yer Englishman Churchill steadied himself after his rough ride, he was in fine enough voice as was Lord Pirrie. And although Redmond outshone them both, the crowd roared to hear the British Home Secretary pledging his government to stand side by side with us to bring in Home Rule. Pirrie got a roar of approval too, when he opened the proceedings, for saying that the Ulster Liberals were every bit as determined as Redmond and the Irish Parliamentary Party to see Home Rule. 'It is in the best interests of all of Ireland,' says he.

Father stroked his chin. 'It's good to have the Ulster Liberals saying the same as the I.P.P. With all the hoo-hah from the Ulster Unionists, you could easily forget that there are Protestants as well as Catholics who believe Home Rule is what we need.'

Bridie was still gazing at Michael like he was Redmond himself. 'An Englishman and a Lord and you a steward, Michael,' she gushed.

I got up from the table. 'C'mon Bridie, we need to be going before my brother's so full of himself, we won't be able to get him and his head through the front door.'

Bridie stood up, her eyes never shifting.

'So, Michael, what exactly is Home Rule?'

I paused as I was gathering my own shawl round me. Bridie had done me the favour of asking my question. And well she might, for Michael would not banter her like he bantered me at times.

Michael choked on his mouthful of broth. He stared at Bridie, his eyes narrowing and his lips twitching, as if she'd asked him to add up a long set of numbers and he was figuring it out in his head. Father opened his mouth but thought better of it. I knotted my shawl round me.

'If we got Home Rule, Ireland would have self-government.' Michael spoke slowly, as if working words out as he was going.

'So England wouldn't rule over us any longer?' Bridie shook her head. 'Would you ever credit that?'

'Not exactly.' Michael paused. If he was picking potatoes as slowly as he was picking his words, he'd be starved to death.

'Not exactly. We would still be part of the United Kingdom.'

It was Bridie's turn to narrow her eyes. 'Well now, how would that work, I wonder.'

'Bridie, we need to go! Imelda hasn't all night and nor have we.' I had my hand on the door handle and clattered my clogs for good measure.

Bridie stirred herself.

'Maybe you can tell me a bit more another time, Michael.'

And with that we bade them good night and stepped onto the pavement.

'Look!' Bridie'd stopped and was spinning round, arms outstretched. 'Now we've come round that bend, we can't see where we've come from, and we can't see ahead beyond that tree where the road turns again.'

It was the Sunday before St Patrick's Day and we'd taken ourselves for a walk in the direction of the Black Mountain, looking for shamrock for all of our ones to pin on their clothes. I stopped, looked to my right, and left and then at her. Her face was one big smile.

'Yes. I can see that.' I shrugged.

'I love that about walking in a glen – how everything we've passed suddenly disappears and another bit of the road opens out – like one of them books with pictures that pop out and then fold away when you turn the page.'

'Where'd *you* see a book like that?'

Bridie looked as if she'd been caught stealing. All red and couldn't look me in the face. 'Lizzie Balfour showed me it at the meeting last week. It was a present for one of her nieces.'

'So you managed to get out of the Women's Confraternity again, despite yer Aunt Imelda?'

Bridie nodded. 'Yes. I went to the suffragette meeting instead.'

'Has Imelda changed her tune then? It was only last week you said she was going on and on to you and yer mammy about you missing the Women's Confraternity.'

'She's still doin' my head in with all that.' Bridie raised her head and herself to her full height. 'But I wasn't going to stop going to the suffragette meetings, whatever she thought.'

She'd started to walk again and was striding out as if the Kingdom of Heaven itself was round the corner. I upped my pace to keep alongside her and for a while, we walked with only the panting of our breaths for company.

'Do you remember that day Jenny McAleese brought a poem she'd writ into school?' Bridie had slowed down and was looking straight at me. 'And after she'd let her read it out, aul Donegan says, in her hoity-toity voice, looking over her glasses and down her nose at her, "People like you, Jenny McAleese, would be better paying attention to washing your clothes than scribbling on paper."'

'Yeah, I remember. And I remember we all laughed including you.'

'I did, more shame on me, siding with that hatchet of a woman. Why shouldn't any one of us write a poem if we want to?'

'Ach Bridie! The problem wasn't writing the poem. It was being stupid enough to think aul Donegan would do anything other than mock her for it.'

'That's not the point Nan Rose. What right has she to

tell any one of us what we can do? And how can she get away with saying that to us? She wouldn't say that to someone like Lizzie Balfour.'

'That's cos she'd know someone else washes her clothes.' I managed to throw that last line off, so that after a second, Bridie laughed at the joke. We walked on, arms linked until the path curved to the right again. The sun that had shone so brightly at the start of our walk was hidden in cloud and now that the path had narrowed, twisted fingers of hawthorn tugged at my skirt, as if warning about what lay ahead. Bridie stopped.

'And look, Nan Rose. This bit where we're standing is about to disappear.' She turned to take in the whole view. 'But we know it'll be here, just as it is, when we come back.'

'It depends on what happens in the meantime.'

Bridie's eyes narrowed.

'What do you mean?'

'When I went back with Father to the cottage after Granny died, he said it wasn't the same.'

'What'd changed?'

'Him.'

Bridie burst out laughing. 'Well, that's diffrint. He hadn't been back for years. We're just goin' for a walk.'

I sat down heavily on a flat rock by the oak tree. I looked up at her. For the first time I felt like the wee one between us and I didn't like it. I folded my arms tight round my chest, the better to hold myself together.

'Life can change in the blink of an eye. Look at Martha Reynolds. She came into work on a Tuesday morning and an hour later, when her sleeve caught in the frame, she'd lost two of her fingers.' I looked hard at Bridie. 'Why don't you tell me now what you haven't been tellin' me all week? I know it's something about yer woman Balfour. And then we can decide if we're going on or going back.'

Bridie came over slowly and sat down beside me. I watched as she placed both hands on the grass and rocked a little back and forth. I watched as she crossed and then uncrossed her ankles. I watched and I waited. When she spoke, it was into her lap, so that I'd to lean into her to catch her words.

'Miss Balfour wants me to come and work as her personal maid.' She stretched over to pick a buttercup and twirled it under her chin. 'And I'm going to accept.' In the silence, there was a sudden flurry and a chirruping in the tree above us. Gazing up, I could see two robins flitting from branch to branch in a squabble. One of them was going to lose out.

Bridie was due to start work for Lizzie Balfour the Monday after Easter week. With each day that passed, her excitement grew. Sunday fortnight before Easter, her mammy and her had made their way to the Balfour's, where they'd met Mrs Balfour and were introduced to the cook. After that, she could barely contain herself. I was beside myself too but with what I couldn't say. She was like a bright farthing newly minted. The more she gleamed, the more I felt like a squashed lump of lead.

Even when she pleaded with me to walk over to The Balfours with her and her mammy on the Sunday before she started work, I felt no pleasure at being so wanted. But I determined to go. For one thing, when I thought of her in the future I'd be able to picture where she was. I decided my best bet was to wait till I got Mammy and Father together and then bring the matter up, for if I asked Mammy first, she'd say no. Ever since the Celtic Park meeting, she'd been like a mother hen with her chickens, flapping and clucking at any suggestion of anyone of us straying off our beaten tracks. To make matters worse, there'd been a big demonstration against Home Rule at Balmoral on Easter Tuesday and afterwards, in Royal Avenue the crowds had thronged the

English Conservative fella, Bonar Law, as if he was the Angel Gabriel, himself.

I got my chance on Friday evening. Michael'd taken himself out as soon as he'd swallowed the last mouthful on his plate. Father had sat himself down by the fireplace to tend his pipe and Mammy and me were still at the table. I stood up, as if to clear the dishes so I was standing between them.

'Bridie and her mammy are walking over to the Balfours on Sunday, and they want me to go with them.' I'd barely finished the words when Mammy was in like a ferret down a rabbit hole.

'I don't want you crossin' the city, Nan Rose. If Bridie Corr wants to take herself off over there, that's her business – though you'd think her mother would have thought again, after all that business on Tuesday.'

She looked over at Father, who was bent over the Irish News, fingering the words. 'With all this palaver, there's going to be trouble sooner or later. Better stay close to home. Aren't I right, Father?'

Even as Father was tearing himself away from the paper, I nipped in quick, for once the two of them agreed on something, there was no way of getting' round it. 'Mrs Corr said she'd be glad of the company on the way back, for it'll be hard leaving Bridie there. And yous are always sayin' to give a neighbour a hand when you can.'

Father looked from one to the other of us.

'Let her go, Agnes. Nobody'll bother them on a Sunday.' He beckoned me to him. I walked slowly to where he sat by the side of the empty grate. He put a hand on my shoulder. 'Just remember, when you're over that way Nan Rose, and seein' those big houses,' he said softly. 'Just remember where the money came from to build them.'

On the Saturday you'd have thought it was me starting work over on the Malone Road for Mammy insisted I should have a bath and wash my hair. 'And keep on your good skirt when you come from Mass tomorrow and wear it when you're walking over. For I won't have anyone lookin' down at a daughter of mine.'

So, after I came in from the mill, I fed the fire more wood and turf and put a half pot of water on the stand at the fender and hung a kettle of hot water over the fire. Later that afternoon, while Father and Michael were round at the Hibernians Club playing a game of cards and Mammy was visiting Maggie, I fed the fire more turf and sat the tin bath down in front of it. I filled it with a kettle of boiling water and a kettle of cold. I half-filled the kettle again with cold water to mix with the half pot of hot so I'd lukewarm water to rinse my hair with. When all was ready, I clambered out of my clothes and stepped into the clear water. I suddenly felt special. This was the first time I'd been head of the queue for the bath. In the quiet of the house, I squatted down, scrubbing first and then dipping the flannel in the thin grey suds and squeezing the water all over me. Soak, squeeze, soak, squeeze. After a while, I found myself giving in to the trickle and tickle of the water down my back and by the time I stepped out of the bath, I felt I could just sit and be quiet for the first time since Bridie'd told me about her decision. I took my time, drying and dressing myself. I combed out my hair so that it hung straight and damp down over my shoulders, all the while enjoying the bit of heat from the fire. I glanced at the clock. It'd be another half-hour before Mammy'd be back.

I tiptoed upstairs and took out my secret tin that I kept hidden right at the bottom of the metal trunk in the bedroom. Back in the kitchen, I sat in Father's chair. I prised off the lid and fingered through my treasures. The shells from Tyrella beach caught my eye. They'd been two hinged shells, but each had separated into two. I lifted the four of them carefully out and placed them in my left palm. At first, I just looked at them, remembering that morning, on our way back home from visiting Granny. Father had stopped by the beach so as I could have a proper look at the sea. For a moment I could see and hear again that single lark, that morsel of sweet sound, rising straight and high out of the dunes until it disappeared into the blue. I could see us, Father ahead, steady and slow on the damp sand, and me meandering across the blanket of dry sand, picking shells until my apron pockets were full. As we turned and headed back, I paddled along beside father, the water playing at my ankles. He'd laughed at my bulging pockets.

'Nan Rose, you'll have to leave most of those behind, for the sea doesn't like us plundering its belongings. And your mother won't take too kindly to a pile of shells.' We paused by a low rock near the beginning of the track. Father sat and lit his pipe while I emptied my booty near his feet. He smoked and I sifted, and in the peace between and all around us, I felt as if time had stopped. I chose my two pairs of hinged shells.

'Look Father, if I press them gently between my finger and thumb they open and close a tiny bit.'

'Like you and your friend Bridie, whispering away at the front step. I swear I could never have imagined two wee girls would have so many secrets.' And with that, he tapped out his pipe on the rock and we headed in the direction of the pony and cart.

Now I fingered the shells in my palm. The flatter pair were the colour of cream and sand with three darker lines running across their backs so that I could fancy it as a soft shawl draped across a woman's shoulders. The other pair were fuller with a scalloped edge like ladies' skirts falling in folds from the waist but with layers of petticoats peeping out from the bottom.

I imagined Bridie helping Lizzie Balfour dress and undress, imagined her starch and iron petticoats and blouses. For a moment, I allowed myself to wonder how I might feel with the finest of linen next to my skin. 'Nan Rose, that's the road to nowhere,' I told myself. I sighed and chose one of each pair of shells. I took out the long yellow ribbon that Maggie'd given me, fetched the scissors and cut it into two equal lengths. I pocketed the two shells and the one length of ribbon and returned their other halves to the tin and closed the lid.

On Sunday afternoon, I set off with Bridie and her mother, all three of us smelling of Lifebuoy soap. Bridie's hair was plaited tight into a long rope and she'd tied it with the ribbon I'd given her on Saturday evening.

'Ach Nan Rose,' she'd said, when I gave her the ribbon and shells, 'They're lovely. I'll keep my halves safe, knowin' you'll do the same with yours.' She'd suddenly laughed. 'Wait till you see what Granny gave me.' It was a wee tin St Christopher medal. "To keep you safe on your journey," says she. You'd think I was going across the water instead of across the city. I said to Granny that I'd be home every Sunday and do you know what she said? "I hope so, Daughter, but sometimes it's easier to leave than to come back."'

I'd laughed with her and didn't tell her that I'd heard Mammy say something the same to Maggie. I still had that childish notion that somehow if you didn't talk about what you feared, then you could keep it at bay.

We crossed the city centre and came out at the bottom of the Lisburn Rd. As we walked up the road, heading out of town again, the streets became wider and cleaner. They looked as if somebody'd scrubbed every one of them from end to end. And they were even called something different. 'AV… EN…

UE'. The houses were bigger, wider, and grander than I'd ever imagined when Bridie had been telling me about them on the way over. But what I couldn't credit, even though I was seeing them with my own eyes, were the wee squares of garden between the front door of every house and the pavement. Like having yer own bit of countryside. In the ones that were not hidden by tall hedges, I could see daffodils hemming a square or circle of grass. One had a hawthorn tree with its blossom decking it like lace. Now, if we had the likes of that instead of mucky cobbles, the childer would be out playing in it, women would be talking across to their neighbours and we'd maybe have planted a few spuds, scallions or carrots. Whereas here, there wasn't a soul to be seen.

We turned into Wellington Avenue and walked up and past No. 12 as slowly as we could without stopping. The brass knocker shone like gold against the gleaming black paint of the door. Even though Bridie'd described it all, I hadn't imagined it would be as grand as it was. Mrs Corr seemed as flustered as me while Bridie almost throbbed with excitement. We stood at the nearest lamppost and bade Bridie goodbye. I suddenly felt shy, but Bridie'd already left us, for she could barely wait to knock the door on her new life. She birled round.

'I'd better go, or I'll be late. I'll see yous next Sunday.' We hovered between a hug and a handshake and did neither. She spun round, walked to No.12 and we watched as the door opened and swallowed her up, closing after her with a smack like lips on a piece of potato apple bread.

I noticed my hands were curled into tight fists and it came to me in a rush that I wanted to shake Mrs Corr. I wanted to shake her till she rattled and then run home as fast as I could. I wanted to shake her, all the while hollering 'You shouldn't've let her go. You should've told her to stay. She's gone now and our Bridie won't ever be back.'

Six

September 29th, 1912

I'd barely stepped out the front door onto the pavement in response to Bridie's knock, when she linked my arm close and leaned into me.

'You'll never believe where I was yesterday,' says she.

'Well, if I'd never believe it, there's no point in me trying to guess it,' says I. I'd a bit of a face on me for Bridie was late and we'd have to near run to get to Clonard for the start of the Mass. Otherwise, we'd be walking up the aisle trying to find the odd space on a pew to squeeze into, and all the while, standing out like two sore thumbs. I unlinked my arm, the better to walk as fast as I could.

Bridie wasn't fazed. 'I was down at the City Hall,' says she.

That stopped me in my tracks. I looked at her with my jaw dropped open.

'The City Hall yesterday? I don't believe you!'

She smiled as sweet as any angel. 'I'll tell you after Mass. C'mon, we need to run now or we'll be late.'

I might as well not have been at Clonard that morning for my head was buzzing as to what on earth would possess Bridie to go down to the City Hall on the very day it would be thronged with Unionists chomping at the bit to sign their Ulster Covenant agin Home Rule.

As it was, she didn't open her mouth until we'd begun our usual loop round Dunville Park. Since Easter when she'd started work for Lizzie Balfour, she and I walked to Clonard every Sunday for the ten o'clock mass and afterwards, come rain or shine, circled one or two times through Dunville Park, on our way home. If the weather was bad, we'd just sit down in the shelter for a wee while. It was the only way to get a bit of time to ourselves, what with her only being off from Saturday evening to Sunday tea-time. We'd talk about anything and everything that was on our minds – family, fellas, the goings on at the odd suffragette meeting that Bridie managed to attend. We'd have a right geg, for I'd give her chapter and verse on the goings-on at the mill and the street and she'd mimic the cook giving off about Mrs Balfour behind her back and then smiling to her face, so polite her jaws nearly cracked with the strain.

'So, as I was telling ye, Nan Rose, I was down at the City Hall yesterday. I went down with Miss Lizzie.'

'What was she doing down there? You told me her father was one of them that supported Home Rule.'

'He is one of them Liberals, yes. And yes, they all support Home Rule, even though it's only him that can vote.' She paused and I knowd she was wanting me to tease it all out of her. Paying me back for not playing along when she told me earlier. My curiosity swallowed my pride whole.

'So, c'mon Bridie, stop beating about the bush. Otherwise, we'll be back home before you tell me what you want me to hear.'

'Well.' She linked my arm and leaned in close again. 'You know there's women who are agin Home Rule and that they're organising for women to sign their own declaration, seeing as only men are allowed to sign that covenant?'

I nodded.

'Now, according to Lizzie, there's been a bit of an

argument at some of the suffragette meetings about whether or not they should be signing the declaration just to make the point about women having a say.'

'So, Lizzie Balfour went down to sign something she didn't believe in just for the sake of signing? That's like cutting off your nose to spite your face.'

'Noooh! She just wanted to go down and see what was going on. She took me along, so as I could get into town and out the other end, for she was afeard for me walking home myself with crowds everywhere.'

'I'll give her that,' says I. 'She's right and good at lookin' out for you.'

'Most of the time, she does, yes,' says Bridie. 'And she was right about Saturday. I've never seen a crowd like it. From Shaftesbury Square on, it was heavin' for they were streaming like a river down the Lisburn, Malone and Donegall Roads on their way to the City Hall. To tell you the truth, I thought I wasn't going to make it past Shaftesbury Square, for we were being pushed one way and then the next as all three roads met. I've never been in a crowd that big and tight. Not to mention their Union Jacks flying and some of the ones from the Donegall Road hollerin' at the top of their voices "Home Rule means Rome Rule. No to Rome Rule. No to Home Rule."'

By this time, me and Bridie'd circled the park once. I looked over at her, for I could hear her breathing suddenly ragged. The colour had drained from her face and her eyes were gazing at somewhere beyond the park.

'C'mon and let's head down towards the fountain,' says I, taking her by the elbow. 'We can sit by the water where the air's a bit fresher.'

She turned and met my eyes then. 'For a minute, I was back in that crowd,' says she, rubbing her chest just below her throat. The life had gone out of her voice, leaving her words slow and heavy. We walked to one of the wooden seats circling the fountain. I could feel the wood warm agin me as I settled myself beside Bridie. While I waited for her to gather herself, I watched the wee rainbows where the sunshine played on the drops.

'It's all just catching up with me now, talkin' to you, Nan Rose. You're the first one I've told, for I didn't want to worry Mammy.' She spoke soft and low. Her right hand clutched a fold of her skirt and twisted it this way and that.

'There were a crowd of fellas behind us, about the same age as your Michael. They were boastin' they were going to sign that bloomin' covenant with their own blood. I thought they were just showing off, but I heard older ones saying the same to each other as we passed through the crowd. And I nearly lost my footing once or twice in all the jostling.' She stopped twisting her skirt and brought both hands to her chest. She gulped in air.

'Mother of God, the fear's hittin' me now. Every so often, it's as if I'm back there, feard I'd go under and be trampled or that they'd find out I was a Catholic. God knows what would've happened then.' She crossed herself at the thought, her hand trembling like a leaf all the while, before resting her hands in her lap. I put my hand on hers. Signing with their own blood! That alone would put the wind up ye, never mind all the rest. We sat there with no words between us until the bells striking noon roused us to be on our way. I went to take my hand away, but Bridie clasped my hand between both of hers.

'Just let me finish this, before we set off back, Nan Rose.'

I settled back against the seat.

'We finally got in sight of the dome of the City Hall when there was this almighty roar from the crowd along with the banging of those huge Lambeg Drums. I'd never seen one of them properly before, let alone heard them up close. I nearly fainted, for I felt as if I was being hit with the thunderin' boom of them again and again. "That must be Lord Carson and the others coming out from signing the covenant," says Lizzie. I could see she was getting agitated herself, for she had taken hold of my sleeve at the elbow and was lookin' this way and that as if to see a way out. "Hold on to my coat, if you need to," says she. "I think we need to head towards the back of the City Hall, what, with the high and mighty coming out the front."'

Bridie took a big breath in and out.

'That got us out of the crowds, and we were able to make our way through side streets and back streets to the bottom of King Street, which is where Lizzie left me.'

She unclasped my hand and raised herself slowly from the seat, as if she was her granny. It was on the tip of my tongue to say to Bridie that she was going to get into trouble sooner or later, if she carried on taking herself places where she wasn't among her own. But then it struck me that none of the rest of us might be any safer.

As it happened, despite their blood writing and them forming the Ulster Volunteer Force and them drilling up and down streets all over the place, the government got its Home Rule passed on the sixteenth of January, the day before our Michael's birthday. He was that pleased with himself, you'd've thought they'd done it as a gift to him personally.

He must've run the length of the Springfield Road that day, for Maggie and I had only walked from the mill to the corner of Conway Street and were turning on to the Falls when he came up behind us and grabbed each of us round the waist and near knocked us both over. We managed to right ourselves just in time, and grabbing an arm each, we steered him out of the flow of women and against the wall.

'Have ye taken leave of your senses, Michael Murphy?' says Maggie, her arms akimbo and every bit the older sister.

'Yous haven't heard?!' says Michael, looking from one to the other of us. 'Redmond's done it.' He punched the air. 'What did I tell yous all? They've defeated Carson's amendment to exclude the north of Ireland. The Home Rule Bill's been passed for ALL Ireland. And the Lords can't stop it. The most they can do now is to veto it for two years.' He was laughing with so much glee that I started laughing too.

Maggie shook her head, opened her mouth and thought better of it. She linked his arm and beckoned me to link the other. 'We'd better walk you home, our brother, for I've never seen a body drunk with delight before.'

If he hadn't been, he'd have noticed the half-pitying look she gave him.

It took Michael until the middle of March to sober up. St Patrick's day fell on a Monday, and with it being a holiday, there was a big ceili at St Mary's Hall on the Sunday evening. Bridie'd called round for me, and Michael said he'd walk down with us. 'I'll be the envy of many a fella there, walking in with two fine lasses like yourselves,' says he, placing himself the other side of Bridie.

'And there'll be many a girl at the ceili envying me and Nan Rose and us walking in with yourself,' says Bridie. 'Isn't that right, Nan Rose?'

'I don't know about that,' says Michael. 'Maybe you'd each save me a dance, so's I don't be holding up the wall the whole night.'

'I'll save you a dance, Michael, certainly,' says Bridie. 'And we could both partner ye for The Fairy Reel, couldn't we Nan Rose?' She gave a quick nod and smile in my direction. So I knowd I wasn't expected to say anything. Which was just as well, for I was feeling that out of step in the craic between them that I hadn't a word in me.

'Nan Rose! Michael! Wait on us. We can all walk down together.' Was I glad to hear Maggie's voice. We turned round to see her and Charles walking along with Jim McAnearney. Walking slower on account of Jim's limp. They caught up with us, Maggie stepped in, and Michael fell back so the three fellas were behind the three of us. We carried on at the slower pace, the fellas talking among themselves and us the same until Charles suddenly raised his voice.

'So Michael, Jim was telling Maggie and me that they reckon Carson must have a hundred thousand volunteers drilling to fight agin Home Rule. What do ye make of that?'

We fell quiet, waiting for Michael's answer.

'They can drill all they like,' says he. 'Bits of stick for rifles aren't gonna take them far.' His jaunty tone of earlier had dropped.

'There's talk at the foundry that they'll not have a problem getting the genuine articles when they're ready.' Charles worked up at the Falls Foundry on Howard Street, where there were quite a few in the Ulster Volunteers.

'Aye,' says Jim. 'According to the ones I know in the polis, the reckoning is the Kaiser'll be more than happy to supply the necessary, if the English Unionists don't.'

There was a silence.

'That can work both ways' says Michael. His voice couldn't match the certainty of his words.

'It can,' says Charles. 'But don't expect the authorities to treat both sides the same.' I was glad we'd arrived at St Mary's Hall for any fighting talk rattled me. My feet were heavy as we joined the end of the queue, but the sound of the fiddle and accordion striking up a reel brought the spring back to my step. I looked over at Michael. He'd his hands shoved deep in his jacket pockets, and he was staring hard at his boots. I could see the clench of his jaw. He was that much in a world of his own, the rest of us might as well not have been there. Maggie, Charles and Jim were talking over and round him, with Bridie out on the edge at the other side of them. She had wrapped her arms round her waist and was chewing her bottom lip. By this time, the queue had shuffled along, and we were three people away from the paying-in table. I reached past Maggie, took hold of Bridie's arm and pulled her over towards me so that she Michael and I were closer together. I was going to have to puff some life back into the two of them, one way or the other.

'So, Michael,' says I, 'before we get inside the hall, do ye want us to keep you a dance or not? For Bridie and me like to be up dancing, with or without fellas. Isn't that right, Bridie?'

Bridie straightened herself up and tossed her head so that her plait swung over her shoulder and down her back.

'It is that, Nan Rose. For I've already promised Imelda Dobbin last night that we'd do the Siege of Ennis with her and her sister, seeing as she taught it to us last week.'

Michael roused himself from his shoes and got a jolt to realise we were at the doorway.

'They'll surely call the Walls of Limerick first,' says he, looking at Bridie. 'Will ye partner me for that one?'

Bridie didn't answer straight away. She waited until we had stepped into the glow of the gaslit hall, before turning to Michael.

'I will that,' says she, as if she was bestowing a great favour on him.

Michael rubbed his hands, before clasping them together to his chest 'That'll get me off to a good start, this evening, thank ye Bridie.' He glanced over to his left where Charles and Jim had joined the rest of the men, huddled in wee groups, hands in their pockets, as if they were on a street corner. 'I'm away over to have a word with a couple of these fellas. I'll be back over as soon as they strike up that tune.'

'And they have the nerve to talk about women blethering away all day,' says Maggie, as we walked to the other end of the hall where the women were seated near the table, all set with a clean white sheet and cups and saucers, ready for the tea break half-way through the evening.

As soon as the Walls of Limerick was called, Michael and Bridie were on their feet along with a few other couples. They stood on the floor, looking over at the rest of us, with Michael beckoning with both hands to encourage us up. Charles looked at Maggie. I caught the quick look between them and Maggie's nod in my direction.

'May I have your hand for this first dance, Nan Rose?' Charles held one hand out and the other clasped to his chest in a show of doing the honours properly. I didn't need to be asked twice. Charles was a good dancer, which is more than you could say for most of the fellas I knowd. You'd never credit how many men had two left feet when it came to dancing with them. We sauntered over to face Bridie and Michael to make a foursome.

Between the cajoling from the caller on the stage and the chivvying from those on the floor, we soon had a good circle of foursomes back-to-back. The music struck up and the caller got us going.

'In, two three and out, two three.'

Charles and I danced in to meet Bridie and Michael and back out again. We repeated the movement. Now Michael and me took each other's right hand and danced away from Charles and Bridie who were dancing away from us. Fair play to Michael. He could manage the sevens out to the side without tripping himself and he was smiling which was the main thing.

'Now right hands in the middle and round for four.'

The four of us clasped hands and danced round for four threes.

'Now left hands in the middle and back to your places in four.'

Bridie was concentrating so hard on getting the steps right that she was jumping the threes rather than stepping them. No matter how many times Imelda and me had told her to drop her shoulders and take it easy with the feet, she'd be so busy thinking about where she was putting them, she'd get in the way of them doing it for themselves. I caught her eye and we grinned at each other. Her shoulders dropped a fraction.

'Now swing your partner round for eight.'

With a good partner, the swing was the best bit of any dance for me. Only then, could ye find that point where both of yous were matched, holding and being held. Only then could ye let yourself birl round, knowing the grip of right hands together and the light touch of left hands on waists would carry ye through to the end.

I glanced over at Michael and Bridie. They had gripped right hands together. As they placed their left hands lightly on each other's waist, their eyes met, and they each smiled shyly at the other.

It was a Saturday, about a month or so after the St Patrick's Day ceili. I was in the scullery, blattering hell out of the washing with the dolly-stick when I heard Michael come in with one of his mates. I paid them no attention for the sweat was lashing off me and I wasn't in the mood to talk to anyone, least of all him. For to tell the truth, my nose was still out of joint with him and Bridie. Easter Sunday had followed hard on the heels of St Patrick's Day and so we'd had another Monday off and another ceili on the Sunday night. There was the same rigmarole as when the three of us walked down to the hall on St Patrick's night. And although, Bridie and me'd walked home again with some other girls and the two of them had barely seen each other since, I was right discombobulated with it all. I didn't want to be begrudging, but I couldn't help it. That made matters worse for I was angry with myself for being that mean.

'There's a fella out here says he knows you, Nan Rose.' Michael was standing behind me in the narrow doorway that separated the front room from the scullery. I gave the dollystick a vicious twist and didn't take him under my notice.

He moved to lean against the wall beside where I was working and spoke softly.

'Nan Rose, what ails ye? You'd think I'd done something agin ye, you've been that huffy with me this last while.'

I made a show of a big sigh, wiped the sweat dripping from my forehead and turned to look up at him. He gave me a baffled smile.

'And here's me bringing home somebody I knowd you'd like to see.'

I wiped my hands on my apron and gave him a ghost of a smile.

'So who's this fella that I'm supposed to know?'

He grinned, taking me by the elbow. 'Come on in and see.'

I pulled back. 'Give me a minute to splash my face and tidy my hair,' I whispered. 'There's a drop of tea in the pot if you want to offer him a cup in the meantime.'

'We're on our way to a meeting at the Hibernians. We'll get something to wet our thirst there.' He went back into the living room. I straightened myself up and followed after him. A red-haired lad not much taller than me stood with his back to the fireplace, cap in hand. He was stocky with an open face which creased into a big smile when he saw me. He looked familiar but I couldn't place him.

'So, you don't remember me Nan Rose, but I bet you haven't forgotten that aul ginger tom, Red Rory.'

I peered hard at him.

'Oh My God, it's Johnny Harper!' I let out a gulder of laughter. 'I haven't seen you since we were both with Granny Dwyer, down the street. Didn't your ones move to The Ardoyne?'

'That's right we did. And I forgot all about Granny and that brute of a cat, until I started in Boyle's sawmill and recognised your Michael here.' His grin widened, wrinkling his eyes.

Our shenanigans with the apple of Granny's eye were coming back to me, and I started to laugh, slapping my thighs with my hands. Michael was looking from one to other of us.

'Do you think one of yous would stop behavin' like a lunatic and tell me what's going on?'

'Ah, so you kept our wee secret,' Johnny says to me, in no hurry to let Michael in.

'I did that,' says I. 'I haven't breathed a word to a soul, not even to our Maggie.' I looked over at Michael, my lips still twitching with laughter. 'But we'd better let Michael here in on it or he'll be torturing us both for the story.'

'But will he swear on his blood not to let on to anyone else?' says Johnny, stringing out our game. I clapped my hands to my mouth.

'Well, do you know? I'd forgotten that bit.'

In my mind's eye, I could suddenly see the both of us, me five and him six in the shadows of Granny Dwyer's scullery. He's taken the sharp pointed knife from the table drawer and nicked the skin of his second finger. He takes mine. I gasp as the knife breaks my skin. I watch a bubble of blood ooze up. Johnny presses our fingers together. 'Swear on your blood that that's our secret.'

I caught sight of Michael's glare. There was only so much he was going to bear before he took the huff.

'Do you remember that cat, Rory, that Granny Dwyer doted on?' I said, walking over to the fire to put on a few coals.

'Aye, I remember,' says Michael 'and I remember you didn't find him that funny. You were terrified of him.'

'Indeed, I was. It was bad enough when you were still there, but it was worse when you left to start school. Anytime that cat found me alone, it would stalk over to me, its big tail twitchin' like a whip. And if I didn't get up right and quick, it would jump onto my lap and paw my thighs. I was that afeard I couldn't move and me waiting for him to dig his claws in and tear a lump out of me.'

'Until I came to the rescue,' says Johnny, taking up the very same lion tamer's pose I remembered from way back then. He'd planted his feet firmly on the ground. Hip width apart. His left hand gripped his waist and with his right he made as if flicking a whip. I could almost hear it crack. I let out another guffaw.

'So, Michael,' says I, 'this day we're doing the messages with Granny. There's wee Teasie O'Callaghan in the pram and me and Johnny here. Granny stops in front of a circus poster in Mrs Dempsey's window. I can still see it clearly for that was the first time I'd ever seen a lion.' I shivered. 'There's a circle of them round a big brawny man in animal skins. They're all fangs, claws, and eyes that'd kill ye. And yer man in the centre – he just stands there, with his hair slicked down and his moustache slicked up, as if he was taking the morning air.'

Michael raised an eyebrow and glanced over at the door. I put on my best show. '"Would ye ever look at those lions. Isn't that a sight that would scare the livin' daylights out of ye?" Granny says, pulling her black shawl more tightly to her and gripping it at her heart. "And to think that Rory boyo's related to them." Well, at that, Johnny here – his eyes lit up like lamps "Rory's a wee lion?" says he, studying the poster, and standing just like he was a minute earlier. That was the start of it.'

Michael looked from one to the other of us, shaking his head, every bit now the older brother.

'It was indeed.' Johnny drew nearer to Michael. 'I remember saying to Nan here on the way back, "I'm going to be like that man when I grow up." Says she "But yous don't have any lions." Says I "I'll start with Rory."'

'The very next day he arrives with a wooden spinning top and whip. When Granny's out the back, he pockets the top and flicks the whip. "I've been practising with our dog," says he, taking up his pose again. "Now for the cat!"' I put my hand on my hip, mimicking him.

'Now Nan. I never waggled my hips like that in my life,' Johnny protested. He looked at me, rubbing his chin. 'But don't let that stop you.' There was something in the lift of his eyebrow that flipped me from being five to fifteen. My cheeks flamed and I lost what I was saying.

He picked up the story. 'I find the cat. I stand in front of him, and I flick the whip. He opens an eye. I flick it again and the end catches his ear. This time he flashes a claw and catches the string. We've a tussle and he lets go of it. By now, he's sitting up – and eejit that I am, don't I think I've got the better of him.' He looked over at Michael and shook his head as if he still couldn't credit it. 'I flick the string again and what does he do, but leap at me. Three of his paws get caught in my jumper and the other latches on to my right hand. He digs in his claws and tears the back of my hand from wrist to fingertips. Look!' He holds out his hand to both of us. 'You see that scar there. That was Rory's doing.'

By this time, I was as good as back at Granny Dwyer's.

'Oh, it was awful,' says I. 'Seeing Rory do to your hand what I'd been afeard he'd do to my leg. And the blood drainin' from your face! I thought he'd done for ye.'

'Yer sister here, lets out such a scream that Granny runs in to see what the commotion's about.'

'Oh God, yes,' says I, starting to laugh again. 'She hollers, "What are ye doing to that cat, ye wee buck."' I looked over at Michael. 'Granny's about to clout him when she sees his hand.'

'And Nan Rose says, all matter of fact like, "He was just practising to be a lion tamer, Granny." Well, the aul one roared with laughter. "That'll teach ye," says she. "First blood to the lion."'

Michael scratched his cheek.

'It's a good story but I don't see why all the secrecy.' He looked over to where his cap hung, his mind now on a pint at the club.

'That isn't the end of it.' I put my hand on Michael's arm as I spoke. 'Johnny here, more power to him, wasn't for giving up.'

'And Nan Rose offered to be my assistant.' He made a mock bow in my direction.

This time, I was able to play along. I smiled and curtsied as Johnny carried on.

'Ever the practical one, she decided Granny's carpet beater would come in handy – though, why on earth Granny had a carpet beater when there was only a scrap of a rag rug at the fireplace, I'll never know.'

We'd slipped into an easy double act by now and I picked up the thread. 'Rory knew we were up to no good, so we bided our time. This particular afternoon, Granny's at the top of the street, nattering. We spot Rory, licking his paws in a corner of sunlight in the back yard. Johnny grabs the whip from the corner where he always left it on the ready and I grab the carpet beater on the way out of the back door. We're on him before he stirs. He stands up on tippy claws, archin' his back, every hair up on end and his tail too, up and twitching.'

'I cracks the whip above his head shouting at him to do what he's told and sit. The bloody cat just stands there staring. So I crack it again close to his face and blow me if he doesn't catch it in both claws. I try to pull the whip away, but Rory holds on and springs towards me as the whip springs back.'

I squeezed Michael's arm. 'And quick as a flash I get the carpet beater up between the two of them and Rory lands on that. He totters on the head of the beater. It bends like a fishing rod that's hooked a big catch. My arms is nearly breakin' with the weight of him. I let go just as Rory springs again to land on the tin roof of the lavatory, his claws screeching so hard my teeth were on edge.'

'I was sure the commotion would bring Granny running so I grabbed Nan by the arm, and we backed into the house, never taking our eyes of him in case he leapt on us. But he just stood there, hissing and giving us the evil eye.'

'And then he turns and disappears into the entry. Never to be seen again.'

Now it was Michael's turn to stroke his chin.

'Well, Nan Rose, I'd never have thought you had it in you. All those times, Granny Dwyer would stop us to talk about poor Rory and you all smiles and sympathy as if butter wouldn't melt in your mouth.'

'Are you telling me you'd have done something different in the same situation?'

He smiled sweetly. 'I just hope you were able to make a good Confession of it all.'

My jaw dropped. I'd never thought of it as a sin.

'Pay no attention to him Nan Rose.' I looked up at Johnny. 'He's just getting' his own back for us teasing him earlier. I'd better take him off to the Hibs to put him in a better mood.' He turned to Michael. 'Are you right, then?'

As they went out the door, Johnny paused, looked back and smiled.

'You'd make a fine assistant to any lion tamer now you're all growd up, Nan Rose.' He lingered on my name, as if savouring a piece of warm potato bread. 'I'm glad you offered to be mine first.'

I couldn't think of anything to say, for all I was feeling was that my name had never sounded as beautiful as at that moment. It was like hearing it sung in a hymn. I watched them as they passed the window, joshing each other. Michael was punching Johnny on the arm as Johnny slapped Michael round the head with his cap. I could hear their laughter after they'd disappeared from view. And as it died away, I birled all the way round the table, feeling like Cinderella at the ball.

When I eventually returned to the washing, all my fretting had gone the way of Rory boyo. I rubbed the shirts and blouses on the glass of the washing board and wrung them out with my bare hands, smiling away to myself.

Michael arrived back by himself just in time to eat. He came over to where I was giving the pot of stew a final stir and made a great show of savouring the smell. Bent over, and talking under his breath, as if to the pot, he said, 'I was telling that Johnny Harper about the craic at the ceili at St Mary's. He's going to call here and walk down with me to the May one. Maybe if you and Bridie are going, we could all walk down together.'

'I can't speak for Bridie. Sometimes she doesn't finish early enough on a Saturday, but I'll walk down with yous. And I'll talk to Bridie tomorrow morning.'

With that, I shooed him out of my road so as I could start serving, but not before I gave him a smile that went all the way to my eyes.

Seven

7th June 1913

The first Saturday in June was bright as a new shilling. I walked to the mill with a spring in my step, for in my mind's eye, I was already at the ceili that night. Throughout the morning, I fed myself memories of the last one, sucking their sweetness like a mouthful of Cherry Lips. I brought to mind that first sight of Johnny as I came downstairs into our hallway and him looking every inch a grand fella in a freshly ironed shirt and best waistcoat and trousers. I smiled again at how he took a sharp breath in when he turned and saw me on the bottom step and me delighted with how I looked with the blue and navy ribbons I'd borrowed from Bridie and Maggie. I'd tied them round my neck and at the end of my plait. Then there was the ease in the four of us walking down the road like two sisters and two brothers, with Michael and Johnny as taken with each other as with Bridie and me. Best of all was the moment when we took to the floor for The Walls of Limerick, and I realised that Johnny moved as if the music was in him.

It had been a grand night. After The Walls of Limerick, the four of us lined up for The Siege of Ennis. Later Maggie and Charles joined us for The Fairy Reel, the last set before the refreshment break. We had the two of them in the middle for that one, what with them both being a head taller than the rest of us. Afterwards we all made our way over to where the teas and soft drinks were being served. The fellas took our orders and fetched drinks for them and us. I glanced over at them while they waited in the queue. Charles was in the middle, one arm round each of the other's shoulders and in fine form, laughing and joshing with them. When they returned with the drinks – a peppermint cordial for Bridie, ginger and clove cordial for Maggie, a lemonade for me and a ginger beer for each of them, Maggie and Charles bantered the rest of us as being 'these young 'uns that we have to look after'. And indeed, for the first time Charles felt like an older brother, warm and good natured and keeping an eye out for all of us. My own heart warmed to him in return.

Maggie told me later that with him being an only child and his mother having lost two babbies after him, he was enjoying the thought of Michael and Johnny as the wee brothers he never had.

We finished off with us all up in our pairs for The Waves of Tory, before traipsing out into the night, arms linked and the craic flying between us.

I was that taken with memories and thoughts that I nearly jumped out of my skin when the factory horn sounded. Twelve o' clock already! We were finished for the week. Maggie and me walked as far as hers together. She was that quiet I knowd something was on her mind and I didn't think it was the night's entertainment.

'Charles and me will maybe see yous in the hall later on tonight,' says she. 'Jim McAnearney and us are going to a meeting James Connolly has organised to talk about what's going on in Dublin and how the Union's organising down there.'

Even I knowd that Big Jim Larkin was hell bent on

organising for better pay and conditions in Dublin, for there wasn't a week that passed without some mention of him in The Irish News. It was him that set up the Irish Transport and General Workers Union and Mr Connolly was their Belfast organiser. In fact, that's what he was when we first met him. We just hadn't knowd that then.

'I didn't know there was anything anybody here could do about what's happening down in Dublin,' says I.

Maggie snorted like a horse that's got its dander up. 'Well, if you'd joined the Irish Textile Workers Union when Bella Dwyer and me and the rest of the strike committee did, you'd have more of an idea about what's going on.' She snorted again for good measure. 'And it's not for want of me mentioning it to both you and Bridie at the time. But yous were off on another track by then.'

I'd never talked to Maggie about feeling dragged along by Bridie's new-fangledness with them suffragettes, for I felt I'd be letting Bridie down somehow. Not to mention that I thought Maggie would give me short shrift for being so easily led. And now here she was giving off to me. I huffed myself up an inch or two.

'It's all well and good you sayin' that Maggie. But just you remember that when you were my age, you weren't that bothered yourself. It was only after you got married that you started standing up and steppin' forward.'

'That's true Nan Rose' says she. She pursed her lips. 'I suppose I thought you two were that keen, you'd have stayed with it.'

'Well, there wouldn't be much point in Bridie joining the union, seeing as she's gone into service.'

'But you haven't, Nan Rose. And yous aren't joined at the hip.'

I changed tack.

'So, is Charles in Larkin's union?'

'He joined a month or two back. Out of sympathy with the Dublin ones.'

'I hadn't knowd that. He never said.'

'Charles isn't Michael. He keeps himself to himself.'

We were at the front door of the house she and Charles had rooms in. I left her at the doorstep, for I didn't want to carry on the talk about the union until I'd time to think again about what she was saying. Right then, I was more interested in getting home to build up the fire to heat the water for a bath.

I'd just turned into our street when I saw Bridie turning in from the other end. She saw me at the same time and came scurrying towards me. Even before she opened her mouth, I could see something was wrong. She had a face as long as a poker on her and shoulders so drooped you'd've thought she was carrying a sack of spuds on her back.

'You're finished early today, Bridie. Are ye coming in?'

'Are ye expectin' any of your ones back?'

'Not until three or after. I'm first in the queue for the bath. I just need to put a bit of turf on the embers before the fire goes out so as to finish heating the water.'

We had reached our front door. I turned the key and stepped into the hall, leaving the door open to let some light into the front room. I set to coaxing the embers into flame, feeding the fire with morsels of turf.

'Just give me a minute here, Bridie, and then we can sit down and talk. Do you want a cup of buttermilk?' It was then I realised Bridie was still stood in the hall, as if she was visiting for the first time and not knowing where to put herself. She came in and sat down on Father's wee stool, for all the world as if she was walking through a bad dream.

'I can't go tonight, Nan Rose. I told Lizzie I'd go back over this evening and stop over. It grieves me sore to be missing the ceili, but I can't do anything else. It wouldn't be right.' She sighed long and hard.

I stopped what I was doing. The fire would take care of itself for a bit. I poured us both a cup of buttermilk from the jug. I put the cup into her hands and took mine over to the end of the table and sat down on a chair there. A long band of sunlight cast by the open door lay between us.

'What's going on, Bridie? What ails ye?'

'Lizzie knew that suffragette, Emily Davison, that threw herself in front of the King's horse the other day. She'd met her at some meeting or other last year and yer woman was very kind to her. They'd kept in touch since. Anyway, she'd a telegram this morning from one of the other suffragettes telling her that she's that badly hurt, she's near death.'

Bridie sighed again. 'I'd brought it into her room and was there when she opened it. She'd no sooner read it than she sunk her face into her hands. I couldn't pretend nothing was happening. I went to the kitchen and made her a cup of tea. When I came back, she was still sitting like that.'

I took a long drink from the cup, all the better to get my bearings. Bridie went through the motions of lifting her cup before cradling it back in her lap.

'God only knows what made her run into a gallopin' horse,' says she. 'The thought of it sends shivers through me. I know I couldn't do it. For one thing, at the end of the day I'd rather be alive.'

'Bella was saying much the same this morning as we walked home from the mill,' says I. 'But could ye imagine what would've happened if any of us had run out under a cart horse? They would have hired somebody else, and that would have been the end of it. With only our families being worse off. Talking of which, what about Mr and Mrs Balfour? Will they not think it odd that you are back there on a Saturday night?'

'They're visiting relatives in Bangor this weekend. Lizzie was due to stop over with a friend tonight. But when she got the news, she telephoned her to say she was sick. Said to me she couldn't bear to be with someone right then who wasn't sympathetic to the suffragette cause.'

She finally put the cup to her lips before cradling it again.

'You know me, Nan Rose. I'm forever stepping in when maybe I'd be better off steppin' back and buttoning my lips. The upshot is I offered to stay over in the house this evening and she accepted. Which says how hard it's hit her. She paid for my bus fare into town and back so as I could let Mammy know what was happening.'

Now it was my turn to sigh, remembering Michael's words as he went out the door in the morning. 'This is one mornin' that'll fly by, for I'll be thinkin' of the craic the four of us will have tonight.' Bridie stood up, smoothing down her skirt. She put the half-drunk cup of milk on the table.

'I'd better be going, Nan Rose, for it'll be easier to talk to Mammy and get the bus back before Aunt Imelda comes back from Sinclair's. The last thing I need is for her to put in her two ha'pence worth and start muttering about mad women.'

I stood up and hugged her to me, for she looked like she had the weight of the world on her shoulders and my heart went out to her. As we stepped back, she took my hands in hers.

'Will you tell your Michael I'm sorry to be missing him and the ceili tonight?'

'I can, but you could call in yourself and tell him before you get the bus. He'll be about in the middle of the afternoon.'

'I can't do that, Nan Rose. I wouldn't trust myself to not get upset and then, that might look as if I thought he and I had an understanding.'

'Do yous not? I'd swear our Michael thinks you do.'

If Bridie'd seen the face on him when I told him, she'd not have been in any doubt how Michael felt. He crumpled his face like a paper bag before turning away from me and staring hard out the window.

But fair play to him, he didn't let Johnny or me down. He put a brave face on, even if it needed our banter to help him keep it there until the music and the craic lifted him enough for Johnny to persuade him to find a partner and join the two of us for The Siege of Ennis. As it happened, who should he ask but Gemma Locke with her black curls, her plump face like a full moon and with that half-simper permanently pinned to it. When I saw Michael and her walking over to join Johnny and me, I had to pin a smile to my own face.

I managed to pass myself for the dance, for there's no time for talking once the music starts. But after Michael and Johnny had accompanied us back to where the women sat and then headed back to talk with the men, didn't she stick to me like a fly to flypaper and her gushing about what a grand dancer Michael was and what a fine pair Johnny and me made, and would I like to have a wee Cherry Lip or two. She held out her paper bag of sweets. Well, I nearly took a couple, for I felt I deserved something for putting up with her company, but I thought it better to leave her in no doubt as to where I stood.

'No, thank ye, Gemma. You save them for yerself,' says I. 'For I've still got some here that Bridie and me shared at the last ceili. I'm just sorry she had to work tonight, for I've no doubt that the four of us would have had as good a night's craic as we did last time.'

It would have helped if Michael had been that clear. As it was, he only danced thrice all night. He asked Eileen Peoples up for the dance just after the refreshment break and then didn't he ask Miss Gemma up for the last dance. Anytime I glanced over in their direction she looked like a cat with a saucer of cream.

The walk back to the corner of our street was difficult. Michael was making a hollow show of what a grand night he'd had, while I was beside myself with annoyance at him and curiosity about what'd happened at the meeting that meant neither Maggie, Charles, nor Jim McAnearney had made an appearance all night. To make matters worse, I was hardly able to bid Johnny good night, for didn't Michael linger at the corner with us, like a dog in the manger, until I walked ahead up the street, leaving the two of them standing.

Maggie and Charles called in after 12 o'clock mass the next day. Michael was barely in the door ahead of them and Mammy, Father and me were having a cup of tea with some of yesterday's soda bread warmed near the fire.

'There's a few pieces more keeping warm there under the cloth,' says Mammy, rising from her seat.

'Sit yourself down Mammy. We can sort ourselves,' says Maggie, fetching a couple of cups and a plate from the shelf.

'So, what was the news from last night's meeting?' says Father, ignoring Mammy's dark look from across the table.

'James Connolly was there himself, having only come back up from Dublin on Friday,' says Maggie. 'So we got it from the horse's mouth. The engineers have struck now, following on from this second shipping strike and the building strike.'

'Two of the dockers spoke at the meeting,' says Charles. 'They were telling us that the city's full of it. There's Larkinite processions and banners all over the place.' He stopped to take a swallow of tea. 'They've messages of support from unions in England, Wales and Scotland, with workers there ready to join a general strike. They reckon they could've a complete close down across the water.'

'Mother of Jesus!' says Mammy, crossing herself.

I looked from Charles to Maggie to Father, but I couldn't make out what he thought of the news, for he sat there, rubbing his chin and keeping himself to himself.

As if all of that wasn't enough to be contending with, the Twelfth of July parades were even more unbearable than usual. Not only did we have the Orange Men flaunting themselves with their flutes and drums to be heard for miles around, but all the papers were full of their speeches bragging that they'd defeat any threat to their Ulster. Which they did – for, a few days later, didn't the House of Lords throw out the Home Rule Bill for the second time. Not that that wasn't expected, but Michael took it bad, despite him knowing that they could only stop it for two years at the most. For the rest of the week and right up to the hour of us going to the ceili, Michael was beside himself and ready to take it out on anybody, bar those who felt exactly like himself.

On the Saturday evening, Bridie called round to ours so we could walk down together. Hardly was she in our front room when she said for us all to hear how disappointed she'd been to have to work the June Saturday. Glancing to and from Michael all the while, she said it'd made for a long four weeks and how she was so looking forward to the evening. Michael behaved as if she hadn't said a word. By which time, I was that angry with him for behaving like a baiting bear all week, I had to button my lips tight lest I said something that'd mean one of us would lose the bap altogether.

When Johnny arrived we set off with him and me stuck like pigs in the middle between the two of them. Bridie was that agitated, she couldn't stop talking about having helped

Lizzie Balfour pack that day for a fortnight's trip to the north of England so that she could take part in a suffragette gathering to remember yer woman Emily Davison. Meantime, Michael was giving forth to Johnny at the top of his voice about the Lords letting Carson dance rings round them. As if we all hadn't had enough of that in the week and none of us being able to do anything about it one way or the other! I linked Bridie's arm and started to walk faster, so as to leave Johnny and Michael behind us, hoping that Johnny might talk some sense into him.

More power to him, he must have spoken in tongues, for when they caught up with us, as we turned into Chapel Walk, Michael went to the outside of Bridie, while Johnny went to the other side of me. I unlinked Bridie's arm and let her and Michael walk a little ahead of us. We couldn't hear what they were saying, but at least they were talking.

'I've given him a nudge in the right direction,' whispered Johnny.

And that might've been all that was needed, if Gemma Locke and a couple of her friends hadn't squeezed in behind the four of us as we shuffled along in the queue. Bridie was chatting away to her, thinking Gemma had squeezed in to talk to her. I was pinching myself for not saying anything to Bridie about Michael and Gemma at the last ceili in case it made matters worse between him and her. Forewarned is forearmed, after all.

Johnny told me later that Michael'd only asked Gemma up for the second dance of the evening because he felt obliged, what with her hovering around Bridie and me like a spider – my words, not his – all evening. And, further it was Bridie that'd suggested they ask Gemma to make up the third person to form one side of The Fairy Reel. Maybe so, but he didn't give that impression.

I know, for Johnny, Imelda Dobbin and me had formed another three to make up the other side and so I was facing him, Bridie and Gemma for the whole set. It didn't help that Gemma's light on her feet. Every time Michael turned to her to repeat the same steps he and Bridie'd just done, she was so dainty that you'd have thought the two of them were dancing on air. I could see Bridie was put out, even if she didn't know exactly what she was put out about, for didn't her every step get clumpier.

Johnny and Michael'd barely escorted us back to our seats and gone off to join the men, when Bridie elbowed me and nodded in the direction of the door. We stepped outside and into the shadow of the building.

Says she, 'I'm going home, Nan Rose. I don't feel myself and...' She hugged herself tight. 'And Michael'd enjoy himself more being with ones that have more life in them.'

I pleaded with her, 'Bridie, don't go. Come back in and we'll get a taste of lemon squash or a cup of tea. You'll feel better then.'

'I won't, Nan Rose.' says she. 'I've got a bad feeling about the evening. I want to go home.'

'Well, I'm not letting you walk home by yourself,' says I. 'Come back in so as I can tell Maggie or Johnny that we're leaving.'

'I'll wait for ye here,' says she.

She didn't. I came out again as quick as I could, and she'd gone.

Nor did she call for me next morning for us to go to Mass. I walked to Clonard fed up to the teeth with both of them, for what can you do when bodies are not only not talking to one another, they don't want to talk to you neither? I was fretting and fuming that much, I wisht I was a fella, for at least they can stand, shuffling at the back of the church and nip out just after the Communion, without anybody being pass remarkable. As it was, I squeezed into the last space on a pew, right beside Bella Dwyer.

'Is Bridie not with ye this morning?' she whispered as she shuffled up to give me a bit more room. I shook my head and was saved from having to say anything else, as we all stood for the priest and altar boys entering.

There was something comforting about being squeezed between Bella's ample body and the end of the pew. I must have drifted off not long after the priest ascended into the pulpit, for the next thing I knowd, Bella was elbowing me awake from a dream of being wee and snuggled into Maggie in bed while Michael tossed and turned at her other side. Even as I roused myself to kneel for the Our Father, I heard Maggie say "Michael, a chroí, settle yourself and don't be bothering about tomorrow. It'll sort itself out." I felt my annoyance with him and my fretting about him and Bridie slip away. What would be, would be. It'd be as much as I was able for to be true to each of them and pay mind to Johnny and me.

With that settled, I decided I'd call round to Bridie's on my way home. Furthermore, seeing as Maggie had come to help me in the dream, I decided once and for all to follow her lead and join the union. The last piece that struck me was that depending on what happened, the next few weeks could be a test for Johnny and me. It was one thing being in a foursome. It was another thing altogether being in a twosome.

Johnny must have been thinking along similar lines, for the following Saturday, I was walking home from the mill with some of the others, us linking arms and singing, when I spotted him at the corner of Albert Street and the Falls. He saw me, smiled and beckoned me over. My feet gave a skip as I realised that he'd been looking for me. I glanced round at the other girls. No one else had noticed.

'Yous go on ahead and I'll catch up, I've just remembered Mammy asked me to call in to see if I could get a soup bone from the butcher's.' I walked, as lackadaisical as I could, over in Johnny's direction.

'Well, what's got you up this way, Johnny Harper?'

'What does it look like I'm doing, Nan Rose? I've been waiting for you.'

I paused to hear what else he had to say, for he had something on his mind to take him all the way straight from the timber yard to meet me at the mill.

'I thought I could walk ye back towards your house,' says he, taking off his cap, fidgeting with it and putting it back on his head. 'And if we dandered slowly it'd give us a chance to talk.'

I nodded. 'But we'll be at our house in next to no time. We could wander up to Clonard before turning back down to ours. That way we've the excuse that we were calling to light a candle for a good cause, in case anybody wants to know.' We started to walk back up the Falls.

'It mightn't be a bad thing to do that,' says he. 'I'd never realised how thran your Michael can be. He's as bad as that boyo of a cat, Rory.'

'That he can be,' says I, laughing. 'Although to be fair, mostly he's easy-going. Then every so often he gets a notion about something, and he clamps hold of it and won't let go for dear life. Like this Home Rule business.'

'Politics is one thing. I could understand that. But this is to do with Bridie.'

I turned to look at him, all ears.

'Seeing as you were that concerned about him and Bridie, I've been trying to talk to him over the week.' He drew a breath. He took off his cap again before jamming it back on his head.

'The last thing I want is to get caught between you and Michael, Nan Rose. And I don't want to be talkin' about Michael behind his back.'

'So, what are ye saying, Johnny?'

'What I'm sayin' is between you and me, Nan Rose.'

'I'm hardly going to be running back to Michael to tell him we were talkin' about him.'

'Nor Bridie neither?'

The penny dropped.

'How about I don't say anything to anybody unless we agree?'

'That's the docket,' says he. 'But before we get to that, you need to hear me out before ye say anything.'

I nearly took umbrage at the insinuation that I was one for interrupting, but I thought better of it. At this rate we'd be at our house before we talked about whatever he needed to tell me.

'Done,' says I.

The gist of what he said was that Michael was convinced Bridie didn't feel the same towards him as he did to her. 'Otherwise, why did she choose to go back to work the night of the June ceili, when she didn't have to?'

Well, I'd to bite my bottom lip hard more than once while Johnny was talking, but I'd given my word. I held fire. I even managed to walk on a few paces after he'd finished before opening my mouth.

'How is it that fellas have no problem spending time with their mates in a club or hanging about street corners passin' more than the time of day, but when it comes to women helping a friend in need, it's held agin them?'

'Ach, Nan Rose. That's not fair. We're talking about Michael, not all fellas. And…'

'So, you put him right then, did ye?'

Johnny suddenly took a couple of strides ahead and then turned to face me, stopping me in my tracks. He shoved his cap back from his face and shook his head.

'If my back was agin the wall, Nan Rose, I can't think of

anyone I'd rather have on my side,' says he. 'But this isn't about sides. I thought ye wanted to bring the two of them together. That's what I want.'

I folded my arms tight across my chest. I looked at him straight in the eyes. I could see from how his lips were twitching that he wanted to laugh. I started laughing, so did he and then we were laughing together. We carried on walking, but with an ease between us now.

'And it's not that your Michael doesn't understand women helping women. Sure, he's got his two sisters and his mammy. It's more it's hard for him to understand being that friendly with your employer. And if I'm honest so do I.'

I was quiet then, for I wanted to pick my words so as not to let Bridie down.

'I know it's hard to understand. And if Lizzie Balfour wasn't a suffragette and if Bridie hadn't started going to meetings, they wouldn't be so friendly. But that's how they were before she offered Bridie a job.' I chewed my lip. 'How it all turns out remains to be seen. But I like what I know of Lizzie.' By this time, we'd already passed Clonard and were heading back in the direction of our house.

'The other thing I know from talking to Bridie is that she's as fond of Michael as I thought he was of her and that she's hurt sore by how he was at the last ceili.'

'In that case, we'll just have to sort them out, one way or the other, won't we?' says Johnny. 'And that means putting our heads together.' He paused. 'So, what do ye say I meet ye coming out of the mill next Saturday again?'

I looked over at him. His eyes were full of mischief and for a minute, I was back again in Granny Dwyer's with the carpet beater in my hand. We grinned at each other.

'That's a grand idea, Johnny. At this rate we'll all four of us be back on track in next to no time.'

Eight

23rd August 1913

By the week before the August ceili, Johnny and me had everyone lined up. I'd asked Maggie if she and Charles would call for us, for I thought it'd be easier walking down with more of us. The more craic, the less awkwardness. Johnny'd convinced Michael and I'd finally persuaded Bridie that July was all a misunderstanding that should be left behind. We were right pleased with ourselves walking back from the mill that Saturday midday. We sauntered as far as the corner of our house, well pleased at what a fine pair of plotters we were.

But there were bigger plots than ours afoot. On Monday, yer man, Murphy that owned the Dublin tram company and the Independent Newspapers had sacked men in the parcels office of the tram company because they refused to leave Mr Larkin's union. He'd already sacked messengers delivering his newspapers in July for being union members. It was the first time I'd heard Father say he was ashamed of his name 'with that divil William Murphy sharing it'. And on the Tuesday after Johnny and me'd put everything in place, didn't Big Jim call the tramworkers out on strike.

'Giving as good as he got,' says Maggie, as we walked home from the mill with Bella Dwyer, Ellen Kavanagh and the Peoples sisters on Thursday.

'Aye,' says Bella. 'That'll hit Mr William Murphy where it counts – in his pockets.'

'Read all about it! Riots in Dublin! RIC drafted in. Read all about it!'

The newspaper seller was brandishing a newspaper in one hand and pointing to the poster on his newsstand with the other. We joined a small crowd gathered round him. Bella raised her hand with her coins clasped between her thumb and forefinger and the seller reached her over a paper.

We huddled round, looking over her shoulder as she read out the headlines.

RIOTING IN DUBLIN AS STRIKE BRINGS DUBLIN TO A HALT
ROYAL IRISH CONSTABULARY DRAFTED IN TO HELP DUBLIN POLICE
Led by Jim Larkin, The Irish Transport and General Workers Union has brought disruption and disorder to Dublin. With Dublin brought to a halt by the tramworkers strike during the Royal Horse Show, rioting breaks out at Ringsend Power Station

Bella read on for a sentence or two, before folding away the paper and turning round to look at the rest of us. Nobody spoke.

'God help us,' says Bella. 'The RIC and the Dublin polis.'

'We'll need to get our hands on The Irish Worker as soon as it comes out tomorrow. That way we'll at least know what's happenin' from the union itself,' says Maggie.

To tell ye the truth, right then, I was thinking less about the strikers and the union than about whether or not all of this'd pull the rug from under our scheming about Saturday night. Maggie didn't look like a woman that was in the mood for a dance. Ellen Kavanagh must have read my thoughts.

'It's right and handy we've got the ceili coming up,' says she. 'There's always a good crowd there. Maybe we could say to Oliver at the union office that we could take some extra copies of The Worker to sell to any of them that's going.'

We all looked at her.

'Do ye think we'd be allowed to sell them?' says Imelda Dobbin. 'Ye know the priests don't have much truck with the union.'

'We don't have to make a song and dance about it,' says Maggie. 'If we each take a half-dozen newspapers under our shawls and just put the word round that we're sellin' them, who's to notice?'

And that was that! It was as much as I could do to stop myself taking hold of Ellen and birling her round with delight.

On Friday, I called round to Bridie's on the way home from the mill and asked Mrs Corr to tell Bridie to call for me as soon as she got in from the Balfours, for after the business with Gemma Locke at the last ceili, I was going to make sure Bridie wasn't wrong-footed this time. She needed to know what we were up to and not to be gabbing away about Lizzie Balfour and the suffragettes.

On Saturday midday, I walked back from the mill with the usual ones and the talk was mostly about the news in The Irish Worker that Jim Larkin had called a mass meeting in Sackville Street for the Sunday.

'That man's got the gift of the gab,' says Bella, '"An Injury to One is the Concern of All". Never a truer word spoken. It makes you want to be there with them tomorrow.'

Maggie was walking in front with Imelda Dobbin and so they hadn't heard what Bella said. None of the rest of us answered right away. I was thinking that it'd been hard enough not to be afeard during our wee strike. I doubted I'd have the heart for a huge meeting with the polis all round.

'You're a better woman than me, Bella,' says Mrs Smith. 'A meeting like that'd frighten the livin' daylights out of me. The best I can do is to give them what little bit of support I can.'

'Ach don't get me wrong, Josie,' says Bella. 'I can't help my spirit rising when I hear what he says. But I'm glad I'm here rather than there. And, for sure, I'm glad it's the men he's calling out rather than the women.'

I felt the shame lift off me at those words. So, it wasn't just me then.

By the time Bridie and Johnny arrived at our house on Saturday evening to head down to St Mary's Hall, some magistrate had banned the big meeting Larkin'd called for the Sunday. Neither Father nor Mammy were at home so there was nothing to stop the four of us talking about what Big Jim'd do now.

Maggie and Charles arrived with the latest news. Charles knew a fella that worked on the Dublin Belfast train who'd gone to a meeting on Friday where Big Jim had publicly burned the magistrate's proclamation forbidding the Sunday meeting.

'You've got to hand it to Larkin,' says Charles, flushed with the excitement of it all. 'Do you know what he said?'

We waited for him to continue while Maggie who was in the know started to laugh.

'He said he cared as much for Magistrate Swifte as he did for the King of England!'

Michael and Johnny roared their approval while Bridie and I looked at each other open-mouthed. Larkin's daring was hard to credit.

"Mind you,' says Charles more quietly, 'it remains to be seen how he'll get to the meeting. They've issued a warrant for his arrest and Dublin's crawling with polis on the hunt for him.'

We headed down to St Mary's, united in our admiration for Big Jim's defiance. And when we got to the queue to get in, there were sufficient ones that felt the same that we'd no problem selling the newspapers.

It was a grand night, for it's easy to dance when your spirits are high. So, even Bridie moved as if on air. And although Bridie and I were civil with Gemma, neither of us made any move to include her in our sets. Maggie did her bit as well, for when she saw the four of us on the floor, looking for another two to make up a set for The Fairy Reel, she stepped up quick as a flash, pulling Ellen Kavanagh along with her. I caught sight of Gemma who'd taken two steps in our direction. She'd stopped in her tracks with her jaw dropped, staring at Maggie's back as if she couldn't quite take in what'd happened. I clapped my hand over my mouth to smother the grin on my face.

Maggie and Charles left before the last dance and so the four of us were able to saunter together as far as the corner of Bridie's street, whereupon Michael said he'd walk Bridie to her door. Johnny and me walked the last wee bit to our house even slower.

We turned into the silence of our street, dark bar for the glow of candlelight through a thin upstairs window blind here and there. Johnny slipped his arm round my waist, drawing me ever so slightly towards him. I felt the heat of his body and of his hand. I softened into his shelter and a sigh I never knew I had in me gave itself over to the night air.

'Are ye alright, Nan Rose?' says he, bending his head towards mine.

'Indeed, I am, Johnny. Indeed, I am,' says I, looking up into his face. Eyes dimmed by darkness, I breathed in the smell of Lifebuoy soap from his face and of ginger beer on his breath. I turned towards him and our lips homed in on each other. The kiss, when it came, sent a warm judder through me. I fell into betwixt and between. We moved ever closer until the shock of chest touching chest jolted us apart.

I straightened my shawl and pulled it closer to me. I looked round the street in case we'd missed approaching footsteps. All still dark, still silent. I took his hand in mine.

'I need to be home, Johnny, and so do you, for you've still a couple of miles to walk.'

'I have that, Nan Rose,' says he as we reached our door. 'But don't worry, I'll be walking home on air.'

'And I'll be lying in a dream,' says I, as we allowed our lips a lingering goodbye kiss.

Next morning, I got the shock of my life when Bridie arrived at our door right on half past nine, which meant we could take our time walking to Clonard for ten o'clock mass. As soon as we set off, I could see by the skip of her that she was in bright form. Usually neither of us could wait to tell our news to the other, but I was suddenly shy at the thought of talking to Bridie about Johnny and me kissing. It didn't seem right somehow to let Bridie into that special place between him and me. It was just as well she was ready to gab for both of us.

'What a grand night that was Nan Rose and I thank you and Johnny for it.' She linked my arm and leaned into me. 'Aren't I the lucky one to have you as my friend and you to have a brother like Michael.' She suddenly sighed. 'And I'd be even luckier if I didn't have an Aunt Imelda.'

'Aunt Imelda?'

'Aye. We'd barely turned the corner into our street, when didn't I see the light from our front door as it opened and who should step out, looking from one end of the street to the other, but Herself. The divil himself appearin' wouldn't have put the wind up me more. "Michael," says I, "just keep walking but let go of my hand for that's the aunt at our door." Fair play to him, he didn't miss a step and he knew how to pass himself. "Good evening, Miss Corr," says he, "It's a fine night to be takin' the air." Thanks be, before she could say a word, didn't Mammy appear at her side. "Ach Michael Murphy!" says she. "You're a sight for sore eyes. If it wasn't so late now, I'd tell ye to come in and give us a bit of your craic." And with that, she shooed me in past Imelda, so the only goodbye I could give Michael was a backward glance.'

Later, Maggie and Charles called in after eleven o'clock mass. When the talk turned to the goings on in Dublin, Mammy was that agitated she couldn't sit still. She clattered about making the noisiest cups of tea I'd ever heard.

'I don't know what Larkin's thinking about,' says she. 'Who's going to feed the families? What about the childer?'

'The childer are going to suffer whatever happens, Mammy,' says Maggie, 'for without better conditions, what chance do they have?'

I saw Mammy look Maggie up and down. So, I knowd it wasn't just me wondering how long it'd be before there'd be any sign of her having a babby.

Mammy's question and Maggie's answer kept coming back to me over the course of the week. Jim Larkin did address the meeting in Sackville Street on the Sunday – for all of five minutes before the polis arrived on the balcony and arrested him in full view of the crowd. By the end of the week, four hundred other employers had joined with yer man Murphy to lock out any union members. Dublin ground to a standstill while twenty-four thousand men went without a wage.

The same question and answer stayed with me as we moved into September and the lock-out and hunger bit deep in Dublin. I thought of our strike that'd only lasted the two weeks. That was hard enough – and we'd three other wages coming into our house and Maggie had Charles to support them. I'd never knowd until then that Dublin didn't have the mills we had and so there was less work for women. What was it like for families where there was only the man working and them with no wage for over a month?

Bella called a meeting of the union committee in her house after work on the first Saturday in September. 'And you come along, if you can Daughter,' says she to me, 'for it'd be good to hear what a young 'un thinks of what I'm puttin' forward.'

So, I crushed into her front room along with the eight committee members.

'I know you've all things to be getting on with,' says she, 'and I can't even offer yous a drop of tea for I haven't that many cups or the tea to go round. So, I won't keep yous. But I wanted to talk about what we could do for the Dublin ones.'

The gist of it was that we should organise a wee social night ourselves to raise money instead of going to the September ceili. 'For with the priests involved at St Mary's Hall and the clergy across Ireland seemin' set agin the strikers, it's hard enough even to sell The Irish Worker to the queue waitin' to get in. So why are we giving our hard-earned money to them, when we could be helping people like ourselves?

There was a nodding of heads.

'More power to ye, Bella, for you've always an eye to the next step,' called out Ellen Kavanagh. The rest of us clapped our agreement.

'And knowin' you,' says Maggie, 'you'll already have an idea of how we're goin' to make it happen.' A tickle of laughter went round us all.

'Well, I did have a word with John McAvoy and he's willing to give us the upstairs room above his public bar and to throw in a couple of jugs of cordials. Them that want something stronger can bring it up from the bar.'

We knew the room from holding a couple of meetings there during our strike, so we knowd it was a quarter of the size of the hall.

'But sure, we're not goin' to get even a quarter of the ones that go to the ceili,' says Bella, 'for we'll need to pass the news by word of mouth in case we put the wind up the parish priest. We wouldn't want him to take a notion to denounce us from the pulpit.'

I hadn't even thought of that.

'We may just be grateful that we've got the Redemptorists at Clonard and them outside of any parish,' says Mrs Smith. 'For at least we can get to Sunday Mass without fear of being shamed.'

'I'll not have any priest shame me for doing what's right,' says Maggie.

'It's well seen you're no longer living at home with Mammy,' says I. Another tickle of laughter went round.

'Don't you worry Daughter,' says Mrs Smith. 'Agnes's heart is in the right place and, if necessary, I can call round and remind her of that – for she and me go back a long way.'

So that's what we did. On the night, it was more of a crush than expected, for there were some from the union that weren't from the area. But the craic more than made up for the cramp. And when Bella stood up at the start of the last dance and announced that between the thruppence entrance charge, the farthings for soft drinks and money from the collecting tins in the public bar and the sale of The Irish Worker, we'd raised seven guineas for the Dublin ones, the clapping and cheers near lifted the roof.

Even Mammy gave her blessing when I told her the next morning about how much we'd collected. She gave me sixpence. 'That's from your father and me,' says she. 'Ye can't stand by and see families starved to death.'

The only fly in the ointment was Aunt Imelda, yet again. Bridie was near in tears as we walked to Sunday Mass. 'There was I that relieved at her not standing at the door waitin' for us last night, and didn't she set on me before I came out this morning, with her face as long as a poker. One of them Holy Joes that passes round the plate at the eight o'clock mass told her about the 'do' at McAvoy's. He also told her that me and you, Maggie and Michael were among those choosing to side with Jim Larkin. Says she to me, "I was mortified when he said he would have expected more from a niece of mine and me being a pillar of the church." I wouldn't mind for my own sake, but she was giving off to Mammy "for letting her daughter go to rack and ruin with those Murphy ones." So help me, Nan Rose, I don't know what I'm going to do. At this rate, I'd be better off never coming home.'

I didn't know what to say, for the aunt made Mammy look like one of those wee angels hovering round the crib. And besides, Bridie'd set me off thinking in another direction altogether. What would happen if we wanted to run another 'do' in McAvoy's now that those close to the parish priest were in the know about what we were up to?

As it happened our wee efforts were soon overtaken. By early October, The Irish Worker announced the union was setting up food kitchens for women and children in the union headquarters at Liberty Hall in Dublin and there was a day or two after that when the papers were full of the news that a ship had come all the way from Liverpool, England, laden with so much food that it was low in the water.

Father brought a day-old Irish News in from the warehouse. After we'd eaten, he sat by the hearth to read out the news. Mammy and I huddled at either shoulder as he read, all the better to see the picture on the front page. Under the headline YOU HAVE BROKEN THE STARVATION BOOM SAYS JAMES LARKIN was a drawing of him addressing the crowds waiting at the docks while crates were unloaded from a ship decked with bunting and banners.

'Sure, wouldn't it have been easier just to send money?' says Mammy, as she settled into the opposite chair and pulled out her darning basket.

'Aye, maybe it would, Agnes,' says Father, 'but you can't gather a crowd at the Docks to see you open an envelope, never mind announcing that it's broken the starvation boom. You've got to hand it to Larkin. He knows what lifts a body's heart – and he's got an eye for the front page.'

As it was, we'd have needed a ship arriving every week in Dublin to keep our spirits lifted throughout October. The union's defiance was matched by the employers' determination to not give an inch.

Meantime in Belfast, the stories and sightings of Carson's Ulster Volunteers readying to fight agin Home Rule fed our talk at the mill and at home with fear. Some nights I'd lie in bed with their slogans rattling in my head. 'Ulster will fight. And Ulster will be right.' 'A Protestant Parliament for a Protestant People'. I'd fall into sleep wondering what would become of us.

And as if all that wasn't enough to be contending with, we'd the matter of the ceilis at St Mary's Hall. I'd told Maggie what the Aunt Imelda had said to Bridie, as I walked her back to her place after work one evening.

'I'm heart sick of men using the power of their cloth agin us,' says she. 'It's all the same, whether they be Protestant politicians, priests or employers. I'll give the money I'd spend at the ceili to the union.'

'I know what you mean, Maggie,' says I. 'But nobody's

going to stop you and Charles being together in your own home. Whereas Michael and I've got Mammy, and Bridie's got Imelda to be dealin' with. Those two are the match of any man in not budging.'

Maggie laughed then and linked me closer into her. 'In that case, I'll have to think about that, for I've never seen you nor Michael stuck before and I'll not start now.' I glanced up in time to catch that soft smile of hers that took me all the way back to being a wee 'un. I smiled back as I squeezed her arm agin me.

As it was, Johnny'd also been pondering our problem, and more power to him, had come up with the idea that the best way for the four of us to get a bit of time to ourselves was for him and Michael to take themselves to ten o'clock mass at Clonard and then they could join us in our dander round Dunville Park. That suited Bridie and me well, but it meant an effort for the two of them. Johnny would have to get himself across from the Ardoyne and Michael would have to forego his one lie-in of the week.

Bridie's jaw dropped when I told her. 'They'd do that for us?' says she, stopping stock still by the fountain in the park. She took a big breath, the better to take in the news.

'Yes, but let's not get carried away. They'll probably only manage it for a month – which will maybe give time for things to sort themselves out with Saint Mary's Hall.'

'Even so,' says she, 'to give up your one lie-in of the week, and for Johnny to walk the whole way across the city!'

'Yes,' says I, 'which is why it'll not last. But their hearts are in the right place.'

So, the four of us dandered our way through November and who knows, we might have managed longer, but once again bigger plans than ours overtook us. In the middle of

November didn't James Connolly set up the Irish Citizen army to protect the Dublin strikers from the polis. And then barely a week later, didn't fellas I'd never heard of set up the Irish Volunteers to counter the Ulster Volunteers set up by Carson.

When the four of us met the last Sunday in November, Michael could barely talk about anything else.

'It's about time that somebody organised those of us for Home Rule. No wonder that Dublin Hall was packed at the meeting to launch it. Thousands of men inside and the same again outside. Would you believe they signed up nearly ten thousand volunteers on the day? And who wouldn't with a man like that Eoin McNeill leading it, and him a professor at University College Dublin?'

'They seem to have a notion for teachers,' says Johnny. 'There was a schoolteacher named Padraig Pearse sharing a platform with McNeill. Seems a bit odd to me … I don't think of teachers as fighting men.'

Michael waved his hand in the air as if swatting Johnny's opinion like a fly. 'You need men willing to fight but you need leaders that are steady and not given to rushes of blood to the head. Otherwise, the British will not take them seriously.'

I wondered who Michael'd been listening to but thought better of asking. At this rate we'd not get a word in edgeways round the politics.

Worse was to come. Within a couple of weeks, Michael and Johnny'd signed up as Irish Volunteers. 'I couldn't leave him to do it alone,' says Johnny when he and I got a chance to talk. 'At the end of the day, you've got to stand up and be counted.'

The following Sunday, they'd to go to some local meeting for Volunteers at the Hibernians, leaving Bridie and me to circle the park by ourselves. I could tell there was something not right, for either Bridie wasn't saying much, or she wasn't paying much attention to what I was telling her. I was about to ask her what was going on, when she said, all soft like, that she'd something to tell me. Right away, I'd a bad feeling in my guts.

The gist of it was that Mr and Mrs Balfour were afeard of how things were shaping up here. They reckoned it wouldn't be long before there'd be fighting on the streets of Belfast, what with the Ulster Volunteers parading here, there and everywhere and the Irish Volunteers set to do the same. They were planning to send Lizzie to England to stay with an aunt and uncle for God knows how long. And who could blame them? Everybody I knew was a bit afeard, but we didn't have anywhere else to go.

Still, every cloud has a silver lining. 'Good riddance to Lizzie Balfour,' I thought to myself. Not that I'd anything agin her personally. It was more about her interfering in other people's lives.

'Well, don't worry Bridie. I'm sure you'd be able to get your old job back at the mill,' says I, not gloating nor gleeful, though in my heart I was dancing a jig. The look on her face put a stop to that. She was peering at me as if trying to make me out from a distance. She drew back the arm that'd been linked to mine.

'Nan Rose, how could you think I'd ever go back to the mill? Do you think I'm an eejit?' She took a big breath in. 'Lizzie Balfour wants me to go with her.'

She might as well have slapped me across the face. I was that shocked I nearly lost my footing. She put her hand to my elbow to steady me and then linked arms again. I bit my lip hard and squeezed my eyes for I felt small enough, without crying like a babby. We walked on in silence for I don't know how long until I found my voice again.

'You're thinking to go across the water to strangers?'

She nodded and I could see she was biting her lip too.

'But what about Michael? ... And what about ...me?' I could feel the tears near choking me, so I unlinked my arm and started to walk faster. Bridie caught up with me.

'Nan Rose, once I'm over there, I could speak up for you. I could find you a place. I'm sure Lizzie Balfour'd help for she's awful fond of you and she knows you're like a sister to me.'

Now it was my turn to stop and peer at Bridie as if I wasn't sure I knew her.

'And could you see me, spending my days pandering to those that need others to lift and lay them, while never setting eyes on all those I love dear? Could you see me leaving Johnny this side of the water?'

'Ach Nan Rose, I'm sorry. I don't know what I'm saying. I don't know what I'm doing.' I could see the tears tripping her now. I started to walk on, but slowly this time. Bridie kept pace with me.

'You're the only one I've said this to, Nan Rose. I haven't even mentioned it to Mammy.'

We were passing the small shelter with its single bench facing out towards the fountain. It was empty.

'C'mon and let's sit down here for a minute Bridie, for we can't be walking home with faces like cry-babbies.'

Bridie nodded through her tears.

We sat down folding over the tail end of our shawls to give us another layer against the cold bench and shuffling together for warmth. I was still churning inside. So, I sat staring out over the park and waiting for Bridie to speak. It was a while before she opened her mouth.

'I don't know that I've ever said to you, Nan Rose, that if I wasn't working for Lizzie Balfour, I'd not last long as a maid. I always feel she's keeping an eye out for me and when she talks, she's talking to me – Bridie. I never feel she just sees me as her servant. It makes the world of a difference having your employer treating you…with…respect. And every so often, we've a wee laugh together.'

I didn't look round, but I nodded.

'I've been hearing bits and pieces of chat at the Balfour's this last while, what with the gossip in the kitchen and the odd piece of conversation ye hear as you to and fro between the front rooms. But I took my cue from Lizzie. Many a night as I was helping her get ready for bed, she'd say "That's what can happen as people get old. They worry about anything and everything." And she'd shake out her hair and I'd feel she was shrugging all the cares off herself, and me as well.'

'Bridie, there's been talk and a lot of people afeard for months. You don't have to be over with the Balfours to know that.'

'I know, Nan Rose. I know. And when there's nothin' ye can do about any of it, ye just get on with it. But now … now I've got a choice.'

I stamped my feet and not just from the cold.

'Ye know Bridie, if I hadn't thought you were serious about Michael I'd not have put Johnny and me to all the trouble to sort things out between the two of yous.' I stood up, desperate to carry on walking, for the churning in my stomach had started again.

'If I wasn't as serious about Michael, and if I didn't know I'd miss you sore, Nan Rose, it'd be a lot easier for me.' Bridie stood up and faced me. 'But you know, and I know what Michael's serious about over anything else.'

I couldn't say anything, for I knowd she was speaking the truth.

'If there's fighting, he'll be in the thick of it. Johnny too, maybe. But you'll have yer job and Maggie and your family round you. I'll be at home with Aunt Imelda ruling the roost, and Lizzie Balfour, who's been as daecent to me as anybody could be, on the other side of the water.'

We started to walk then. We even linked arms again, but there was nothing more to be said for now. The churning in my guts had stopped. Instead, I felt my heart that heavy, it was all I could do to drag it and me home.

Nine

The Manor House
Oakdale Rd
Sheffield

25th January 1914

Dear Nan Rose
    I am sitting here this Sunday morning in the bit of time I have off in the week. Sometimes its the morning and sometimes its the afternoon. The rest of the time I am run off my feet for Mrs Archer thinks I can do a little for Lizzie and a lot for her. You know me so you know I like to be in the thick of things and not twiddling my thums. But I dont like being taken for granted.
    Lizzies been helping me spell more words in the bit of time we have together after I help her dress in the morning and again at the end of the day before she settles into bed. I have to ask her how to spell any new word I have heard. Or she gives me a new one. She asked me if I wanted to write a letter to her so that she could see how I wrote sentences. You know me. When do I ever say No? But I am sorry I did for she says I have a habit of droppin the g off words.

Now she wants me to write her a letter every so often to help me learn. At least I know WE understand each other Nan Rose whatever I write.

Its the third Sunday since I arrived here and the third time I have started to write you. Believe it or not the hardest times are when Im off. You will not credit this but I have sat through two Sunday masses this morning. Just to pass away the time somewhere thats half warm. I might even have stayed for the 11 mass but I saw the sexton glancing down at me as he tidied the altar. I looked round and apart from an aul biddy who looked like she was asleep I was the only one there. So when he came down the altar steps and through the gate at the communion rail eyeing me all the time I jumped up crossed myself and skedaddled out the side door.

But I was prayin for all of yous and for all them poor fellas and men from Larkins union that had to go back this week with their tails between their legs without makin a blind bit of diffrince to anything. Lizzie told me on Monday evening as I was brushing and plaiting her hair for bed. I nearly dropped the brush I was holdin. I forgot she could see me in the mirror on the dressing table. Sit down on the settee Bridie says she. All the colour has left you. I did as I was bid for I was suddenly shivring and my heart was that sore I was bent over with the ache in it. I couldint say anything for I didnt know if I was coming or goin. But when I went up to my own bed I cried myself to sleep. It wasnt just the strike. It was for everything. All I could think was that all of you were over there and I was here with only Lizzie Balfour to understand.

Anyway I have pulled myself together since. For what else is there to be done? And as youre not here to see where I am, I will tell you. Im squeezed right up under the roof. You come in the door. At your left shoulder and jammed up agin the wall is a WARDROBE. Straight ahead is a wee fireplace. To the left of it is Sarahs bed shoved up into the corner. Mine is shoved up into the corner to the right. There should be two of us but Sarah thats the other maid is living at home for now. Her mother is poorly and she needs to be there at night.

There is a chamber pot under the bed. Its like a huge teacup with big red roses painted round its middle. Near the end of my bed and right under the roof window theres a pine table thats so narrow it looks as if its been chopped in half along its length. I am sitting there right now with me sharpened pencil and paper.

We are allowed to light a fire an hour before we go to bed these winter nights but the coal scuttle is that small I have hardly got the fire going and its out. The only heat I get is from carrying it up the two flights of stairs.

I dreamt the other night that you and I were running out on the street after the coal cart and fetched so much in we sat for hours in front of the fire talking. As it is the snow is thick on the ground. So you would have a job even finding a piece of coal on the street let alone sneakin it upstairs.

I hope you and Johnny are well. When I opened my bag after getting here, I found a wee poke of paper with four cherry lips in it. It was in the pocket of my other skirt. I sucked one as I sat in this chair. Would you believe I could still taste the cherry particular if I closed my eyes and remembered the four of us at that last ceili in October. I put the other three with those two shells and the ribbons you gave me when I started work for Lizzie Balfour. They are all safe and sound in that linen purse you made for me when I set off across the water. Where did you get that scrap of yellow that you cut into a daffodil head and stitched on the front? I keep it under my pillow and go to sleep thinking about you all. How is Michael? Is he still set agin me?

Your good friend Bridie

'I notice Daughter, that every time your mother or I mention Bridie's name you take a bit of a huff.' I put down the darning into my lap and I took my time to look up at Father. I shrugged for I didn't know what to say. He and I were alone in the house so there was no hope of interruption from Mammy or Michael.

'You've taken her moving to England very personal.'

I couldn't contain myself. I was that agitated the darning landed on the floor.

'She shouldn't have moved to England. And now that she has, it's not the same. She nivir thought about that before she left.'

'Daughter, dear! You'd think she went to England to spite you.'

'She shouldn't't've gone. She didn't need to.' If I hadn't been sitting down I'd have stamped my feet hard and loud on the flagstones. I saw Father shake his head. Says I 'Mammy thinks the same. That Mrs Corr shouldn't have let her.'

'Your mother has never had the need or inclination to leave the place she was born in. Not everyone is the same.'

Father took out his baccy tin and started to tap and fill his pipe. I buttoned my lip for I could feel he was gathering himself to say something that I needed to hear. He lit the pipe, sucked in and then settled himself back in his chair.

'From when I was a wee 'un, to the day I left home, any spare time I had I spent with Niall Deeny. We climbed trees, we walked the fields, we fished, we swam. Where there was one you were as likely to find the other. Now Niall was the only son in his family so from the beginning he was set to stay working the land. And I was the second son in mine, and so, from the beginning, although I didn't know it, I was set to leave.'

By this time I'd settled back into my chair.

'There was many a time after I came to Belfast when I wished that Niall was beside me. Or that I had the means to get a message to him or him me. For even when you know you're doing what you need to do, it doesn't stop it being hard and it doesn't stop you wanting the company of the ones you hold dear. I'd hate to think of you in England, Nan Rose, the way I was when I first came to Belfast. The same goes for that wee Bridie one for she's been in and out of here that often that she's nearly like a daughter to me.'

'Did you never see him again Father?'

'Ach, I saw him the few times I managed to get back for a visit. But it was never the same. We'd lost contact with the parting of the ways. Maybe it would've happened anyway as we grew up. But maybe not.'

I unfolded Bridie's letter from my skirt pocket. I spread it on my lap, taking my time to smooth out the creases. The pencil marks were beginning to smudge with the sweat from my hands for I'd fingered it time and again during the two weeks I'd had it.

'Bridie writes well. Lizzie Balfour is still helping her learn.' I must've said it very low for out of the corner of my eye I saw Father lean forward to catch my words. He didn't say anything and in the silence I could feel a hot tear trickle down my cheek.

I bent my head lower.

'There's no shame in not knowing, Daughter. The only shame is in not learning when you've got the chance. And did I not hear Maggie say that she was going to go to some class or other in Albert Street?'

I nodded. Maggie'd finally got her prayers answered and was expecting a babby in early summer. She'd the bit between her teeth about making a better life for her childer. In the autumn she'd joined a class run by one of the trade union women and was doing a bit of Irish history and more reading and writing.

The Manor House
Oakdale Rd
Sheffield
22nd February 1914

Dear Nan Rose,

Just in case you did not get my last letter I have put the address on the top again. I am going to write this one in wee bits and then post it when both sides of the page are filled up to save on stamps. And maybe by the time I come to the end your letter will have arrived.

I will tell you about the house. Lizzie Balfour says it is grand but not that grand. Well. It may not be grand to her but I have never been in a house like it for it puts the Balfours house to shame. That maybe gives you some idea for you saw the outside of that. There are three big downstairs windows looking out over the garden and as many panes of glass on the floor above. I know. For last week Sarah and I had the job of cleanin and polishin every single one of them. Sarahs a bit older and taller than me. Shes built like a long drink of water but she prickles like a hedgehog. When we were doing the windows, I noticed the garden is full of stones. Now I know from Miss Lizzie that rock is easy to come by round Sheffield but even so. Says I to Sarah I dont see the point of going to the trouble of digging it all up and then scattering stones over it. Well she looked at me as if I crawled out of the gutter. She put on the voice she uses when shes talking to Mrs Archer. Like her mouth was full of marbles. IF says she you are still here in three months you will see the ROCKRIE in full bloom. Seems they paid someone specially to put those stones there and you get all sorts of wee plants growing in and round them. Anyway. That will teach me to open my mouth to say what I think. Every so often I forget that Im not with my own kind and it does me no favours.

When I went to Lizzies room that evening she was staring at the window. She turned round as I came in and I could see by the set of her lips that she was annoyed about something. Bridie says she and my heart sank to my feet for I thought it was me she was annoyed with. It would be too much if Lizzie ever turned agin me.

As it turned out it was her aunt was the problem. What is it about aunts? I crossed the water to get away from Imelda only to find Lizzies aunt is just as difficult. Anyway. Lizzie says that her mother said that I could go with Lizzie as a maid and a COMPANION (thats a sort of friend that you pay) as long as I helped out a bit in the house. Seems Lizzie thinks her aunt is takin a mile instead of an inch and feeling bad that there is nothin she can do about it for now. She is hoping that as she gets settled and the better weather comes that she will get out and about more and take me with her some of the time. Even her saying that helps for at least I know where she stands on the matter.

Now seeing as Im talkin about Mrs Archer I will say a bit more. To look at her you would think butter wouldnt melt in her mouth for she looks like a soft plump cushion. And if you heard her talking to her own kind she talks soft and sweet. But when she talks to Sarah or me its a diffrint matter. More often than not she is so hard and sharp, I think she is crunchin glass, but then every so often she is soft and sweet and I dont know whether Im comin or going. At least I knowd where I stood with Aunt Imelda.

As for the ones like me I have the divil of a job to know what they say and them me. It is no skin of their noses for they can talk to each other. But Nan Rose you know how hard it is for me not to have somebody who I can be at ease with. I have to talk so slowly and listen so hard Im wrung out with the effort.

And I dont like how they are always trying to change what I am sayin. You do not say Woy. You say Why. It is not NottingHAM. It is NottingM. Well if it is why do they not write it like that? Im fed up with them sayin one thing and writing another. And Im beginnin to think that its not just the words and how they talk them. For I met a woman in the church this Sunday in between the two masses. I was hiding myself away behind a pillar in the side altar out of sight of the sexton. Besides I like the wee altar to Our Lady. Sitting there I feel shes lookin out for me. Anyway. This woman slipped into the pew behind me and the first I knew of it was when she put a hand on my shoulder. I nearly jumped out of my skin. Its alright DUCK says she. DUCK here is like us sayin daughter. Its alright DUCK but I seen you here the last number of Sundays and Im wondring if youre a stranger and away from home. Oh Nan Rose my eyes just watered up. I couldint stop myself. Says she I live five minutes down the road and if you were not set on hearing another mass you are welcome to a cup of tea. Well at that I welled up so inside that all I could do was nod. She took me to her wee house and we sat and talked til the clock on her mantelpiece struck 10 30 and she had to be getting the breakfast ready for her man who was having a lie in. Now the point Im makin is I talked to yer woman Mrs Baker longer than I have talked to anyone bar Lizzie. And I had no trouble knowin what she was saying and she me. I tell a lie. I had to tell her what hallion meant. And then she laughed that much but in such a way that I started laughing with her. So theres people like me this side of the water after all.

8th March

Nan Rose

I am so happy. I got your letter yesterday. Just when I was thinkin you were in the huff with me. And beginning to fear I would never hear from you again. It near burnt a hole in my pocket all day for I was itching to tear it open. As it was, I read it again and again once I was in bed. and woke this morning still full of your news. I am so glad you and Johnny are still managin to have a bit of time together in between the marching and the meetings of the Irish Volunteers. Maybe you could thank Michael for wishing me well and give my good wishes to him. And Maggie is going to have a babby. She must be

over the moon. I will pray that it arrives safe and sound. How are all the ones at the mill?
    I am going with Lizzie to a suffragette meeting tonight. So I will post this then.
    Your good friend
    Bridie

I glanced up at the clock on the mantelpiece. Eight o'clock. I had the house to myself and no rush to do anything, what with us all being off for St Patrick's Day on the morrow. As soon as we'd eaten supper and I realised mammy, father and Michael were all going to be out for a couple of hours, I got the tin bath in. I poured in a kettle of warm water and a half kettle of cold. I got everything off me and stood in the couple of inches of water and soaked myself down with a flannel and a bit of soap. My hair was grand as I'd already had a bath on Saturday. But with tomorrow a holiday and a whole crowd of us going to walk up towards one of the open fields near Hannahstown after mass, I wanted to feel Sunday clean. Johnny, Michael and me were all going. And if Maggie could get a lift in one of the carts heading up there, we'd have her and Charles as well. We would play games and eat our pieces while taking in the sight of Belfast below us. If the weather held, we'd maybe manage a set dance or two before walking back home in our own good time.

    I settled myself into Father's chair and lifted Bridie's envelope from Father's stool where I'd put it while I washed. Bandit settled herself, her muzzle resting on my feet. I took my time to read it again. For all the grand house and being with Lizzie Balfour, I could hear it was hard going for Bridie. Maybe she'd have been better off putting up with Imelda? But then she'd still have had to find work. I let out a long sigh. It was all very well for Father to talk about me writing, but I felt miles away from Bridie. I was miles away from

Bridie and her in a different world. At least when she was with the Balfours, we'd seen each other every week. I read the letter yet again. I was glad me saying Michael wished her well lifted her spirits. What I didn't say was that it took Johnny and me on either side of him a good quarter of an hour, wheedling and cajoling for him to mutter even those few words.

Bandit suddenly sat up and then scarpered forward to greet Michael as he walked through the door, He slung his cap on the hook and came over to stand in front of the embers of the fire. He glanced down at the letter in my lap.

'How is she?' says he, pulling a chair across from the table and sitting down square to the grate. I looked up at him.

'How's Bridie?' says I, my jaw nearly dropping off me for it was the first time since she left that he'd shown any interest.

'There's no one else you write to, is there?' He glanced again at the letter.

I picked my words with care. 'She's upset about how the strike ended. She's pleased that you were asking for her and she said to tell you she was asking for you.' I drew breath. 'It's not easy for her being by herself and that far away.'

He shrugged. 'She's made her bed…so she'll have to lie in it.' He stood up suddenly and just managed to catch the back of the chair before it toppled.

I looked down at the letter for I didn't want him to see how disappointed I was at our talk ending before it began. He was as thran as a dog with a bone. But he was still standing there, his hands now on the mantelpiece, his arms at full stretch so he leaned over the embers.

'She didn't have to go, did she? Yer woman Balfour was clearly better company than any of the rest of us.'

My heart went out to him at that moment, for didn't I have the same thoughts myself at times. I stood up and rested my right hand on the mantelpiece near his. He glanced at me and as quickly away but not before I caught the pain in his eyes and his lips pursed tight so they wouldn't betray him. I stayed where I was but looked down at our feet as I near whispered, 'Ach Michael, you know what the aunt is like and you know what you yourself are like. There isn't much give in either of you when yous get the bit between your teeth. Bridie was heart sore at leaving but there wasn't enough space for a life between you and Imelda. She knew she'd come a poor second to wherever the politics took you. Lizzie Balfour was her one chance and she took it.'

He placed his hand over mine and nodded and we stood still and silent with our own thoughts – until Bandit who was sitting between us could contain her patience no longer and started barking. Michael reached down and held her head between his hands before ruffling her hair. He straightened himself and put his hand at my shoulder.

'I'll have to keep an eye on you Nan Rose, for I can't have my wee sister becoming as wise as my big sister now, can I?'

Sheffield
5th April

Dear Nan Rose,

Now what with it being warmer here in between the rain and Mrs Baker bringin me round to hers for a cup of tea I have less need to sit in the church half the morning. So today after I left her house I decided to walk the streets round here. Lizzie gave me one of her old hats when I was helping her unpack. Old to her but as new to me. It is ROYAL blue felt with a brim that you can turn up as well as down that fits me if I pile my hair up under it and nip it in at the side with a hat pin. She gave me that as well. But I have to not let on where they came from in case it annoys other people. So she says. I do not know if she means Sarah or her aunt. I cant think she means Mrs Wright the cook for shes never out of the kitchen if she can help it. She reminds me of your mammy. As long as you know that she runs the kitchen and act ACCORDINGLY. That means not a foot out of line. Mrs Wright will be fine by you. There was only her and me on yesterday. I fetched in the breakfast dishes. Do you want me to wash these for I have a bit of time on my hands says I. She gave me a long look. But then says she You do that Bridie duck. Smiling. And then you and I will have a cup of tea and a slice of this tea loaf. She and Sarah do not get on. I think thats because Sarah fancies herself as the housekeeper. The other day Miss Lizzie was poorly and in bed. I fetched her up her breakfast and then afterwards brought the tray in to the kitchen. I was turning to go when Sarah sailed in. As if she owned the place. Good morning ladies she said. Made me think of aul Campbell that did. Well she paid no heed to Mrs Wright but I did. Do you know the way a cat stops stock still every hair bristling at the sight of a dog? That was Mrs Wright at the sight and sound of Sarah.

Anyway back to the hat and pin. I do as Im told and dont be flauntin them. But with them and the grey coat mammy made me from an old one of Aunt Imelda I look as if I have as much right as the next one to be walking out of a Sunday morning.

You can see my new word in this next sentence. Mrs Archers forever telling one or other of us to CONCENTRATE. For her that means listen to what I am saying and do exactly as I say. Lizzie is hell bent on helping me write. She was on at me last night about still dropping the g. And then she started to talk to me about COMMAS and some upside down comma that had a name like apostle.

17th April
I am by myself in the house for an hour or two so Im writing this from my favourite room in the Archers - the MUSIC room. Can you credit that? A room where you only go to play or listen to music. The only furniture is a big black piano that is so shiny you can see your face in it and two rows of chairs sitting opposite it. Im sitting on the floor with my paper on the end chair in the back row. They keep calling this the grand piano. Well it is grand. It is a very diffrint shape from the old brown one in our school. But I still think it is showin off to keep talking about how grand it is.

The first time I came in here I was supposed to be dusting and polishing but as soon as I closed the door behind me I stopped still. It is so quiet and light for its got these glass doors that they call FRENCH WINDOWS looking out to the garden. Right now theres a CHERRY tree blooming. I only wish I had the dress its wearing. The floor is a special polished wood - its PARQUET Lizzie says. Instead of just putting down straight planks and having done with it, the woods cut into wee rectangles and then pieced together like a jigsaw. It would have taken some doing. I think your father would like it with him being so handy with wood. I take off my shoes when I come in for otherwise Im creaking like a door in need of oil – and without them I feel like I am gliding ever so quietly in the soft light. In here all the sounds of the house and the street fade and all I can hear are the songs of the birds.

24th April

You will never guess what is happening. There is a painter coming from London to stay in a fortnight's time. Can you see I have put the apostle in that last sentence? He paints pictures not houses. Would you believe it? Somebody who can get by drawing and colouring in. He is the Archers godson and is coming to teach at the School of Art here. I know what yer thinking, Nan Rose. Do they TEACH people to sit around painting one another? Have they nothing better to do? But what would you and I do, if us and all our ones had more than enough money?

One of his pictures is hanging up in the music room. On the wall above the fireplace. Mrs Archer pointed it out to me as I was dustin. Take extra care with that BRI-die says she, for she PRONOUNCES my name funny like that. Lizzie says her aunt PRONOUNCES rather than talks and she wrote down the word so I could learn it. We will have the ARTIST himself arriving to stay shortly says Mrs Archer puffing herself up as if she painted it herself and not just been handed it on a plate. After she left me in peace, I took my time and had a good gander at it. There is a woman sitting in some garden or other. And Nan Rose I swear it is the Garden of Eden itself, the flowers are that big and bright. The white flowers are nearly the size of yer face. Lizzie told me they were hazalyas. There are yellow and purple and pink ones and yer woman is sitting in the middle of them. Beyond the bushes in one corner you can see the sea and across from that, a line of sand and a hillside.

But this hillside is purple not yellow. So there is no gorse there like there is along the road we walked to Hannahstown.

I think the painting would be far better on the wee bit of wall by the French windows. That way the two gardens could sit side by side, one right here that you can walk into and the other a warm dream away. But sure what do I know? Anyway Nan Rose. I can hardly keep my eyes open. So Im away to rest my head.

Bridie

With Bridie miles away – a world away even, me and Maggie drew even closer. Now that she and Charles had moved and were renting a first-floor room in a bigger terrace in Dover Street, they had a living room and scullery to themselves with the bed partitioned off in one corner to make a sort of bedroom. So it was easier to catch her by herself. I'd taken to calling round to give her a hand round the house, for she looked heavy and tired these days with the babby due in a month or so. And if I wasn't behind myself of a morning, I'd wait at the corner of her street for her to join me and we'd walk up to the mill together.

So Saturday morning that's what I did. As I stood waiting at the corner, I let myself bask for a minute or two in the blue sky, the sunshine and the warmth of the day. I could feel my spirits lift, just thinking that we were nearly in May and the days inching longer each week. And then I caught sight of Maggie walking towards me, heavier and slower than just a couple of days back. As she drew near, I could see she was white with tiredness, her eyes cradled in dark shadows.

'Maggie, you look like death warmed up, says I. 'Have ye not slept?'

'Did none of yous hear the racket going on in the early hours of the morning,' says she. 'Coming from the Shankill Road direction?'

I shook my head. Maggie sighed and rolled her eyes.

'I think yous'ns would sleep through the Last Trumpet,' says she.

By this time we'd turned the corner onto Divis Street and could see Bella Dwyer, Peggy Arthurs and Ellen Kavanagh walking a bit ahead of us. Maggie quickened her pace.

'Bella! Ellen!' she called. They stopped, turned and waited.

'Did any of yous hear some of that commotion in the early hours of the morning?' Maggie looked from face to face.

'I didn't,' says Peggy Arthurs, 'but our Mal came in from doing his night watchman shift at Mackies foundry just as I was going out the door. He says he was stopped and checked by two separate Ulster Volunteer patrols as he walked to work. And he says, there was a stream of lorries and waggons going down the Shankill early evening and then back again at eleven at night. He says it was about midnight before the sound of men's voices and footsteps stopped and the last door slammed shut.'

That put the fear of God in me. And by the silence and sideways looks we were all giving each other, I wasn't alone. For months there'd been rumours that them Ulster Volunteers were hell bent on arming themselves – and very little word that our ones were managing to do the same.

We carried on walking to the mill. Together but each of us alone with their own thoughts. We were nearly at the gates when Bella says, 'Maybe we might hear a bit more from some of the ones that live on the Shankill.'

Ellen Kavanagh sighed loud and long. 'I'm heart-sick of all this. We used to be able to come to work and have a bit of craic and not mind who came from where. There were ones from the Shankill as well as ourselves when we went on strike. But now, it's whatever you say, say nothing unless you know you're with your own. I'm wound up like a clock with it all.'

In fact, it was near six o'clock on Saturday evening before we found out from Charles and Maggie what was behind all the shenanigans on Friday night. They called round to our house with him brandishing a copy of the Belfast Evening Telegraph. I was keeping an eye on the bit of lamb bone stew simmering over the fire and waiting for Johnny and Michael to call back in after yet another meeting of their Irish Volunteers. Mammy was patching a couple of bedsheets with squares cut from an aul flour bag that Mrs Hegarty had given her for Mrs Hegarty's brother worked in Hughes bakery. And father was out the back repairing one of the kitchen chairs.

Charles laid the paper out on the table and we gathered round.

'Will ye give yer father a shout, Nan Rose?' says he. 'I think he'll want to hear this.'

I went to the back door and called him in. He nodded, picked up an old rag to wipe his hands and followed me. As he came to the table we shuffled aside so that he stood next to Charles. I shifted to stand behind Maggie who had sunk into the nearest chair at the table when she arrived. Mammy sat down the other side of Father, resting her elbow on the table and her chin in her hand.

Charles began to read out the headlines. 'Amazing Night at Larne. Wholesale Gunrunning. Thousands of Rifles Landed. Three and a half Million Cartridges. Motors from Far and Near. An Astounding Achievement.'

I slumped down on the chair beside Maggie for the fear was mangling my guts. Mammy glanced at me and reached over to touch my arm. I squeezed her hand and managed a thin smile.

'Well if you'd ever any doubt as to where The Telegraph stood, it'd be clear now,' says Father. 'Yer man writing can barely contain his jubilance.'

'Aye,' says Charles. 'It says here that this piece is "special to the Telegraph" which means he was there by invitation. They knew he was on their side.' He straightened himself so he was talking to all of us.

'They landed at Larne and unloaded the whole lot within a few hours. Yer man here says, "there was no rush or bustle… it was done in pur-su-ance of a well-formed plan." Now listen to this.' He looked up and round at us all. '"All the arms were landed at Larne Harbour, and a vast transport of motor cars, lorries and waggons …came to the town…hundreds of motors reached the assembly point at an identical moment. It was an amazing sight to see this huge procession of cars nearly three miles in length descending upon the town with all their headlights ablaze." They're organised and they're moving with impunity.'

'Mother of God protect us,' says Mammy crossing herself. 'What's to become of us?'

Father was still studying the paper.

'They had another two ships there as well. So they loaded those up too…and "The authorities might as well have been in Timbuctoo in so far as knowledge or inter-fer-ence was concerned." Now why does that not surprise me?' He went over to sit in his chair by the fireplace, picked up his baccy tin, opened it, lifted his pipe and set to filling and lighting it – as if he was all by himself and had all the time in the world.

Mammy bustled over to shift the pot of stew off the flame and shift the kettle of water to boil.

'Yous'll take a cup of tea?' says she, looking over at Maggie and Charles. 'And there's a wee bit of soda bread left from yesterday, Maggie. Kept special for you.'

Charles straightened. Hands on his hips, he stretched backwards. 'I wonder what our two Irish Volunteers will have to say about all of this?'

Sheffield
5th May

Dear Nan Rose

I was so relieved to get your letter today. I'd barely posted that last letter when Lizzie told me about those Ulster Volunteer ones landing all those guns at Larne. We were sitting in the garden at the time as we had the house to ourselves, for Mr and Mrs Archer had taken Harry Wharton, yer painter fella to visit some friends in Hathersage. A village not far from here. Lizzie said she was not feeling well and they seemed happy enough to leave her.

Thats when she told me all the news about home. She was right agitated even if she was trying to stay calm. You remember Mr Archer supports Home Rule? She said he was APOLECTIC with what yer man Carson is getting away with. That means he's raging. Whereas her mother talks as if there was nothing out of the ordinary happening. Which Lizzie says is a sign she is sick with worry.

Well, after that I was sick with worry. Thinking of Mammy and all yous. I was never so glad to get a letter from you. Thank you for calling round to see Mammy and check that she and Granny and Aunt Imelda were alright. It was very kind of your parents to think of them.

From what you say, Michael and Mr Archer would get on well seeing as they are both APOLECTIC. But I suppose Michael must be heart sore. I can see him now sitting at your kitchen table explaining to me what Home Rule was and him so pleased to be a steward. It is good he has Johnny as a friend. What with Johnny not taking it all so hard, maybe because he has you. I have written Michael a wee note and put it in with this letter for you to give to him. Please. I wanted him to know I was thinking of him right now.

8th May

To tell you the truth Nan Rose, my heart is not in anything that is happening here right now. I keep thinking of all yous that I know and love back home. I even thought of Gemma Locke. I was thinking it would be good for Michael if he had a girl to walk out with. Even if I would be sad. I know you would tell me if he had. Would you not?

Anyway, it's not doing me any good for my heart to be across the water and the rest of me here. So I will tell you about life here right now. Apart from Lizzie, nobody else seems to be at all interested in what is happening in Ireland. Even Mrs Archer. And she has a sister there. She is too busy doting on Harry Wharton.

As for him, I had a proper gander at him last Wednesday. Sarah's mother had taken a turn for the worse so it was left to me to bring in a tray with a pot of tea, the best cups and these tiny wee sandwiches that would slip down your throat without you as much as noticin. He looks nothing like his painting. I do not right know what I was expectin but he just looks pale. As if all his colour and life was brushed into his pictures. He must be a bit older than yer Maggie's man Charles. And not a patch on him for looks. He is plump with fair wispy hair and beard. For all the world like a badly plucked chicken. Except for his hands. As I laid the tray down on the table beside Mrs Archer I caught his hands move out of the corner of my eye. He was telling a story and was describing a curtain bill o in and his left hand was like a bird on the wind. I must have gotten distracted for the next I knew Mrs Archer was staring hard at me. Thank you Bridie. That will be all says she all sweet and with a smile that she prised out from her jaws.

10th May

I would love you to see where I was on Friday. It is called Padley Gorge. Mrs Archer was poorly so she insisted Lizzie take this painter fella there and as Lizzie could not go alone, I went with them. We travelled in a train for about half an hour and walked for another half hour from the station into the woods. The sun was flitting in and out through the trees and we were stepping in and out of splashes of light. All the time the sound of water in our ears. I never noticed before all the diffrint sounds water makes. BURBLING, TRICKLING, ROARING. But thats whats interesting about being out with yer man. Every so often he just stops dead and stands there looking or listening. He stopped at a clump of primroses and as I watched him fingering the leaves, I swear I saw that primrose like it was being born right in front of my eyes, like it was breathing. And when he stopped to sit on a rock and I watched him listen, thats when I heard the water. All the time Mr Harry

Wharton, thats his name, had a funny wee smile like a child thats been let play in mud to its hearts content. I dont warm to him as such but watching him I see things in a DIFFERENT way.

We had a PICNIC. That is a spread of food you would give your eye teeth for, all laid out on a tablecloth on the grass. Lizzie insisted I ate with them. I am not having you stand there behind us like a tin soldier, Bridie.

Well Nan Rose, there were plates of sandwiches, chicken and ham, salmon and cucumber and another plate of chocolate cake and wee buns with cherries in them. All washed down with some ginger lemonade. I was glad she had him carry it the whole way and not me. It is wonderful to have a strong man about the place. She said that to him with her sweetest smile. And without a blush and her a suffragette.

Afterwards I packed it all into the basket. Lizzie sat on the blanket writing in her notebook and he took out an even bigger notebook and started drawing. I picked daisies and made a daisy chain, with each daisy being someone from home. When I looked up he was staring from me to his book and scribbling away like a man possessed.

17^h May

I can hardly write for my hands shaking that much Nan Rose. Im a bit afeard. Yer man has asked to paint me. Paint Me. Can you credit it? And that has set the cat among the pigeons.

Lizzie told me all this last night. Seems yer man got the notion that afternoon of the picnic. Now this is the odd thing. Mrs Archer is dead set against the notion. Mark my words. No good will come of it says she. But will she say to him that she forbids it? No. Because says she he is her only godson and an artist. Well for all her mighty ways, she could learn a thing or two from your mammy or Aunt Imelda. For they would cross Saint Peter himself if they thought he was in the wrong.

Lizzie thinks it is a bit of a geg. She says it seems you have the face of a FAERIE queen, Bridie. What do you say to that? I was brushing her hair at the time and I stopped and stared at myself in the mirror. How would he know? says I. Has he seen faeries? Well at that she burst out laughing. You will have to ask him when you sit for him. Sit for him? says I. Yes, you have to sit very still while you are being painted. Im not a great one for sitting still says I.

But this is what takes me to the fair, Nan Rose. Nobody, not even Lizzie asked me would I mind doing it. And Lizzie says that even though her aunt does not like the idea she would like it even less if I said I was not for doing it.

I hoped to see Mrs Baker this morning at Mass and could have a word with her. But as it was, I could only talk to Our Lady and as you know, she answers in her own way. So I am glad I can write to you here in my wee room before I start back this afternoon. I will post this tomorrow. I hope you can write soon.

Bridie

Ten

Wednesday, 10th June 1914

Ever since Bridie'd mentioned that painter fella, I'd had a bad feeling. I was expecting trouble. And I couldn't say anything to anyone for I didn't want word to go round and people start casting aspersions on Bridie. As likely as not, she'd get herself out of trouble as easily as she walked into it. Still… The only thing I could think to do was to make sure Mammy didn't get a whiff of anything. That meant me getting to the post before her for Mammy had the same attitude to whatever came into the house as she had to wages. She was the woman of the house and by rights everything should come to her to manage as she saw fit. She'd open any letters. So I'd taken to coming straight home from the mill as quick as I could whereas what I was used to doing was to walk with Maggie back to hers.

    I got a jolt to find not one, but two letters for me on the mat. The other envelope put Bridie's to shame. It felt like linen while Bridie's was little more than thin newspaper. The writing was bold and all of a piece. *Miss N.R. Murphy.* I traced Bridie's careful big print on the other envelope, for unlike her letters where she wrote as small as she could to save paper, she seemed to think that if my name and address didn't take up most of the space, it wouldn't arrive. I fingered the linen envelope, fat with paper. The same postmark as

Bridie's. That put the fear of God in me. Then, thinking Mammy'd come in, I folded both carefully and slid them deep into my skirt pocket. I slipped out the back for if I bumped into Mammy she'd know as soon as look at me that I was hiding something.

You'd never credit how hard it is to find a place to read a letter in peace and quiet. In the house, I'd have to be in my own bed after everyone'd gone to sleep which was no good to me for more often than not I was the first one to close my eyes. Or I could wait for the odd time I'd the house to myself. But this time, those letters were burning a hole in my pocket.

You might think it would be easy enough to find a quiet place outside – but there was nothing more likely to invite nosiness than a girl sitting alone and looking like she was doing nothing but minding her own business. I wondered about taking myself down to St Mary's Chapel for it had a grotto for Our Lady outside. I could kneel at the pew below the statue and prop the letters between my elbows. But in the end, I decided to just go on up to Maggie's, for she'd understand and give me peace when I needed it.

I found her dozing in the rocking chair with the light from the window splashed over and about her. She looked like an angel with her hair falling loose over her shoulder and chest, except you never see pictures of them looking tired and worn out and with chapped hands. As I watched her sleep, I'd a notion to go over and stroke her cheek and tuck her hair behind her ear as she used to do with me. But as I'd be far better use making her a cup of tea, I stepped softly over to the jaw tub, put a taste of water in the kettle and sat it over the embers to heat. It suddenly came to me that Mammy might've looked like this when she was carrying Maggie. And that there'd come a time when that might be me lying there exhausted. A shiver ran through me. It was well seen that God was a man, for he'd let them off easy.

While the kettle was boiling, I sat in the chair opposite Maggie, fetched out the letters and opened the one from Bridie.

6th June

Nan Rose I got your wee letter yesterday. I was so pleased for I kept thinking what would happen if it arrived and me not here? So now I do not have to worry about that – which is good for I have enough to be worrying about. I swear the only thing that keeps me right is talking to you on paper. I have been scribbling away this last week or so. And carrying it round in that little cloth purse you made me and it pinned to my petticoat. Whats eating away at me is that it must have been my fault, even if I can not figure out how. For thats what they all say. That its up to the woman to keep things right. No matter even if you are just a girl.

So now I can not stay here and I will not be sent back. Not like this. But if it is my fault, how have I not been struck dead when I went to the novena on Thursday? Instead, Our Lady helped me for who came and sat down beside me but Mrs Baker. I have not seen her the last two weeks and there she was. We walked back to her house for a cup of tea, me keeping my head down and just listenin to what she had to say for herself. But with a cup of tea in my hand, I was able to tell her. Not much. But enough. Says I Its not going well with Mrs Archer on account of me and her visitor. Says she And is this visitor a man or a woman? When I told her it was a man who was a painter fella and who was painting me, she gave such a start that her cup of tea near went flyin. Then she sat back and looked at me without saying a word before crossin her arms tight in front of her. That does not sound like a house for a young girl like yourself to be in, Bridie. What would yer mother say if she knew there were carry-ons like that?

I nearly dropped my own cup then at the thought of Mammy blamin me as well. For did she not say to me when I started work for Lizzie Balfour and then again on the Docks to be sure and do as I was told and to be obligin when I could. And thats all I was doing. How was I to know where it led to? And now the thought of Mammy, or God help us, Aunt Imelda finding out what happened makes me go cold with fright. So Nan Rose, whatever you say, say nothin to anybody about what I am telling ye. As soon as Im settled again, I will let them know. Thank God, I have a wee bit of money saved. Also Mrs Baker says there is a widow woman down the street that I could lodge with for now and she knows ones at the factory that she will ask to speak up for me. What with all this talk of war, says she, they will have a lot of places to fill for the young lads are champing at the bit to have a good reason to fight.

Well that was news to me. Have you heard talk of war? That's the diffrince between working as a servant and working in the mill. Everybody in this house is that caught up in fighting their own corner here, you forget there is a bigger world out there. Anyway Nan Rose, I need to go. Lizzie gave me my pay today and there is nothin to keep me here after that. I will write you as soon as I know where I am.

Maybe if you get a chance you will light a candle for me. Bridie.

Well by the time I got to the end of the letter, my thoughts were galloping like racehorses round a track in my head. I read it again thinking I'd missed some clue as to what had happened with yer man. Nothing. And now I didn't even know where she was living! Bridie'd never felt so near nor so far away.

Maggie stirred and I folded the letter quick and put it back in my pocket. It was the first time I'd hesitated to tell Maggie whatever was on my mind. She stirred but she didn't waken even though the kettle was blowing. I took it off the hob and set to opening the other envelope. My hands were trembling as I fished the letter out.

A cloth pouch stuffed with a wodge of paper fell on my lap. I'd have recognised it anywhere for it was the purse I'd given Bridie when she set off across the water. I fingered the scrap of yellow that I'd cut in the shape of a daffodil head and stitched on the front. I'd wheedled that from Maggie. She'd just dyed an end strip of finer linen with gorse to make a sash for her waist for Easter Sunday. And Bridie, God love her, was as pleased as if I'd given her a purse of gold and silk. Bridie! My heart started thumping for she wouldn't have given letter nor purse to anyone else if she'd any choice in the matter. I put the purse back in my pocket and unfolded the sheets from which it had tumbled. I went straight to the end. *Elizabeth Balfour.*

I don't know who else I thought would have been writing to me from Sheffield, but I was that relieved that it was Lizzie, that it took me a good few minutes to remember I'd a big bone to pick with her. Remembering my anger steadied my hands and I picked up the letter to see what she'd to say for herself.

7th June 1914

Dear Nan Rose,
I am writing to you in the hope that you will be able

to help. Bridie has disappeared without a word or note to anyone.

I cannot but think that I am in some way responsible for this. I only ever wished Bridie well but I can see now that good intentions are not enough.

However, I feel if I could speak to her, I might still be able to help. I could at least give her the choice of returning home or support her to find suitable lodging and other work if she wanted to stay for I have no doubt that neither she nor my aunt would wish her to return to service here.

However, if I am to be of use, I must act quickly. So, I am writing to you because I think you are the only person likely to know where Bridie has gone. If you do, I ask you to trust me and tell me. I have spoken to Mr Frazer, the manager at your mill and he has agreed that if I telephone at the midday break on Friday, 12th June, he will allow you to speak to me in private.

I know that you had misgivings about the wisdom of Bridie leaving all that she knew to come to work with me. And events appear to have proved you right. I do hope that you know that I have acted in good faith. I do believe that we women can and should support one another to live fuller lives.

Having set this whole chain of events in motion, I am determined to do all that I can to resolve the present situation in Bridie's best interests. And I know, that as Bridie's dearest friend, you too will want the same for her. So, I do hope and trust that you will be willing to speak with me when I telephone.

In the meantime, I enclose some writing that I found in Bridie's room. It is addressed to you. I hope you will forgive me. When she did not return from her morning off, I feared ... I have taken the liberty of reading it in

the hope that it would give me a clue as to her intentions and whereabouts. No matter that it has not. It has added to my regret and strengthened my resolve to make amends.
    Yours sincerely,
    Elizabeth Balfour.

I don't know how long I sat staring at the letter in my hands. Although I couldn't work out every word, I got the gist of it. The clock on the mantelpiece sounding the hour roused me. It was only then I realised that Maggie was awake and looking at me. She made the effort to smile.

'That looks a quare interesting letter you've got there, Nan Rose, for I've been sitting here awake these last five minutes and you've been sitting as still as a statue. It must be grand to have someone write to you. How Bridie finds the time to do it I don't know for it's as much as I can do to get through what needs done round here after a day's work.' She raised herself slowly out of the chair, one hand on its arm and the other at the small of her back.

I folded the letter away and stood up to put the kettle back on the hob.

'I suppose if you or I were across the water, Maggie, and nobody about that we could talk easy to, we'd make the time.' I managed to smile over at her.

'Now this kettle's not long boiled. I'll make us a cup of tea and then I'll peel these potatoes.'

While the tea was brewing and I was making short work of the potatoes, I heard Maggie raise herself to standing and start setting the table, her every step slow. When I glanced round, she was stopped still, one hand leaning on the back of the kitchen chair, the other holding her left hip.

'Maggie, for dear's sake sit down and let me do that. Put your feet up on the wee stool and take it easy for another while.'

She didn't speak but gripped the back of the chair with both hands. She let out such a gulder of pain that I nearly dropped the pot of potatoes.

'Mother of God, Maggie, what's happening?' I was at the table beside her and could see her white as a sheet and the sweat breaking on her forehead. Every so often a shudder passed through her and her hands gripped the chair even harder.

'Hold on, Maggie, hold on. I'll fetch Mammy.'

She shook her head. I stood there not knowing which end of me was up. I'd never wanted Mammy as much as I did right there and then. As I scoured Maggie's face for some clue as to what to do for the best, I suddenly remembered the time Father and I visited Granny and I came across one of the sheep with the lamb coming out of her backside covered in blood. So help me, I thought my insides would drop with dread for that's when it dawned on me that we maybe did the same.

'You may fill that big pot with water and put it on to boil.' Maggie had straightened up and returned to herself. 'And do the same with the kettle.'

She could as easily have been telling me how to lay the table. How did she know what to do when she'd never had a babby before? I did as I was told as quick as the tremble that had spread from my hands through my body would let me. By the time the pot and kettle were on the go, she'd returned to the rocker, her hands on her belly, rockin' to and fro in the chair as if she was a child on a swing with not a care in the world. I eyed a little pile of sheets and squares of cloth that she must have put on the table.

'Don't look so afeard, little sister. It's going to be a while yet.' She gave me her big sister smile, sweet as ever despite the strain in her face.

'But how do you know, Maggie?' My feet were itching to

run as hard as they could home to fetch help. I trusted them more than I did Maggie at that point.

'That's only the start of the labour pains. When they come quicker and stronger, then you know it's all going to happen very soon.'

'But how do you know? Did Mammy tell you?'

'C'mon Nan Rose, could you see Mammy talkin' to anyone about anything to do with what goes on here?' She rubbed and patted her belly as it curved in and down. 'It's just as well there are other women that are more than happy to tell you, whether you want to know or not.'

I kept thinking about that sheep. Maybe we didn't do it like that after all. For if Maggie knew what was going to happen, she wouldn't be so calm, so…easy…would she?

And still my feet were twitching and itching. The sound of the two Marley girls talking as they walked down the hall and opened the door to the room immediately below us drifted up to us. I sagged onto the nearest chair. At least there was somebody else in the house, and not a minute too soon. Not that they'd be of much use for they were single like myself and were probably in the dark as much as I was… but at least they were a bit older.

'Right, you can go now, Nan Rose.' It took me a minute to notice that Maggie was speaking. She looked at me and her lips were fighting back laughter. 'Oh Nan Rose, you couldn't look worse if you'd seen a ghost.'

'I don't know how you can sit there laughin' Maggie. For if anything happened, you'd be relying on me who hasn't a clue what to do.' I was nearly in tears with agitation.

'I'm sorry Sister, for at your age I'd have felt the same. Anyway, give me over the brush there.'

'The brush?'

'Yes, the brush. And on your way out, tell the Marley girls that you're going to fetch Mammy and would they keep an ear out in the meantime for me banging on their ceiling if I need help.'

'Sure they'd be as little use to you as I would be.'

'You'd be surprised Nan Rose. They grew up in the country where birthing and dying is just part of life. They've delivered a lamb or two in their time, and even a calf.'

Mother of God, it was bad enough thinking of a sheep. My feet took me to the door and I'd just the wit to grab my shawl.

Eleven

11th June 1914

Well, the prospect of delivering a babby all by yourself is one thing. Being left out of it altogether is another. And neither was to my liking. So when Mammy said that she'd head round to Maggie's and fetch Mrs Deakin on the way, leaving me to sort tea for Father and Michael 'and lay a place for Charles for I'll send him round here out of the road', I folded my arms to give me the strength to stand my ground.

'I'll gladly sort the tea out, but as soon as that's done, I'm heading back to Maggie's.' My voice sounded more certain than I was. I straightened up and looked Mammy right in the eyes. She pressed her lips tight and bristled like the big mongrel that guarded Brown's scrapyard.

'It's not a circus we're goin' to. You'd be more use here than hanging about gawking.'

'You've never brought us up to be ones to hang about and gawk, Mammy – but I've been helping Maggie these last lot of months and I don't want to be pushed out now.' She snorted, for all the world like a wee bull. Her lips tightened to the thinnest of lines.

'Mammy, I wish you would stop treatin' me like I'm a child. I'm bringing home a full wage and Johnny and I are going steady. Can you not see I'm a woman now too?'

'You may be a woman but you're not a married one yet and that makes a big difference. And you make sure you don't forget that when you're with yer fella.'

I didn't say anything but I didn't move either.

In the silence between us, the clock on the mantelpiece tocked louder. Mammy broke first. She let out a long sigh and shook her head before she picked up her shawl.

'Well... as long as you remember that you're there to help and don't be looking for help yourself if you suddenly get cold feet, we'll see you round there in a while.' And with that she was out the door.

I stood there in the emptiness of the house with Mammy's warning lingering round me like a shroud. I was back at Granny's the afternoon that lamb was born and this time I remembered how I'd broken into a cold sweat. It'd been all I could do to stop my stomach heaving itself inside out. It was now my turn to press my lips tight. That was then. When I was a child. And for the life of me, I wasn't going to let myself down in front of Mammy and Mrs Deakin. Not even if the effort killed me.

Mind you, later on, when Maggie let out a scream that pierced the room, I nearly passed out with fear. For I was sure she was dying. But I didn't even get a chance to draw breath when I heard a babby cry out. I was caught between crying and laughing.

Mammy came out of the bedroom, holding a wee bundle in her arms.

'You may run round home and tell Charles he's got a son.' She smiled. Such a big smile, it lit up her face like sunshine. 'But you might like to hold your nephew for a minute or so first.'

'Does Maggie not want to hold him?' I was in the middle of reaching out for him when fear squeezed my heart so that I stopped, my hands clutching only air.

'Yer sister's getting' her breath back. She'll have him soon enough – and for the rest of her life after that – so you may make the most of your chance now.' She placed him in the crook of my arm. I eased back the swaddling from his face the better to see this new wean. His eyes were open, big and navy blue. I caught my breath, for I was looking into eyes that were so old they went all the way back in time. I stroked his cheek with my finger, dandled the curve of his chin. I held a tiny fist, marvelling at the perfect nails. I swear no holy picture has ever moved me like the sight and feel of that scrap of new life, torn from and still clinging to somewhere altogether beyond us.

I looked up and caught Mammy with a look as soft as spring rain on her face. We stepped towards each other and for a moment, we were side by side, me holding the babby, her arm holding my waist.

'We'll be having Charles Patrick back in here. His mammy's askin' for him.' Mrs Deakin's call broke the spell. Mammy scooped wee Charlie out of my arms and shooed me off to fetch his father.

Well, it was no wonder that I forgot all about Bridie until I was undressing for bed that night and felt the purse of paper in my pocket. Maybe it was that I couldn't keep my eyes open or maybe it was that I didn't want to spoil the memory of my acquaintance with my first nephew – whatever, I left the rest of Bridie's news for the morrow.

I woke from a dream where I was cradling the child while Lizzie Balfour banged at the door and rattled the windowpane with her umbrella handle, the shape and colour of a crow's head. She was dressed from head to toe in black.

A sliver of light was edging its way between the blind and the window frame. The house was silent bar father's snoring. I tried to burrow my way back into the bedclothes and beyond into sleep. But from nowhere came the thought that Lizzie Balfour had said she was going to speak to me through a telephone. That wakened me like a bucket of cold water. I rose, pulled on my clothes in the half light and tiptoed across the floor and downstairs as quiet as a cat. Michael was out for the count in his bed by the hearth, his face buried in the bedclothes, one arm dangling loose to the floor. I lifted my shawl and crossed the front room, into the scullery and lifted the latch of the back door as lightly as any fairy. I fetched the washtub from its hook on the outside wall, upended it and was about to settle myself to hear what else Bridie had to say, when I heard a soft bark from Bandit's box. Her head was juking out the opening, the better for her to see my every move. I gave her a stern look and pointed hard at her to stay where she was. She sniffed the air as if making up her mind what to do, before dropping her head back down between her front paws. I gave a look round to check nobody else was stirring, lapped my shawl under me and crossed myself for good measure before unfolding her wodge of writing.

19th May 1914

Nan Rose,

I was sitting for that Harry Wharton fella a couple of hours today. From three o'clock til five. And thats how its going to be til he paints this faerie queen he has in his mind's eye. That way I can still do my bit to prepare for lunch and clear up afterwards. And then be at hand to help with dinner. Says Mrs Archer, you can fit the dusting and polishing in between times, waving her hand in the air as if all of that can be done in a twinkle. She must think I am being paid to twiddle my thumbs if she thinks I can lose two hours in a day and still be on top of what Im supposed to be doing. Lizzie says not to worry, just enjoy the EXPERIENCE and says she can manage mostly for herself for the next week or so.

Enjoy the experience. Sure is that not what I always think? Is that not what took me first to work for Miss Lizzie and then to cross the water with her? For I am forever one to fancy that the door ahead opens on a brighter place than where I am standing. And so it is with this sitting business. Though why they call it sitting, when I have been standing all the time, I do not know. Standing til my legs could crack under me. Standing by the open French windows with only one hand resting on the door frame for support. Me that can hardly stop still for two minutes let alone two hours.

21st

Well, its been a bit of a diffrint story these last two days. When I arrived in the music room yesterday, Mr Wharton had sat one of the straight backed chairs at the door frame and had it piled high with cushions.

Sit there Bridie says he. Yes, just perch there and sit tall. He hands me a length of satin, green as the fields, with gold swirls traced through it. And drape this over you as if it were a cloak. I do as Im bid. He pulls here and there at the cloth until it falls just right for him. Now pin it together with this brooch so that it sits just there. He hands me a gold hoop and points to the centre of my chest He walks to and fro, eyeing me this way and that.

Ah, says he, stopping in front of me. I need you to let loose your hair. I dont know why but that did not feel right to me.

Come, come Bridie. Have you ever seen a faerie

queen with her hair tied back off her face? I shook my head. Well then, make haste for we do not have much time. He strode back to his easel and I unplaited my hair so that it fell long and loose over my shoulders.

22nd

I do not know what to make of all this being painted. Sitting there, stock still, only seeing him out of the corner of my eye. I swear, what with looking out on the garden and dressed for the part, I begin to think Im away with the little people myself half the time. And if I am not with them, Im getting carried away in a worse direction. For knowing he is looking at me and knowing that Im worth someone like him looking at, is enough to turn my head. So when I remember I say a prayer to Our Lady for was it not pride that sent the divil himself to hell? Mind you, theres nothing like scrubbing a floor at the end of the day to remind me of my place here.

24th

I should never have juked at that picture, but you know me Nan Rose, always wanting to see what is going on. And if Im honest I was wonderin how long all this palaver is going to take. So today when they were all out having Sunday lunch at Hathersage, I slipped back into the room to have a good gander.

I should never have juked for its put a spell on me. For it is me and it is not me. She seems older, this her he has painted. So still and KNOWING. As if she knew some secret I dont.

I keep wonderin what it is like to be her.

God forgive my vanity for that picture of his keeps coming back to me. This morning when I got up, I peered hard in the mirror, this way and that, trying to see who he sees. I suddenly wanted to feel my hair. I ran my fingers through it. I swept it up. I let it fall. Is that how it would feel to him? I asked myself. And it did not stop there. I ran my hands over my shoulders and my hips, still asking myself that same question. And do you know what came to mind – Eve in the Garden of Eden after she bit the apple.

Oh Nan Rose, what a day I have had and it is all my own doing. I dont feel right in my own skin. Im outside myself watching my every move and still with that same question.

I have lost my stride. I have lost myself.

And Im sitting here writing when I should be sleeping. And Im feard to send this to you for you will think Im an awful eejit. But I can not stop writing.

I laid Bridie's letter on my lap, leaned back agin the wall and looked up at the rectangle of sky above. At least, it was blue and set for a fine day. How could Bridie have thought I wouldn't understand?

A warm tingle ran through me as I remembered that first kiss with Johnny as we walked back from the August ceili and how I felt the next morning. Sitting with Bridie's letter on my lap, I could still smell and taste the ginger beer on his breath as his lips pecked and then lingered on mine, I could still feel the warmth of his lean body pressing against me and the shivers running through me as his fingers sank into my hair coiled at the nape of my neck. And the next morning, sure I was that delighted with it all, I felt like a queen of the land.

The difference was I knowd Johnny since we were childer and I knowd I could trust him. This painter fella sounded like another matter, altogether. I picked up Bridie's letter again and read on.

27th May

Oh Nan Rose, whats to become of me? Only for you and Our Lady today, I was lost altogether. It all happened so fast. He was twitching that green cloak this way and that. Brushing my hair back with his fingers to let it fall over one shoulder and away from the other. All the time looking at me. Til I was betwixt and between yer woman in the picture myself. If only I had not looked and got carried away, I am sure I would have put a stop to it before it started.

So when he said If I may, even as he took my chin between his thumb and finger and tilted it up and towards him, I did not push his hand away nor speak a word. For it was happening to her not me. Even when he took me by the shoulders and started kissing my hair and my lips. It was only when he stuck his tongue in my mouth, pushing and waggling for all the world like a skint weasel, that my teeth took on a life of their own. I must have bit him hard for the next thing he let out a gulder and his hands went to his mouth. He was hopping about and makin such a racket I was sure someone would be in through the door at any minute. I ran through those French windows like a scalded cat. I rushed through the scullery, opened the kitchen door and near flattened Sarah. She was carrying a jug of water and half of it spilt over me.

I said the first thing that came to me and it was a lie.

Sarah Sarah, bring that water over to Mr Wharton for hes swallowed a bee. Hes in agony over there. Im that shaken up Im no good to man or beast.

Her jaw dropped. Her eyes widened.

For goodness sake, Bridie says she. You are that full of yourself these days, you are more scatter brained than ever. And with that she flounced off carrying the jug like a jewel case. I practically flew up the stairs to the attic.

I closed the door and leaned back against it, with my heart thumping fit to burst and my stomach churning like it was making butter. I knew I was in trouble though how I got myself there was beyond me. But between Mrs Archer, Sarah and now yer man, there are too many here who will be more than happy to put me in the place they think I belong.

Oh Nan Rose, I wisht to God you were beside me at that minute. But no sooner did I see your face than I heard you say, Bridie, what did I tell ye? What possessed ye to leave your own ones and to take yourself the other side of the water on the word of a girl a few years older than yourself? I started to cry for the thought of you giving off to me as well as everyone else was more than I could bear.

Bridie, pull yourself together. This isn't the time to be drowning in tears. You'd be better saying a prayer than crying your eyes out. So help me, Nan Rose, I heard your voice as clear as a bell and I was that startled, I nearly choked. I looked up expecting to see you sitting on the bed. But there was only me. You saying that though, was all I needed to gather myself. I knelt down right there behind the door. Holy Mary, Mother of God, pray for us sinners now and at the hour of our death. I just kept saying that over and over again until my heart stopped banging against my ribs and my breath grew easy. I was soon able to right myself, open the door and walk downstairs, one step at a time, to face whatever was going on.

As it is, the rest of the day has been quiet enough.

Sarah is like a cat with the cream for he gave her thruppence for her trouble. Not to mention the delight she took in flaunting it to me at the first chance.

And I kept myself in the kitchen, out of the way of him and Mrs Archer. I only wish I could scour my mouth and my soul as clean as I did those pots and pans.

By the time I'd read that far, I was so beside myself with anger at the nerve of yer man, that I was up and pacing to and fro at the side of the wash tub. It was only when Bandit padded out and over to me, barking for good measure, that I caught myself on. I settled her and settled myself to finish reading the letter.

29th

I am at my wits end for everything I try to do for the best seems to only make things worse. I am frettin that much about being by myself with yer man that Im not sleeping well and you know thats not like me. Im that tired Im dragging myself round the house like a sack of potatoes. So I thought to tell Lizzie Balfour that I did not want to have anything more to do with all this sitting.

I took my chance yesterday morning, as she was brushing her hair, and I was laying out her clothes. I thought to be sensible and not blurt it all out. Approach it like I was dancing The Walls of Limerick, in and out, in and out, a slip to the side and back again. But, it is one thing dancing that, its another talking like that. After I said how hard it is for someone like me to sit still and how difficult that must make it for him to paint me, and how it would be much better if he could find someone easier, Lizzie laid the brush on the dressing table and gave me a hard look through the mirror.

Bridie, if there is something you want to tell me, it would be better to come to the point. You have been pacing to and fro that much with that dress, I am surprised you have not worn a hole in the rug. Well, that stopped me in my tracks. I know she was just bantering but you know that you need to be in the right mood to take banter. I bunched my lips tight and looked down at my feet. And if a big tear did not start tricklin down my face. Well at that, she turned round to face me. What is it Bridie? This is not like you.

And do you know, Nan Rose, at that, I was tongue tied. For shes right. None of this is like me. The shame of it all hit me like a bucket of tar. I had no words.

Bridie, sit down on the bed and tell me what ails you? says she. I sat down. I looked at my hands. Im not doing this right, Miss Lizzie. Im afeard for I dont like getting things wrong.

Oh Bridie, dear, says she in her sweetest voice. Like china tinkling. There was I thinking you might enjoy being painted. But of course it can also be such a strain. I looked up. All full of hope. I will tell you what. I will bring my book and my sewing in and sit with you this afternoon for I have no plans to be out today.

Which she did, fair play to her. And yer man was acting like butter would not melt in his mouth. So delighted in your interest, Elizabeth. And for sparing Bridie, says he as he called her over to the easel. I hope you are as delighted as I am with our progress.

Well, she oohed and aahed at the painting and said what a gem I was.

Bridie, come here and look at this, says she. I could see he was not too pleased about that. But what could he do? Or I for that matter? I stood beside her and looked without seeing for I did not want to get caught in the spell again. Well Bridie says she, you are perfect for this painting. And with that she took the ground from under me. I was lost for words.

2nd June

I should be in bed Nan Rose but I can NOT settle and Im pacing the floor. Thanks be Sarah is at home again tonight. So Im doing the only thing that gives me some peace and thats writing to you even if you never see this. Yer man was at it again today. Just when I thought it had all been a storm in a teacup that had blown over with Miss Lizzie's visit. The clock had just struck half past 4 and in my minds eye, I was already out of the music room and back in the kitchen safe and sound when I heard his footsteps coming towards me. My mouth went dry with fright. He came up behind me and pressed down on my shoulder with one hand even as he scooped up my hair with his other and buried his face in my neck. And then I could hardly credit what he said. Do not pretend with me. I know you desire me. I can see it in your eyes as I paint them. You lure me on, you little witch. Your every look and gesture beckons me. And all with a face of innocence. With that he laid his hands on my breasts. And started to knead them like they were dough.

I did the only thing I could. My right hand was loose so I grabbed him by the hair and I pulled for all

I was worth. He let go of me right and quick then. I was out of that chair with a handful of hair in my fist and had opened the door before he righted himself. For I tugged that hard, he nearly fell over. Thank God and his Holy Mother there was not a one in the hallway.

Thats the last time you will be painting any bit of me Mr Wharton says I. And with that I made for the kitchen.

But what he said about it being me keeps rattling over and over. I do not DESIRE him, so how can he think I do? I know all his attention made me feel special. But I have not been leading him on. Have I? I can NOT trust him. Now I feel I can NOT trust myself. And if I cant trust myself to do right, whats to become of me?

4th June

Ach, Nan Rose, I have lost something I never knew I had. Because I grew up with it. I am only now appreciating that I always belonged. Because I do not belong here. But whats done is done.

That Harry Wharton has a right brass neck on him. I was serving at breakfast this morning, for Sarah's mother was bad again last night. Mr Archer had gone to his office and Lizzie and her aunt were taking their time over their tea. I was bringing in a fresh pot when the door opened and yer man came in. I tell ye, if looks could kill, I would have died on the spot. But he was all smiles and sweet words to the two of them. I was at the sideboard clearing the used delph and topping up the dish of egg bacon and tomatoes. You would not believe what these people can eat, even Lizzie. But then again, maybe we would be the same if we had the chance. Anyway, says he, all loud and fancy like he was on a stage, Dear Elizabeth, I hope I can count on your support and that you will ENTERSEED on my behalf with our little Bridie. Well the hair on my arms stood up like a cats when I heard my name. Out of the corner of my eye, I could see Mrs Archer putting down her teacup and giving me one of her long looks. More trouble. I forced myself to carry on what I was doing as if I had not heard a word but my hands were shaking so hard I feared to break one of her precious plates. God only knows what would have happened then. Out on my ear right away, no doubt.

And what would I be asking Bridie to do, Harry? says Lizzie in her quiet voice. So I knew she was thinking hard. Bridie, you may return to the kitchen. We have everything we need for now. Mrs Archer was doing her high and mighty woman of the house. Well, no need to tell me twice. But I was not going to slink out of there with my tail between my legs. You would have been proud of me Nan Rose. I walked to the door with my head held high, like we did when we marched back to the mill that morning the strike was over.

And this is the geg Nan Rose. Theres Mrs Archer living in her own house and yet never realising that particularly when shes PRONOUNCING as she often does you can hear her in the hall if you are going about your business quietly. And believe me, she was PRONOUNCING. All at Miss Lizzie and all about me. How you did not ASK servants, you TOLD them. How she was too soft with me. Treating me like a little sister that she never had. And how she rued the day she had taken us both under her wing and into her house.

Well, when she said that last bit, I started to get frightened for Miss Lizzie for shes been awful good to me and I would not want her getting into trouble on account of me. But then, Mrs Archer says If it was not for dear Harry having started his painting with her in it, I would be sending her home and making sure her mother and your mother knew the reasons why.

Well I think dear Harry must have thought he had took things a step too far for if he does not start saying how Im doing my best and sitting is not easy. That was when I knew I had to get away from him and from this place. For despite everything, I could feel myself all soft towards him for being kind. And thats the road to nowhere.

Anyway, I have this evening off and they are starting a novena at the church tonight. So Im taking myself there as soon as I put my pencil down I need to get my brain showered and ask Our Lady for help.

Bridie

I sat there as the sky lightened, trying to make sense of it all and cursed Lizzie Balfour again under my breath. The road to hell is paved with good intentions. I folded the pages and had barely put them back in my pocket when I heard Father rousing Michael. Bandit heard too and was up and out of her box, her tail wagging. I just had time to put the tub back in place and give her a quick pat. I stepped back into the scullery as Mammy came through from the front room. It was well seen she was still in the glow from wee Charlie's arrival for she just nodded to me as if me being up with the larks happened every day.

Twelve

Friday, 12th June 1914

I was never as glad to hear aul Campbell ring the bell as I was on Friday evening. I was already bone tired when I'd started work that morning, what with all the commotion of the week catching up with me. And then to have a morning on tenterhooks waiting for a summons to Mr Frazer's office – that did me in altogether. My guts were knotted at the thought of making an eejit of myself using one of them telephones. And my head was wracked with wondering what on earth I could say to any of the ones that would ask what was up, with me being summoned to the manager's office. For whatever I said, I could say nothing about Bridie.

As it was, I needn't have worked myself into such a twist. Mr Frazer, to give him his due, managed the whole business so as to attract little notice. The first I knew was when Campbell came over to my end of the frame, ringing his bell for our midday break and said that I was to report to Mr Frazer's office ten minutes before the end of that. I can't say I got much enjoyment out of my piece nor did I take in a word of the story Imelda Dobbin was telling as we sat in a wee circle. I made an excuse that the sun was giving me a headache and made my way over to the shade of the mill and from there up the stone steps. I'd never been up them before. The nearest I'd gotten was waiting in the shadow of the corner for Maggie, Bella and the rest of the committee to come down after putting their case to the manager before we went on strike. I shivered, remembering my fear then. But as I took the steps one at a time, I gave myself a talking-to. I was asking nothing from nobody. I remembered us marching back into work after the strike. I pictured Maggie on one side of me, Bridie and Bella on the other and I marched on up in step with them.

I rounded the landing on the 4th floor into a long narrow hallway. I could see that the first couple of doors on either side had glass panes in their top halves. I walked towards them. There were no names on the first two doors, but through the second door on my right, I could hear Mr Frazer's voice. He was talking to someone. A younger man's voice replied. That threw me. I stared at the fine writing on the glass pane and made out a fancy Mr and an F and an r. I pulled myself up to my full height and tapped loudly.

'Come in.' It was the younger man who spoke. I opened the door, stepped in, paused to get my bearings and closed the door behind me. Mr Frazer was standing in the doorway in the right-hand corner of the room. He looked me up and down and barely nodded before turning to walk through into the next room. 'I leave you in the capable hands of Mr Johnson, our clerk. He will show you what to do.' The door closed loudly behind him.

I looked at yer man, Johnson. He was sitting at a table that would've taken up the whole of our front room but only if we'd taken down the front of the house to get it in. A big black book was wide open in front of him and I could see both pages filled with rows of words and numbers. Behind him, more black books were stacked cover to cover on every shelf of a bookcase that reached nearly to the high ceiling. He looked very small and stooped sitting there, like a wee older Jim Mc

Anearney but without Jim's hump. I felt myself sag with relief. He wasn't the sort could put the fear of God in anyone.

'Sit down there Miss Murphy,' he said in a voice as thin as the rest of him. He nodded towards a chair at the end of the desk right beside a big shiny black telephone. 'Miss Balfour is due to ring at any moment. When she does, I will pick up the telephone receiver and I will pass it to you.' He went back to his black book. I sat down and said a quiet prayer to Our Lady to keep me steady. I'd barely said 'Amen' when that telephone rang. I was so startled I nearly jumped out of the chair. Mr Johnson picked up the arm of the telephone, put one end to his ear and spoke into the other. 'Yes,' he said, 'she is here and she can speak to you for a few minutes.' He handed me the telephone and I reached over to take it as if he was handing me a cat.

His face twitched into a near-smile. 'It cannot bite you,' says he, but kindly.

I took my time to put the arm to my ear. Even as I did so I could hear Lizzie Balfour's voice as if from a long way away. Which she was.

'Nan Rose, are you there? Nan Rose?'

'Yes, I am here.'

'Oh, I am so glad to be able to speak to you.'

I could almost feel the relief in her voice.

'Do you know where Bridie might be? Can you tell me anything?'

'The only thing I know is that–' I looked over at yer man to make sure he was paying attention to his books. And just to make sure, I didn't mention Bridie's name. '–she got to know a woman at the church where she went on Sunday. Mrs Baker is her name. Maybe you could find her?'

'The church…of course. I should have thought of that.' There was a pause. 'But I dare say, you will be thinking I should have thought of many things.' There was another pause. Out of the corner of my eye, I could see Mr Johnson look up in my direction.'

'That's all I can tell you.'

'And I know you need to go back to work. Nan Rose, thank you so much. One way or the other I will let you know how I manage. I do hope you and your family are well.'

'Yes, thank you. They are. And I hope the same goes for you.'

'Thank you. Goodbye.'

I heard a click. I looked down at the round end that I had been speaking into. In my mind's eye, Lizzie Balfour disappeared in a puff of air, even as I could see yer man reaching to take the telephone arm from me.

I was as wrung out as a dish rag when the bell sounded the end of our working day. That bit of a conversation with Lizzie Balfour had left me empty and heavy. She and Bridie were across the water and here was I, not knowing who to talk to or what to do for the best. All I knowd for certain was that none of Bridie's ones nor Mammy must get wind of what was going on. Which meant that I couldn't be blabbing my mouth off, even as I was desperate to talk to someone.

I walked back as far as the corner of Maggie's street with Ellen Kavanagh, Bella Dwyer and Peggy Arthurs. They wanted to know how she and the babby were and in telling them about the arrival of wee Charlie, my own spirits lifted. I walked through Maggie's door, saw him sleeping peacefully in one of the kitchen cupboard drawers, which she'd placed on the kitchen table and all else went out of mind. Which was just as well for although Maggie was up and about, she looked and moved like a shadow of herself.

I did what I could in the couple of hours I had. I pummelled and pounded clean the bed sheets and swaddling for the babby that had been soaking in the tin bath from the day before, along with a couple of shirts and skirts. Meantime Maggie had pushed up the sash window, opened the front door to air the room and set to brushing and wiping. I took the washing down the stairs to hang out the back. When I returned, the babby was stirring. Maggie was bent over him and I watched her pat his chest in a quiet rhythm while shushing him softly. He wasn't for having any of that and was working himself up to a gulder when Maggie lifted him, held him close and sat down with him on the rocking chair. I could see she'd been halfway through peeling some potatoes and had scallions out to chop so I carried on with that. Charlie settled himself to sleep at her chest and when I looked over Maggie was beginning to doze.

For a while the only sound was the tick of the clock on the mantelpiece and my knife tapping the chopping board as I sliced potatoes into quarters and scallions into slivers. As the quiet seeped into me, I felt myself loosen as if I'd put down a heavy sack I was carrying. It struck me that I could do nothing more for Bridie other than to pray and trust that God and His Holy Mother would see her right.

'I haven't even made you a cup of tea since you came in the door, Nan Rose.'

I looked over to see Maggie rousing herself.

'I was about to heat the kettle when this fella woke up.'

'No matter, Maggie,' says I. 'I'll need to be getting home for my supper and Charles'll be in any minute for his. I'll just put these potatoes on to boil.'

Even as I spoke we heard footsteps on the stairs, the door opened and I turned to see Charles stood in the doorway. He looked round at the three of us for a moment.

'Nan Rose, what would we do without you?' says he, hanging up his cap and coat before striding over to Maggie and rubbing the top of her shoulder. 'Yer wee man here has us not knowin' whether we're comin' or going.'

'Well, I know that I'm going back round home for my supper,' says I.

'You'll want to hold the babby for a minute or two before you go,' says Maggie, 'for I could see by the way you were lookin' at him as he slept that you were desperate for him to wake up.' She reached Charlie over and I took him in my arms. He stirred but I patted his back in the same way I'd seen Maggie pat his chest and shushed him as I moved my weight from one foot to the other so as to rock him. Out of the corner of my eye, I saw Maggie heave herself out of the chair with Charles putting his hands to her back by way of support. I glanced up as Charles ran his fingers through Maggie's hair, tucking the loose stands behind her ear, just like Maggie had often done with me when I was young. She must have been bone-tired for she couldn't even manage a smile.

'It won't take me long to get the food on the table,' says she as she moved away from him without as much as a 'how are ye?'

Out of the corner of my eye, I saw Charles's expression darken as he watched her busy herself with fetching crockery.

I looked from one to the other of them and then said to Charles. 'Will I put this fella back into his bed now or would ye like to hold him for a while?' Charles barely looked at me or the babby, his attention still on Maggie.

'If he's asleep better to settle him in the drawer. That way I can clean myself up before I do anything else,' he said.

I did as I was told, wrapped my shawl round me and bade them both good evening. As I walked home, I kept coming back to Charles. Of course any man would want to wash the dirt of the day off him. And he was probably nearly as tired as Maggie. But I couldn't help think that if it were Father, there'd have been more warmth in how he spoke about the babby.

Later that evening after the four of us had eaten, there was a knock at the door. Mammy, who was heading out to visit Mrs Smith opened it.

'Patrick, it's Barney for you,' she called as she left. Barney was the rag-and-bone man.

Father went to the door and after a few words, he came back, brandishing two curved pieces of wood.

'It's an ill wind,' says he.

'The end of that one is split badly and the other one's not much better,' says Michael, leaning over in his chair to peer closer.

'And sure isn't that how I've come to have them?' says Father, so delighted with himself that I found myself smiling with him. 'There was a rocking chair on the top of a high load on Barney's cart and it fell off. These took the brunt of the fall. They're no use to him so he gave them to me. I'll return the favour another day. That's me all set now.' He was heading for the back door.

In the last fortnight, he'd taken the notion that he could make a cradle for the babby. 'Not as grand as you see in the windows of Robinson & Cleaver. But if Maggie had something she could rock with her foot, that'd be a help to her.'

He'd put the word out and had been given a large wooden drawer salvaged from an old sideboard in return for helping a fella fix his back door. Now Barney had given him what he needed to finish the job.

With Mammy and him out of the house, Michael and me had it to ourselves for a while. He was sat at the table, laying out the cards for a game of solitaire while I settled to mend a tear in my good skirt and to sew some buttons on one of Mammy's blouses and a shirt of Father's.

'So did Charles say anything about how it is at the foundry these days?' says he.

'The foundry?' says I. 'Why, what's happening there?'
He looked at me, considering.

'The same as is happening any place there's Prods and Taigs work together,' says he. 'A closing of ranks. And a feeling if you're one of only a few Taigs that you could be out on your ear, if things turn nastier. At least Johnny and me are working for one of our own.'

'Maggie never mentioned it and Charles was barely in when I left. Did he mention it to you?'

'Could you see him talkin' to me who's just a fella, when he always keeps his cards close to his chest? No, a couple of the Volunteers work there. I got it from them. And who knows, maybe if you're an Irish Volunteer working alongside Ulster Volunteers, you've more to be worried about.'

He returned to his cards. But the talk of trouble had minded me about what Bridie'd said in her last letter.

'So have you heard any talk about war? I mean a big war. Not just fighting here. Bridie mentioned it in her last letter.'

As soon as I'd mentioned Bridie, I could've bit my tongue off. I knowd from Johnny that Michael'd finally wrote to her and I hadn't noticed any letters at all arriving for him. Now I watched as he stopped his play but didn't lift his eyes from the table.

'It's well for some,' says he.

'Bridie's got a lot on her plate at the moment, Michael.'

That got his attention. He straightened up and looked over at me, waiting. 'I can't say anymore now. But I'm sure when things quieten, Bridie will write to you. And in the meantime, don't even breathe that to anyone, bar Johnny.'

He carried on looking at me for a good minute before he shrugged his shoulders and returned to his cards.

'And have you heard any talk about war?' says I.

'Nan Rose, you've put the jinx on me with all this talk,'

says he, eyeing the cards laid out to see if he'd missed a way of moving a card to open a space.

I decided not to mention that it was him that started it. I watched as he gathered in the cards, stacked them and shuffled the pack. He put the deck face down and then pushed himself back into the chair so he was balanced on its back legs.

'You'd be better talkin' to Jim McAnearney than me,' says he, 'but seeing as he's not about, I'll tell ye what I know if you'll sew a button back on my waistcoat for me before you put your needle and thread away.'

'Give it over,' says I

He rocked back so the chair was back on four legs, before fetching his waistcoat from the peg. He came over and handed it to me. 'The button's in the pocket,' says he, turning to put both hands on the mantelpiece and leaning forward on them.

'According to Jim – and who better to say than him whose head's always in a newspaper or a book when he has a chance? According to Jim, there's been trouble in the Balkans – that's a handful of countries in the south of Europe – this last lot of years. He says it's like a tinderbox. And he says if anything sparks off there, who knows where it'll end.'

'But Bridie said there was talk of England going to war. What have the Bal… kins got to do with England?'

'Ach Nan Rose, you must know better than to ask that! Hasn't England got its finger and nose stuck into many a pie? And isn't it the divil to get them and their fingers out? You've only to look at us here.'

'So what will happen to us if England goes to war?'

'According to Jim, there's some say that England's trouble is our opportunity – and there's others say if we want Home Rule, we'll have to be good allies to England. That's as much as I can tell ye.' He looked round and down to see what I was sewing.

'Now if you would sew that button on before you start anything else, I could take myself off to the Hibernians – and I might've something else to tell you when I get back.'

I made a show of rolling my eyes but I did what he wanted. That way I'd have peace and quiet to hear myself think.

Maggie took a week off work. She and Mrs Smith had come to an arrangement about looking after Charlie. It was Mrs Smith who'd been the first of us to get fined that time before we went on strike. The pouce dust had finally done for her chest and there were times this last winter she was so racked with the cough she could hardly get her breath. She stopped working in the mill in February and now looked after her daughter's two wee 'uns. She lived right and handy to the mill which meant that Maggie'd be able to walk to hers and back in the midday break and feed the babby.

So Maggie started back to work on the third Monday in June. I remember because that Friday I had a letter from Bridie.

4 Edmund Court
Sheffield
Sunday 21st June

Dear Nan Rose

This is just a wee note to let you know I'm still in the land of the living and at this address. I'm lodging with Mrs Myers in a wee terrace not much different from the Townsend Street home I left behind. It's a quare change from the Archers but Mrs Myers is a decent woman and I feel safe and sound here. She is not long a widow with a daughter married to a fella from Chesterfield and living there. She is looking to find another lodger or two, but for now, there's just me and her in the house with her in the front bedroom and me in the back. I cannot tell you how much having a wee room to myself suits me, Nan Rose. If truth be told, I'm a bit heart sore. And a bit weary. And wanting no truck with anyone, for all the ones I'd want to see, like yourself and Michael are across the water.

I have a job sewing cotton shirts and blouses in a wee corner place ten minutes walk from here. Me and two women twice my age bent over sewing machines all day long. Do not be laughing Nan Rose – for I bet you are thinking I would be better off never leaving. And maybe I would. But I am here now and got to make the best of it. For now, it gives me enough to pay my way with Mrs Myers. Thank ye for telling Lizzie Balfour about the church. Where would I be without you? More power to her, Lizzie found Mrs Baker. Who gave her a mouthful about looking after young girls in her care. Despite that, Lizzie must have charmed her enough for her to agree to take a note to me.

The upshot was that Lizzie and I met. She told me she was so worried that she had read my letters to you in the hope of finding out what had happened and was scundered to hear about Harry Wharton.

She offered to pay my passage back to Belfast. But I am not going home with my tail between my legs. If I go back, I need to be able to hold my head up. That is the only way I can hold my ground with Aunt Imelda. I saw Mrs Baker on Sunday at mass and had a cup of tea at her house afterwards. She is still talking about if and when war comes and the fellas go off to fight. Mrs Myers also. Who knows other than

God and His Holy Mother? But maybe I might be able to get better work.

Anyway, Lizzie gave me two weeks wages to tide me over and told me if I ever changed my mind about home, the fare would be there for me. And then she says I feel I have a responsibility to you, Bridie, as a suffragette and a friend. So let us stay in contact. And there you have it Nan Rose.

Will you give this other wee note inside to Michael? One thing about meeting a bad fella like Harry Wharton is that I appreciate even more a good fella like your Michael even if he is across the water.

Please write as soon as you can Nan Rose for I want to hear how yous all are.

Bridie.

That set me to thinking again about a big war. And then, lo and behold, on the following Monday, didn't Maggie come back into the mill yard with a minute to go before the gates closed after the midday break, and heading straight to where I sat with a crowd of the others. She was walking faster than I'd seen her move for many a day. The rest of us were gathering ourselves to go back in. She was that breathless she could barely speak.

'There were crowds round the newspaper seller when I passed him going and coming,' says she. 'I didn't have the time to stop, but he was yelling about a murder in somewhere I'd never heard of. "Sara something". Some duke or other. Then I heard a fella in the crowd say that was the Balkans.'

By Sunday when Johnny met me outside ten mass, the talk at the mill and at home about the murder of the Archduke and his wife had exhausted itself. There wasn't a fresh word to be said about how terrible it was that she died trying to save him and their poor wee 'uns losing their father and their mammy; but as nobody rushed to declare war on somebody else, the steam went out of men and fellas talking themselves in circles about what might happen here if war broke out.

As for myself, I'd enough on my plate that morning, for I was going over to Johnny's house for the first time. I'd knowd them all when I was little, for Johnny was the youngest. His sister Anne was the same age as Maggie and they'd been friendly at school.

Now, as he and I walked in the direction of Carlisle Circus, from where we'd head up to the Ardoyne, he gave me a bit more chapter and verse. Thomas, the oldest, had been a sickly child on account of his chest but that hadn't stopped him holding down a job nor stopped him getting married and having three childer. His mammy looked after them as Thomas's wife, Kate, was a spinner in the same mill as his sister, Anne.

We hadn't seen each other in the week and as we walked the last couple of miles from Carlisle Circus our talk turned to the recent news. It was then I remembered what Michael had said about what would happen here if there was a big war.

'Johnny, when they say England's trouble is our opportunity, do you know what they mean?' says I.

'Who was talking about that?' says he.

'Michael mentioned it a while back. He said there were volunteers that thought that.'

'It's them Republican ones. They reckon the only way we'll get independence is to fight England for it. And the best time to do that is when England's fighting somebody else. Though how they expect to take the country with them when they can't even convince most of us Volunteers, God only knows.'

We had linked arms together and I was leaning into him as we walked the last uphill stretch.

'It's not only the Republican ones arguing that,' says he, and he was picking his words now. 'There's some say that yer man James Connolly thinks the same.'

'That may be so, Johnny,' says I, 'but right now I'm back to thinking about meeting your mammy and sister. And looking round me to see what it's like around here.'

'In that case Nan Rose, we'll go this way,' says he steering me round to the right, down a narrow street a bit like ours. 'I can show you the school that I went to at the bottom here and take you round the back way to ours.'

Well, we traipsed past the school and came through the field where Johnny said the wee fellas used to kick a pig's bladder about while the wee girls played skips out the front of the school. By the time we reached the corner shop where he said he'd go, now and again, to buy a poke of broken biscuits, we were laughing like childer ourselves. And we were still laughing as we turned the corner into his street.

'So this is Nan Rose Murphy!' We turned to see two women standing on the doorstep of a house four doors away. The woman who'd spoken came towards us with a wee cup in her hands. Her red hair was streaked with grey. She was taller than Mammy and soft rather than round.

'Mammy,' says Johnny, 'you took us by surprise there.'

I let go of his arm.

'I was just borrowin' a taste of sugar for we've run out and I wanted to be able to give you a cup of tea, Daughter,' says she, coming up to me. 'You're a Murphy alright. I can see yer brother in ye and yer sister Maggie. Your Maggie and our Anne were always in and out of each other's home.'

I could see Johnny in her, for she had the same eyes and cheekbones with a rosiness round the cheeks.

'I'm pleased to meet you, Mrs Harper,' says I. 'And Maggie and Mammy said to remember them to ye and to say they hoped you were well.'

'And the same to them and to your father,' says she. 'We're just a few doors up here.' She linked my arm and I could feel she was heavy on her feet. I thought of Mammy. She more often than not had a spring in her step. I wondered how it was for Mrs Harper to bring a family up by herself the last ten years since Mr Harper had died suddenly. He had been unloading barrels from a cart when the horse reared. A barrel caught him hard on the chest and he fell down and was then flattened by the rest of the barrels in the line as they piled on top.

Later Johnny and I sauntered back towards our house at our ease. 'That went better than I'd thought it might,' says I. 'Yer mammy and sister between them made me feel right at home. And your Anne wanting to know all about Maggie and Charles and the babby made the talk right and easy.'

'Aye. Anne's been wanting to meet you, if only to hear more about Maggie. She says a man is no good for giving the wee details that a woman wants to know.' He unlinked his arm, put it round my waist and squeezed me to him. 'And I could see they took to you as I knowd they would. For who wouldn't?' He gave my waist another squeeze. I was sorry it was a Sunday morning rather than a Saturday evening for we would've dared a wee kiss or two and a longer squeeze under cover of darkness.

Thirteen

I picked up two envelopes in Bridie's handwriting from the hall floor as I came in the door. One for me, one for Michael. So, as I was the first one back, I put his on the mantelpiece and took mine out the back to sit on the aul crate at the door. Bandit padded over as soon as I'd sat down to rest her muzzle on my knee.

Sheffield
7th August 1914

Nan Rose,

Since England declared war on Germany theres been posters going up everywhere. BOYS COME ALONG YOU'RE WANTED. RALLY ROUND THE FLAG. EVERY FIT MAN WANTED. With soldiers holding bayonets and union jacks flying.

Do yous have them up round yous? I cannot see anything with the Union Jack going down well round home. Men here are signing up in their hundreds. And a lot of the women are all for it. Theres talk women will do their jobs when the men are away fighting, and we will get higher wages.

Well, its an ill wind that blows nobody good. Mrs Myers reckons there will be no shortage of jobs in the factories. For Sheffield is a big place for steel. Lizzie told me that before but it never meant anything til now. We are one of the cities to be making all the weapons and what have ye. Mrs Myers says her brother is a foreman in one of the steel works so she will ask him to put in a word for me. And to tell you the truth, Im now desperate to get out of this sewing place.

What is going to happen in Belfast? I had a letter from Michael last week and he was telling me about the Irish Volunteers landing German rifles and ammunition near Dublin. Germany doesn't seem to mind who they give weapons to in Ireland. He was giving off about how the powers that be had turned a blind eye when the Ulster Volunteers ran guns a couple of months back but had sent a troop of soldiers to try to stop this landing.

I had a letter from Mammy the very next day and she was talking about the same incident. Shame on them soldiers for shooting into the crowd even if they were throwing stones she said. Why not just fire over their heads?

It's hard to credit that after all this last year of wondering if and when there'd be fighting on the streets in Belfast, that the first four people killed were in Dublin.

So I'm hoping that all of you are alright. I pray for yous every morning and night.

Bridie.

After reading the letter, I leaned against the back wall. I scratched Bandit's head and ears while I thought back to Saturday evening.

Maggie and Charles had called in with the babby. I'd

been to the corner shop and had come in the back to find Charles and Michael sitting either end of the scullery table with father sitting between them. He was facing the back door which was open to let in some of the August heat. He glanced up at me and nodded.

Maggie was standing behind him in the doorway between the scullery and the front room. She was rocking back and forward with wee Charlie at her chest. I stopped where I was, smiling and taking in her and him, the wee dote. She was humming and patting him on the back as she rocked to and fro. His head was resting at her shoulder, his small mouth pressed into her neck and his little hand clutching the collar of her blouse.

Michael was talking and the anger in his voice hit me. I turned and caught the last bit of what he was saying. A week on from the shooting in Dublin and he was still beside himself with rage at what had happened.

'But Michael, what do you expect? I told you when the Ulster Volunteers landed weapons at Larne that it'd be a different story if and when our side did the same.' Charles was leaning back into the chair so its front legs were off the floor. He wasn't bantering. He looked as grim as Michael. 'Meantime the same Germany that's dishing out guns left, right and centre here has now invaded France.'

He suddenly leaned forward so the front legs of the chair banged the floor hard. Father looked over at him, opened his mouth, thought about it and closed it again. Charles leaned forward over the table, his eyes still on Michael. 'One thing that has finally united the Ulster and the Irish Volunteers – they get their guns from the same Devil!'

I couldn't take my eyes off Charles's face for he was gripped with a fierceness I'd never seen. When I did glance back at Maggie, she'd stopped humming and patting. She'd stopped stock still and so stiff that in a minute the babby started crying. She began to rock him again but her face had set in a frown.

Needless to say, the others missed that. But it struck me, for once again I felt the difference between them. As long as they'd been together, whatever he said and did seemed right by her and the same the other way round. And to tell the truth, I was more worried about them falling out than all the talk about a big war. As long as the two of them were right, then I could hold on to the notion that Johnny and I would be right.

Father got up from the table. He put his hands on his hips and arched backwards. 'Well, I'll leave you fellas to it. I'm going to take a dander to Mrs Dempsey's for a twist of baccy.'

Michael and Charles nodded but sat where they were. I stepped into the scullery so as he could step through the back door.

'And I'm going to walk back with the babby,' says Maggie. 'I'll see you back home in your own time, Charles.'

'I'll walk round with you Maggie,' says I. 'That way I can have a cuddle of yer wee man.'

Maggie looked over and smiled – a ghost of her big sister smile that she kept for me.

Outside, she lifted wee Charlie up and rubbed noses with him before settling him into the crook of my arm. She linked up with me and we walked slowly up the street, only speaking to bid the time of day to one or other neighbour that was on their doorstep. The August air was gentle on us. I shuggled myself closer to her. We were turning the corner onto the Falls before she spoke.

'His granny's people came from France. Not that that mattered one way or the other, until all this palaver started.' Her voice was flat.

'Charles? Part French?' says I. 'I never knowd.'

'Well, if you call two great grandparents that you've never seen being French, yes, there's a part of him that's French. Seems his mother, who was born and bred in Dublin, always made a thing about having French blood. As if it was a shade or two bluer than anyone else's. And Charles takes after his mother.'

I dared to say that she sounded annoyed with him.

'Yes, I am, more's the pity,' says she. '*I* don't know. It seems it's easier for men to fret about what's happening to those in a far-off country than to worry about their own ones right beside them.'

I tightened my hold on the babby and pressed my lips to his forehead.

'But Maggie, Charles and you…' I struggled for words.

'You wouldn't credit the difference a babby makes.' She sighed. 'Sometimes, to see Charles, you'd think it was a competition between him and his son.'

I thought about all the times I'd seen Maggie with wee Charlie.

'Well, if it is a competition, the babby's winning, hands down.' We'd turned the corner into her street. Maggie stopped and turned to look at me.

'What do you mean?'

'All that I meant was that since the day and hour he was born, you've only had eyes for him. And why wouldn't you? To have that wee bundle of life with only eyes for you in return.'

Maggie didn't say anything but she looked as if I'd told her some great secret instead of something that was there for all to see. We walked in silence to her door. I noticed that as she reached out for the boyo, she was lost in thought. She opened the door and walked into the hall, without a word, as if in a dream.

Now, as I sat fingering Bridie's letter, I thought again

about what Michael had said about the foundry where Charles worked. Neither Charles nor Maggie had ever mentioned it. Maybe Maggie mightn't even know?

30th August

Well, Nan Rose, things are moving right and quick around here. I went over to that steelworks on Wednesday night after work and Im starting tomorrow at nearly TWICE the wages I was getting. It is the other side of Sheffield but I just have to walk into town to get the 20 to 9 bus in the morning. Well, with the hours we did in the mill and I did for the Archer family, that makes an easy start to my day.

I waited til I got paid Thursday night before I told yer woman thats in charge here that I was not coming back. She was none too pleased. Said a big order was coming in and it was wrong of me to walk out like that. But the truth is I can. And I have. For one thing all that business with the Archers taught me was not to put myself out for ones that have no time for me other than what they can get out of me. No matter what they think as they do not think much of people like me anyway.

Im away off now to ten mass. And to light a candle of thanks to Our Lady. It is hard to credit I have a proper job with a decent wage. And do you know what Nan Rose? Next Saturday morning, I am going to some meeting Lizzie Balfour is organising at the Town Hall and afterwards we are going to a GALLERY. For they are showing some paintings yer man did. Says she to me when I saw her last week, that picture of you, Bridie, has pride of place. You should go and see it for without you, it would not be there. Well do you know, I went white at the thought of it and my heart started galloping. Says she You did nothing wrong. It is him that should be ashamed of himself. I just stared at her open mouthed. The last thing I wanted was to bump into him or any of the Archers. She must have read my mind for she told me then that they were all out of Sheffield next week. Your good friend, Bridie

Belfast
17 September 1914

Dear Bridie

You have more lives than a cat. More power to you. And I have to hand it to Lizzie Balfour. She knows how to stick by you.

Things are moving right and quick round here as well. Michael is scundered for the English government decided yesterday to delay Home Rule for a year or until the end of the war. Charles signed up for the war the same day. We could all see that coming for everyday he was full of the news of how badly the British were doing against the Germans in France. So he is now one of the New Army set up by Lord Kitchenr. In the 10th Irish Division. Maggie told me as we walked to the mill on Tuesday. She did not say much but I could see she was biting her lip in between speaking. And the way she was carrying herself, hunched over, she looked as if she'd been winded by a punch to the stomach. The gist of it was that Charles reckons sooner or later nearly every fella able to fight will sign up and that he'd rather join up now to save France than a Home Rule bill that is not worth the paper it is writ on. We don't see eye to eye on this she said. But when he tells me that those that sign up for a few months fighting will have more chance of work here afterwards I almost believe him. I want to. And I know he wants to believe it himself. For he is not sure how things will work out in the foundry.

Charles is not the only one on our side to volunteer. But those shipyard fellas in the Ulster Volunteers have signed up in their droves. They have even got their own Ulster Division. But there is no sign of the Irish Volunteers doing the same.

21 September

I spoke too soon Bridie. There was a meeting of Irish Volunteers somewhere in the south yesterday and didn't John Redmond call for the Irish Volunteers to enlist in the new Irish regiments of the British Army as well. The Irish News was full of it today. It has set the cat among the pigeons in our house. Michael says Redmond is right. If we all stand up and fight on the side of England, they will be more inclined to stick with their word and give us Home Rule. Father says and what about the Ulster Volunteers? Do you think they would be signing up on the side of England if they thought Ireland would have Home Rule at the end of it all? Mammy is beside herself with worry. For with Michael turned 19 last month he can sign up if he wants. Thank God, Johnny is only six months older than me and will not even be 18 until October.

Nan Rose

22nd September

I was going to post this on my way to the mill today, Bridie. But Mrs Dempsey's son Tommy called to us first thing to tell us that your granny died in her sleep last night. May her soul rest in peace. Your mammy wanted us to know straight away. I called round on my way to the mill and spoke to your mammy. I told her I was about to post a letter to you and she said she'd be grateful if I would let you know. She says she will write in a few days after the wake and the funeral are over. She says that your granny went peaceful and to tell you that she prayed for you every morning and night.

I am awful sorry Bridie. We will all call and pay our respects this evening.

Nan Rose.

Barely a week from me posting my letter to Bridie, I'd called for Maggie as usual so as to walk up to the mill together. She was at the corner ready and waiting but I could see she wasn't right for she was lurching from one foot to the other so that she was more shaking than rocking wee Charlie from side to side.

'Charles got his papers yesterday. They were waiting for him when he got home from work. He's to report for training at Barracks Street on Monday week.' She bit her lip hard, even as I could see her eyes fill with tears. Wee Charlie must have picked up on her agitation for he started gurning.

'Let me take him,' says I, reaching out my arms.

She did as I bade her. I wrapped him in my shawl and rocked him and me to and fro waiting for Maggie to gather herself. He settled to playing with my plait as it fell over my shoulder. In a minute or so, Maggie linked arms. 'We'd better go for I wouldn't want both of us to be locked out for the morning on account of me keepin' you late.' We began to walk at a pace.

'It seems they'll do their first lot of training in Belfast at one of the army depots. After that they'll ship them off to barracks either down South or in England. So, he'll be to and fro home for the first wee while.' She sighed loud and heavy. 'I'm glad he's not being shipped out right away, but so help me, it'll stick in my gullet to see him in a British army uniform.'

All I could think to do was to keep pressing her arm tight agin me as we walked. In a while, she sighed again, quieter.

'There's nothing else for it, but to put up with it,' says she.

It must only have been a week after that, when Johnny met me from work one weekday. It was a fine early October evening. He looked as if he'd scored the winning goal in a hurling match, his chest puffed out and him carrying himself a good three inches taller. Even as I walked towards him, he ran towards me, put his arm round my waist and twirled me round. I burst out laughing for his jubilation was contagious. I thought maybe he'd backed a winner at the greyhounds, and for a few minutes, we circled each other in high spirits. We'd no sooner come to a stop, his hands still at my waist, when he was out with it.

'I enlisted on my way back from work, Nan Rose.'

I was like a pricked balloon with the air seeping out of me. I could hardly get my breath, never mind my words.

'With Michael?' says I

He just nodded. I must've turned in a daze and started walking home. He kept step with me.

'I couldn't not, and still call myself a man.'

It was my turn to nod. No words would come.

'Sure it'll be over by Christmas. That's what they're all saying – and I'll have played my part.'

'What'll your mother say, and you her youngest?'

'She'll get used to it. She has to. Anyway she has my sister at home and Thomas can't enlist'.

For the first time it occurred to me that frailty has its advantages. Thomas's chest would keep him out of any war.

We walked the rest of the way to our door, with me not able to speak and Johnny making light of it all.

'I could meet you again tomorrow evening, Nan Rose?'

I nodded. I hadn't the heart for anything other than a peck on the cheek. I walked in the door to find Mammy white-faced and red-eyed. She waved me to silence even as I opened my mouth.

'Your brother and that Johnny one have enlisted.' She shook her head and pursed her lips even tighter together. Her voice broke and she turned on her heels to go into the scullery. Then she turned back on herself and came towards me. She clasped me by the shoulders and squeezed. Her eyes filled with tears. She turned and made for the scullery again. I stood there not knowing which end of me was up. I wisht to God Bridie was back and living round the corner.

Even though Michael and Johnny had enlisted in the 16th (Irish) Division, the only change in our house was that instead of going to the timber yard every morning, Michael reported for duty at Barracks Street and swapped his work clothes for a uniform that was rough and scratchy with newly shod boots that rang on the flagstones.

When Michael was about, I'd catch Father looking at him every so often, across the kitchen table, as if he was trying to work out some question he never managed to ask in the chit-chat about how it was all going. Only Mammy bustled around, fussing over Michael, trying to spin him closer, even as he was spinning away.

As for Johnny and me, I took it hard that he hadn't even talked to me before he'd signed up. I lurched from being so angry with him that I could hardly give him a civil word to desperately wanting to enjoy what time we still had together.

And I could see him lurch from barely being able to hide his excitement at the adventure of war to sometimes sighing as if his heart'd break when he held me close. It was as if we both suddenly had two left feet and could only make a hames of dancing together. Every so often though, when we were birling round in a ceili dance or having a bit of banter at his house or mine, it felt like it'd always been for an hour or so.

We'd all no sooner settled into this state of betwixt and between, when Charles announced that his lot would be moving to the Curragh in County Kildare in the New Year. Michael and Johnny were near beside themselves with excitement at the news, as they reckoned they too would be going soon. Father, Maggie and I, we each fell back into ourselves, with not much craic for anybody. The more the three of us sank, the more agitated and determined Mammy was to lift us all up.

One Saturday in late November, she drummed it into me before she and I left that morning for the mill to cajole Maggie round after our shift for she'd have a treat for us. She was as good as her word, for no sooner had Maggie and me sat ourselves at the table with Charlie on her knee, than Mammy put a plate of her potato apple, hot from the griddle down in front of us. She had even managed to salvage a bit of butter to lather over the top. As she sat down at the table, she reached over to take Charlie onto her lap.

I looked over at her, my mouth full of warm sweetness. She didn't notice for she'd eyes only for Charlie. There it was, that expression that I'd only seen before when she served Michael a bit of sausage and onion in gravy or a piece of liver and kidney, for, more often than not, since he and the others enlisted, in her mind's eye, it was him she was cooking for.

Just then, Maggie, licking the last trace of butter off her

lips with the tip of her tongue, put her hand on Mammy's arm as it rested on the table.

'I don't know how you do it Mammy. No matter how many times I've made potato bread or potato apple, it never tastes as good as yours.'

Well, Mammy leaned back in the chair, a big smile on her face. She was as happy as a pig in muck.

I suppose that's when it struck me what a sea change had happened between them. I hadn't noticed it because with Father and I, Mammy was the same as ever. She was the woman of the house, she knew what was best for the home and all we needed to do was to fall in line. Which, by and large, we were happy to do. But with Maggie – ever since the strike, I realised now – and with Michael from the day and hour he came back to tell her he'd joined up, it was as if she was wrong-footed. She looked to please them rather than expecting them to please her.

Wee Charlie was gazing at Mammy as she made babby noises. He held on to the plait of her hair as it fell across her chest, working it with his wee fat fingers. She laughed and kissed the top of his head. Maggie and I smiled at each other.

'He's the spittin' image of Michael when he was that age,' says Mammy. Every time she said that it was as if for the first time. And no doubt, we'd be hearing it a lot more often when Michael went.

'He's got Michael's mouth and colouring but across the eyes, I can see Charles,' says Maggie. We all studied him.

'God help him,' says I, 'for between us we'll have him carrying the weight of the two of them.' As soon as I'd said it, I could have bitten my tongue off. It was as if I'd flipped a coin and the other side landed face up.

'God spare them to live,' says Mammy, crossing herself and looking round at me and Maggie. We did the same.

There was a pause, but before a silence could settle on us,

Mammy says, 'Now, Maggie, how about you, Charles and the babby coming round here to eat on Christmas Day after Mass?' She looked round at both of us. 'I may not be able to make a silk purse from a pig's ear, but with a bit of onion and potato, we can make a decent enough stew for all of us from a few pigs' trotters.'

'That'd be grand Mammy,' says Maggie. 'But are ye sure?'

'Would I have said it if I wasn't sure?' says Mammy.

'I'll talk to Charles then. It'd certainly be easier to keep our spirits up if we're all together.'

Well the thought of Christmas burned like a candle in our midst all through November. When I found myself worried about what the New Year would bring, I just reminded myself it was wee Charlie's first Christmas. And I don't think I was alone in that. Halfway through December, Father took to bringing in bits and pieces of wood and set to whittling and chiselling them in a corner of the scullery when he had a chance. Maggie told me she was raiding her bag of scraps of material to make a wee rag boy. I'd scavenged old newspaper and was like a child myself, cutting it into strips, folding and cutting them into a diamond pattern all set to glue them into four chains to hang round the walls on Christmas Eve. A few days before, Mammy steamed a bread and raisin pudding. I suppose we were like childer ourselves. Childer round a fire, warmed and lit by the flames and with the shadows thrown back and behind us, for the time being.

A few days to go and Father arrived in with two boiling fowls, ready for plucking. He set them on the scullery table with a thump that set their heads and necks wobbling as they dangled over the edge. Michael and I cheered with delight.

'So, Agnes, you see? I told you aul Barney never forgets a favour. He's settled a year in one go, here.'

Father folded his arms and smiled at the birds. I half

expected him to go and tousle each of their heads, he looked so pleased with himself and them.

'Well, there you are, Michael. That's your Christmas job for you,' says I, as soon as Mammy and Father were out of the scullery.

'And since when did you become woman of the house?' says he, but with no malice. 'Or maybe you're practising for when your turn comes?' His grin widened as I reddened.

'It's just we all need to do a bit.'

'God help that Johnny fella. He doesn't know what he's letting himself in for and him thinking butter wouldn't melt in your mouth.'

I wasn't going to let him faze me a second time.

'And don't be looking at me like that Nan Rose, for all the world like you're Mammy.'

I didn't move a muscle.

He shrugged and looked hard at the chickens.

'Well, as it is, I don't mind plucking these fellas. For Johnny and I have sorted what we're bringing the wee fella for Christmas.'

Well, he'd hooked me there. I went to open my mouth but he just tapped the side of his nose with his finger and smiled at me like an angel.

I didn't have long to wait. On Christmas Eve night, Father was polishing shoes for Mass in the morning while Mammy and I peeled potatoes and chopped soup vegetables, when we heard a kerfuffle at the front door. Bandit, who had been dozing in the corner, was on her feet in an instant, growling.

The door opened and Charles came in, carrying a sack in one hand and clutching three bottles of stout in the other. Johnny and Michael carried in a small tin bath with a wee holly tree planted in it. They put the bath down gently on the floor while Charles set the bottles on the mantel piece. He turned round and upended the sack with a flourish and a bow. Ivy, mistletoe and more holly slid into a glistening green puddle on the floor. Bandit, her tail wagging sixteen to a dozen, was snuffling round the greenery when the holly jabbed her on the nose. She started back, then bent low on her forepaws the better to give the holly a good barking. Michael scooped her in his arms and bade her shush, before plonking her at his feet.

'Now what, in the Name of God, do yous have there?' says Mammy, her arms akimbo and her eyes glancing between the bottles and the floor. I put my hand over my mouth to stop me laughing for she looked as if she was about to shush them out the door with all their paraphernalia.

'Mrs Murphy,' says Johnny, 'have ye not heard of those Christmas trees that them with money are having in their homes now?'

'I have indeed,' says she. 'There's one of them in the windae of Robinson and Cleavers for all to see. But they're not holly trees. They're *fur* trees.' She looked round at the three of them, sniffing the air. 'Have yous been drinking?'

'That was me, Mrs Murphy,' says Charles. 'I insisted on stopping for a half at Rooney's bar on the way round here, for these boys were foundered by the time we reached our house. Would you believe they had us up as far as Hannahstown digging up the tree and collecting all this greenery? Just so that my son, your grandson could have a special first Christmas.' He inclined his head towards her and gave her his sweetest smile.

Mammy raised an eyebrow as only she could.

'I'm surprised they didn't take yous all into Purdysburn, for yous must've looked like lunatics.' And with that, she couldn't hold a straight face any longer and burst out laughing.

Well, then, we had great craic as we put our decorations up – holly branches over the holy pictures and the mirror, ivy along the mantelpiece. They stuck my paper chains to the ceiling so that they hung in grand loops from each corner to the centre.

'And now for the last piece,' says Michael. He nudged Johnny to stand on the chair where it sat by the doorway to the scullery and handed him up a bunch of mistletoe to tie to the nail in the centre.

'You're going to have to watch yer man here, Nan Rose,' says Michael. 'For nothing would do, but we had to scour one lane after another until we got him some of this.'

Johnny reddened as he stepped down from the chair. I reddened, feeling all eyes on me, particularly Mammy's. Johnny lifted the chair and then hesitated.

'Ach, Nan Rose,' says Father, 'You'll have to do the daecent thing by yer man.'

I stopped myself glancing round to Mammy. He was my lad and I was his lass. I stepped under the mistletoe and looked up at him. As his lips touched mine, I forgot about Mammy and the war and gave myself over to the taste of his lips and the warmth of his body next to mine.

My head was still ringing with the clapping and Bandit barking as Charles and Johnny gathered themselves to go.

'I'll walk you back part of the way, Johnny,' says Michael as he lifted his coat from the hook.

Charles straightened his cap on his head, lifted the bottles and handed them to Father.

'I hope you don't mind, Mr Murphy. I brought these for the house tomorrow.'

'You're alright, son, thank ye. There's no harm in having something for a being to sup if they're here on Christmas Day.' He put the bottles down again on the mantelpiece and stood gazing at Charles as he bade Mammy good night at the front door and he stayed there, lost in his own thoughts until their footsteps stopped ringing on the cobbles.

Later, as the three of us were having a cup of tea, the mystery of what Father had been working at was solved. He carried in a wee wooden dog on wheels with a plait of twine through its nose.

'Is that the same varnish you used on the hall?' says I. 'It's given him a great chestnut colour.'

'Nothing gets past you Daughter,' says he. 'It is indeed.'

'Oh Patrick, it's a beauty!' says Mammy. 'It won't be long before the wee man will enjoy pulling that along behind him.'

'Well, if he gets half the pleasure I've had from making it, he'll be sorted,' says Father. He sat it in the corner near the holly tree.

Mammy started laughing again. 'I'm still thinking of those boyos earlier,' says she. 'It's a pity the three of them aren't in the same regiment, for it's good to see Charles like an older brother to them two. And to see him come out of himself more and be easier in company.'

'Aye,' says Father. 'Company's a good thing as long as it doesn't go to your head.' He glanced up at the mantelpiece where the bottles still stood like soldiers.

I bade them good night then, for I wanted time to myself. I went to sleep, remembering Johnny's lips on mine as we stood under the mistletoe.

Fourteen

March 1915

And then they were gone. Charles left for the Curragh in Kildare in January. In February, Johhny and Michael headed to another place I'd never heard of before – Fermoy. All I knew was it was even further south. I was in high dudgeon.

'Why do they have to send them to the back end of nowhere?' says I to Father, who was reading the paper by the fire.

He laughed. 'You Belfast ones take me to the fair!' says he. 'Anywhere outside of the city isn't worth bothering about.'

I rattled the wooden spoon round the pot, as if I was just giving the potato stew a good stir. He looked up. My face must have looked like a crumpled bag, for he put the paper down on his lap.

'Ach, daughter, I know it must be hard. But, you'll have to get used to it, for he'll be even further in the back end of nowhere before this war's over.' With that, he went quiet and stared at the fire.

I wasn't only missing Johnny. I was missing Michael. I wouldn't have believed I'd be so aggrieved to see the back end of my brother and all his teasing. I glanced down at Bandit who was lying by the side of the fireplace, her muzzle between her front paws and her eyes returning time and again to the front door. Since the day and hour Michael had left for Fermoy, she hadn't been herself. More often than not, I'd find her, head and tail drooped, whining quietly. I reached over to scratch her muzzle. She nosed my palm. You can say that about dogs – they can't enlist and they can't take themselves across the water without you.

It wasn't only the house that seemed empty. I'd walk to work in the morning and back in the evening, noticing the absences of the familiar huddle of men at this corner or that, noticing their voices and footsteps fainter in the river of bodies and talk streaming to and from the mill gates. I clutched the memories of Johnny at my side closer.

Not that it was all bad news. It meant we finally got shot of aul Campbell, our foreman. And who did they replace him with, but Bella Dwyer? It just goes to show that even the powers to be can learn lessons. They'd finally realised what we'd known all along. Better to have Bella with ye than agin ye. That was the beginning of the change – of women filling the empty spaces at work and at home. In our case, it happened one March evening in the blink of an eye. Maggie'd announced that she was expecting a babby sometime in August.

Mammy must have thought about it for all of a minute before she says, 'Maggie, would you not think of coming home until this war's over? For it'd be easier to give you a hand with the wee 'uns if we were running one home between us rather than two.'

I didn't think for a second that Maggie'd want to be back under the same roof as Mammy. I was wrong. Her face lit up before clouding over as she looked at me. More power to her, Maggie didn't take me for granted the way Mammy did.

'Sure, where would we all fit?' says she.

'What do you mean?' says Mammy. 'Sure, you and Nan Rose could share the bed at the front the way yous always did. There'd still be room for Charlie's cot.' She paused, tracing Maggie's gaze back to me. 'And when Charles gets leave, she and the babby can sleep down here where Michael slept. Isn't that right, Nan Rose?'

I smiled back, even as I shook my head at her. 'It's more than alright by me, Mammy, even if it would have been nice to be asked.'

'Sure, isn't that what I'm doing now?' says she. Maggie and I just laughed. Mammy was, and ever would be incorrigible.

'But what happens when they're all back on leave together?' says I, remembering all the banter on Christmas Day about Father needing to find another two chickens for Easter. Mammy looked down at her hands.

'I doubt they'll all be back at the same time,' says she quietly. 'And if by the oddest chance they were, we'd manage somehow.'

So, it was settled. Maggie and wee Charlie moved in with us within the fortnight.

A week or so after that, I turned the corner from Divis Place on my way home from the mill and saw Mrs Hegarty, who'd been on strike with us, at her doorstep. It struck me as odd that she was huddled into her shawl even though it felt like the first proper day of Spring. I'd barely paused to bid her good day when she laid her hand on my arm. Her hand was shaking so hard, it set my arm off shaking too.

'Daughter, will you ask your mother to call in when she has a minute?' She let out a sigh that ran the length of her. I nodded and scurried past, for that sigh had sent a chill right through to my bones. Her husband had been a Regular for as long as I remember and her only son, Barney, had followed in his father's footsteps as soon as he was able.

Mammy was hardly in the door when I told her. She picked up her shawl from the chair where she'd just laid it.

'I'd better go right away,' she says, crossing herself.

'I'll sort us out here,' says I. 'I've already started peeling the potatoes.' I wanted to chivvy her out the door for the sense of dread was suffocating me. I was holding on to the thought that Mammy would deal with whatever was happening just as I used to hold on to a fistful of Maggie's hair when I was wee and fighting sleep. She turned at the doorstep. 'Make sure either you or Maggie stay in. I might need you.'

I practically shut the door on her face, I was that desperate to keep whatever it was out of our house.

Over the next hour, Maggie and then Father, each fell quiet when I told them. Only wee Charlie was undeterred. If anything, all of us being so preoccupied just made him more determined to get one of us to pay attention. In the end, Father stood up and lifted his pipe and baccy tin.

'I'll take this young fella out the back for a bit of air while I have a smoke,' says he, scooping Charlie off the floor where he was rattling the button tin for all he was worth.

'At least none of our ones are over there yet,' I practically whispered to Maggie, for it seemed an awful selfish thing to say.

'No, not yet,' says she, her words dropping like buttons on the flagstones. She laid down the socks she'd started to darn and gazed after Father and Charlie. In the silence, the clock tocked loud as a heartbeat, ticking off the minutes as they passed.

I was about to put the food on the table when Mammy arrived back. She sagged into the nearest chair, half shrugging her shawl off her shoulders. Her face was grey. We all stopped still and looked at her.

'It's Mr Hegarty, God rest him. He's been killed in France. At New Chapel or something like that.'

All I could think was, 'Thank God, it wasn't Barney.' Mr Hegarty was over forty. Old people die sooner or later.

No sooner had I thought it than Father reached over and put his hand on Mammy's shoulder and it struck me that I'd as good as chosen Michael or Johnny over him. I was that consternated, I nearly dropped the pot of stew on the table.

'If we can save a bit of that, I'll take a bowl back in for Eileen and sit with her for a while,' says Mammy. Her every word was an effort. 'I was trying to think who'd have a bit of black cloth for to make a bow for the front door.'

'I've an old skirt that I've been saving. I'll make one up as soon as I've put Charlie down to sleep.'

Mammy nodded at Maggie before looking over at me.

'As soon as we clear away here, can you let the neighbours know and leave a message in at the presbytery?'

I didn't have to be asked twice. Now that what had happened had been brought into our house, I was better off being out and about.

As soon as I told the ones on our street, I called with Ellen Kavanagh who lived round the corner, for I thought she'd maybe be willing to call to some of the ones from the mill that were friendly with Mrs Hegarty. She had her shawl on and was out the door with me before I'd even finished speaking.

When I got back, our front room was in darkness save for the bit of light from the street. Father was standing, staring into the empty grate. He turned round as I closed the door.

'Yer mother's away to bed and Maggie's gone in to sit with Mrs Hegarty for a while. I thought I'd wait for you and we could go in together.' I nodded.

A handful of neighbours had gathered, the women seated round the grate where a low fire burned, the men standing in the corner, near the scullery door. The one oil lamp on the table threw big shadows on the walls so that a second gathering of larger-than-life figures surrounded us. Bella Dwyer was sitting on one side of Mrs Hegarty with Mrs

Smith at the other side of her. They must've come as soon as Ellen Kavanagh told them.

On the mantelpiece, flanked by two half stubs of candles, and in the place where the clock usually stood, was a framed photograph of Mr Hegarty in his uniform. Father went up to Mrs Hegarty, with me close at his side.

'I'm sorry for your trouble, Eileen,' says he, taking her hand. 'Peter was a good man and he'll be missed.'

'Thank ye,' says she, dabbing her eyes. 'At least, he's gone to a better life than this one.'

'I'm awful sorry, Mrs Hegarty,' says I. 'Is Barney alright?'

She gave me a pale smile. 'He is for now,' says she. 'We'll just have to keep praying to God and His Holy Mother for him and all the other young 'uns, like your Michael and your fella, who are caught up in this war.'

Father joined the men in the corner. In a while, the priest came and led us in the Rosary and Prayers for the Dead.

It was odd to be at a wake without a body. It struck me we'd have to get used to it.

Easter came and went without any of our ones getting leave. There was a steady ration of letters so we weren't starved completely of sight or sound of them. I didn't have to break my neck getting back home after work for Mammy had changed her tune about opening letters. My and Maggie's letters would always be sitting on the mantelpiece waiting for us. At first, I thought she'd realised that neither of us would stand for that carry-on any longer but she wouldn't even open Michael's although they were addressed to Mr and Mrs Murphy and Family. She would hand the envelope to Father as he sat with his pipe at the hearth after we'd eaten. He would open it and smooth out the letter on his lap. He'd sit with it like a prayer, before reading it to himself. He always handed it back to Mammy with the same words.

'Thanks be, Agnes, he's doing alright.'

And then, as if a bell that only he could hear had summoned him, he'd bend over, knock out his pipe on the edge of the fire surround and stand up, his hands rubbing the small of his back for a minute or two. Then he'd walk into the scullery, open the back door and stand framed there, all with the same slow silence as the priest leaving the altar. And like the congregation, we'd sit with our own thoughts for a few minutes before Mammy'd read Michael's words aloud.

I couldn't understand Father's comment, for you'd expect them to be alright, seeing as they still hadn't left Ireland. I said this to Maggie when we were lying in bed one night. She just shrugged. 'But you know Father, Nan Rose. From the day and hour they started this war, he's felt it in his bones that we're in for a long haul. I suppose he's practising for the months ahead.'

Well, that was news to me. I wanted to know how it was that she was so sure of her ground, but Maggie'd already turned over into sleep. Maybe that's why Mammy had stopped opening letters? They were both girding themselves for bad news every time.

Maggie and I would feed each other a sentence or two from our letters in that twilight between lying awake and sleeping. And then I'd turn over, nursing the secret of Johnny's endearments to my heart. Sometimes that would work and I'd fall into a dream from which I'd wake in the morning with the feel and smell of his breath on my cheek. Maggie must have been doing the same thing, for every now and then she'd waken with a smile and say she'd been walking with Charles in the night. At that time there were no nightmares for we knew they were safe and sound down south.

It was May when Maggie got a letter saying Charles had a week's leave and he'd be with us on the seventh. The letter only arrived the day before so there was a flustering and a flapping that evening. Or to be precise, Mammy flustered and flapped like a mother hen. Father and I did what we were bid, for when Mammy was in an organising mood, she was like a strong wind. Better to have it drive you along from behind than walk into it. Maggie didn't seem to notice. She'd fallen quiet, with eyes only for wee Charlie, who was pulling himself up to standing with the help of Father's chair. It was as if she was in some faraway place. So the rest of us worked round her.

Father and I went out to see what we could beg, borrow, scavenge – or if need be, get on tick. I started with Bridie's mammy and didn't get any further for she greeted me as usual as if it was Bridie herself at the door.

'Nan Rose, you're a sight for sore eyes,' says she. 'Come on in and let's have some of your craic, for I'm here by myself until Imelda comes back from the Women's Confraternity meeting at Clonard.'

I didn't need to be asked twice for I was very fond of Mrs Corr and the only thing that had kept me from visiting her more regular was the thought of dealing with the Aunt Imelda. Since the granny had died, the aunt was a law unto herself. I could never figure out how a woman who was so religious could be so proud. I'd see her every so often striding along the street or kneeling at Mass of a Sunday, head and shoulders above any woman in sight. It wasn't just that she was tall. It was more that she wouldn't or couldn't bend an inch. Even at the Sanctus with the bells ringing and the whole congregation with their heads sunk into their chests, the most you'd see from Aunt Imelda was the slightest of nods. I know, for God forgive me, when she was in sight, I was still mesmerised by her. There were times, I couldn't stop myself juking over to see what she was up to even when the priest was turning the bread and water into the Body and Blood of Christ. It gave me the greatest satisfaction to find fault with her, for the truth was, I suppose that I was convinced that, more than anything else, she was the reason Bridie stayed across the water.

Anyway, she was out of the road for the next half hour. So Mrs Corr and I had a cup of tea and we nattered away about our ones and about the news from Bridie.

'She's doing well for herself.' She said it like she was asking me a question, but before I could agree, she carried on. 'God knows I worried when she left for England and I worried even more when she told me she'd parted company with Miss Balfour's aunt and uncle.' I could see her looking over at me out of the corner of her eye, maybe hoping my face'd tell her something my mouth wasn't. I just nodded and said nothing.

'I suppose the money's better in the factory…but …'

I thought I'd be safer making a move to go, what with Mrs Corr's questions hanging in the air and the prospect of the aunt arriving back at any minute. So I thanked her for the tea and stood up.

'Wait a minute, you can have a wee bowl of stewed rhubarb to take with you, for I made some this morning and here's a couple of eggs. I'm sure Charles'll have an appetite from all that soldiering.'

I got back home as Maggie was ladling porridge from the pot into the kitchen cupboard drawer and Mammy was wrapping farls of fresh soda bread in a cloth. I wasn't one for a cold porridge piece myself, but men's appetites are different. They'd shovel anything in to fill a hole.

Father was back before me. A long sack, plump with fresh straw, was squashed into the corner. A smaller sack and a couple of blankets sat on top.

'That should see you and wee Charlie right for the next week, Daughter,' says he to me, when I came in. 'By the time tomorrow night comes, that'll all be well dried out and yous'll have beds fit for royalty.'

Says I, 'Do you think the king has neighbours like ours, round the corner from him, ready to lend him the makings of a bed when he has to fit another body into his palace?' We laughed.

So we were sorted and all that had to be done was to wait for the morrow.

It was an odd week, for, with Charles arrived, we all seemed strangely shy and new-fangled with each other. Wee Charlie spent the first couple of days holding on to the skirts of one or other of us three women when Charles was about and the rest of the week skittering between his father's knee and the arms of whichever one of us had time for him – as if he couldn't quite get his bearings. The rest of us were skittering too, but not being childer, we could only put on our best faces.

I scuttled the most around Maggie. One minute, I'd be sitting beside her at the table, elbows nudging, heads inclined to the other and next I'd be eyeing her and Charles from a distance with every bit of me aching for Johnny. As for Maggie, at times I could see her eyes flicker between Charles and Charlie.

Even Father was affected. He didn't skitter as such. He was too solid for that. It was more that every so often he'd take in that there were two men in the house. So sometimes, he'd take himself out the back as usual when he wanted a bit of peace and other times, he'd catch himself on and invite Charles to take the air with him.

I suppose that was it – Charles was a man now, whereas before he'd just been Maggie's fella. I couldn't quite put my finger on the change but it made me think of making bread. Before you put the dough on the griddle, it's soft and pliable.

After it's baked, it's solid. Something in Charles had baked, for better or worse. And he hadn't even left Ireland.

Every so often he'd tell a story of life in barracks and he'd have us laughing to tears, particularly when he talked about the shenanigans of his sergeant. But it was like swallowing a mouthful of cough medicine. After the sweet taste comes the sour. Underneath his banter, was an anger that made my arms prickle. Maggie'd go quiet.

'With a brute of a man like that in charge of them,' says she to me one night when we were in the scullery together, 'they'd be better off with the Huns.'

Many a night that week, in the quiet of the house, with wee Charlie curled like a pup, asleep beside me, I'd ponder the difference in Charles. I wondered if that's what happened when men are with men and how Johnny and Michael might be when next we saw them.

Charles had no sooner gone back to the Curragh, than he wrote to say they were moving to England, to a place called Basingstoke. His letter arrived the same day as one from Johnny to say he and Michael had three days leave and they hoped to be in Belfast sometime Friday afternoon. I didn't know whether to laugh or cry for I was dying to see both of them but I reckoned that, like Charles, that meant they'd soon be shipped out.

I was in two minds about whether to go to work on the Friday. I wanted as much time as I could with Johnny, but I had to be careful with taking any time off work, for we needed every penny. In the end, I decided to go into work Friday for the chances were they'd be late rather than early.

When I left work that evening, I found myself looking over to where Johnny'd previously stood to meet me. He wasn't there. I stood for a minute, biting my lip with disappointment and scouring the corner, in case I'd missed him. Then I turned and high-tailed it home as fast as I could. I charged down our street to find the door locked. Nobody was home yet. I was that beside myself, I nearly burst into tears on the doorstep.

I was fumbling for my key for the chain had got tangled with the end of my shawl as I'd raced home, when, out of the corner of my eye, I saw the two of them come round the corner. I was that delighted, I screamed. And I was still screaming when Johnny lifted me off my feet and birled me round.

It must've taken another half-hour for Mammy to arrive home – and that was all it took for me to feel the change in them. They'd gone away fellas – and here they were, barely four months later – men. I suddenly felt myself shy with Johnny for he'd an ease in himself that wrong-footed me, even as it delighted me.

Mammy came in, dropped her basket and threw her arms round Michael and then Johnny, while I got a better look at this man of mine. It wasn't only that he'd filled out across the chest and shoulders, nor that he stood taller in his uniform. It was the way he held himself. I watched Mammy fuss over them both, cupping each of their faces in turn in her hands. Johnny was smiling and bantering with her. That's when it came to me. Before he would've been keen to please her. Now he was content to let her fuss – it didn't feel to me that he'd the same need for her approval, nor mine, for that matter. He looked up and caught my eye. I smiled back, even as I thought we'd be dancing a different step from here on in.

He stopped at ours, long enough for Father, Maggie and Charlie to come in, before heading over to his mammy's. As I walked him to the corner of Townsend Street and Divis Street, he announced that, as well as us going to the Saturday night ceili, he wanted to take us both to Botanic Gardens on Sunday. 'That way, we'll have a bit of time to ourselves, somewhere different,' says he, before he took me in his arms and gave me the kiss I'd been longing for since I'd set eyes on him that afternoon.

I'd heard tell of Botanic Gardens, of course, but what would I want to be traipsing across the city by myself for, in the bit of free time I had? With Johnny, though, that'd be another adventure.

Seeing as he was home, I was given first place in the queue for the Saturday afternoon bath. I looked grand enough at the ceili on Saturday, but when I'd told Maggie about the plan for Sunday, she said, she'd give me a hand to look my best.

True to her word on Sunday morning before mass, she combed and plaited my hair for me and pinned it on top of my head, twisted in with a navy blue ribbon.

'That'll show off your eyes,' says she.

I looked in the mirror on the wall, just big enough to frame her face and mine. It was the first time I thought that my navy eyes were every bit as good as her light blue ones.

I was still admiring her handiwork when she shook out her Sunday blouse and handed it to me. 'You can wear this for the day.'

Her hand was resting on my shoulder. I lifted it and kissed it.

'I don't know what I'd do without you, Maggie,' says I.

'Get away with yourself,' says she, 'for you'll be putting me off what I'm doing and me not finished with you yet.' She stooped and opened the tin chest that held anything and everything that was dear to us.

'You can borrow this, as long as you take good care of it, which I know you will.' She lifted out the shawl that Charles had given her to wear on their wedding day. It'd been his mother's and her mother's before that. It was crocheted in grey wool. Wool so soft, it must've been from lambs and grey like the morning mist on the hills. She cast it over my shoulders and then crossed it at the front, looped it round my waist and tied it at my back. She took the mirror from its nail on the wall, stepped back as far as she could and slowly moved the mirror down so that I could see myself from head to waist.

'Oh Maggie!' I was nearly in tears with delight. I was that made up, I nearly forgot my Cherry Lips, but I remembered just in time. I reached over to the windowsill for the paper poke of them I'd bought for a farthing as soon as I'd got Johnny's letter. For there's nothing like that wee sweet to scent your breath and put an extra bit of colour on your lips.

When I came back from mass, Johnny was already sitting in the front room, talking away to Father and Mammy. He glanced up at me and the words died on his lips as he stared at me, his mouth open. It was the first time I'd ever seen him lost for words. And knowing it was the sight of me that'd stopped him in his tracks, well, it made me go all tongue-tied too. God knows how long we would've stood there staring at one another, all shy and without a word between us, if it hadn't been for Father.

'Well, if you two are looking for company, I'm sure Agnes and I can oblige.'

That got us over ourselves and out the door and once we were on the street with the sun beaming at us, we began to pick up our own rhythm. We were walking along King Street when Johnny says, 'If we walk down to Royal Avenue, Nan Rose, we could get a tram up to Botanic Park.'

I stopped dead and turned to look him square in the face. 'Have they made you a general already?' says I.

He grinned. 'Not yet but give it a month or two.' He squeezed my hand. 'In the meantime, I'm doing what I've been dreaming about ever since one of the lads told me about this Botanic Park – taking you and me out on a day to remember.' He gazed at me, all soft then so that I had to blink away tears.

'Well, I can't think of better company for a day to remember,' says I, squeezing his hand in return. 'And even the weather's on our side.' With that, we traipsed our way down King Street, swinging our arms like childer.

We clambered on to the open top of the tram and I sat in state the whole way from Royal Avenue to the Queen's University, right beside the park. I'd been over in this direction once before – the afternoon Mrs Corr and I walked Bridie over to the Balfour's house. But it's a very different thing to be looking across at a grand place like the City Hall with your feet on the pavement and you jostled by passers-by than sitting at your ease while a horse does all the work. I sat back in my seat and when I wasn't glancing sideways at Johnny, to take in the fine cut of him in his uniform, I was enjoying the sights. To tell you the truth, I had to stop myself waving at people as we passed, for they'd know then that I was only an eejit who'd never been on a tram before in her life.

Well! After all the excitement of the journey, I didn't know what to make of Botanic Park as we walked to the gates. What I mean is that it had a grand entrance with the people taking the air a cut above anything I'd seen except for Lizzie Balfour and some of the rest of them suffragettes. But it was still only a park and by the way Johnny'd been talking, I'd thought there must be something special about it. Still, for his sake, I was determined to show willing. So I stopped just inside the gates and took the view in all directions. I paused at the first flower beds which were full of early roses and made a great show of sniffing the air and bending over this one or that one, the better to appreciate it. I was even beginning to get into it all when I noticed Johnny studying the signpost.

He caught my eye.

'You take your time there Nan Rose,' says he 'and then, we can head in this direction. There's something I want you to see.' I did a bit more sniffing and oohing for good measure before linking arms with him again.

'Right you are then,' says I, 'lead on.'

We rounded the corner – there, right in front of our eyes, was a palace of glass…and not a cracked pane to be seen anywhere. I stopped still and stared, with my jaw near hanging off me. Johnny hollered with delight.

'This is The Palm House, Nan Rose,' says he, 'and it's even better than that fella, Baxter, said.'

I stirred myself to take a closer look. 'They've built that just for plants?' I was thinking of our street. It's not that I'd have wanted to live in a house made of glass, but all that light and our houses so dark.

Mind you, it was darker once you were inside, with leaves of every size and shape spreading out in all directions. I half expected one of them plants to wrap itself round me and swallow me up. I stepped closer to Johnny. He pointed in the direction of a white spiral staircase and we clambered up, his boots ringing out on each iron rung before we stepped on to a balcony that ran the width of the building. A husband and wife and their two small boys were already there, looking down at the wildness below. The man had one of them proper hats on, the sort that perch on a man's head and look as if the slightest gust of wind would send it tumbling and rolling away. She'd on a wide-brimmed straw hat trimmed with silk roses that looked as fresh as if she'd picked them that morning. There was something about those hats that did for me. I felt thick and shabby, despite Maggie's best efforts and I'd have skedaddled back down those steps if it hadn't been for the two boys. They were staring at Johnny as if the Lord himself had come to earth again. Johnny nodded at them and they both stood straight as a die and gave him a proper salute. I bit my lip to stop laughing. The man and woman had turned round also. She smiled at both of us but yer man tipped his hat at Johnny before chivvying the boys down the steps.

Do you know, I felt so two-faced! For there was I, who'd no time for all this war business, feeling like the cat that'd got the milk and all because my fella was in uniform. I stroked Maggie's fine shawl again, smiling as I remembered the reflection of her and me in the mirror earlier.

'Nan Rose.'

I looked over to where Johnny was standing right at the railing at the edge of the balcony. He beckoned me over and we stood side by side, elbows touching, looking down. From here, I could see how the plants and trees climbed up steeply on either side of a stream which gurgled its way the length of the building into a dark pond. Every so often, through the forest of green, candles flickered from hollows in the stonework. Flowers, the like of which I'd never seen before, rested on leaves that sat on the pond like giant dinner plates on a table. Some of the flowers had opened creamy petal after creamy petal so I could see right into their yellow hearts, while others held their secrets tight.

'Oh Johnny, it's like we're looking down into a faerie glen,' says I, 'what with them candles and flowers ... it's the sort of place the little folk would like ... I can almost see them playing in those big flowers by day and tucked in cosy at night.' I kissed him on the cheek. 'I'd never have thought it'd be this special.'

He took my hand where it rested on his right shoulder and kissed it. He looked up into my face, his eyes shining and with a big grin that reached from one cheek to his other.

'I've got to hand it to Baxter. He said this was the place for me and never a truer word was spoken.' With that, he dropped to his knee, still holding my hand.

'Nan Rose Murphy, will you marry me?'

I clapped my hands over my mouth. I didn't know whether to laugh or cry. I was that beside myself I must've jumped up and down with the delight of it all, for the wrought-iron platform rang out like bells. Some of the ones admiring the plants below looked up to see what sort of a hallion was causing such a racket. I got that flustered, I pulled Johnny to his feet and buried my face in his shoulder.

'Yes, Johnny Harper. Oh yes, I will.' I felt his breath tickle my cheek, his lips warm on mine and we kissed long and hard before the steps sounded to let us know we were going to have company.

Over the next couple of hours as we circled the park, we laid our plans. Johnny'd come back with me and ask Father and Mammy for their blessing and on the morrow we'd walk over to tell his mother and ask her to bless us as well.

'This war can't carry on much longer, Nan Rose. And once I'm back we can make our plans to be wed.'

'God spare us to live, we will Johnny,' says I. What I didn't say, for I didn't want to knock the shine off the day and the smile off his face, was how could he be sure when it had only been a few months back that he'd been convinced it would be all over by December.

Fifteen

July 1915

By the beginning of July, while the other two were still in Fermoy, Charles had been shipped off to a place called Gallipoli. None of us knew exactly where that was. In fact, if it hadn't been for big Jim McAnearney, we might never have been any the wiser.

It was him who told Maggie that Gallipoli was at the edge of Turkey. That always stuck in my mind for up until then, the only turkey I'd heard of was the one that ran about a farm. He offered to show Maggie where it was on the globe they had in the hall, if she came down any evening before the classes started. So it was that she, me and wee Charlie wandered down to St. Mary's of an early July evening to meet Jim. Maggie was heavy with the babby inside her and so I had half-toddled, half-carried Charlie as far as the hall. I held him in my arms as Jim brought us in to have a look at this here globe.

I can still see Maggie that evening, looking to and fro, to and fro from Jim's right index finger on Ireland to his other index finger on Gallipoli. With every word he spoke about how long it would take to get to one from the other she grew paler and quieter. When Jim lifted his fingers away, she placed her own where his had been. Still she stood, her eyes moving from one to the other and the silence growing between us.

I'd sat myself and Charlie down at one of the desks. Jim came back over to us. He ruffled Charlie's hair. He brought over some chalk and a slate and drew a dog in one corner. Charlie clapped. Nothing would do but that Jim would draw more dogs. After he'd finished the third one, Jim looked up and caught my eye. His eyes flicked to Maggie, who was now standing, arms folded, still staring at that line between Charles and herself. He glanced back at me and I could feel him willing me to do something. But sure, I felt as helpless as he looked. After what seemed like an age in which he and I enquired after every member of the other's family, the door opened and the first ones in the class started to arrive. Jim shuffled his feet, coughed and said he was sorry but we'd need to go as the class was about to start. Maggie looked up as if she'd been miles away. We thanked him and left.

She was as quiet as the grave on the way home until we turned the corner into our street. I set Charlie down on his feet for he liked to toddle that last little stretch himself. As I straightened up, Maggie turned to me. 'I'll not see him until this war's over for he's never going to get home and back there in a week's leave.'

Even though I didn't put much store by it myself, says I, 'There's some as think this year will be the end of it.'

She gave me a pitying look. 'That'll be the same ones that thought it would all be done and dusted by Christmas last.'

After that evening, Maggie went more into herself. As July gave way to August, she grew heavier, said less and sighed more. Johnny and Michael were still in Fermoy and that distance between our fellas lay between her and me.

To make matters worse, all of us were still rattled from all the hoo-ha back in May when a couple of the English newspapers were raging on their front pages about the Army having men fighting all over the place and without the shells to back them up. The papers had come out when Johnny and Michael were still on leave, but when you're relying on word of mouth from someone who's seen a paper telling someone else who hasn't and so on, it can take a while to catch up. So, by the time we knew there was a 'Shell Crisis', they were back in Fermoy, there'd been ructions in the government and they'd made your man, Lloyd George responsible for 'Munitions'. That August was the nearest I'd come to seeing Father angry. Every now and again, he'd clatter the front door shut as he came in, fling his cap on the nearest chair and stride right through the front room and the scullery to the back door, without a word to any of us. The one time I'd tiptoed after him into the scullery, I could see him framed at the back door, muttering and every so often shaking his head as if he was talking to himself. It was the only time I didn't dare speak to him.

Now, while you could say it was good that there was somebody now supposed to sort things out, how could you trust they would when they'd all made such a hames of it in the first place? So, I knowd that on top of her not wanting Charles to be there in the first place and reckoning she'd not see him again until it was all over, Maggie must be even more worried he'd be killed. Whereas I could at least breathe easy for a while, with the other two still safe in Ireland.

Not that Johnny saw it that way. I got a letter from him around then.

> Dear Nan Rose
> I am still marching up and down lanes in Fermoy five months on. Sure what use is that to man or beast? I will not get a whiff of proper fighting at this rate. Meantime, I am miles from you, Nan love, bar in my dreams.
> Your loving Johnny

I took to picking my way with Maggie as carefully as if I'd been in a peat bog for I'd no wish to go up to my oxters in muck. And as far as I could make out, Father and Mammy were doing the same. It put the wind up me when I realised they were afeard of putting a foot wrong with Maggie, too. The only good thing to come out of all of that was that wee Charlie got fussed over and played with to his heart's content. I'd never appreciated before how having a child about could smooth over the most awkward of silences.

We still walked to work together in the morning, dropping the child off at Mrs Smith's on the way but to tell you the truth, I was glad when we parted company on the mill floor to go our separate ways. It felt like a weight slipped off my neck as I watched Maggie walk to the other end of the spinning hall. After that, my agitation would settle and I could lose myself for a while in the rhythm of the spinning. I'd never have thought I'd have looked forward so much to a day's work.

Mind you, that wasn't just about me. What with so fewer men, and them that were about keeping quiet, as if they didn't want to be seen to still be here, we women had more of the run of the place. Time and again, Bella Dwyer's banter as she walked up and down the lines cracked a smile out of the greyest of faces.

It must've been towards the end of August that Maggie got a letter from Charles. We'd walked home from the mill together – slowly, for she was that heavy, she looked as if the babby'd come anytime. We'd picked Charlie up from Mrs Smith, so at least we'd a bit of chatter on the last bit of the way.

We both looked at the mantle-piece as soon as we went in. There was an envelope right beside the clock. Even from across the room you could see it was from Charles, for his writing was small and smooth. Maggie pocketed it, and in a while she went upstairs, leaving Charlie with me. Father and Mammy must have called round to a neighbour's for we had the house to ourselves. She'd no sooner gone upstairs than wee Molly Cush from three doors up called to ask if she could play with Charlie. So I settled them both at the back step, with the scullery door open so's I could keep an eye on them. I'd just made myself a cup of tea and was sitting at the table, being soothed by their innocent chatter from the back step, when Maggie came back down. She was tight-lipped and red round the eyes. I was that afeard something had happened to Charles that I could hardly hear myself speak over the thumping of my heart.

'Maggie, what is it? Has anything happened?'

She pressed her lips even tighter and shook her head. She bent over the fire and poked a couple of coals to smithereens.

'No. Charles is fine. He sends us his love and tells me that despite it all, the coast off Gallipoli is beautiful.' She attacked another piece of coal. Eejit that I am, I didn't know when to let words be.

'Ach Maggie, it's not fair him being posted so far away.'

She turned round, her hand gripping the poker that hard, her knuckles were white.

'There's nothing unfair about it. If he had't been so damned keen to join up, if he'd even waited the few weeks until Redmond called for the Volunteers to enlist, then he'd be with the others. But no, not Charles. He had to be off playing the hero and to hell with his family.'

'I hadn't knowd you were still angry with him for enlisting.'

She dropped the poker, stood up and walked over to the door to the scullery, from where she could look out at the two childer. She rubbed the palms of her hands up and down the small of her back before turning back to face me.

'I didn't know either until I heard where he'd been posted to. I keep thinking I'm over it but then something starts me off again. Only this lunchtime, Maisie Radcliffe... her man's over there as well... was giving off about her childer growing up without their father for all they were likely to see of him.'

I opened my mouth.

'And before you say anything, Nan Rose, be warned. I don't want you or anyone else telling me that what can't be cured must be endured. I swear I'll hit the next biddy as says that, over the head with the frying pan.'

Despite ourselves, we both burst out laughing. But Maggie's died as quickly as it had come. She came back over to me.

'Look at me, Sister. I'm twenty-five and instead of being in my own home with my man beside me, I'm here and dependent on my family to make ends meet. All this talk of doing the right thing by your country, how brave our men are, but what about their families?'

She looked back at the poker. I looked down at my hands. My right hand seemed to have a life of its own, twisting the tie of my apron this way and that.

'God forgive me, I should be grateful I've got a family. I should be grateful Charles is alive and in one piece and that in his own way he still loves me. But if I'm telling the truth, I'm not. Time and again, I come back to the fact that he thought more of his mother's country than he did of me and his babby. I can't get beyond that. If I could, I would, for it'd make life easier between us. Believe me I've tried, but right now, I can't.' She began to tap her feet on the floor.

I didn't know what to say. I was sorry I'd asked, for it hadn't done Maggie any good and had just made me miserable.

'Maybe It'll all be over sooner than we think. Johnny seemed to think so. Then yous could pick up where yous left off.'

Maggie rested her palms on the table and leaned towards me.

'Nan Rose, you be careful with Johnny. Think twice about getting married until this war's over. That way you'll know where you stand in relation to each other.'

Maggie might as well have punched me in the guts. It was only the week before that I'd mentioned to her – and only her – that Johnny'd asked in his last letter if I'd marry him when he was next home on leave. I opened my mouth and I closed it again tight, for I couldn't trust myself to speak. I stood up slowly so that there we were, each of us, with palms on the table staring at each other hard.

'That's up to Johnny and me to decide. There's no more to be said about it.' I couldn't help myself sounding harsh.

'Suit yourself,' says she, lifting her hands off the table and turning away to look out at Charlie.

It was just as well that the babby was due, for otherwise I don't know how long we might have gone on, with each of us drawing more into ourselves. As it was, a few days later, Bella Dwyer came bustling across the spinning hall floor to me halfway through the Saturday morning to tell me Maggie needed taking home. She came with me to where Maggie was sitting on a bench just outside the spinning hall doors. She was breathing heavy and gripping the edge of the bench as if her life depended on it. At the sight of her, my heart jumped into my mouth, for my first thought was there'd just be her and me at home, if we even managed to get there. But as I went over to her, I did my best to look as if I was taking it all in my stride. Bella and I sat either side of her, waiting for the pain to pass. Between us we helped her up and gathered her shawl round her. We were at the front step before Maggie spoke.

'Bella, would you ask one of the neighbours to call at Mrs

Smith's and ask her to keep Charlie until one of our ones goes to fetch him?'

'I'll do it myself, Maggie. That way I'll know it's been done. You just get yourself home.' Bella walked down the steps with us and gave my arm a parting squeeze. 'Take it easy walking home. I'll be saying a prayer to His Holy Mother for all to go well.'

Maggie and I reached the corner into our street, before another spasm gripped her. She leaned her back against the wall, clutching my arm with one hand while the pain bent her over.

Out of the corner of my eye, I saw Betty Cush, Molly's older sister, on the other side of our street. She'd stopped in her tracks at the sight of Maggie. Although she was only nine, she'd a good head on her, that one.

'Betty,' I called. 'Can you do us a favour and run round to Mrs Deakin and tell her that Maggie needs her now?'

She shot off like a greyhound, with me muttering a prayer to Our Holy Mother that Mrs Deakin would be in, for it'd be another few hours before Mammy finished work.

'Do yous need a hand?' Bridie's mammy had turned into our street from the top end and was walking down towards us on her way home. I was never as glad to see a body, for although Maggie was now able to walk on slowly, I needed to get her up to our bedroom, where everything'd been laid out on top of the trunk, ready – and I didn't think I'd manage if she was gripped again on the stairs.

As it was, Maggie clambered the stairs herself, with me behind her for support, while Mrs Corr stoked the banked embers of the fire to bring the kettle of water, that had been warmed there during the day, to the boil.

We'd barely got into the bedroom when Maggie juddered, holding on to the wall for support.

'Can you get onto the bed?' says I.

'I'm better off standing,' says she, when she could speak.
'Standin'?'
Just then, Mrs Corr came through the door. 'I've brought yous up a basin of warm water to get yous started,' says she, laying it on the floor beside us.
'Maggie reckons she's better off standing?' says I. Bridie's mammy didn't bat an eyelid.
'Well then, we may get some of that newspaper and clean flour sacks on the floor under her.'
Maggie was getting her breath back. She was white as a sheet and the beads of sweat standing out on her forehead.
'Help us out of this blouse and skirt, Nan Rose. Before the next wave starts.' We helped her step out of her skirt and had barely pulled her blouse off her, so that she stood only in her petticoat when she gripped my arm so tight I thought she'd break it. She let out a gulder that had my ears ringing. I broke into a cold sweat. What in hell was keeping Mrs Deakin?
'I'm going down for the kettle for it'll have boiled by now,' says Mrs Corr. 'If you get behind your sister Nan Rose and put your arms high up round her waist, that'll give her some support.' I did as I was bid. Maggie leaned into me, breathing heavily. In an odd way, feeling her weight against me, her heart thumping alongside my own, calmed me. My breath followed hers. When the spasm passed, we sagged into one another. In the quiet, we heard Mrs Deakin in the hall, heard Mrs Corr's answering voice, heard their footsteps on the stairs.
I kissed the back of Maggie's neck. 'You'll be alright now, Sister. We've all the help you need.'
Maggie put her hand on mine. 'We'd have managed, whatever, you and I,' says she.
The other two were barely in the room with Mrs Deakin positioned at Maggie's feet, when the juddering and guldering

started in earnest I did the only thing I could, which was to hold Maggie tight at the top of her waist and just go with her every move. I was near blinded with the sweat lashing down my face. Through it all, though, I could hear Mrs Deakin's voice, taking charge.

'Bunch up the petticoat, Teresa, and give the end to Nan Rose to hold. That way, we can see what we're doing.'

'Take it easy, Maggie. EASY. Ready for the next time.'

God knows how many times she said that. I don't know how many times Mrs Corr wiped mine or Maggie's forehead. I was beginning to feel my arms would drop off me when Maggie started heaving fast and heavy.

'Now, push, Maggie, Push. PUUSSHH.' I heard Mrs Deakin's sharp intake of breath. 'That's it Maggie, I can see the babby's head. C'mon, one more PUSH.'

I heaved and pushed alongside Maggie, my ears ringing with her hollering, for what seemed an eternity. I thought we couldn't keep going any longer, when Maggie gave one enormous judder. She sagged in my arms, spent with the effort. I heard Mrs Corr sing out.

'It's a girl.'

Her first cry sent a thrill right though me. I burst out laughing with relief.

Between us, we sorted Maggie into bed with the babby beside her. While Mrs Deakin tended to what needed doing underneath, Mrs Corr wiped the babby clean and I edged Maggie into the bed, before mopping her face and arms and helping her into a clean petticoat. I could as easy have slumped onto the bed beside Maggie, for I felt well and truly spent. Then, Mrs Corr handed me the wee one for me to hand into Maggie's arms. She was light as a feather and my heart lightened too at the sight of her tiny wee face, peeping out of her swaddling. I stood there for a minute, with my body like clay and my heart like a lark, taking in the line of her tightly closed eyelids and the wisps of fair hair on her head. I looked up at where Maggie sat, propped up with the bolster and our rolled shawls. She was grey with the effort of it all and her eyes had that expression, where she seemed to be here and not here at the same time.

'Looks like this one's got your colouring, Maggie,' says I, settling the babby into her outstretched arms.

'That's my girl,' says she, smiling from me to where the wee one cradled in her arms. My eyes filled with tears then, for even as I looked at them, I was remembering those mornings as childer, and me waking up at one side of Maggie, clutching her hair and Michael on the other side of her, with his arm flung over her waist.

I slumped on the bed at Maggie's feet, even as Betty Cush's voice rang out clear from the hall.

'Mr Murphy's coming up the street NOW!'

'Thank ye, Betty. You can let him in. We're all sorted.' Mrs Deakin paused in her piling of the blood sodden sacking and clothing into the tin bath and swept the rest of us into her smile. 'He's right on time … arriving back when all the hard work's over.'

Mammy wasn't long behind him, but by that time, Maggie and the babby were asleep, Father had gone to fetch Charlie and I'd wet a pot of tea for the rest of us. The sight of the three of us at the table stopped Mammy in her tracks. She stared at me as if she'd seen a ghost and it was only then I realised that the roll-ups of my sleeves were stained with blood from when I helped Maggie out of the petticoat she'd been standing in.

'Mother of God, where's Maggie?' she cried.

'She and her wee daughter are settled upstairs, Agnes,' says Mrs Deakin. 'Sure you wouldn't be expecting us to sit around at our ease if there was anything the matter, would you?'

Mammy turned in the direction of the stairs and then back to nod at Mrs Deakin and Bridie's mammy, before staring hard again at me. It was as if she couldn't figure out how I'd managed to get in on the act rather than herself.

However discombobulated she was about the birth, Mammy was easily soothed by the sight of the babby and, even more so, by Maggie's announcement that she was calling her Agnes Rose, after her and I. If I'm honest, I was puffed up with pride and delight, myself. Even more so, when Mammy suggested 'Let her be Agnes Rose, but better if we call her Rosie, before others start calling her Aggie.'

Sixteen

Friday, September 3rd 1915

Maggie stayed home for a week after Rosie's birth, for Mrs Smith's chest was terrible bad. It was a peaceful week. In between, looking after the wee'uns, she looked after the house. So, the rest of us came home from our day's work to find the fire banked, the kettle boiled and whatever could be stewed, simmering on the hob, with a bit of onion. We'd have time to sit and gather ourselves or have a bit of time with Charlie or the babby before eating and bed.

    I suppose I was lulled into a doze. I began to think that maybe Johnny and Michael might never reach the war, for they were still in Fermoy, six months on from arriving there. I even began to see myself as married, as having my own child. In other words, I was ahead of myself.

    So, I didn't think there was anything untoward about a letter arriving for Father and Mammy the same day as one from Johnny to me. I saw them as I walked through the door for Maggie had set them side by side on the mantelpiece. I flung my shawl on the chair, took the wee knife with the pointy edge and slit open the envelope as I stood there at the fireplace.

    29th August 1915
    Nan love, at last we are on the move. We will be

in England by the time you read this. And finally doing our bit not long once we get to wherever we are sent. I am sorry I will not hold you in my arms before crossing the water. I hold you in my dreams. Your loving Johnny.

I stood there, biting my lip with one hand on the mantelpiece taking my weight and the letter in the other. For a while all else faded away.

'Nan, Nan, look me.' Charlie was tugging at my skirt. I roused myself to pat his head and saw that my hand was shaking.

'Be a good boy and let Nan Rose be, Charlie.' Maggie's voice came from behind me. I turned to see her standing in the scullery doorway, her shawl wrapped round her and tied at the waist so that the babby was snug at her chest.

'You're alright, Charlie,' says I stooping down to look at the twigs he had in his hand. And with that, I realised my legs were joining in. I straightened up so as I could put both hands on the mantelpiece.

'Johnny and Michael have left for England,' I says to Maggie, not looking at her.

She came over to me, put an arm round my waist and drew me towards her. I laid my face on her shoulder. Charlie must have knowd something wasn't right for he pressed himself against us, holding on with each hand to each of our skirts. I picked him up and we stood, Maggie and I looking at Michael's handwriting on the other envelope.

'What do you think, Maggie? Should I tell them when they come in or let Father open Michael's letter first?'

'Better to tell them.'

I thought about it. 'Can you tell them, Maggie? I don't trust myself not to blabber.'

I took myself out the back with Charlie and we sat on the upturned tin bath talking to Bandit. I managed to tell my news to the dog with my voice only breaking once. When she heard Michael's name, she looked over towards the house before looking back to me. She started to lick my hand and I had to stand up then for otherwise the tears would've undone me.

When I came back into the house, Father and Mammy were sitting at the table and Maggie was serving out herring and potatoes. The meal went easy enough. Charlie had only eyes for Father, and Mammy was nursing Rosie on her lap while she ate. While I cleared the plates away, Charlie clambered down on to the floor to play with his twigs. Maggie took her chance then.

'Nan Rose had a letter from Johnny today.'

I turned back to the table as she spoke. Their faces had furrowed as they looked from Maggie to me to Michael's letter on the mantelpiece.

'He and Michael have been shipped across to England. At some point they'll go from there to join the war.'

Mammy's face crumpled. She bent over and kissed the top of Rosie's head. She stayed like that as she rocked herself and the babby to and fro. Father stood up and walked over to the fireplace, squeezing my shoulder as he passed. Charlie stopped playing and toddled up and over to sit at Father's feet, gazing up at him. Father stayed standing as he slit open the envelope, put the knife down, took out and unfolded the letter. He stayed standing as he held the letter in both hands and read aloud.

29th August

Dear Father and Mother and dear Maggie and Nan Rose

Johnny and I are finally being sent across the water to fight. All we know is that we go to England tomorrow evening and from there we will be sent to fight. God alone knows when and to where. But we will not be back home before we go. I hope and pray that I will do what needs to be done and that it will serve the cause of Ireland. And I hope and pray that we will see you all again before too long.

Your loving son and brother, Michael

There was silence except for the ticking of the clock. I bit my lip to stop it wobbling and blinked hard. Father looked round at each of us.

'May God have mercy on us all and bring the three of them home safe.'

'Amen.' Mammy was still rocking Rosie, but she looked at Maggie and I as she spoke.

A week or so after that I had a letter from Bridie.

15th September 1915

Dear Nan Rose

I still cannot credit that Michael and Johnny are somewhere in England now. Michael wrote me from Fermoy telling me they were due to board ship within the week. And your letter arrived not long after. I spilt tears on each of the letters, for I got to thinking about when we were all back in Belfast and going together to the ceilis. And then thinking of how it is for you. No sooner has Johnny gone to all the trouble to bring you somewhere special so as he could ask you to marry him – when he and Michael are off across the water. Johnny is some fella, Nan Rose. You know, I have been praying ever since you wrote me that if somebody ever asks me to marry him, he will pull out the stops too. For now, I pray every day that your three all come home safe.

My big news is that Lizzie Balfour is taking herself off to London to train as a nurse. You have to hand it to her, for shes one that does not need to be working at all, let alone doing such a hard job. She says that she and I will have to meet up before she goes. She also says to pass on her kind regards to you and your family.

I will write a longer letter next time Nan Rose. I just wanted to let you know I am thinking about you and praying for you all.

Your good friend Bridie

I folded the letter and put it in my skirt pocket, thinking of Lizzie Balfour, more power to her, off to play her part in the war. I thought of Charles somewhere in the back of beyond with no prospect of seeing home until this war ended, of Johnny and Michael about to head off to God knows where, and even Bridie in Sheffield caught up in it all. And then out of nowhere it struck me that if people like Bridie were not working in munitions, none of the others would need to be sent anywhere. That threw me until I remembered that if our ones weren't fighting over there, they'd as likely be fighting on the streets of Belfast even now.

I sighed. It was beyond me. The best I could do was to look after those that were dear to me and close by – and to pray it would all be over soon.

With the letters from Michael and Johnny, a different mood settled on us and chivvied us into October. Mammy went about, her lips tighter, her temper shorter. More often than not, I'd catch Father stare at the photograph of Michael and Johnny by the side of the clock and sigh, before looking over at the one of Charles on the other side. Only Maggie seemed to go about her business easier, despite going back to the mill and leaving both childer with Mrs Smith. I supposed she maybe didn't feel as alone now that Charles wouldn't be the only one of ours fighting somewhere in the back of beyond.

We went into October with all our attention on the big war but on Wednesday of that first week weren't the papers full again of what was going on right here in Ireland. Maggie and me heard about it from Mrs Smith when we stopped to collect the childer.

'Did yous hear about James Connolly and a handful of his Citizen Army making a mock attack on Dublin Castle?' says she, as we were leaving. 'The Irish News is full of it for I stopped at the newspaper seller when I took the wee 'uns out for a walk this afternoon and he told me all about it.' She looked from one to the other of us. 'What is that all about, I wonder? For whatever you're up to, you're not going to do much with a hundred men or less.'

I shrugged. Maggie nodded. 'We'll maybe find out more in a while,' says she. 'In the meantime we need to be getting these two home.'

As we walked back, Charlie's chitter-chatter eased the silence between us. I was remembering the conversation with Johnny on the way up to his mother's in June about those that thought England's trouble was Ireland's opportunity. He'd mentioned then that James Connolly was one of them. I realised it hadn't bothered me then, but now with our ones signed up, it didn't sit so easy with me. I glanced over at Maggie. She had eyes only for the childer. I couldn't help but think that was her way of not talking about the news. She still kept in touch with Nora Connolly, his daughter. Mammy knowd that and her ears pricked up like a hound any time Maggie showed she'd a mind of her own about the state of the world. If Mr Connolly hadn't been down in Dublin, she'd probably have had more to say about the company Maggie kept.

From time to time throughout October, Father would bring a day-old Irish News home from the warehouse and read out bits and pieces after we ate. That's how we knowd the British Army weren't faring well against the Germans in France. And that's how we knowd that it wasn't only James Connolly and his Citizen Army who were out parading and drilling. So were them Irish Volunteers that hadn't followed John Redmond's call to support the British in the war so we'd have Home Rule. They'd stayed with Eoin MacNeill who set them up in the first place.

Father did not have much truck with talk of an uprising against the English. 'I'll believe in that when I see the Germans landing in Dublin, for without them, the rump of the Volunteers and a couple of hundred of the Citizen Army haven't a hope in hell of raising much more than a pitchfork against England.' He concentrated his attention on what was happening in the big war for that's where all of our ones were – not only our three, but all the other one hundred and seventy thousand Irish Volunteers that'd followed Redmond.

I'd always been able to talk to Father – but now, I could see how much the talk of an uprising upset him. Anyway, it was difficult to get him by himself and I couldn't bear the thought of talking when either Mammy or Maggie were about. That'd be like setting the cat among the pigeons.

So I couldn't make sense of it all. And the less sense I could make of it, the more I missed Johnny and Michael, for I could always talk to one or other of them about what was going on.

Right at the end of October, I got another letter from Bridie.

26th October 1915

Dear Nan Rose,

I met up with Lizzie Balfour on Sunday. She had invited me back to the Archers for afternoon tea as she leaves this Saturday. Mr and Mrs Archer were away visiting friends. I says to her What if Mrs Wright or Sarah are there, for I am sure it will get back to your aunt and uncle? That is for me to worry about says she. But if it puts your mind at rest, there is no one in the house for I said they could have the weekend off as I could manage by myself for once.

So I got myself dressed up with the hat that Lizzie had given me way back and a coat I have just had made by one of the women I knew when I worked in that sewing place after I left the Archers.

I was glad I went to see her, for even though my insides were in knots all the way there, once I was inside and knew that we did have the place to ourselves, I was able to take my ease. It was not long before I was itching to have a good nosy round the house in a way I couldnt when I was working there. Lizzie is a great one at reading minds, for says she, Bridie, you have not sat still in that chair for twisting your head round this way and that. If you wish, take your time and have a walk round the downstairs rooms while I arrange afternoon tea.

I did not have to be asked twice. I walked round every room as if I was one of those that had time on their hands to stroll as long as the fancy took them. I stopped and stared in the glass cabinets, for there was many a little trinket or piece of china that had caught my eye when I was dusting and they gave me as much pleasure as I had when Mammy gave me that spinning top when I was wee. I looked out of every window to take in the view and waved at the last of the roses. I might still have been there, but Lizzie called me for tea. I am in the music room. That stopped me in my tracks, for the last time I was in that room was, you know. I stood in the hallway, looking at the door and could not put a foot forward. The next thing the door opens and shes standing there looking at me as if I had two heads.

Bridie, what has happened? You are as white as a sheet says she. Come in here and sit down. With that, she took my elbow and chivvied me inside. The first thing that caught my eye was Harry Wharton's painting of that garden. I could not take my eyes of it even as she took me by the shoulders and put me on the chair as if I was a big doll. She turned round to see what I was staring at and the penny dropped. She clapped hands on her cheeks. Bridie dear says she, I am so sorry. I was only thinking of how much you liked this room. She lifted the other chair over nearer the open French windows with its back to the painting. Sit here. I did what I was told and after a while, with the air and the sound of the birds, the life came back to me.

Well Nan Rose, I walked back to my lodgings as slowly as if I had two wooden legs. Taking my time. I thought I had got over all that business. So it was a shock to be so thrown being back in that room. But by the time I got back here, it came to me that I had finally gotten rid of that divil of a man for I felt light and free. The last time I felt like that was the day we had the picnic in Padley Gorge.

Lizzie and I were talking about the government plans to bring in CONSCRIPTION for any single man between 18 and 41. We were remembering how we all used to think men had it easy but how we have now changed our minds. I know I wouldn't want to be in any of their shoes now. But, God forgive me, when I think that Harry Wharton will have to sign up, I am not one bit sorry. Better over there than over here making life difficult for the likes of me.

At least, Michael and Johnny are still here in England. I do appreciate Michael's wee letters. He was writing that he and the other fellas find it hard to understand the English ones. And the English ones say they can't make out a word the Belfast fellas say. He said it must have been hard for me when I came over with me being the only one. I felt like laughing and crying when I read that.

They are two good fellas, Nan Rose. May Our Lady keep them safe.

Your good friend Bridie

I folded the letter and put it in my skirt pocket. I kept being surprised at how different it was between here and there. There was Bridie talking about conscription. And here was I not long in from walking home with the ones from the mill and all the talk was on a different track altogether. It was Peggy Arthurs that started it.

'Did any of yous see what James Connolly writ in his paper yesterday?'

'No. What?' says Maggie. 'My head's that turned with first Charlie and now wee Rosie snuffling and coughing, that I've had time for little else.'

'I'll bring it in tomorrow if you want to see. But the sentence I remember is, "Now with arms in their hands, they propose to steer their own course, to carve their own future." You can see him saying that to a crowd, can't yous?'

'I can,' says Bella. 'And it makes for hard hearing, with so many of ours following Redmond's call.'

'He's never made any secret that he's for fighting the English not supporting them,' says Ellen Kavanagh. 'But it's one thing to talk ...'

I couldn't help myself glance over at Mrs Hegarty and as I did, I caught Bella doing the same.

'Well, whatever happens, it's out of our hands,' says Bella. 'Even if it's us women will be picking up the pieces.'

The days shortened. The nights lengthened. The darkness pressed against us going and coming back from the mill. In the evening, shadows gathered closer to the glow of the oil lamp and the flicker of flame from the fire. Some nights I felt myself heaving for breath, squeezed as I was between some rising fear and the thickening shadows.

It was the beginning of December when another two letters from England arrived. I was the first home. I stood in the hall, staring at Johnny's, and then Michael's writing on the identical envelopes. I knowd it could only mean one thing – but until the envelope was opened and the letter read, I could hold on to them being safe in England. I decided I'd wait and let Father open the one from Michael first.

We'd no sooner finished eating and cleared the table, when Father rose. I was sitting, face to the mantelpiece. I watched him pick up Michael's envelope and pause at Johnny's. He glanced round at me and back to the mantelpiece, before lifting Johnny's as well. He came back to the table, handed it to me before sitting back down heavily. I pocketed my letter and clutched it tight under the table as he cut open Michael's and smoothed out its single sheet of paper before reading aloud.

'Dear Father and Mother,
We are bound for France on 1st of December. It may take a while for you to get another letter. So I wish you all a good Christmas. I will take the memory of our last one with me.' Father swallowed hard. I could see his Adam's apple jiggle. 'Give my love to my sisters and the wee ones.
Your loving son, Michael.'

Mammy sniffed loudly. I looked over to see her lips pursed tight and her eyes fastened on where the letter lay on the table.

'May God spare them and Charles to live,' says she, crossing herself. The three of us followed suit, while Charlie looked from one face to the other, his bottom lip a-tremble at our silence. Only Rosie was oblivious, her little snores reaching us from where she was sleeping in one of the cupboard drawers at the side of the fireplace.

I waited till everyone was in bed before sitting in Father's chair, warming my feet at the embers. I fished out the crumpled envelope from my pocket and took my time opening it. Two small rosebuds, the ones you see stitched on to the end of a collar or a blouse pocket, fell into my lap. With that, the tears were tripping me, and I hadn't even read his note.

My dearest Nan
Rosebuds for my Rose. To keep close while I am far away in France. The war does not matter to me now. You do. Pray God, I do my duty. And return safe to your warm embrace. I love you.
Johnny.

I folded the letter back over the rosebuds and put them

back in the envelope. I held it close against my heart, closed my eyes and let the tears come. After a while, my crying stopped. Still clutching the envelope, I heaved myself out of the chair and pulled myself up the stairs to bed.

The week before Christmas, Field Marshal French was sacked as Commander of the British Expeditionary Force. I only remember because Father said 'That's the best Christmas present any of us is likely to get, for yer man Haig surely couldn't do any worse than that John French fella. Maybe we'll fare better in 1916'.

Their names didn't mean anything to me, but I took his word for it. Maybe Johnny'd be right and the war'd be over soon. Maggie wasn't convinced.

'I wouldn't bet on it,' says she.

Father gave her a long look but said nothing.

Christmas itself came and went, a shadow of the one previous. The only good thing was that we gathered from the Irish News that winter meant there wasn't much fighting on the Front. According to some who'd men over there, their biggest enemy was the mud and the rats. I couldn't help thinking it must've been a fierce let-down from all Johnny's thoughts of daring-do. Still, at least he and Michael were safe. Other than that, there wasn't much to lift our spirits, and remembering our last one only made it worse. Looking ahead to the next one didn't help either, for there was no knowing if we'd be in a better or worse state by then. Still, between us, we managed to put together a few bits and pieces for wee Charlie. We put his into a wee sack Mammy'd made by folding a flour bag twice and stitching round the edge. That did the trick.

Watching him take out his treasure piece by piece was the one bright spot of Christmas day, for he delighted in each and every item. At the top were the three tin soldiers I'd bought for him.

'There's your father and your uncle Michael and your other uncle Johnny,' says I as he stood them at the edge of the hearth.

'Dada...Mike...ill...Johneee,' says he, lifting up each one in turn for us all to see.

Mammy'd knitted both him and Rosie a pair of mitts and a scarf from an old red shawl that she'd sometimes worn in bed at night. He stood at her knees and waited like an angel while she put each one on him in turn, fussing and chucking his cheeks as she went. Nothing would do him then but that Mammy should put Rosie's hat on her.

'When she's awake, Charlie. When she's awake.' Mammy pointed to the sack. 'What else have you in there?'

In the heel of the sack was the smallest of Jack-in-the-boxes that Father'd made. He helped Charlie slip the hook. The child jumped like the Jack himself and for a second we didn't know whether he was going to laugh or cry. Father ruffled his hair.

'Well what do you think of that, son?' he says.

Charlie still wasn't too sure so Father pushed the Jack back in and slipped on the lock.

'There,' says he, 'you can keep him locked in and let him out any time you want to make yer mammy or yer aunt Nan jump.' Charlie looked round at Maggie and I with the wickedest grin I've ever seen on a child and we both burst out laughing so that he got carried away, laughing and bouncing up and down with the excitement of it all.

Maggie lifted up the sack.

'Do you not want to see what else you've got in there?' she says.

He was immediately all eyes and hands. She held it open so he could root around at the bottom. He pulled out a ball.

Maggie'd done well for she'd scavenged a piglet's bladder from the butcher, filled it with newspaper and stitched it up with green and yellow wool.

'There you are!' says she, laughing. 'You've got an Irish ball there – green, white and gold.'

It wouldn't have made any difference to him if it'd been red, white and blue. He immediately started throwing it at her to play catch. After a while, she jiggled the sack.

'There's still something else in here. Are they for me, do you think?'

He dropped the ball in a flash and rooted some more. He brought out an apple.

'Abbel,' he shouts, holding it up. Mammy was up and stirring rabbit stew at the fire. She reached out for it.

'Will I cook this in the pot for you?' says she. He stepped back, clutching the apple to him.

'Nooo. Miiine.'

'So who's going to keep that safe for you?' says Maggie, opening her hand. He looked round each of us in turn and then marched over and gave it to me.

'Nan.'

'You see, Maggie,' says Father. 'She's been spoiling him rotten every chance she's had.'

Maggie gave me a big smile. 'I won't have a word said against her. No child could have a better aunt.'

I rested back against the chair. I smiled over at Rosie, sleeping, warm as a cat by the fire. Between Maggie and Charlie, I'd been given two of the best Christmas presents ever. For even though, the wee fella took his apple back and gave it to each of us in turn to keep safe, I was still warmed to the heart, for I'd been his first choice and Maggie hadn't minded.

Seventeen

January 1916

We'd barely seen 1916 in, when didn't they bring in conscription in England, as Bridie'd said – but not in Ireland.

'I wouldn't have credited them with that much sense,' says Father. 'But even they must know they're sitting on a powder keg here.' I looked over at Maggie but she was saying nowt.

I thought the British Government would've been bloody stupid not to know. Still, as Father said, it was hard to take anyone plotting a secret uprising seriously when they were flaunting themselves in armed manoeuvres at every opportunity. Every time I heard about yet another parade, I thought of Michael and Johnny and all them other Volunteers that signed up because of Ireland, eye to eye with rats in the mud even before they contended with the Germans, while other ones here were trying to make a deal with the same Germans to invade us and England, all in the name of Ireland as well.

There was more talk than action both here and in France. God knows what was going on with Charles in Gallipoli, for, from what Maggie said, his letters didn't say much about what they were up to. There was only once that I remember her smiling after she'd opened a letter. That was right at the beginning of February, on St Brigid's day. It was only a little smile on her lips but by the way she carried herself that day, it must have been a big smile inside. She was humming 'Believe me if all those endearing young charms' as we walked to work in the morning. Later, I could still hear her singing it to wee Charlie and her repeating, '*Oh! the heart, that has truly loved, never forgets, But as truly loves on to the close.*'

That night in bed, she turned to me, resting up on her elbow, her hair falling loose over her shoulder.

'Do you know what Charles said in his letter today?'

Well, I'd been dying to know all day what Charles could possibly have said that brought such a change in her. So I didn't banter about not being a mind reader. I just smiled and asked, 'What?'

She looked past me, resting her hand on her fist. I couldn't see her eyes but I knew her faraway look well enough. She was probably in Gallipoli.

'He says they were marching along the coast and him looking out over the sea and thinking of all the water between us. "There was a breath of wind on my cheek and it brought with it the memory of your hair soft on my face and neck. I was with you again then. And, more than anything, I wish I was back with you and the children right now."'

She sighed and lay back on the mattress.

'That's the first time he's said something like that. It's the first time he's said he wants to be here with us.'

It was just as well she wasn't expecting me to say anything. Here she was, my big sister, the one that always knew what to do for the best and her talking as if she'd no more sense than a wee half-timer on her first day in the mill. Sure it was as plain as could be that Charles loved her as much as any man could love a woman. But men are men. There was Johnny. He wanted to be with me *and* he'd wanted his adventure. More's the pity!

It must've been coming up to the end of March when Mammy came in, all business, from her evening novena at Clonard for I remember Maggie was nursing wee Rosie with Charlie curled up at her side while I played a game of solitaire and Father dozed in his chair, Bandit at his feet.

'Mrs Pick's just told me that James Connolly's wife Lily and her daughters have quit their house. Gone in the blink of an eye over the weekend.'

She was standing in the middle of the room, taking off her shawl. She looked hard at Maggie.

'I'd have thought you'd've got wind of that seeing as you visit every so often.'

Maggie lifted the child so that Rosie's head rested on her shoulder. She rubbed her back to burp her.

'Mammy, just because Mrs Connolly remembers me from the strike and is always welcoming, and just because I'm friendly with Nora, doesn't mean they tell me their business. No more than I tell them mine.'

She looked straight over at Mammy.

I marvelled at Maggie's bare cheek and her never letting on that Eilish Canavan that was another one that was friendly with the Connolly family, had called in on her way home from the mill to tell Maggie the very same news.

Says she, 'Nora Connolly says to tell you she was asking after you and the babby, for I called in on Saturday evening as they were packing the last of their things.'

I bent my head closer over the cards, for Mammy could still read my face like a book and I didn't want to be giving the game away.

I needn't have worried for Mammy still had her eyes on Maggie.

'Mrs Pick says there's something definitely afoot if they've moved so sudden, for she says they were good and settled there.'

'Well, if there's something afoot, Mrs Pick's the woman that'll give us chapter and verse before too long.' Father had roused himself from his doze. 'That woman's got a nose like a ferret for any piece of gossip.'

I choked on a giggle.

'Patrick,' says Mammy, all flustered, 'it's not like you to bad mouth a neighbour.'

Father was unrepentant.

'Well now, Agnes, I didn't think I was badmouthing anybody, so much as saying what everybody knows.'

He winked over at me, sitting with my fist stuffed into my mouth. I fell to spluttering giggles.

'I can see I'll get no sense from any of yous this evening,' says Mammy, turning tail and marching into the scullery.

I looked up and caught Maggie smiling at Father. A big smile. And well she might, for it wasn't easy to knock Mammy off course when she'd the bit between her teeth.

By April, I didn't know which end of me was up. My heart was with Johnny and Michael, for the fighting had resumed with the good weather but my head was here and turned this way and that with all the gossip and reading of the tea leaves that was going on. You couldn't bid a neighbour the time of day or sit down at table to eat without someone or other wondering would there or wouldn't there be a rising.

'It'd be madness for them to even think about it, what with the bulk of the Volunteers taken up in the War.'

'You'd think they'd have more respect for our ones that are out there, losing life and limb. After all, they're only there because Redmond called for them to enlist so as to help Ireland.'

'And what better time than now, when all the English might is across the water? All we need is a wee bit of help from Germany.'

'Germany's more sense than to faff about with them'ns that've wild words and little to back it up.'

'What are they thinking of? Making deals with the country that's killing our ones! It's not right.'

And so the talk went on, round and round and in and out, like a huge Fairy Reel, with everyone back where they started, after all the steps and turns were over.

Meantime, the papers were as full of the planned Irish Volunteers assembly in Dublin on Easter Sunday as they were of the war news. I was affronted that our three and all them as were fighting and dying were being shoved out of the news by them'ns that were parading and play acting. I stomped about for days with a scowl that would have frightened the divil himself.

The only thing that lifted me out of it was a card from Johnny. I'd never seen the like of it before. On the white card was a square of embroidered leaves edging a circle of flowers with pink petals and white bobbled centres. Right in the centre, fine neat stitches said 'With love'. I turned it over to feast on his own clumsy pencil marks.

Dearest Nan Rose

It is so good to just say your name. I do not know where we are as it is all much of a muchness. But you are always with me before I sleep. We passed through a village yesterday and some women were selling these by the wayside. I have put down for special leave for us to get married. Otherwise I might not see you til all of this is done.

All my love Johnny

I could almost hear him say the words and with that, every bit of me ached to have him beside me and us in each other's arms. The thought that he might get special leave, that I might see him soon had my guts somersaulting, for even as I thought of that, it struck me that I might not ever see him again. I clutched his card to my chest, caught as I was between laughing and crying. In a while, I remembered to cross myself and thank God and His Holy Mother that Johnny was still alive.

With Good Friday came the news that Roger Casement had been arrested at Banna Strand, north of Tralee in County Kerry, trying to smuggle in German guns. He was one of them high up in the Irish Volunteers that had stayed with Eoin MacNeill and ignored John Redmond's call to fight with the English. A couple of others were arrested with him and three others drowned driving off the pier in the dark. The German boat was taken.

I bumped into Jim Mc Anearney coming out of St Mary's Church that evening. He pushed his cap back and shook his head. 'It's like Kinsale all over again,' says he. 'When will we ever learn?'

I didn't want to show my ignorance but my face must've betrayed me, for he went on.

'It was in 1601. We'd defeated Elizabeth's army the length and breadth of the country. We were pitched for the final battle.' He paused for effect. 'And sure didn't the Spanish turn up, with a fraction of their fleet at the wrong bit of the coast. The rest's history. In 1798, The United Irishmen depended on the French and where did that get them but the gallows?'

'Does that mean we just have to put up with England lording over us?' says I.

'Now that's a question I can't answer,' says he, 'for it's easier to see what went wrong in the past and harder to know what'll work in the future.' And with that, he straightened his cap and shuffled away.

Maggie'd persuaded me to go to early Mass at Saint Peter's on Easter Sunday morning, while Mammy kept an eye on Charlie and Rosie. As we made our way on to the Falls, she mentioned, all casual, that any Volunteers from Belfast bound for Coalisland where the Northern ones were gathering to travel to Dublin would likely be there.

'I'm with them in spirit,' says she, 'so the least I can do is to see them off with a prayer and a blessing.'

So help me, I felt like grabbing her by the shoulders and shaking her. For, as far as I was concerned, she'd taken leave of her senses to be supporting any notion of a rising when her own fella and brother and my Johnny could even now be dead from a German bullet.

I'd never seen St. Peter's so full of men for an early Mass. The pews were awash with green for many of them had managed the green jacket and cap of the Volunteers. God only knows what weapons they'd been able to put their hands on for they must've left those at home to collect on their way from the church.

We slipped into a pew near the back, the better to see whoever was there. Looking round, I could see one's I'd gone to school with, and here and there a neighbour or one from the mill that'd always been civil and willing to lend a hand. My heart softened and I could unbutton my lip, for I felt better able to say a prayer for them all, mad eejits though they might be.

When it came to the sermon, the shuffling and coughing that always accompanied the priest's walk up into the pulpit took longer than usual to die down. I suppose most of them just wanted the Mass to be over and done with so's to get on with the journey to Dublin. Father Mc Bride bade his time and waited until there was silence before setting the cat among the pigeons.

'Brothers and Sisters,' says he, 'I can see that many of you are gathered here before setting off for Coalisland.'

At that the silence tightened until you could hear a pin drop. Men straightened their backs and dared him to say anything to dissuade them.

'I assume that you have not seen this morning's paper and the announcement communicated to the Press last evening by the Staff of the Volunteers.'

No priest ever had a more attentive congregation. All eyes were fixed on him and I couldn't've been the only one catching my breath. He savoured his moment before pronouncing every word loud and heavy as a bell.

'"Owing to the very critical position, all orders given to Irish Volunteers for Easter Sunday, are hereby rescinded, and no parades, marches or other movements of Irish Volunteers will take place. Each individual Volunteer will obey this order strictly in every particular." This is signed by Eoin MacNeill, himself.'

There was a second of stock stillness before a babbling broke out in every direction.

Even as I turned to look at Maggie, I could see the man in front turn to his neighbour.

'Mother of Jesus,' says he, 'That's finished us before we're even started.' His face was white, his voice shaking. He stood up and shuffled his neighbour and himself out of the pew. Other men were doing similar. A stream of grim faces were heading for the door even before Communion.

Well at that, there was a roar from the pulpit. I wouldn't've thought Father McBride had it in him for he was getting on in years. Those that were trying to shuffle out of pews were stopped in their tracks and those that had made it to the aisle skedaddled out as fast as their legs would take them.

The rest of us turned our faces to the pulpit. I found Maggie's hand and held tight.

Father Mc Bride was gripping the edge of the pulpit with both hands. He looked as if it was only his arms that were holding him up for his face and body had crumpled. But when he spoke you could hear the anger strong in his voice.

'On this holiest day of the year, when our Lord Jesus Christ triumphs over death, when we celebrate that through his sacrifice of suffering and dying, we have all been redeemed, is it too much to ask that we spend one hour with Him? Is it too much to ask that we take the meaning of the Resurrection into our hearts?'

He slowly surveyed those of us that were left and found his answer in the agitation that was there for us all to see in the shuffling of bums and in faces turning this way and that. He cut his losses. I've never seen a priest before or since give such a tired blessing.

'May the Peace of the Lord be with you all,' says he as he stepped down from the pulpit. Well, by the looks of himself and some of the Volunteers, there was little peace about. Consternation was the order of the day. As soon as the Communion was over, the church emptied of men.

We came out, when all was finished, to crowds of them queued up at the two newspaper sellers at the gates or huddled in wee groups reading the news from a shared paper. In the light of day, I could see that there were some as looked as if they'd been punched and were still gasping for air, never mind words. There were others who didn't seem that fazed. By the look in their eyes, I'd say they were relieved.

Maggie threaded her way slowly through them, with me trailing in her wake. I could hear snatches of argument as we passed.

'We've got our orders so we need to be heading home.'

'What put the wind up MacNeill for him to be calling off the manoeuvres at such a late hour?'

'I don't care what he says, I'm heading for Dublin. Are any of yous for coming with me?'

'Who are we to go against the man himself?'

'There's no point in doing anything other than go home, for we're divided among ourselves – again!'

Maggie was clearly looking for someone in particular, for although she bade the time of day to one and other that we knew, her eyes kept searching the circles of men. She must've spotted him for she suddenly turned right and upped her pace. We were bearing down on two men conferring together. The taller one had a newspaper rolled up and was slapping his thighs with it as he talked. From the distance, he cut a fine figure for he'd on one of the proper wide brimmed hats with one side furled up. I stuttered in my steps for I suddenly remembered that first time Charles had come round to our house. 'So here was another fine clothes horse of a man' to use Mammy's expression.

'Dia duit, Seamus. Dia duit, Eamon,' says Maggie, greeting them each in turn.

The taller one doffed his grand hat, the other his cap.

'Dia is Mhuire duit, Maggie,' yer man says. They both nodded at me.

'You must be Nan Rose,' says the Seamus fella. 'You're the spitting image of your sister.'

I managed a smile, even though I felt far from it. There was something a bit too familiar in this stranger knowing who I was.

'So, what do you make of all that?' Maggie looked from one to the other, before resting her eyes on the Seamus one.

'I'd say MacNeill's got wind of the Republican Brotherhood's plans at the eleventh hour,' yer man says, still tapping the newspaper against his thigh.

'And what are yous for doing?'

Her eyes were still on him. Eamon and I nodded, one stewed prune to another.

Seamus glanced round him and then at his comrade.

'We'll need to talk to some of the other lads, but I'm for heading to Dublin. We've come too far to turn back now.'

Maggie folded her arms tight to her.

'May Our Lord and his Holy Mother protect yous both.'

And with that we parted.

I was glad to be away from them all, for it only agitated me seeing all these'ns dressed up for soldiering but well away from where all the real fighting was happening.

'So who were they?' says I.

'They're just ones I met at the night class I used to go to before I had the childer.' And with that she upped her pace again, without saying another word.

Eighteen

April 24th 1916

By Easter Monday night, the word on the streets was that there'd been a rising after all. They'd taken Dublin City, and Padraig Pearse had proclaimed an Irish Republic from the steps of the GPO. There were some that claimed to have seen a copy of the Proclamation and knew them as signed it. James Connolly was one of them.

If you'd seen us walk to the mill that Easter Tuesday morning, you'd have thought we were going to a wake. It wasn't that there wasn't talk. More that we were all being very picky as to who we said what to – for you didn't know who was raging at the rebels and who was rooting for them. 'Whatever you say, say nothin'.' That's what you did unless you knew for certain that you were talking to someone on the same side.

By Tuesday, them'ns that'd seen sight of the only Dublin newspaper on sale, were able to tell the rest of us that the British Army had arrived in Dublin and there was fighting all over. The next day, Father came home from work and announced that all licensed premises in Dublin had been closed.

'I never thought I'd see a day where there was none of the demon drink in our capital city,' says he. 'Maybe we could do with a bit of martial law here, if that's what it takes to stop ones drinking themselves to death and their families to ruin.'

By Saturday morning, when Maggie and I walked through the mill gates, I couldn't wait for the midday horn. All this stepping on eggshells and buttoning your lip was getting on my nerves. In fact, the only thing that'd saved me the last few days was the clatter of our spinning jennies. You couldn't get stuck in awkward silences with all that racket rattling your eardrums.

We caught sight of Bella Dwyer as we walked through the mill doors. She was standing on the landing by the doors of the spinning hall, near the steps that led up to the offices of the powers that be. She'd one arm lapped round her waist while her other hand clasped her mouth tight. It struck me that if she were to loosen her grip an inch, the floodgates would open.

'Are you alright, Bella?' says Maggie, 'You look like death warmed up.'

'Ah, Maggie, don't start me, for I've got to get through the day,' says Bella, her voice groaning with the weight of feeling. 'I just don't know how my sister's going to get over it. Both her sons… it's terrible, terrible.'

'Your sister's boys were in Dublin?' Maggie was trying to piece it together, but her head was still with the rising.

'Dublin?' Bella almost spat the name out. 'I'm talking about Hulluch.'

'Hulluch?' says Maggie. 'Where's Hulluch?'

Bella's sigh could've been heard on the Falls Road.

'Have yous not heard? While all that palaver's been going on in Dublin, there's over five hundred of the 16th Irish Division gassed to death in France.'

'The 16th?' I could barely get the words out, what with the fear squeezing the life out of my heart. Johnny? Michael?

'The 16th?' I heard Maggie echo as we clutched each other.

'Ach, sisters.' Bella stretched out and gripped each of us by the arm. 'Sisters, I'm sorry – but yous are alright. Your ones are alright. It wasn't the Belfast ones that were in the front line. It was the lads from Eniskillen. The Iniskillings… our big Frankie, our wee Stephen…'

Her voice finally cracked and she staggered into us so that now it was our turn to grip her. Maggie had her arm round her while I caught her shawl as it slipped off her. For a minute, we stood there, all three of us shivering and shaking.

'Come and sit down, Bella.' Maggie helped her down on to the steps. I was still shaking as I took up guard in front of them so as we wouldn't be inundated with ones wanting to know what was going on, for the horn had blasted and there were still ones traipsing past.

'I'm so sorry, Bella,' I heard Maggie say. 'I knowd those two were like sons to you.'

'What is going on here, ladies?'

I'd been so busy sheltering Bella from the women walking past that I never even heard Mr Frazer come down the steps. But I made up for my mistake right and quick. I took the first three steps like a cat so as I was between him and Bella. I drew myself up as tall as I could and summoned up all my courage.

'Mrs Dwyer's just heard her two nephews were gassed at Hulluch.' He stared at me and I couldn't read his look. This was yer man that'd been so high and mighty when Bella, Maggie and them went to talk about our demands, five years ago, practically to the day. I'd be damned if he was going to play that game now. I ploughed on.

'She reared them when they were little and her sister was bad with pneumonia. They're like her own.'

Still he stared at me. From behind, I could hear Maggie and Bella pull themselves up from sitting.

'My dear Mrs Dwyer.' His voice was so respectful, I stepped aside.

'My dear Mrs Dwyer, I am so sorry to hear of your and your family's loss.'

Bella was straightening herself up. 'Perhaps Mrs Rice could accompany you up to my office where you could have a more comfortable seat and time to recover. This is grievous news.'

'Thank you kindly, Mr Frazer,' says Bella, gathering herself, 'but I think I'd be better getting on with the work. It'll steady me.'

He studied the three of us.

'If you are sure, Mrs Dwyer?'

Bella nodded. And still he stood.

'Mrs Dwyer, I do hope you and your family can take some comfort from the valour with which they fought even in those terrible circumstances.' Bella nodded. He nodded.

We went our separate ways.

It was only later in the week that I heard he'd lost his youngest grandson in the same attack.

All the rest of that Saturday, I was like a wasp in a jar. Not for the first time, I was glad of having to work the jenny for it kept my head and my hands occupied. When I got home, nothing would do me, but to be busying. I was that much on tenterhooks, I couldn't eat. I was desperate to hear from Johnny and Michael. So I did the only thing I could do. I looked round for jobs to be done and I set to. I gave every one of the windows a good clean with vinegar and water. I scrubbed every pot and pan we had in the house. Not that that took me long. I must have been making such a racket that I hadn't heard Father come in. He walked into the scullery as I was putting the frying pan back on its shelf.

'Daughter dear, you're making more noise than a dozen trumpets tuning up. I'm surprised the walls haven't fallen down. What ails ye?'

I turned round and looked everywhere but at him for I was sure I'd start gurning like a babby. It was all I could do to hold myself together.

'I was thinking I'd take a walk up to the Falls Park to get my brain showered,' says he. 'Maybe you'd like to come with me? It's a fine day for a bit of fresh air.'

I nodded and rushed past him to get my shawl.

We walked as far as Albert Street in silence, Father slow and steady, me chomping at the bit to charge ahead but holding myself back to keep pace with him. After a while, I found myself breathing easier, felt my feet lighter on the cobbles. I began to notice what was happening round me rather than being caught in fearful fancies of Johnny and Michael sliced to death with bayonets or choking for air with gas all round them.

'Do you remember that time we went to see Granny, Father?'

'Now, do you think I would forget that, Nan Rose and it being the only time you and I ever sat in a pony and cart the whole length of a day?'

I smiled and looked up at him, remembering us rocked side by side that day as the cart trundled towards Clough. It was a shock to see his face grey in the sunshine, his shoulders stooped. I'd never noticed he was old before. Fear had me in its grip again. What if he were to take sick? You didn't have to be in a war to die.

'Are you alright, Father?'

He glanced over at me and smiled. A sort of sad, tired smile, despite himself.

'I'm grand, Daughter, and it's enough for your mother to be worrying about all of us, without you starting as well.' I could hear he was bantering me, but I wasn't that easy swayed off course.

'It's just you look ... awful tired.'

'And sure, aren't we all tired? Aren't we all sick and tired of this needless bloodshed, everywhere we look?'

I felt the weight of his voice on my shoulders.

'Do you ever stay awake worrying about Michael?' says I.

'Daughter, I'm too tired at the end of a day's work to be tossing and turning at night over what I can do nothing about.'

We walked on a few paces.

'All I can do is say a prayer for him and all the rest of them – even the ones in Dublin that should have more wit.' He sighed heavily. 'Even if prayers don't seem to be making much difference.'

By Sunday, the rising was all over. According to them as were in the know, or knew ones that were in the know, Padraig Pearse had surrendered on Saturday. James Connolly'd countersigned the surrender to cover his Citizen Army fellas. The centre of Dublin was in ruins and Dubliners were raging at the rebels for causing all the trouble in the first place. Only Mammy seemed to know what to do.

'I'm for going to the Holy Hour at Clonard,' says she, 'for God alone knows what'll happen next.'

God and Jim McAnearney. Maggie and I bumped into him on the way home from the mill on Monday. He was standing with some other fellas at the corner of Dover Street, huddled round a newspaper.

'What's the word from Dublin?' says Maggie. They shuffled apart to make a space for us.

'Not good,' says Jim. 'Looks like the Dublin papers are baying for blood.'

An old woman, plodding past with the help of a stick, caught what he said and stopped.

'Mother of Jesus,' says she crossing herself. 'Will we ever

be done with one or other calling for more men dead?' She pulled her black shawl so close round her that she looked like a crow. 'There's four men from our street buried in France, God knows where, and another two caught up in all this Dublin business.'

There was a nodding of heads in sympathy.

'So, what are they saying, Jim?' says Maggie, bringing us back to her question.

'Ach, they're talking about "crime and destruction" and giving off about the looting.' He took hold of the paper and flicked through the pages until he found what he was looking for. 'Listen to this,' says he, straightening up and talking to us all, like a priest in the pulpit. '"The surgeon's knife has been put to the corruption in the body of Ireland and its course must not be stayed until the whole *malignant* growth has been removed."'

'And what does that mean?' says yer woman, saving me from having to show my ignorance yet again.

'It means they're wanting the leaders executed,' says Jim.

'Why do they never write what they mean?' says I.

'They're getting paid by the letter,' says one of the other men. 'So they're stringing as many big words together as they can.' That raised a hollow laugh.

'Blood money,' says another, his voice, like a knife cutting the laughter dead.

It went from bad to worse. The British Army started court-martials on the Tuesday and executed Patrick Pearse, Thomas McDonagh and Tom Clarke the next day. By the end of the week, they'd executed nine more. Meantime, yer man in charge, General Maxwell, had decided to round up all Sinn Feiners, even ones not fighting in Dublin. Thousands of them were lifted all over the country.

On Sunday, Maggie and I were that struck by the headline in the Sunday Pictorial, one of them English papers, that we put together a penny to buy it.

DOOMED REBEL'S WEDDING: MARRIAGE BEFORE EXECUTION

Even Mammy'd a tear in her eye when we read out how Joseph Plunkett had married his sweetheart Grace Gifford hours before he was shot.

'More power to her for standing by him to the end,' says she.

I brought the front page into work on Monday. At twelve o'clock, the weather was fine so I took myself, my piece and the paper out to the yard and sat on the yard wall with my back against the railings and my face to the sun. As I unwrapped the scrap of muslin round my bread, the usual crowd gathered round. Some of them sat down either side of me and others lifted a couple of empty crates so we were in a bit of a circle, our pieces in our laps. Thank God, we weren't tiptoeing round each other any longer. The week before had put an end to that, for even the ones like myself that had no truck with the rebels, had no truck at all with what the English were doing. Well, you know how it is. It's one thing me falling out with our Maggie, but well dare anyone else say or do a word agin her. That's the same the world over.

'Mind you,' says Bella Dwyer, 'our Frankie never got a chance to marry his lass – and many's a one lying dead on foreign soil the same.' She bunched her lips together, before letting out a long sigh. 'Not that I begrudge them being able to do it, for we all need whatever comfort we can find in these times.'

I thought of Johnny. A shiver ran through me so that the page trembled in my hands. I laid it down and crossed myself, praying that he'd be spared, along with the rest of them.

'Has anybody heard any word about James Connolly?' says Susan Kavanagh.

'Just that he's still in hospital. His leg must've been badly shot up,' says Lily Johnston.

'Do you think that'll mean he won't be executed? They'd hardly shoot a man in hospital,' says Imelda Peoples.

'Well, there wouldn't be much point in nursing him better, and then shooting him dead,' says Mrs Hegarty. 'More's the pity.'

I looked round at the crowd of us, every one of us involved in that strike. It wasn't only me that had a soft spot for Mr Connolly. And no wonder, for whether you agreed with him or not, he'd done right by us.

Mind you, not everybody felt the same. A day or two later, that divil, William Murphy had his Irish Independent calling for the blood of James Connolly in particular. Murphy was a powerful man in Dublin. When Big Jim Larkin was organising people into the union some years back, it was Murphy that'd organised the employers to lock out any workers who refused to leave the union. You'd have to be a particular hard sort of divil to starve people into knuckling under. And he'd had it in for Mr Connolly ever since he took over from Big Jim.

'We need more people like yer man, Shaw here,' announces Father as soon as he came through the door that same day. Maggie was sorting the childer before bed, Mammy was tending to the lamb bone stew. I was darning socks, with my heart in my shoes. We all looked over at him.

'Shaw who?' says Mammy narrowing her eyes. She always looked suspicious when she couldn't place a body's name.

Father produced a folded up paper from his pocket. Mammy's eyes narrowed more.

'Is that another one of them English papers?' says she as he smoothed it out on the table and found the page he was looking for.

'Aye, but don't worry, Agnes. I didn't pay a farthing for it. I was that taken with what this fella Shaw says that I borrowed it from one of the men at the warehouse. I've to give it back to him tomorrow.'

'So who's Shaw?' says Mammy again.

'George Bernard,' says Father. 'He writes plays for the theatre. And, according to some, he's the most famous Irishman in Britain.'

'Never heard of him,' says she, bunching up her lips.

'Well, wait to you hear this,' says he, tracing the words and making their sounds slowly. '"An Irishman raising arms for the independence of his country is only doing what Englishmen will do if England was conquered by Germans in the course of the war." I couldn't've put it better myself.' He traced the words back and nodded to himself. We waited for him to carry on.

'He's saying if they carry on with these executions, they'll turn them into heroes and saints.'

Maggie folded her arms tight and straightened up.

'They're heroes already, whatever the English do,' says she.

'Maybe to the likes of you, Daughter, but not to lots of others. What he's saying is that if they keep shooting them, they'll be heroes all over.'

'More power to them,' says Maggie, paying no attention to Mammy's bristling.

'Will they listen to somebody so famous?' says I, thinking Mr Connolly might be saved yet.

'Have you ever known the English government to listen to anything sensible in yer life, and particular if it's coming from an Irishman?' Father shook his head.

He was right. We walked out of the mill at twelve o' clock Saturday to be met at the gates by lads selling The Irish News.

'Read all about it. Connolly and MacDermott executed. Read all about it.'

I was that beside myself, half of me was standing there and half of me was back on that Saturday, five years before, when we gathered round Bella and her wanting to organise some of us to call round to see yer man Connolly that was organising the Deep Sea Dockers. I reached for Bridie's hand before realising what I was doing. I looked round for Maggie or Bella, even as I was carried along by the rush of women pouring out onto the street. I managed to step out of the stream of bodies and reached one of the newspaper sellers. I was standing there, neither able to ask for a paper nor walk away, when I heard Bella's voice behind me.

'You may give us one of those papers, Son, even if it is grievous news.' She paid the lad with one hand, even as she put her arm round me with the other and steered us both over to the side against the mill wall. It wasn't long before a wee crowd had gathered round her. Maggie came over and put her arm round my waist and I did the same with her. I was practically in tears even before Bella began to read out loud. When she got to Mr Connolly being tied to the chair because he couldn't stand, Lily Johnson let out a wail like a banshee and somebody at the back started keening with her.

Bella stopped reading, pulled herself up straight and looked round us.

'I know it's hard,' says she, her own eyes bright with tears, 'but if Mr Connolly could face death without wailing, the least we can do to show our respect is to hold ourselves together.' Lily stopped mid wail and gulped down the rest of her sobs. Everybody else fell silent and straightened up.

'Now, before I carry on,' says she, 'I want yous to know that as soon as I finish reading this, I'm for walking to Clonard to say a prayer for the soul of Mr Connolly and for all those other Irishmen who've died in Dublin and beyond since Easter Sunday.' Her voice caught. I held my breath, remembering the state of her after Hulluch. But she gathered herself.

'We can read the rest of it later, Bella. It's better if we go to Clonard straight away for some of us need to get home for the childer,' says Maggie.

Bella nodded. She looked round. And without more ado, twenty or so of us sorted ourselves into linked arms, four abreast and set out in silence for the monastery.

We unlinked arms at the steps and slipped quietly, one after one into the silence of the monastery. Our footsteps echoed each other as we followed Bella down the side aisle and knelt before Our Lady of Perpetual Succour. When Bella rose to light a candle, I followed her up. I lit one for them as died and lit another for Johnny, Michael and Charles.

As soon as we were back outside, Maggie ran on ahead for she was late picking up the childer, The rest of us walked slowly back, one or other peeling off as we came to the corner of their street until there was only Bella and me left.

'You know, Bella, when I was standing outside the gates this morning, I was remembering that Saturday you roused us all to stand up for ourselves.'

She gave a snort of laughter.

'Aye, your Maggie and your wee friend, Bridie, first in line to stand up and be counted.'

I reddened, remembering how all I could think of was Mammy's rage if both Maggie and I had set off to the Connolly's.

'Do you still keep in touch with her?'

I nodded.

'And how is she?' says Bella

'She's grand,' says I 'She's still working away.'

'She and your Michael made a grand pair.'

We'd reached the corner of Bella's street.

'They're still in touch,' says I.

'And is there no sign of a fella over there?'

'Not that I know of,' says I, 'and I'd have thought I'd know as soon as Bridie knew.'

'So she's still over there by herself?' Bella shook her head. 'That takes some doing. Tell her I was askin' for her.'

I took my time to walk back home, for now that I was by myself, I realised I was like a jelly inside. I was remembering the first time I saw Mr Connolly, and me thinking he was smaller than I expected. And then he'd begun to speak.

'Working women of Belfast on whose labour the prosperity of this fine city has been built.'

We'd all grown taller then. I let my hand touch my chest where I'd pinned Johnny's wee card, wrapped in a piece of muslin, to the strap of my petticoat. God spare the rest of us to live, we might all be together again when the war was over, even if Mr Connolly wouldn't be there to see it.

I dawdled my way down the Falls Road and did two laps of the square for good measure. I arrived home, feeling more of myself.

The front door was open to let some light in. As I stepped through, the first thing that struck me was the silence. For a minute, I thought they were all out, but no. I could pick out Father standing with his back to the mantelpiece and Mammy sitting on the chair like a statue with Charlie on her knee. He came to life quick enough when he saw me, wriggling off Mammy's lap before she could grab him and throwing himself at my knees. It was only as I picked him up that I saw Maggie standing in the scullery doorway, shoogling from side to side to soothe wee Rosie. I'd no sooner thought that they looked as if they were waiting for someone, when I realised that the someone was me. Maggie stepped towards me, stopped and looked over at the table. I turned round, following her eyes to see Johnny's mother tucked into the corner, her arm propped up on the table and her head resting in her hand.

'Mrs Harper,' says I.

She reached out to hand me a piece of paper.

'I'm awful sorry, Daughter,' says she.

I smoothed out the telegram, my hands shaking so hard, I could hardly keep hold of it. I heard Mrs Harper speak, as if from far away.

'At least if he'd died here, there'd be some hope of burying him proper.'

Nineteen

May 1916–February 1919

15th May

Dear Nan Rose. You have lost your fella and I have lost my friend. I cannot stop thinking of him and of you. Any spare minute and you are both with me – but I seem to have lost my tongue let alone write. Maybe it will be easier when we next meet. Theres talk of leave sometime in the next month. Your loving brother Michael

Sheffield
18th May 1916

Oh Nan Rose

I have been sitting here thinking of you all evening – ever since I came in from the factory and opened a letter from Mammy. I have been in tears on and off since I read about Johnny. I dont know what else to say. But I wanted to let you know I will be praying for you every day that you find strength. I wish I was there with you. I will write a longer letter soon.

Bridie.

Belfast
18th May

Your letter came today Michael. I have lost my tongue as well. I too think of you and him constantly. I long to see you. Please God you stay safe. Even if that was not meant for Johnny. Nan Rose

27th May 1916

Dear Bridie

Thank you for your letter. And for your prayers. I have found it hard to pray this last fortnight. So you doing it for me is appreciated. It is as much as I can to rise in the morning and get through the day until bedtime. Words are hard. Either they are not there or they come to me and I want to lie down and cry until I have none left. I cant be doing that so its better to let the words be. Wee Charlie and Rosie make me smile sometimes despite myself. And every so often Father and me will dander up to and round Dunville Park like you and I used to do. We do not talk much but then Fathers quiet is very easy. Please write even if it takes me a while to write back. It is always good to hear what you are up to. Nan Rose.

3rd June 1916

Well, Nan Rose,

If it helps for me to tell you what is going on here, I am more than happy to oblige. And maybe like with the childer, my letter will bring a smile to your face. I am now working at FIRTH'S NATIONAL PROJECTILE MUNITIONS. Its that big, you could fit four or more mills inside it. Ever since all that palaver about not enough shells last year, Sheffield has been going toke with munitions factories. This place opened in January and with them bringing in conscription here, they were desperate for women workers. I got a job in April. So I am still finding my feet. I spent the first few weeks learning how to use a LATHE. You know you could not have a mill without a spinning jenny. Well, you can not have a munitions factory without a lathe. It is not as noisy as the mill and not as wet and damp.

I remember that time I decided to go into service with Lizzie and me saying to you I wasnt going to end up with a chest racked with coughing and hands like the bark of a tree. Sure what an eejit I was, for if you are like us that have to work hard for our living, it is going to take its toll one way or the other. So I may not end up with a bad chest, but if we ever meet again, you may not recognise me for it seems working in munitions gives you yellow skin.

Thats the least of my worries right now. What is annoying me the most, is the number of ones, women as well as men, that dont think any woman should be doing a man's job. Who they think is going to do them, I do not know. So manys a night I am coming back on the tram that tired that I can hardly keep my eyes open, when one or other that cant mind their own business starts in on one or other of us.

You should be at home and doing what a womans supposed to be doing says this aul fella to me yesterday.

I have never been one to twiddle my thumbs in my life says I. And that would be true even if I had a choice in the matter. So leave me be and give my head peace.

That will tell you how tired I was – for it was as much as I could do to say that.

Even the ones that want us working seem to think

a woman doing the same job as a man is somehow not doing the same job and so can be paid less. Still the pay is better than what we got back home and theres talk here about organising for equal pay with men. Would you ever have credited that back when we went out on strike just to be allowed a bit of craic?

Do not feel any rush to write back, Nan Rose. Just when you are good and ready. You are always in my prayers. As is Michael. I have had a few wee notes from him. He says words are hard but sometimes sitting without Johnny beside him is harder. So he's glad he has me and you to talk to on paper. I suppose that's why he is sending me a note every few days with a couple of sentences about what is going on round him as he writes. And every so often a sentence about what Johnny and he would be doing right then if Johnny were still with him.

Bridie.

Etaples, France
20th June 1916

Dearest Nan Rose,

A letter arrived from Bridie today in which she told me of the death of your fiancé Johnny. I am so sorry to hear of your loss and grateful that you have the support of your family and friends in coming to terms with a future without your beloved at your side.

War is indeed grievous. I have been based at this field hospital here for the last two weeks, tending to severely injured soldiers. I appreciate that this may be of little comfort to you – but time and again, when faced with those most seriously wounded, I think that it might have been a mercy if they had died instantly. My only hope is that with others here, I am able to do something to alleviate their suffering.

In addition to praying for a speedy end to this war, I hope and pray that I may see you and Bridie again in more peaceful times.

Yours sincerely
Elizabeth Balfour.

30th June 1916

Dear Bridie

It is as if a door has been shut tight inside me. Not just any door. A big heavy one about the length of me. Shut tight. I am alright when I am working for I just keep going. But mostly I am on one side of the door and everybody else on the other. Except with the childer. Theres no door with them.

Michael came back on leave in the middle of June. I thought maybe with him it would be diffrint. I thought maybe it would be like it was. He was always easy company even when he was bantering me. But so help me I got such a shock when I saw him. He looked as if he had been trailed through the mud all the way from France. He walked in the door just as we sat down to have a bowl of soup and potatoes. Mammy stood up and then it was as if her feet left her for she sat back down as washed out as her blouse. I was no good to anyone for I kept seeing Johnny beside him and then not beside him. I did not know whether I was coming or going.

It was just as well Father and Maggie had their wits about them. Between them they had him out into the back with every one of his clothes stripped off and a bar of carbolic soap and a kettle of lukewarm water to wash with. At Maggies bidding I fetched him a shirt and trousers from the trunk in our bedroom. I couldint tell you if they belonged to him or Charles. But I can tell you they hung on him like he was a clothes hanger. By the time he came back in and sat at the table, mammy had roused herself and was frying him a couple of eggs and a piece of soda bread to go along with the remains of the soup and potatoes.

I went to bed early for I couldint bear how hard it was with him there. As if he was a stranger. All I could think was that a door had closed for Michael as well. He slept with Father. Mammy came into the bed with Maggie me and the childer. Head to toe.

Father and Mammy were both up early the next morning. As I came downstairs I heard Father say that Michael had slept screwed up in a tight ball all night.

He was like a lost soul among us and I could see Father Mammy and Maggie wrung out with the effort to be with him. But from the minute Maggie and Father had him out the back, Bandit was straining at the leash to be with him and after the first night Father let the dog in. He had some notion she might do Michael good. Which she did for she sat at his feet and followed him whenever he moved. After a while he was talking to her if not to the rest of us. And then would you believe it? Wee Charlie lost his shyness and came and sat as near as he could to Michael and Bandit. Not saying anything. Just sitting close. After a while he brought his ball and put it in Michaels lap and stood with his hands resting on Michaels knee. Michael threw the ball up in the air and gently headed it to the wee fella. Who squealed with delight and brought it back for more. That started Bandit barking but as they played it began to feel more like Michael was home. And I was home with him. At least for a while.

He had four days leave. I was first home from work on his last evening. I found him out the back sitting on the stool with the photograph of him and Johnny cupped in his hands, Bandit at his feet. He looked up as he reached his hand to take mine. I held his like I was holding on to life itself. All that I wanted to ask him died on my lips. No words. No doors.

12th July

No marching today. The Orange Order cancelled them all. Reeling like the rest of us from the turnaround in news from France this last week or so. It's hard to take in. Thousands of those shipyard fellas that joined up to save their Ulster from Home Rule killed or wounded. I thought of Lizzie Balfour maybe in the middle of it all. Father got hold of a Belfast Telegraph the day after it all started. The first time we had one in the house. Battle of the Somme they called it. Said they sang songs with light hearts. I found that hard to credit. But maybe it helped them hold their nerve. God forgive me I couldint help thinking that at least it wasint the 16th Irish and Michael wasint there. At Sunday Mass I prayed for them all and for their ones at home with broken hearts.

Nan Rose

30th September 1916

Dear Nan Rose

I was so glad to hear from Michael after that battle at GUILLEMONT. My heart was in my mouth with all the newspaper reports of so many from the 16th

Irish wounded or dead. For when I think of the men fighting it's either him or you and your ones that I see in my mind's eye. Yous are like family to me Nan Rose and I miss you all terrible.

The longer this war goes on the harder it is working in munitions. Never mind it may be turning the colour of my skin, it is doing my head in. Or maybe its my heart. I know our side need shells and more shells. But I keep thinking it is young fellas fighting young fellas. More often than not, I wake up from dreams of dead bodies. At least in the mill we never did anybody harm.

Thanks for calling round to see Mammy so regular. I know she appreciates it. She told me in her last letter that you brought the two childer round. She said she smiled more at the two of them in those couple of hours than she had in the last year. I suppose it is hard enough with all of this fighting, without getting old and failed.

Bridie

16th November 1916

Dear Nan Rose,

Fancy your Michael ending up beside them 36th Ulster Division ones. I will look up where Flanders is the first chance I get. I always remember you telling me that Michael reckoned that fighting a common enemy was better than fighting each other. In his last letter he said he still feels like that. He says it gives him some comfort being on the same bit of ground as them shipyard fellas and hearing so many Belfast voices. I have been sending him some sweets and tobacco and this time I put those together with a pair of gloves and a scarf that I sewed up from a piece of thick felt I bought with him in mind. For with winter, he surely can't have too many gloves or scarves. A wee parcel for Christmas that I hope will give him some cheer.

I am so glad that you are not waking up each and every morning with a heart of lead. And that every so often you forget for a moment and find yourself having a wee laugh at a bit of craic in the mill or with the childer at home.

Well, I hope you might laugh at what I am up to now. I joined a football team. The factory here set up a few teams to play other works teams. I am not one for charging up and down a field after a ball, but it is a bit of a geg and a bit of company. So I help out by being a LINESWOMAN. You only have to keep an eye on half of the pitch at one side and wave a flag if the ball goes out over it.

Most of our team dont have husbands or childer so when theres a Saturday match, we go to a tea room afterwards for an early tea and then the pictures. That and the odd local dance does me, for some days by the time I'm back at Mrs Myers, it is as much as I can do to eat the evening meal, do a wee bit of washing and go to bed.

That is no bad thing for since that artist fella, I have no time for any of the men here, no matter how they come across. And it means even after paying my bills and sending money back to Mammy, I can save some of my wages every week. That way, when all this war ends and I am out of a job with all the rest of us women, I will have a bit to tide me over while I work out what next. Would you credit me being that sensible Nan Rose?

Your good friend
Bridie

1st February 1917

Dear Nan Rose,

Well, its Saint Brigid's Day, the first day of Spring, despite the weather. It is grey, wet and I was that cold this morning I could barely button my blouse. Given I was called after her, I was hoping something would happen to lift my spirits but the day went from bad to worse and by the time I was on the tram home I was like a baitin bear. I was with a couple of the ones I am friendly with and we were sitting opposite two women about the age of your Maggie. Dressed in fine thick coats and with two childer between them. You would not credit the dirty looks they gave us. The one says to the other in a voice loud enough for all to hear, I do not know where it is going to end, with young women out working instead of at home and with money to burn on FRIVOLITIES. I was about to give her a piece of my mind when I caught sight of a policewoman further up the tram. I shut my mouth tight then, for I knowd it would be me that would be seen as the troublemaker. But I had the last laugh. The policewoman got off the tram first and as she passed the three of us, she smiled and said in a voice as loud as yer womans, You must be ready for home after a day's hard work supporting the war effort, Ladies. Well done.

I gave her a big smile and stuck the smile to my face as I stared hard at the other two.

Mentioning your Maggie, how is Charles? You dont hear so much about any of them thats fighting outside of France. I am sure she must be glad that she has all of you round her and him gone so long.

2nd February

When I did get back up to my room, there was an envelope from Michael propped up at the bottom of the door. I was that delighted to see it I wanted to take my time in opening it. Like you and I used to do if we were sharing a few cherry lips between us as we sat on our step. So I took off my coat slowly and hung it up and then I sat down at the wee table by my bed, opened the envelope and lifted out this BEAUTIFUL card. It has daisies embroidered on a piece of green silk stuck on a square of card the colour of cream. I sat reading and rereading what Michael wrote. This is what he said.

Dear Bridie,

I hope this will come in time for Saint Brigid's Day. I did not know what I could find to send you, but yesterday we were tramping through a small village and a woman the age of your mammy or mine was at her doorstep selling a few cards. God love her, she looked very failed. The fellas knew I was looking for something for you and let me choose first. Mind you, I had to put up with their banter for the rest of the day. I remember Johnny sent a card like this to Nan Rose and he told me she was over the moon with it. So I hope it pleases you. I send it with all my love. Michael.

Ach, Nan Rose I sat there with the card in my hands, remembering the time when the four of us were stepping out together. Before any and all of this fighting and dying. The tears were tripping me for I just wanted to be back home in Belfast with us all together again. Even Aunt Imelda. So that will tell you how bad I was.

Anyway, I have Michael's card sat on the table beside my tin of treasures with those shells and ribbon you gave me when I left Belfast. To keep you close even though we are so far away.

Bridie.

12th April 1917

Dear Bridie,

I was telling you last time I wrote what little I knew about how Charles. is. As it happens Patrick Reilly that you will remember from the mill came home from the war for good this last month. He was one that signed up the same time as Charles. He lost his left arm from the elbow down. Maggie and I called to visit him a couple of times, for he was at school with Maggie and his mother worked with Mammy.

Oh Bridie the sight and sound of him makes me thank God and His Holy Mother that Johnny died. For it would kill me if he was like Patrick. The arm is bad enough but he is not right in himself some of the time. As if hes back there and not here.

Anyway, from what we could make out, him and Charles and the rest of them had it hard. I cannot write everything he told us but one thing that struck me was they were out there in clothes only fit for summer in the middle of winter and the mountains twice as high as anything we know here and cold as ice at night. He said frostbite got many of them before the enemy did.

Maggie is beside herself for she feels bad that at times she has been thinking Charles was having it easy. Who could blame her for there is so little news from that far away. Nan Rose

Etaples,
9th June 1917

Dear Bridie,
I have a few days leave from next week, the 18th. My aunt is not well and so I am planning to visit with her in Sheffield as my mother is keen to have my opinion on how she is.

I wonder if you might be free to meet me of an early evening after your work. I would so enjoy spending an hour or two in conversation with you. Who knows? We might even find time to share news on the division within the Union. I'm somewhat out of touch with being in France, so I am very interested that your heart is with Sylvia rather than Emmeline Pankhurst. However, most of all, I am interested in how you are.

I suggest I will book a table for us two at the Lyons Tea Room on Friday 20th at 7 o'clock. If you cannot make that, perhaps you would leave a message for me at the tea room and suggest an alternative arrangement?

Yours sincerely,
Elizabeth.

3rd July 1917

Dear Bridie
I was glad to hear that Lizzie Balfour is still well even if she is looking failed. I often think of her in the middle of all them wounded and dying. More power to her. Thanks for passing on her good wishes and for letting me know she got my letter thanking her for writing to me after Johnny. Your tea sounded right and nice.

Imelda Peoples got married last Sunday and she had Maggie and me and some of the ones you know from the mill round to her house on the Saturday evening for tea and a bit of cake. Her fella is a fisherman from Ardglass. So she is moving to over there.

That aside there is very little good news. Other than us all still being here and the two childer still making me smile. I will write more next time.

Please God, by then maybe this fighting in Flanders will have stopped and Michael will be still alive. And Please God that will lift Father a bit. There is barely a day goes by when he does not come in sighing about yet another young fella he knows crippled or dead. It is as much as he can do these days to take himself out the back after work and sit on his stool staring into the air. Nan Rose

1st September 1917

Dear Bridie

Yes. Thank God Michael is still with us. It is a miracle any of them are still standing after all that fighting at Passingdale. Since early July every day has brought news of more dead and wounded.

We are drenched in blood from both sides says Father last night. And even in grief we are divided. We talk of our ones slaughtered in England's war and on the other side they talk of courage and sacrifice.

I know what he means but I wish he did not take it so hard. He is beside himself. Despite the best efforts of Mammy Maggie me and the childer to coax him out of himself. The only one to get near him at times is Bandit. When he is sitting outside the back he lets the dog settle at his feet. Maybe she gives Father comfort with him being Michaels dog.

Despite it all Mammy continues to put her faith in God and His Holy Mother. And her hope in the next life. Heaven seems a long way off to me. But wee Charlie and Rosie are at hand. Like all childer of 3 years he is into everything. He plays with those soldiers I gave him last Christmas every day, calling each by their name. As far as he is concerned, Johnny is still with the other two over the sea.

Maggie heard from Charles last week. They are being moved to Egypt. Last night she and me walked round to see Jim McAnearney before he started his night class. To see where Charles is going. The way Jim was talking, you would swear he fancied going there himself. The land of the Fairoes. Says he. Peramids. He could see neither of us knew what he was talking about. Come back next week and I will bring in a book I have from the library says he. I will bring the wee lad with us then says Maggie. He will enjoy the pictures. Nan Rose

2nd November 1917

Dear Nan Rose

You were asking am I still going to suffragette meetings. No, not now that there are two sides to it. I have joined the NATIONAL FEDERATION OF WOMEN WORKERS. They are fighting for our rights, and for equal pay for equal work. I think that is the best place for me to be. Theres a crowd of us go to meetings together. One of them, Alice Dent, is now lodging here with Mrs Myers. She was in service the same as myself. So we can usually find something or other to talk about. She has no brothers either and when she saw me putting together some tobacco and chocolate to send your Michael, she asked if she

could maybe send something as well. I said yes, for it means Michael will have more people thinking of him. She is a great knitter and she is clacking away so he will have a pair of socks and mitts from her as well as from me this Christmas along with other wee treats. Do yous manage to send anything out to Charles with him being away that far?
Bridie

10 December 1917

Dear Bridie,

Christmas came early for me. Thank you and your friend Alice. Some of the fellas here are bantering me for having two women as well as my ones sending me gifts. You know what fellas are like. No matter how many times I say it is you and a friend of yours they do not want to know. They know I am lucky. Some here have no family at all. But between us we are saving cake chocolate and tobacco to share on Christmas Day. The only thing I have to send back is this handkerchief trimmed with lace and sent with love for you and a piece of shrapnel each. I hope the shrapnel will bring you both luck. They were lucky for me as they missed my face by inches and landed in the mud at my side. Michael.

8th February 1918

Dear Nan Rose

That was a lovely Saint Brigid card you sent me. Thank you for remembering that it is a special day for me, what with you being so worried about your father these last months. It is hard for me think of him as you say. Silent as the grave. For, although he was never one that would talk the hind legs of a donkey, he always had a kind word. I pray for him every day for he was like a father to me too.

A letter from Mammy arrived the same day as yours. So I was well pleased when I came back to my wee room after work. I must have spent a good hour thinking of you and everybody else back home.

It is a strange thing. Here I am, four years away this month and I feel no more at home now than I did at the beginning. Now dont get me wrong. I am better used to how they do things here, and I have friends that I can have a laugh with. But that is not the same as feeling you belong. But having crossed the water once, I am not sure I can cross back again. For it would not be the same, would it?

Mind you, your Michael and Charles and Lizzie Balfour are all going to come home, please God, along with all the rest, once this war is over. So it can be done. Or has to be done.

I will write again soon.

Bridie

23rd April 1918

Dear Bridie

I am on strike today. So what better day to write to you? Its not just a handful of us at one mill this time. All of Ireland is out on strike against Conscription. Well not here in our own county Antrim. Full as it is with them Unionists. Still, Maggie, Father and me decided we needed to do our bit. Mammy was contrary as always. What good would it be me losing a days wage for even if every Catholic in York Street Mill came out it would still keep going. Says she. And one of us needs to remember we cant live on air.

Anyway if she can live with us on strike I suppose we can live with her at work. For one thing we can all take it a bit easy whereas Mammy would have a list of jobs the length of her arm to keep us all busy. Maggie has taken the two childer round to call on Ellen Kavanagh. With Ellen having her babby not long after Maggie had Rosie and with her man away fighting, they are right and close.

Father is off to give Mr Deakin a hand to repair his front door. Some boyos the worse for wear staggered into it as they came along the hall to their own room. Took the door off the hinge and nearly landed on top of Mr and Mrs Deakin in their bed. The sooner they ban drink altogether the better for all concerned says Father.

One good thing with all this palaver about bringing in conscription is that Father is in better form than he has been for many a month. He thinks the Anti Conscription Pledge is the best thing since the Pioneer Pledge. I never thought I would see the day when Irish priests and politicians were all agreed about what needed to be done says he. That is nothing short of a miracle. Them unionists do not agree says Mammy. They never saw themselves as Irish and never will says he. So I am not counting them.

If only his chest would clear up he could be right as rain. He has been coughing since he got a drenching a month or so back. Mammy has been putting mustard poultices on his chest and dosing him with this cough concoction that Mrs Deakin made up. And still he coughs. Patrick will you not take a wee drop of whiskey in hot water as a medicinal says she the other night giving him one of her stares.

You know the one where she bites her bottom lip and her eyes narrow. He would not hear of it.

By the way Bella Dwyer was asking for you. I bumped into her on Sunday as we came through the church gates for ten mass. You would not credit the queues of people before and after the mass waiting to sign the Anti-Conscription Pledge. I counted six tables outside the church where you could put your mark and even with that, the queues were nearly out the gates. Well, you know what Bella is like. We had barely stood a minute and did she not have the ones on either side of us bantering away. By the time we were signed up, we were all in good spirits. Maybe they could get us to sign something every week says she for it has been far too long since I had such quare craic.

My hand is sore writing Bridie. So I will stop.
Nan Rose

25th May 1918

Dear Nan Rose

Ever since your last letter, I have been thinking of you and the others. I have been remembering our strike these seven years back and wishing I was with you now. I do envy you being part of a united campaign for something that is worth fighting for. But I have not forgotten how nerve racking it was at times that week we were on strike, with us just up against one mill owner. And there you all are standing up against the British Government.

Please remember me to ones I knew and say I wish them well.

How is it since they arrested all those Sinn Feiners

last week? 73 of them! I was right afraid when I read that. As well as raging. 73 of them taken on jumped up charges of treason.

The good thing is I am not alone. Some of the newspapers are saying that aul general French is still hell bent on conscription and is just gaoling those opposed to avoid even more trouble.

As for ones I know, you could have knocked me down with a feather the other night. It was after the Federation meeting and about half a dozen of us on the committee were clearing up the room. These are not women that I have ever heard show much interest in happenings in Ireland, although they are all good souls. Just like us I suppose. We never had time for anything other than what was under our noses.

So I could not believe my ears when one of them starts saying that the government is doing in Ireland what they did with the Suffragettes. All these military ones, says another, all they understand is fighting and more fighting. But the words that struck me most came from the two Grey sisters. They tend to keep their thoughts to themselves, but they are right and sharp and are never without a book or a paper. I suppose with there being only the two of them and them being older and spinsters, they have more time on their hands of an evening. Anyway, Martha, the older one says good luck to the Irish, for if they can put a stop to conscription, maybe there will be more can be done here. And Sadie says you would think with the Americans now in the war, they would have enough men without taking even more of our own. You know I had never thought of that.

Other than that, I do not have much to say that would not sound like a complaint. And what right have

I to complain when I am being paid a decent wage for a week's work, have a roof over my head and friends that I can have a laugh with? I suppose the truth of the matter is time is passing and I am not getting any younger. More often than not I find myself thinking about what will become of me. Like many a one of us I always thought I might have wee ones. And the longer this slaughter carries on, the less likely it is that that will happen. Every so often it hits me as I am packing a shell with powder that I am helping kill another mother's son, another woman's husband or fella.

Ach, I am sorry Nan Rose. I am gabbling on here and there is you still grieving Johnny. I wish I was sitting beside you, for it would be much easier to talk about all of this. Well, I fancy it would be, but maybe, like everything else, that might be more difficult than when we were girls.

So I will stop now and light a candle tomorrow for Michael and Charles and another that the efforts of all of you over there will stop more men being killed.

Bridie.

Etaples
26th May 1918

My dear Bridie,

I am sorry it has taken me so long to reply to your last letter. It is not for want of thinking about you and hoping that you are well. Rather it is because on top of dealing with the casualties of war, we have had to contend with la grippe (influenza to us) over these last few months. It has gone round the staff here like a dose of salts, so that at any one day, we have half a dozen or so of us at our hospital laid low with high temperatures, no energy and aches all over. So there is even less time for anything other than work.

However, I was given a few hours off this morning and I have walked up the slope beyond our hospital from where I can see the railway siding, the sand dunes and the mouth of the River Canche as it meets the sea. I am sitting here in the midst of flowers – the tulips are gorgeous in colours of gold and red – looking out on a sea like a mirror, disturbed only by the brown sails of the fishing boats as they head out. It is both a delight to the senses, and incongruous. I only have to walk back down the slope to be back in the Land of the Hospitals, a veritable city of huts and tents and to the chaos, the casualties, the cacophony of war. (Although, in truth, right now the guns are still.)

I have been hearing about the extraordinary events in Ireland, courtesy of one of our Dublin doctors, recently returned from a short period of leave. Mr Barry and I are of a similar mind in our yearning that this river of blood ceases. So we were able to share a mutual delight in his rich account of how Dublin was brought to a standstill on 23rd April by the strike against conscription.

My parents are well, thank you, as are my aunt and uncle. I am sorry to hear that Nan Rose's father is poorly. Please give her and your mother my best wishes.

I am going to take this opportunity to walk a little further into the woods and benefit from the power of Nature to soothe and revive one's spirit. So I will draw this letter to a close and look forward to hearing from you in due course.

Yours sincerely
Elizabeth

Belfast 7th June.
Mammy asked me to write straight away Michael. I am sorry. Father died in the early hours of this morning. His cough went into his lungs and he took to his bed Tuesday morning. It is hard to believe that was only three days ago. I am awful sorry. His last words were to ask for you. He wanted you back safe. It must be hard for you so far away and not seeing him. My heart goes out to you.
Your loving sister Nan Rose.

18th June 1918

Dear Bridie
I told Mammy you had asked your priest to include Father in the list of those prayed for at last Sunday Mass. She wanted me to thank you kindly. Your father was very fond of wee Bridie says she. Which he was.

I knowd your mammy was going to write to you straight away for she told me so herself when she called in at the wake on Friday night. That way you can write in your own good time she said.

It has taken til now for me to gather myself. For it was terrible sudden in the end. At first we thought it was just this dose of flu that has been doing the rounds this last week or so. Although it is hitting ones our age and not older ones so much. I came home from the mill at the midday break to see how he was, for it is further for Mammy to come than me or Maggie.

I got a shock for he was hot as fire but shivering and breathing fast as if he had run a mile. I was that feard I ran into Ellen Kavanaghs to ask her to tell

Maggie and Bella Dwyer that I was staying with him. He dozed on and off. All that I could do was to wipe his face and neck with a flannel and pat his hand.

He wakened up properly once. Looked me straight in the eye. Daughter dear you look as if you have seen a ghost he said. I am not dead yet you know. With that he clasped my hand and only loosed his grip when he fell back into a doze.

By the time Maggie rushed in after work, my bottom lip was chewed to bits for that was the only way to stop from crying. That afternoon stays with me clear as day, but I find it hard to credit how much else I have forgot and it not even two weeks since he passed away. I suppose that is to be expected for between the three of us we were so afeard of leaving him that we took it in turns to go to work and sit with father night and day.

The childer got short shrift in all of that. Rosie was like a wee shadow following one or other of us about downstairs. It is just as well she and Ellen Kavanagh's daughter Susie are of an age. Ellen kept her for a couple of hours after work and that meant Charlie could go charging about outside with the ones his age. At 4 he is not wanting his wee sister to toddle after him.

Mind you, he was still taking everything in. It must have been Thursday and I was making some champ for the dinner. Charlie was sat on the floor by Father's chair. Silent as the grave. Playing with those three soldiers I gave him. They go everywhere with him. I was at the table mashing the potatoes with a drop of buttermilk and was about to tip in the scallions. I turned round to lift the board with them chopped and ready on it. When my eye fell on

Charlie and his soldiers. One was lying flat on the chair with the other two standing on either side. He must have felt me looking at him for he looked up and spoke.

Johnny is hurt. Like Granda. Daddy and Michael are staying with him. That knocked the breath out of me. That was the first time he has said anything about Johnny not being the same as the other two.

At the end it was Mammy and me either side of Father. Maggie had roused me at first light to take over from her. I could see enough to grope my way round the bed and into the back room. Mammy was saying her rosary. Father was breathing as if he had been running ever since Tuesday. But asleep. I went the other side of him. I touched his cheek and got such a shock my hand pulled away. He was that clammy and cold. We must have sat there an hour or so with Father gasping for air and Mammy on one side and me on the other on his wee stool that was the only thing small enough to fit in between the bed and the wall. Mammy praying and me half joining in. Remembering Charlie and his toy soldiers earlier. Feeling Johnny behind me. Knowing he was waiting for Father. Knowing he would keep an eye out for him.

Mammy stood up saying I am going to stretch my legs. Well at that Father half opened his eyes. He looked about him as if the room was crowded and he looking from face to face. He stared at me. He looked up at Mammy. He tried to lift his head. I cradled his head with my hand while his lips shaped words. Mammy and me both leaned over. Is Michael not back yet? He hissed like a fire that is about to go out. Not yet says Mammy. But please God he and Charles will come back safe. He nodded. His head was suddenly heavy and my hand sank under the weight of it. Holy Mary Mother of God Pray for us sinners Now and at the hour of our death says Mammy kneeling down and taking his hand in hers.

My hand is fit to break Bridie. So I will stop. Yes. It was a good wake. A dry one out of respect for Father. He would have been proud of the numbers of people that came to the wake and the funeral except that Father was not a man that let things like that go to his head.

Nan Rose

I hope you are well. Even more I wish you were here.

16th November 1918

Dear Nan Rose

This is the first Saturday morning I have had off since our wee strike. Over 7½ years of Saturday mornings working somewhere or other. And over 4 years of working all day Saturday. I can't believe I slept in until half eleven. Not surprising, I suppose, for since Monday, I have been out every evening this week, celebrating in one way or the other. And I still have to keep pinching myself to make sure I am not dreaming.

The end of the war! One minute, I feel like dancing a jig, the next I am fighting back the tears, as I think of all those who are not here with us to see it. Johnny, your father, Granny. And those like yourself who are grieving. I am like a flipped thruppence. Not knowing which side is up.

Mind you, Monday was a day to remember for always. When the horn blasted at 11 o'clock, there was silence for a minute as it sank in that it was finally over, before the place erupted. Everyone of us downed tools in a commotion of hollering, laughing, stamping of feet and clapping of hands. There were ones twirling and jigging on the spot. As well as ones that had lost a man, be they brother or father or son or fella, smiling and crying at the same time or bent over, head in hands. Even before they announced that we were closing for the rest of the day, most of us were heading for the door.

Everywhere must have closed for the trams back into the town were packed. Those on the top were singing and waving scarves or hats. We walked into the centre, five or six abreast, singing our hearts out. When we got there, it was that thronged with people, we could only move with the crowd towards the Town Hall. I do not know how long I was there and I lost count of the number of times I was hugged or twirled round by some sailor or soldier or other, all in good nature.

Having said all that, now the dust is settling, I am thinking that the war will not be over for me until I hear from Michael that he is on his way home. He told me in his last letter that as soon as he knows he will write to me the same time he writes to yous.

And then that sets me thinking that now the men are coming back, us women will soon be out of work. I do not know what will become of me. Still, that is for another day.

Is there any word of Charles coming home? I am hoping I might see Lizzie Balfour if she comes back through Sheffield.

I look forward to hearing how it is with you.
Bridie

MARY MARKEN

30th December 1918

Dear Bridie

I am sorry not to write before now. But I have been run off my feet with one thing and another. As you will know we are expecting Michael home any day now and even though there is still no word as to when Charles will get back, Maggie and the childer moved up to the ground floor of a house in Dover Street in this last week. Now that the war is over, she wanted to find somewhere that she could settle her and the childer and make the place more like a home for Charles returning.

I am missing them terrible already in between sorting ourselves for Michael coming back. Mammy is going to move into the front room with me and leave Michael the back one. She says it will be quieter for him. That is true. But also she has not had a daecent nights sleep there since Father passed away.

At least at the last count Michael and Charles still have all their limbs. Which is a mercy. Jamie Kavanagh that is married to Ellen Kavanagh came back without his left arm from the elbow down. It happened in the last days of the fighting. It must be terrible hard to have nearly come through and then not. When I see the state of them that have come back I am almost grateful that Johnny has not. In my heart he is forever young and bright with life. Which is more than I can say for myself.

We have that flu of six months ago with us again. As I know you do over there. Do you remember Terence Duffy from Coates Street that went to school with our Maggie? Well he came back the week before Christmas and came down with it Christmas Eve morning. No sooner that than it went into his lungs.

He died three days ago but not before his skin had turned black. I felt for his father and mammy, God love them. The last time I saw Mrs Duffy was at Midnight Mass on Christmas Eve. I have never seen such a big smile on her face. To make it even worse, with all this advice to keep yourself to yourself we could not give him a daecent wake. Mind you at the rate ones are coming down with this we would be doing nothing else but going from wake to wake. As it is they say the bodies are piling up at the cemeteries. How is it over there with you?

Now that Father is not with us I am making an effort to keep up with the news myself. I feel I owe it to him for he was always interested in what was going on. It is not so easy now that Maggie is not here for as you know she took after father in that respect. Anyway I see yer man Lloyd George won the General Election.

Did you see the results for here? The cat is right in among the pigeons now with Sinn Fein running away with the election. Michael told us in his last letter he had voted for them. Not that it makes any difference in this corner of Ireland. Unionist as always.

Maggie was beside herself that none of the rest of us at home could vote. I pointed out that that was what you suffragettes were arguing all along. Says she, when Ireland is able to make its own laws, it will be sorted. In the meantime she has been taking every chance to sound the praises of Sinn Fein.

Strange to remember that when Michael went off to war he was thinking Belfast ones fighting a common enemy would stop us fighting each other. God knows what will happen now as Sinn Fein have said they are setting up their own parlyment in Dublin.

So there we are. Do you know yet what you might do for work? It seems so long ago that day you told me you were going to England with Lizzie Balfour. More power to you Bridie. You have got this far. Please God and His Holy Mother you will find the next step.

Nan Rose.

23rd February 1919

Dear Bridie

I am glad that you and those you know are still standing after that last bout of flu. It sounds as if you had it every bit as bad as us. I know we had bodies queued up here at times, but I never heard tell of as many as the 200 you had waiting to be buried in your Burngreave cemetery. And as for funerals taking place in the dark so as to keep up with the dead – that is hard to credit. Maybe we have more priests and ministers than Sheffield? We seem to be over it here but the papers are saying another bout has hit Dublin and the West of Ireland. May it stay away from the North.

Michael came home two weeks ago. Mammy broke down in tears when she saw him for he was that tired he could barely stand and himself and his clothes looked as if they had not seen water since the last time he was here on leave. He looks better now he is cleaned up but he is very failed. Hardly more than skin and bones.

Maggie and the childer called in to see him the next evening and I could see her jaw drop at the cut of him. Wee Rosie clung to her skirts the whole time. The only one that took it in his stride was Charlie. He walked straight over to where Michael was sitting in Fathers chair and stood by his side. Hello Uncle Michael says he. Will you play with me again? There was a minute when Michael looked as if he had not seen never mind heard him. Then he turned to look at the child as if for the first time. As if a lamp had been lit inside. He tousled Charlies hair. What do you like playing these days? says he. Well at that I felt like crying for neither Mammy nor I had seen as much as a glimmer of life from Michael up until then. Maybe Michael is home safe and sound I thought even if he is not the same fella that left.

Nor are we the same ones come to think of it. It will take a while to get used to. For now we are jostling and stepping round one another and trying to get the measure of each other. Maybe if he begins to sleep through the night that will help. Maggie is now expecting Charles back before the end of March. I do not know what to expect she says to me last Sunday as we walked to Clonard for Mass. But maybe Michael being home first will help the childer and me be better prepared.

I hope so too. But there are days when hope is hard. When I feel that it is not that the war is over. It has just come home.

You asked about your mammy. She is doing alright Bridie. As well as can be expected. I have taken to calling in to see her on Saturday afternoons when I know Imelda is working. The childer come with me sometimes for she likes seeing them and they like seeing her. Not surprising as more often than not she has a wee treat for them. Rosie will not be parted from the rag doll your mother made for her a few months back.

Yes. Her eyesight is failing a bit. And she is slower.

But then it is the same with Mammy. I will keep an eye on her and I will let you know.

Nan Rose

And I forgot to say to give my regards to Lizzie Balfour when you see her in Sheffield in March. She might be there before Charles is here.

26 February 1919

Dear Bridie

It has taken me until now to feel my feet are on Belfast ground despite me being home for a while now. It is hard to explain. There are times when I am back in the trenches. Times when I am back here before there was any talk of war. When everything was still young. But more of the time I am here in Belfast now and getting my bearings. Wee Charlie making straight for me every time he sees me helps. And yesterday Edward Boyle called here to say my job in the timber yard is there waiting for me.

It is odd to be back home and Johnny not. And for me to be here now and you still in England. For I think of you both every day. Can you ever see yourself coming home?

Michael.

Twenty

Sheffield
29th April 1919

Well Nan Rose,
I have finally done it. After all my shilly-shallying over these last two months, I have made up my mind. I have booked my passage back. God spares us, I will be arriving home on Friday, 6th June in the evening. After all those nights at the beginning of the year, lying awake in the early hours, wondering if I would be the next to be hit by that flu and fearing to die far away from all those I hold dear, it is hard to credit that I will soon be putting my feet down on the streets of Belfast.

What decided me was a letter from Mammy. I could barely read it, her handwriting was that bad. So, I knew her eyesight is worse. And I thought to myself what am I doing here when my own mother is ailing and I could as easily be there as here.

And would you believe that the day after I decided I needed to be home, didn't Mrs Turnbull tell me that Miss Barrows, her regular housekeeper was returning for the beginning of June. You remember she had gone home to Stoke to look after her mother who had come down with pneumonia? Well her mother died sooner rather than later and so she is coming back as soon as she tidies up the last bits of business down there. That made it easy for me, for I would not have wanted to let Mrs Turnbull down. She is a decent sort and getting this temporary housekeeping job was an answer to my prayers when the munitions work stopped.

And just so you know me when you see me, I am sending you this picture from the local paper. That's me, two from the right with four of the other girls I worked with in munitions. We met up at the park on Easter Monday for there was a band and a fair there. The photographer fella took a shine for Betty and who could blame him? Thats her in the middle beside me. He would still be chatting away with her, but we dragged her off with us. I only got the paper today after I had posted a wee note to Michael. So maybe you could show him the picture as well.

So there we are. I cannot wait to see you again.

Bridie.

I'd picked up Bridie's envelope from the floor as I opened the door. I'd been first home as usual on Saturday, for since Father had passed away, Mammy had taken to calling in to Saint Mary's Church on a Saturday for an hour or so on the way home. As for Michael, it'd be at least two o' clock before he came in the door, if then. Although him being back in the timber yard had steadied him, he seemed to find Saturdays hard. Not surprising, I suppose, given that was when he and Johnny might have headed down to the Hibs together.

I folded Bridie's letter and took the paper over to the window, the better to see her photograph. There she was with a striped blouse that had a collar like a sailor's but with scalloped edging and with a brooch pinned at the front. She was wearing a straw boater complete with ribbons that wouldn't've looked out of place on one of them suffragettes way back then.

I walked over to where our one mirror hung by the side of the scullery door. For the first time in I don't know when, I stared at myself long and hard. To be fair, I was clean. At least I'd managed that through thick and thin – if only, at times, to stop Mammy muttering about me lettin' myself go to rack and ruin. I looked down at my blouse and skirt. The best you could say was that they were well washed and mended. The same as the other blouse and skirt I had.

I looked back at my face. My hair was parted in the middle and plaited into a single rope. Easy to manage. But when had I started pulling it so tight off my face? Was it when we were nursing Father near the end? And look at those lips – set in a sour slash across my face. 'Surely, I don't look like that with the childer? No,' I told myself, 'for they'd run a mile, if you did.'

Over these last couple of months, I had been so delighted every time I thought that Bridie might come back. In my mind's eye, I'd seen us picking up from where we had left off and her looking just a bit older than when she'd left. Now, faced with a photograph of the woman she now was, I could feel my guts tighten into a knot. A woman like that wouldn't want to be seen with a woman like me, would she?

I walked back to the window and picked up the paper. I stared at it till the clock chimed the quarter hour and roused me. Aye. Roused me. Awake. Awake in a way I hadn't been since Johnny's death.

Without more ado, I went out the back to fetch the tin bath in, ignoring Bandit's pleas for the time being.

Later as I combed my damp hair, I tried smiling at myself in the mirror. It didn't come easy.

'Who's that in the paper?' I nearly jumped out of my skin for I'd been that caught up with myself, I hadn't heard Michael come in. I stepped into the front room to see him holding the scrap of newspaper and staring hard at the picture.

'Do you not recognise anyone there?' says I.

He studied the print.

'Ladies in Norfolk Park? Sure who would I know that lives in Norfolk?'

'I'll give you a clue. Norfolk Park's in Sheffield.'

He gave me one of his odd looks.

'Sure what's the sense in that?' says he, putting the paper down in disgust.

I swallowed a sigh. For a minute there, it was the old Michael. Now the light had gone out again. He stood staring through the window, but God knows what he was seeing. We stood there for a minute with only the tick of the clock for company.

'Sheffield?' says he, picking up the paper again. I caught my breath. Sometimes it'd be hours before the light came back on. I walked over to stand beside him. He turned to me, his finger on Bridie's face.

'Is that Bridie Corr?'

I nodded. He smiled, delighted with himself. I couldn't help smiling with him.

'She'd a way of holding her head, like a bird looking at you. That hasn't changed.'

I looked up at him and then at the picture.

'You're right Michael. Now that you've said it, I know exactly what you mean.'

I stood there, just enjoying him being there beside me.

'She said she got the newspaper just after she'd posted

a letter to you. She wanted me to let you see it – so as we'd both be able to recognise her when she's back.'

'Is that right?' He paused. 'I reckon I'd know her anywhere,' says he. He looked over to the mantelpiece where the photograph of him and Johnny stood. My eyes followed his. There they were in their uniforms before they ever set foot into the war. It was Johnny gave me the photograph, framed and all. 'So you don't forget what yer brother and I look like,' says he as he handed me it. At the time, we'd laughed, both thinking we were talking about months.

Michael put his arm round my shoulder and squeezed me to him.

'Old friends are hard to beat.' He moved away to where the teapot was still warm at the fire and poured himself and me a cup of tea. 'I suppose I'll just have to get used to you two blethering away again.'

He walked on through the scullery and I heard the back door open and heard him talking to Bandit before the door shut behind him. Just like Father, out the back for a smoke. The only difference was that where Father had futtered with filling and tapping his pipe, Michael would take out his tin and roll a cigarette. Once it was lit and between his lips, he smoked it till he was kissing his thumb and forefinger, without another match needed. He'd told me you had to smoke like that in the trenches for there were times that striking a light was taking your life in your hands.

I went over and picked up the cup. My hands were shaking. What with Bridie's letter and then Michael beside me, everything had got stirred up again. I sat down in the chair by the table.

The line between the living and the dead felt very thin these days. I could deal with the dreams, even if some mornings the tears were tripping me or I was lathered in a cold sweat – for every so often there'd be a sweet dream and I'd waken up with the taste of Johnny's lips on mine or Father's arm around my shoulder, just like Michael's had been. It's when it happened in daylight that I got thrown. So, there'd been a moment there when I wasn't sure whether it was Michael or Father squeezing my arm. And now here they were, Father warming his back at the fire, Johnny coming in the door with Michael, and giving me the eye. It wasn't that I minded seeing them. Far from it. It was just that it left me not knowing whether I was coming or going.

At least I knowd I wasn't the only one. More often than not, we'd spend the midday break at the mill, telling each other who'd come visiting in a dream. And every so often, somebody'd talk about taking a funny turn at the sight of one of theirs that had gone, standing on the stairs or at the back door.

There were some, particularly men, who'd shake their heads or roll their eyes if they got wind of such a story. But, as Bella Dwyer said to me one of the times we walked back home from the mill together, 'You've got to understand that more often than not, men that have been fighting have seen too much death to want to talk about it. Even though half the time, they're still back there with the dead and the dying.'

I could understand that, for wasn't that where I, myself, was for some bit of every day? But I couldn't see how Bella knowd that, so I asked her.

'Our Stephen told me,' says she. 'Anytime I go back to Enniskillen to visit our Josie, I can feel her two boys about the place, as close as you are to me. Stephen'll often come and talk to me in my sleep and every so often Frankie comes with him. But then you can understand that, for Stephen wasn't even one when Josie took bad and I mothered him the whole of that year.' She gripped my elbow and I could feel her holding herself. I linked her arm closer and she did the same with me.

'Does Johnny not come with the rest of the dead sometimes?' she asked.

'No,' says I. 'He either comes by himself or with our Michael. And all he wants to do is to go to a dance or back to that Botanic Park.' Now it was my turn to grip her. 'Sometimes,' says I, 'sometimes we're on our way and he starts bleeding or he disappears. But, once in a while, we get there. We walk back into that big glass house together.' I'd never said that to anybody else. But then, ever since she lost her nephews and I lost Johnny within a week of each other, we'd an understanding.

With Mammy it was different, even though Father was often in her dreams. She'd waken up of a morning and be pondering out loud what it was that Father wanted to tell her. If there was anybody else she knew in the dream, she'd be praying for them, in case Father had come back to help them across the threshold. But nobody'd passed away as a result of being in the same dream as Father.

'It would make it easier if he said something,' says Mammy, 'but your Father was always a man of few words.'

Maggie'd shaken her head. 'I've enough trouble with the living during the day to be spending my nights with the dead,' says she.

The sound of the back door stirred me. I looked up as Michael came back through the doorway. He peered at me like he'd peered at the newspaper.

'You look as if you were away with the fairies, Nan Rose,' says he.

'I wish,' says I.

'Well, I'm heading round to the Hibs for an hour or two,' says he. 'I said I'd see Charles there.'

'Do you not want something to eat first?' says I, rousing myself.

'No need,' says he, putting on his cap. 'They make a pot of potato stew there of a Saturday afternoon. A bowl of that and a doorstep of a slice of bread for a farthing. Sure you couldn't beat that. Sets you up for a couple of games of cards over a pint.'

'The one pint's no harm to anybody,' says I.

Michael stopped in the doorway. He turned slowly, shoving his cap back off his head.

'It's hard enough me looking after myself, Nan Rose,' says he. 'You can't expect me to be looking after Charles, too. You don't know him – he can be as thran as a billy goat when he has the drink on him.' And with that he was gone.

I looked at the clock. More often than not, Mammy would go on round from Saint Mary's chapel to Maggie's. We both seemed to have gotten into the habit of finding times in the week when Charles wasn't about. I usually called by Maggie on my way to ten mass of a Sunday. She and I would walk Charlie and Rosie over to St Peter's and back. If Charles was still in bed, she'd make us a cup of tea while I played with the two wee ones to my heart's content.

I roused myself and stood up from the table, ready to set to work. I gave the scullery a clean and put some whites to steep in a bucket of water and bleach. I took a notion to make some soda bread and so I put the griddle on to warm while I kneaded the flour, baking soda and buttermilk. As my hands worked the sticky dough, I settled into the quiet of the house and I found myself humming as I rolled out a circle, cut it into four farls and put them to bake on the griddle.

By the time I heard the call of the butcher's lad, the farls were stacked on their side at the edge of the griddle and I was more than ready to pass the time of day with the neighbours. Wee Alec, scrawny as the meat scraps on his wheelbarrow, would be at the corner. As I headed in that direction, I could see him elbow Mrs Pick and hear her gulder of laughter.

I got a ham bone and then walked down as far as Chapel St to get a few vegetables from yer man that had his barrow at the corner of St Mary's. I couldn't have been gone more than an hour. The front door was open and I walked in expecting to find Mammy back. So you can imagine my shock to see Charles slouched in Father's old chair by the fireplace. His head lolled back and I could see blood dripping from a cut above his right eye, as well as from his bottom lip which was split and swollen. I dropped the basket on the floor and rushed over to him.

'Mother of God, what's happened to ye?'

Michael called from the scullery. 'I'm trying to sort him out before Maggie catches sight of him. Can ye give us a hand?'

I rushed into the scullery. He was reaching up for the baking bowl from the shelf in the far corner. He turned, clasping the bowl and gave me that half smile, half plea that melted my heart every time. There wasn't a mark on him and he wasn't away in that place where I couldn't reach him. I was that relieved, I sagged against the wall.

'Just put a taste of cold water in the bowl and we can top it up with some from the kettle,' says I, reaching for a flannel. He stepped back.

'I'll leave that to you, Nan and I'll go back in to Charlie boy.' I grasped his arm.

'But what in God's name happened? You told me you were going to play cards.'

'Aye, so I was, but I'd no sooner got to the door of the Hibs, when I bumped into John Kavanagh who told me Charles and another fella had passed him at the door of the Hercules. They were going in as he was coming out.' He lifted my hand from his arm. 'And being the good brother that I am, and thinking of both my sisters, I decided to go looking for him.'

'And?' I was that agitated, I nearly bit the face off him. He shrugged. 'Don't ask me. I found him in Smithfield at the end of the fight.' He gave me a big grin. 'If you think Charles is bad, you should see the other fella.'

I glared, but it was like water off a duck's back. He was still smiling as he turned into the front room.

I didn't follow him in straight away but took a minute or two to steady myself, leaning on the jaw tub and saying a prayer to Our Lady. I walked back in to find Michael had pulled a chair across from the table and was sitting beside Charles.

'Here you go, Sister,' says he, standing up to give me his chair. As I sat down, I pulled Father's stool across from the fireplace to between Charles and me and sat the bowl on it. It was only then that I noticed his knuckles. They were skint and scraped like someone had used a grater on them. I dipped the flannel in the bowl and wrung it until it just oozed water and began to dab at his forehead, holding his head towards me with my other hand.

I was nearly drunk with the smell of porter on his breath and on his shirt. I was that annoyed at him for getting into that state that I must have jabbed too hard. His arms flailed up and he made to push me away.

'Easy Charles, easy.' Michael placed his hands on Charles' shoulders. 'It's only Nan trying to sort you out. You wouldn't want Maggie and the childer seeing you like this.'

Charles raised his head just off my palm. 'Whoever the hell likes can see me like this. I don't give a damn.' His voice was slurred, his eyes wild. His head slumped back again. I gritted my teeth for so help me, I felt like shaking him. I dabbed as gently as I could, only for fear of him flailing about again. I rinsed the flannel and wrung it out tight. I pressed it against his forehead to see if I could stop the bleeding.

'If you can keep your hand to this,' says I to Michael, 'I'll go and change the water and see if I can find the makings of a bandage.'

When I returned with a square of muslin and some washed sheep wool, Charles had straightened himself up in the chair and was holding the flannel to his head himself.

'Can you tear that into thin strips?' says I to Michael, handing him the muslin. 'There's a pair of scissors in the drawer in the table.' I gave Charles the wool to press against his cut and took the flannel to rinse out under the tap in the scullery. When I came back into the kitchen I saw Michael had a pile of strips all ready. I settled myself back down on the chair.

'So who was yer man?' says Michael to Charles. 'You must have gone at him right and hard for by the size of him he could easily have flattened you.'

'It was that divil of a sergeant, Taylor!' He grinned like the divil incarnate himself. I shivered at the hate in his eyes.

'Oh, that was the gombeen that was in charge of yous throughout.' Michael laughed again. 'He deserved what was coming to him then. As if we weren't all deep enough in hell, without having a bloody boar for a sergeant.'

I remembered Charles's stories about the same hallion the one time he was back on leave, but I said nothing. I concentrated on cleaning the fingers of Charles's left hand.

'Don't look so serious Nan Rose. I'll live to fight another day.'

I looked up. Charles was staring down at me.

'Have you not had enough fighting to do you a lifetime?' It was out of me before I knowd it.

'And what would any of you at home know about that?' He growled and turned away.

'Ach, Charles. Sure you know Nan's just worried about ye. And look at the way she's looking after ye.' Michael squeezed Charles's shoulder. I buttoned my lips.

'You're a ministering angel, Nan Rose, even if your thoughts are not entirely kind,' says Charles. His tone was light. 'And if you'd known what Taylor was like, I swear you'd have laid into him yourself.' I felt my anger dissolving. I met his gaze, smiling, even as I shook my head.

He freed his hand from mine. He reached up and stroked my cheek, his fingers tracing the line from the corner of my eye to my lips. It set a tremor through me so that I paused, lost for a second.

'I need to change this water again,' says I. I rinsed out the flannel, wrung it out and handed it to Michael. 'You could start on his other hand.' I stumbled into the scullery as he sat himself down in the chair.

I leaned on the rim of the jaw tub, the feel of his fingers still fresh on my skin. Tears stung my eyes. I ran the cold water and splashed it over my face. And still the tears came. I didn't know whether I was crying for the two of them that had come back or for Johnny who hadn't or for those of us left picking up the pieces.

'Get a grip on yourself,' I muttered. 'There's enough trouble in the world without you adding to it.'

At that minute, there was a knock at the door and I heard Mrs Pick's voice.

'I came over to see if ye were alright Charles, for I seen Michael helping ye up the street and then this fella came to my door looking for you.'

For once in my life I was glad to hear the aul biddy. I splashed more water on my face, patted my cheeks dry and bustled in with a fresh bowl of water.

A failed lookin' fella with a thatch of black hair was standing beside Mrs Pick, and both of them looking at Charles as if he was Cuchulain himself. Michael meantime seemed to have forgotten what he was supposed to be doing, for he was standing up, arms folded, with the flannel lying on the stool. I jostled him out of my way and sat myself down again. Charles was sitting even straighter in the chair with a grin splitting his face from side to side.

'This is Albert, Nan,' says Michael. 'He and Charles were in the same squad.'

'Aye,' pipes up Charles. 'He knows better than most that Taylor deserved all I gave him and more.'

'I do that,' says Albert. The two of them gave each other a nod. Like Bella and me, they'd an understanding that wasn't for others.

Albert gave Charles a gentle punch on the shoulder.

'You did us all proud today, Charlie. You blattered him good and proper, you did.' Turning to the rest of us, he says, 'It would've done your hearts good to see this man today. He was a credit to all who know him.' As I bathed Charles's right hand in the bowl, I glanced up at his porter and bloodstained shirt, his bottom lip that looked like a peeled tomato, and his swelling right eye. 'Whatever you say, say nothing,' I muttered to myself.

'So did you see how it started?' says Michael. 'For I only came in at the tail end, just in time to shoulder yer man here away before the peelers arrived.'

'Mother of God! The peelers, did you say?' Mrs Pick clasped both hands to her face. Fair play to her, she knew when to come in to add spice to any story.

Albert ignored her and cleared his throat, aware that his moment had come.

'I bumped into Charlie boy here in Smithfield and we decided to wet our lips at the Hercules Bar. The craic was good and we ordered another. But hardly had we gotten the first sup down us, when who should we see walk past the doorway but aul Taylor himself. You couldn't mistake him, for he was walking every bit like he was still on the parade ground. Yer man here was in the middle of another sup and was that agitated, he spilt a good quarter of the porter down his shirt.'

'You're bloody right I was agitated. I couldn't wait to get my hands on him now we were on equal terms. Many's the time I'd sworn to myself that if God spared us both to live, I'd settle some scores with him, once and for all.'

Charles's hand had tightened into a fist. I looked up. His face was flushed, his eyes blazing. I'd never seen him like this before and I'd never put him down as a street fighter. I began to seriously wonder what Maggie was contending with.

'He'd another sup and told John, the barman, to keep an eye on the rest till he came back. Then he was out the door after Taylor faster than a greyhound from the starting pen.'

Albert turned to Charles and gave him another soft punch on the shoulder. I uncurled his fist, wrapped a strip of the muslin round his knuckles and got him to hold the wool with that hand while I set to on the right.

Albert turned back to the rest of us. 'I caught up with him, just as we spotted Taylor bent over a display of books at one of the stalls. "Sergeant Taylor, you aul divil," he shouts. "Seeing you here is an answer to my prayers." Taylor glances round and straightens up. "Rice and McCollum. It's the bad pennies that always show up." His bottom lip curls into that sneer of his as he turns back to his books.

'Yer man here goes right up to him. "Are ye looking for a book on good manners, Sarge? Don't worry about that for I'm here to give you a lesson in person." And with that he swings him round and knocks the hard hat off him. Well you should've seen the look on Taylor's face. He was like a bull that's had his ring tugged hard.' Albert stuttered with laughter. Not content with words, his whole body was telling the story. I couldn't take my eyes off him, and him weaving this way and that.

'He swings that big right arm of his, Charlie ducks and

then catches him square on the chin. Taylor staggers and then, the dander up, doesn't he charge at yer man here?' Albert paused for breath.

'But sure he has the measure of Taylor. He clasps both hands together in a fist and swings into his guts like a sledgehammer.' Albert's swing nearly did for Mrs Pick but she stepped back just in time. Not that he'd noticed.

'He topples back into a crate of books. By this time the shop keeper is out yelling for them to get away from his shop and a crowd is gathered round, rooting for Charlie here, for I'd told them what was going on.'

Albert looked from one to the other of us, his smile splitting his face. He couldn't've looked more delighted if he'd died and found himself in heaven. He turned back to Charles.

'And you didn't let us down, Charlie, boy. You gave it to him for all of us.' He turned back to us. 'We had to pull this fella off Taylor in the end or he'd've been up for murder.'

We were that busy looking at the two of them that we didn't see Maggie arrive until she pushed past Mrs Pick. She must've run from her house as fast as she was able, for she just stood there, red in the face, panting for breath and with both hands supporting her back. A curtain of hair had worked itself loose from her bun and straggled across her right shoulder. She stood there, staring at Charles. I couldn't take my eyes off her, for the last time I'd seen her so… beside herself, was that night Jim McAnearney showed us that globe and it hit her just how far away Charles was. I started to rise from the chair – whether it was to give her my place or get out of the way between her and Charles, I'll never know. Trust Mrs Pick to not be fazed at all.

'Sit down before you fall down, Daughter,' says she.

'I'm not here to pass the time of day,' says Maggie, shooting her a look that would've had anybody else scurrying for the door. Albert took the hint, flattened his cap on his head, bade us all well and was out the door faster than a mouse with a cat at its tail. And still, Mrs Pick didn't budge. She stood, arms folded across her chest, head to the side and eyes fixed on Charles and Maggie, waiting for the makings of another bit of gossip to play out.

I found my voice.

'Could I walk back over with ye, Mrs Pick, and get that pan you borrowed yesterday? I need it if I'm to have the dinner ready for Mammy coming in.' I didn't wait for an answer but stood in front of her, ready to go. Even she didn't have the brass neck to stand her ground.

As I closed the door behind the both of us, I could hear Maggie half shouting, half crying, 'In God's name, what happened to ye?'

I took my time, crossing back over the street, for I'd no stomach for Maggie's anger or tears. So I was flummoxed to walk back in to hear a gulder of laughter from her.

There they were, the three of them – Michael on the stool and Maggie on the chair I'd been on, resting her elbow on the arm of Father's old chair, where Charles was sitting taller. She'd finished bandaging his right knuckles and he had his left hand resting on her shoulder. They turned as one and smiled at me.

'Ach, Nan Rose, you're turning into a force to be reckoned with,' says Charles.

'Aye,' says Maggie. 'That's the first time I've seen Mrs Pick leave this house before she's good and ready.'

I put the pan on the table. Michael got up from the stool.

'Sit yourself down here, Nan Rose. There's a drop of tea still in the pot, if you want it.'

I nodded and he poured me a cup. I could feel myself growing bigger in the glow of their words. I glanced over as Charles looked up at Maggie. She smiled back, and in that moment, she was nearly as soft towards him as when they first met.

'And what do you think of yer man here?' says she, turning to me. 'Taking on that bull of a sergeant and giving him what was owed him.' She didn't wait for a reply but turned to smile again at Charles. 'You stood up to him, good and proper. There's not every man that'll do that.'

That's true, and if Maggie was happy, who was I to think anything different? We sat on for another little while or so, enjoying the craic, before the clock striking the quarter hour shook us out of ourselves.

'Oh, Mother of Jesus,' says Maggie, 'I've left Mammy with the childer. We'd better be getting back, before she has to come looking for us.'

That night, I sat for a while in Father's chair, after Mammy and Michael had gone to bed. That was the time the departed were closest. Sometimes you could even talk with them, although the words were all inside. Johnny came and sat across the hearth from me. I could feel him there, even if I couldn't see him clearly.

'I don't know, Johnny. I wish with all my heart that you were here,' says I, 'but, every so often, I find myself wonderin' just how it would be if you were.' I could feel his smile, even as he waited for me to go on.

'I don't think I could bear it, if you were here and not the same man that went away. And I've yet to come across a man that's been able to do that.'

The tears were beginning to trip me. I took my handkerchief out of my pocket and gave my nose a good blow. And still the tears came. Johnny was now hunched up on Father's stool beside me. I could feel the heat of his hand on mine.

'We're not the only ones to have changed,' says he. 'I left

a girl behind and I'd've come back to a woman.' I felt him lean to kiss the top of my head. 'And a fine one at that.'

I blew my nose again.

'I suppose it's different if people become more of themselves. It's when you feel they've become less of themselves that it's hard,' says I. 'Look at Maggie and Charles. Before I met you, I thought that's the way I'd want to be in love. And now ...' At the thought of the two of them, I found the tears choking me. I sunk my head into my hands. 'I can't bear to see Maggie so unhappy at times. And those times when she's so ... hard ... and bitter with anger, it cuts me to the quick.' As I heard the words, I realised I'd never said this to anybody before. Not even myself. And still Johnny was there, willing to listen and not hold what I said against me.

As we sat there, him and me in the silence, it came to me like a bolt from heaven. When Maggie was bitter with Charles, I felt bitter with her. She'd no right not to be happy. He was back and they had to make the best of it. They had to keep loving one another. Otherwise, what hope was there for any of the rest of us? I was that shocked at my thoughts, I stopped crying.

'And to think Nan Rose that you were the one always chiding me for expecting too much too quick – and here you are doing the same,' says Johnny. 'Give them time, Nan Rose, give them time.'

I could almost feel him finger my hair as it curved in at my collar bone. And even though I wasn't looking at him, I could see his smile. So soft, it nearly took my breath away.

And with that he was gone, as quickly and quietly as he'd come.

I sat for a while, staring into the coals, before rousing myself to bank up the fire. I was bone tired. I took the stairs, one slow step at a time.

The next morning, Maggie and I meandered back from Mass, linking arms, while Charlie walked, hand in hand with Rosie, ahead of us. Since Charles had come home, Rosie clung to Charlie more. And good brother that he was, he put up with that most of the time.

'When you came through that door yesterday,' says I, 'I thought you were ragin' at Charles.'

'I was that,' says she, 'for when Mrs Bryce came to tell me that her husband had seen Charles in a fight with a man twice his size, my heart was in my mouth. I didn't know if I'd find him alive or dead.' She paused. 'And between you and me, Sister, there was a minute when I didn't care one way or the other.'

In the silence between us, I watched Charlie lift Rosie by the waist and give her a burl round, heard their laughter break open the quiet of the street, and couldn't help smiling.

'God willing, maybe it'll be easier for them than for us,' says I.

'It'd be easier for me, if I could believe God cared one way or the other,' says she.

I glanced up and met her eye.

'Make no mistake, Nan Rose, it's not for want of trying. So help me, it's not.'

I nodded and linked her closer. We walked on, each with our own thoughts and eventually turned into her street. The childer ran on but Maggie called them back before they'd reached their door.

'Just you two stay with your Aunt Nan and me, for I don't want you clattering through the house and waking your father.'

At the mention of Charles, their smiles dropped. They looked at each other and then at the cobbles, before prising the two of us apart so that the four of us walked the last few yards, hand in hand.

I felt like a child myself, almost tip toeing into the wee square of a hall. As we stepped through the doorway of the front room, we heard a volley of snores from upstairs, so loud they seemed to be glancing off the walls. Between the drink and the fight of yesterday, it sounded like Charles was dead to the world. No fear any of us disturbing him. If anything, it'd be a miracle if Maggie managed to rouse him for the twelve o'clock mass.'

It wasn't the first Sunday Charles's snores had met us at the front door. But it was as if today, I was hearing them for the first time.

As I helped the two childer out of their church clothes, swapping Charlie's shirt and Rosie's pinny for their weekday ones so they could go out the back and play in the sunshine, Maggie busied herself with teapot and cups. I could feel the tightness that had come over her since we'd begun to walk down her street. Gazing round the room, I could feel its through-other air. Nowadays it seemed as much as Maggie could do to get through a day, let alone bother washing the half of the crocheted curtain on the front window or dusting and polishing her few treasures on the mantelpiece.

I ran my eye across the framed linen sampler that stood at one end of the mantelpiece. The young half-timers under her charge as doffing mistress had given it to her as a wedding present. Overlooked by a crescent moon and encircled with stars were the words 'moon and stars pour their healing light on you and your home'.

At the other end was a photograph of her and Charles on their wedding day in its frame of elm. It was a studio photograph taken in a wee studio near St Mary's. Charles had taken to going up to the hare coursing at Hannahstown on the first Saturdays of the spring months. He'd felt in a lucky mood seeing as he and Maggie were agreed on marriage and had placed a bet on the wining lurcher. When he'd told

Maggie where he'd gotten the money, she agreed to have the photograph taken but on condition he never again bet on any animal killing another.

I stared at Maggie in the photograph... to think then she was younger than me now. Even though you were supposed to be solemn, you could see her happiness in her eyes, feel a big smile twitching at the corner of her lips. And there was Charles, looking every inch of a fine gentleman.

As I sat there, a gloom was shrouding me thicker with every snore fired from the bedroom above. I must've been sleepwalking these last number of months, for all this to have passed me by. Yes, sleepwalking – until yesterday's incident had shaken me awake.

'You must think me awful ungrateful, Nan Rose.'

Maggie's words elbowed me out of my thoughts. She was standing at the table in the corner, one hand holding the teapot and the other resting on her hip. I shook my head to clear it for I couldn't quite take in what she was getting at.

'What I mean is that there you are with your man dead and gone, along with lots of others we know – and here am I begrudging the fact that Charles has come back a bit different.'

'More than a bit,' says I, 'although to tell you the truth, I've been that caught up in nursing my own trouble and worrying about the difference in Michael, that I hadn't really taken in just how much Charles has changed.'

She'd poured the tea but was still standing. I got up and went to her. We sat ourselves down either side of one of the table corners so that our elbows nudged one another. She set her chin into her hands like a cup in a saucer. Over her head, the wedding photograph caught my eye again.

Says I, 'I don't know which is worse - your man dying or your man changing in ways you'd never reckoned. Either way you lose the man you fell for.'

She sighed and took a sup of tea. From the back I could hear Charlie and Rosie playing with the wee ones from down the street.

'It's a quare business,' says Maggie, 'for half the time, he's the man I know and the other half the time, he's a stranger. Not that that's all bad. Sometimes of an evening, when the childer are in bed, he'll sing me a song, for he's picked up tunes from across the four corners. And although I don't often understand the words, they usually make me think of him and I taking our ease by a wee stream of a peaceful summer evening.' She eased her chin from her hands and began rubbing the back and side of her neck with her fingers.

'Other times, with or without drink on him, he's cold as ice, hard as nails and you feel as if you're walking on eggshells. If there's no drink on him, then I just keep the childer and myself out of his way until he comes out of it. But with the drink, he can turn on a sixpence.'

'Has he? ...' I couldn't get my words out.

'He hasn't laid a finger on me, if that's what you're asking,' says she, 'but that's because the one and only time he lifted his hand, I told him, if he ever did, I'd take me and the childer out of here and not come back.'

'Mother of God, Maggie,' says I, for want of anything better to say.

The sound of snoring overhead stopped. Maggie heaved herself up from her chair. 'You'd better be getting on,' says she. 'He's liable to be like a bear with a sore head.'

I did as I was bid but as I was going out the back to say cheerio to the childer, I could hear Maggie behind me talking as if to herself.

'The thing is, if he ever did cross that line, then I don't know what would happen, and nor does he.'

Twenty-One

Sunday 29th June 1919

'And to think, I was worried about coming home to Aunt Imelda ruling the roost. If you'd told me that her not being able to get out of her bed would be even more trouble, I'd never have believed you.'

It was Sunday morning and Bridie and I were sauntering round Dunville Park after ten o'clock mass. It was the first chance we'd had to have an hour together since she'd arrived back, for between her mother and Aunt Imelda, she'd been run off her feet. When she'd first arrived home, I'd called round a couple of times to her. But her head was that turned between the state of her mammy and the demands of Imelda that it was hard to do more than pass the time of day. After that I'd left it up to her to call when she'd a chance but the most Michael or I had seen of her was the odd time she'd call in for a quarter of an hour or so on her way somewhere else.

I could see that had thrown Michael into not knowing where he stood with Bridie. But for me, it'd given me a chance to gather myself. From the day and hour she'd sent me that newspaper photograph, I was minded to not let myself down in front of her. I'd begun to get back into the habit of taking a bit of pride in how I looked. I started washing my hair and myself every Saturday afternoon. I'd bought a blouse second-hand through Bella Dwyer and made up a skirt from an end of a roll. Navy blue it was, with tiny white dots. Over my one Sunday best petticoat, it swished as I walked and the sound brought a smile to my face, for I felt I could hold my own beside Bridie.

I glanced over at her. I noticed the shadows under her eyes, the slight stoop of her shoulders. The last few weeks had taken their toll.

'There I was thinking I was getting Mammy back on her feet and I'd be able to look for some work myself, out of the house.' She stopped still and turned to face me. 'Even though I know it was an accident, in my bad moments I think Imelda fell off that stool to spite me.' She was looking that cross, I daren't say a word. She leaned in closer. 'And in my worse moments, God forgive me, I wish it'd been a bloomin' stepladder and we'd be done with all of this.'

Well, at that, we both burst out laughing. And, in the laughter, I felt us come back together. I could've been seven, twenty-one or any and every age between, for hadn't we been part of each other's life throughout?

Says I, when we'd recovered ourselves, 'You've got to give her her due. Over the years, we've laughed more at Imelda than anybody else we know.'

'Yes,' says Bridie, 'because laughing's better than crying, any day.'

'It is that,' says I, 'but it's not everybody you can do both with.' For me, I'd never come as easy as with her and Johnny. But maybe that was because we hadn't been much more than childer then.

We walked on, linking arms.

'So are you all square with the two of them that run the shop, Bridie?' She had come back to find that not only was her mother failed but that she was behind with orders from the dress shop where she got most of her work from.

'Mammy and I are bringing the last of the orders down this afternoon. We'll see then what's what.' She sighed, loud and heavy. 'It's taken a while to get through them, even though Mammy has done most of the work. The futtery bits, like buttonholes and fancy trimmings that I've been sewing can take an age. It is just as well I've a bit of savings, for those two have refused to pay over a penny until all the orders were complete.'

'I have to hand it to you, Bridie. I wouldn't've thought you had it in you to be able to do that.'

'Well, remember I had those months in that sewing shop between leaving the Archers and Firth's Munitions. I realised then that I'd taken in more from Mammy than I knew, only until then, I'd never sat still long enough to put it into practice – and working there certainly sharpened and quickened my sewing.'

We stopped by one of the benches near the fountain to take in the couples and families out for a dander.

'Would you look at the brim on that hat,' says I, gazing at a woman wearing a hat the colour of clouds before a soft rain. The brim was wide and swirled with mother of pearl lace and pinned with two dove feathers on one side. 'It's just as well he's a bit smaller than her for otherwise they wouldn't be able to link arms without her doing him an injury.'

'A hat like that's not for walking in,' says Bridie. 'You'd need a horse and carriage to sit in and show that off.'

After a while of sitting there and being pass-remarkable at the fripperies of fashion, we rose to head back. Bridie was easier in herself.

'At least I managed to say a prayer for Imelda as well,' says she. 'Our Lady will have more sympathy than I do.'

As we meandered our way back, I took my chance.

'Would you have time to call in for a cup of tea at ours, Bridie? There'll just be Michael and me there, for Mammy takes herself round to Mrs Hegarty's for an hour or two of a Sunday morning.' I'd two fingers crossed as I spoke, for I didn't know myself how things were with Bridie and Michael. Still, I'd said to Michael before I'd gone to bed that she and I might get a chance to call back in.

'That'd be grand,' says she.

As I looked over at her, I caught the flush on her cheeks.

We turned into out street to see Michael standing on our front step. He was looking for all the world as if he was just taking in the air. We were nearly on top of him before he affected to notice us. But I caught the smell of the Lifebuoy soap off him as he stepped back to let us in. Washed and shaved and his hair drying in a neat parting. He followed us in.

'There's a drop of water in the kettle, if yous are wanting a cup of tea,' says he, his eyes on Bridie. You'd've thought the cat had gotten Bridie's tongue. She didn't seem to know where to look. I glanced from one to the other and bit my lip to stop a grin.

'I'll get us a cup of tea, then,' says I, busying myself with cups and tea pot. 'Do you want one, Michael?'

'I don't mind if I do,' says he, as if the thought had just occurred to him.

So, we sat and talked in fits and starts for a half-hour, like one of them automobiles that ye see juddering their way along the road every so often.

'I'd better be getting back round to the house,' says Bridie, picking up her shawl.

'I'm heading down to St Mary's for the next mass,' says Michael, grabbing his cap and jacket. 'I'll walk that way with ye.'

Bridie paused in the doorway.

'If I don't see you before, will you call round on Monday evening? Mammy's going to the seven o'clock Women's Confraternity at Clonard.'

I nodded and they headed off.
I stared at the back of the door, after them.
'You might've given him a few tips, Johnny,' says I.
'Ach, Nan Rose, it came easy with you,' I heard him say. 'And anyway, what's to stop you giving one or other of them a nudge in the right direction?'
'You've got a point there,' says I, gathering up the cups.

Bridie was keeping an eye out for me at the front window. She tapped the pane before I could knock the door. When I looked across, she put a finger to her lips before disappearing and reappearing at the doorstep. She still had her finger at her lips, while with the other hand, she beckoned me in. I followed her into the living room in silence. Even after closing the door on us, she spoke softly.

'Aunt Imelda's nodded off barely a quarter of an hour ago. And before that she'd both Mammy and me run off our feet, up and down those stairs.' She glanced up at the ceiling. 'I'm surprised she hasn't worn a hole through the floorboards with all her thumping with the broom handle.'

She sank down onto one of the two chairs by the hearth and I sat down in the other. They were a grand pair of chairs, for although they were basically the same as Father's chair – wooden spindled with arms and a high back, Mr Corr had upholstered them with leather at the head, arms and seat for a bit more comfort. It was well seen that Mrs Corr polished them every week, for the leather was supple despite being nearly as old as Bridie. It wasn't that she was house-proud. Bridie'd told me a long time ago that that was her mother's way of being with her father.

A pot of tea and two cups sat on a wee stool between us.

'I've just this minute wet that tea, Nan Rose, so we'll need to let it brew.'

I unwrapped the muslin from the top of the two pieces of

potato apple that I'd baked on the griddle just before coming out and sat them and the muslin by the teapot.

'I thought we could both do with a wee treat with our tea,' says I, looking over at her. She smiled, but I could see the effort it took. I'd never seen her look so much like a beaten docket before.

'How did you and yer Mammy get on this afternoon?'

I saw her blink away tears that'd sprung all of a sudden. To let her draw breath, I leaned over and gave the tea a long stir.

'May those two roast in hell, for the way they've treated Mammy. She's been making up orders for them these last fifteen years, and she's never been late once until this last while. And the number of times she's been sewing into the small hours when they wanted something right and quick! You'd think that'd count for something, wouldn't ye? Not with that pair. Mean as razors the both of them.' She gripped the arms of her chair that hard, I could see the white of her knuckles.

'On not one of the days we've been bringing the late orders down, have they as much as bid us good day, nor asked Mammy how she was. They've never offered her a chair – and today she was drawn as a ghost – while they combed every item with their eyes and fingers, ready to pounce on a stitch out of place. I'll tell ye, Nan Rose, it has been worth every painstaking minute of that sewing to see the sour look on their faces when they haven't been able to find a single mistake, not even in this last batch.'

'So yous got what was due?' says I.

'You must be joking,' says Bridie. She mimicked a woman with a lemon in her mouth. '"Better late than never, I suppose, Mrs Corr," says yer woman. While that excuse of a man that's her brother counted coins onto the counter as if they were glued to his fingers. "I've only deducted ten percent for the orders being overdue," says he, looking at us as if he'd done her a favour. Before I could open my mouth, Mammy just nodded her head, turned and headed for the door. She managed to keep her head up, but I could see the effort every step took out of her. I swept up the money as if I was brushing crumbs off a table and gave them each as vicious a look as I could muster.'

Even as she looked at me, her defiance crumpled.

'I don't know what I'm going to do,' says she, and her voice was as small as wee Rosie's. 'There wasn't a mention of giving Mammy another order.'

I didn't know what to say, so I poured us both a cup of tea as slowly as I could manage.

'What about yer Mammy looking after Imelda while you go out and work, Bridie?'

I never got her answer, for right then, there was a soft knock on the door. Bridie pushed herself slowly out of the chair to go answer it.

I heard the door open and Bridie shriek, 'Miss Lizzie!' Barely had she ushered Lizzie Balfour in, when there was a thumping on the ceiling.

Bridie sighed. 'Mother of Jesus, give me patience.' She turned to Lizzie. 'Sit yourself down. I'll be back in a minute'.

I stood up as Lizzie came towards me, her hand reaching out for mine, her smile warmth itself.

'Dear Nan Rose,' says she. 'I am so pleased to find you here as well. I've often wondered how you are.'

She took my hand in both of hers and held it while we each took the other in. The image of the girl that she was when she left Belfast slipped from my mind's eye, in the face of the woman before me. She was wearing a bottle green suit with a blouse and hat, the colour of the palest primrose. That gave a bit of colour to her face, and her smile plumped out the hollows under her cheekbones – but there was no mistaking that she was war-worn, like the rest of us.

'And I'm glad to see you, back safe and sound. More power to ye, for taking yourself off to the Front.'

As we settled into our chairs, I couldn't help noticing her shoes. They were fine polished leather to match the suit, with wee heels, a round toe and a button strap at the ankle. She certainly hadn't lost her eye for a fine cut of a shoe.

'I'd just poured Bridie this cup as you walked in,' says I. 'It's still warm, if you'd like a drop of tea. And there's a piece of potato apple here that I brought round.'

'That would be perfect, thank you,' says she, taking the glove off her right hand.

As we sat there, her sipping her tea and me minded not to slurp mine, I remembered her letter. I kept my eyes on my cup to steady myself.

'Thank you kindly for the letter you sent after Johnny.' I swallowed down his death again. 'I appreciated it.' I managed to look up. 'I've kept it to this day.'

'Oh Nan Rose! I was… I am so sorry. Bridie told me about him and you. From what she said, you seemed made for each other. I can only begin to imagine how hard it is to lose the man you love.'

My eyes went back to my cup.

'There's many a one is in the same boat,' says I, my voice suddenly hoarse. 'And, even worse, there's ones that have never been in love in the first place.' That was a new thought to me and it lifted my spirits so's I could look up at her again.

A silence was no sooner gathering between us, when it was scattered in all directions by Bridie bustling through the room and into the scullery.

'I hope yous two are alright there for another wee while. I've nearly settled her.' She called and then she was off back up the stairs.

'Bridie wrote to tell me about her mother and her aunt.

I'd written to suggest she and I meet up, maybe after one of our women's meetings. How is Mrs Corr?'

It took me only a minute to decide to put Lizzie in the picture. For hadn't she been a good friend? I'd barely finished when Bridie returned.

'You sit down here,' says I, rising from the chair, 'and I'll add some water to the pot.' I came back in to hear Lizzie ask for the name and address of the shop. I pulled out one of the chairs from the table and settled myself while Lizzie rooted about in her basket for a notebook and wrote the details down. Then she fetched out a pair of spectacles and a large brown bottle.

'These are a pair of my mother's old reading glasses that I thought might be of use to your mother, Bridie. And this is an embrocation to be rubbed into your mother's hands and arms morning and night.' She sounded every inch the nurse on her ward round. She fetched out a brown paper parcel. 'This is a piece of beef to make some beef stew, for you will need to build up their strength and keep up your own.'

'Miss Lizzie, you shouldn't've …' Bridie couldn't finish for her eyes had filled with tears. Just as well she'd a handkerchief in her sleeve. She gave her nose a good blow.

'Thank you,' says she, her voice steadying. 'I pray for you every day, Lizzie. That's the only way I have to repay you.'

Lizzie shook her head.

'There's no need for payment between friends, as I'm sure you two know. The friendship itself is enough.'

We sat on, Bridie brightening by the minute as she and Lizzie chatted about one or other that Bridie remembered from when she was first taken with them suffragettes. Before we knew it, the clock struck the hour.

'Oh my goodness!' Lizzie began gathering herself to go.

Bridie stood up. 'Well, with all of this that you've brought, Mammy and Imelda will be sorted in no time.' She beamed. 'You'll see me at one of your meetings yet. I for one can't be waiting around to get to thirty before I can vote.'

Lizzie paused, glanced over at me and hesitated. She took a big breath.

'That depends on how soon you make one, Bridie. I will be moving to Dublin at the beginning of December.' She took another big breath. 'I'm engaged to be married to a surgeon from there. I met him in France – a Mr Joseph Barry.' She looked over at me again, as if she'd wronged me.

'It couldn't happen to a better woman,' says I, and I meant every word. 'For you've the heart of a lion.'

Well, at that, she flushed with pleasure. 'Thank you, Nan Rose. Thank you. Your good wishes warm my heart.' Her eyes were bright with tears as she smiled over at me. I could feel my own fill up in response.

'You're a quiet one, for sure,' says Bridie, her eyes flitting over Lizzie and resting on her gloved left hand. 'I wondered why you'd one on and the other off. Are you not going to let us see your ring?'

Lizzie laughed and removed her glove. A single clear white stone sparkled from a ring of gold. I suddenly felt the absence of Johnny's brass one on my finger. I'd put it in my treasure tin for safe keeping a few days after Mrs Harper had brought the telegram. I studied her ring a little longer, the better to collect myself. When I looked up into her face, it was as if the years had slipped off her. In that moment, she looked as carefree as the girl we'd first met.

'So, are you getting married here or there?' says Bridie.

'Here. On the first of December. It will be a quiet family wedding. Out of respect for all those who have not returned.' She buttoned over her jacket and stood up. I could see by the way Bridie's eyes had narrowed that she was working something out.

'So there'll be another meeting or two before then?'
'The third Monday of every month.'
'If I don't see you before, I'll see you at the November one.' Bridie nodded in my direction. 'Who knows, I might even be able to persuade Nan Rose here to come, if only, for old times' sake.'
'You might at that,' says I, laughing.

I'd barely got in the door after work on Wednesday, when Bridie called. Her cheeks were flushed, her eyes bright and she was jiggling with excitement. Just looking at her made me smile, despite being bone tired.
'I'm not stopping, Nan Rose,' says she. 'But I couldn't wait to tell you what's happened.'
She barely drew breath.
'Yer ones that own the shop sent a wee lad round this morning with a message to Mammy for her to call in "as soon as was convenient". That put the wind up me, for the only thing I could think of, was that something I'd sewn had come undone and they were looking for their money back. Mammy, God love her, just sank onto the chair, as if she'd been punched. I could see she wasn't up for facing those two again. So I says I'd go. I'll tell them you've an order for someone else to finish off, for I won't let them think we're hanging on their every word.'
I was pouring myself a cup of buttermilk as she talked, for I was dying of thirst. Bridie shook her head when I held up a cup to her, and carried on.
'Well, I was no sooner in the shop than Miss Elliott, herself, bustles over to me. It was only then I realised that she could smile like the best of them when she put her mind to it. You'd've thought butter wouldn't melt in her mouth, she was that nice. Apparently, they'd been telephoned by a Miss Balfour from Osborne Park to order a dozen blouses, on

condition that they would guarantee that Mrs Corr would make them up.'

Bridie paused to put on her Miss Elliott voice.

"'It seems that your mother's reputation stretches on to the Malone Road." says Her Ladyship. "Who would have believed that?" You'd have been proud of me, Nan Rose. I kept my face as straight as a poker. "Indeed," says I. "Who would have believed it?"'

With that, we both fell about in glee. As we gathered ourselves, Bridie leaned towards me.

'To tell you the truth, my first thought when yer woman mentioned Lizzie's order was she'd have been better giving it direct to Mammy. But then, I realised she knew what she was doing. There'll be other orders after this one, I'm sure.'

'So, will your mother be able to manage the sewing, Bridie?'

'I hope so. What with the glasses and embrocation that Miss Lizzie brought and with me helping, I'm hoping she'll be able to manage for a bit longer. I just need to get Imelda back on her feet so as I can get out to work.'

It took Michael another fortnight to make his move. He asked Bridie out to a ceili in the Ard Scoil. To be honest, he'd asked both of us to go, but I'd enough of being a stewed prune and so I nudged them in the right direction and was well pleased with myself at that. But from the moment Mammy realised what was afoot, she'd been in high dudgeon. She didn't have the energy any more for pacing and clattering about, banging pots and doors, to let the house and all in it know something was up. Since Father died, she'd drawn more into herself. But you could still cut the agitated atmosphere round her with a knife.

The evening of the ceili, she was sitting by our bit of a fire, with her hands never still. When she wasn't bent over stitching a tear in her blouse, she'd be tapping one hand with the fingers of another or twisting the tie of her apron as she stared into the dying light.

'What ails ye, Mammy?' says I. 'I can see there's something eating at ye.'

'What ails me?' says she. 'I'm surprised ye have to ask. I'm even more surprised you're able to go about as if you hadn't a care in the world.'

I shrugged my shoulders and opened my palms to her, for I didn't know what she was on about. At that she scrunched up the blouse she was mending and flung it on the stool beside her.

'So your brother, Michael, courting Bridie Corr is fine by you?'

'It's got nothing to do with me, other than I'm pleased for both of them. They're both dear to me.'

At that, Mammy grabbed the blouse again. I thought she was going to throw it at me.

'So, how do you think we're going to manage, two women by ourselves without a man's wage coming into the house?'

The thought had never occurred to me.

'But sure Michael's going nowhere in a hurry. It's taken him the guts of two months to get round to asking Bridie out.'

Mammy looked at me as if I wasn't wise in the head.

'I don't know what you're looking at me like that for, Mammy.' says I. 'Sure even if Michael and Bridie wanted to get married tomorrow, they're not going to move into a house with Aunt Imelda, are they? She wouldn't have it, I'm sure. They're more likely to move in with us.'

Mammy gave me a pitying look – the sort of pity that withered the life in ye.

'I take it you haven't seen the Aunt Imelda recently,' says she. 'I called in yesterday to pay my respects.'

'Bridie says she's just taking a while to get over that fall.'

Mammy shook her head. 'The one of yous is as bad as the other. Not a titter of wit between ye, at times.' She gave me a long look. 'Imelda Corr'll do well to get out of that bed again, never mind out of the house. No matter what's going on with the leg, the heart's gone out of her. And once you're not able to earn your keep, you can't expect to be laying down the law.'

We sat for a while in silence. I let the tick of the clock and the odd splutter of the fire keep me company as I watched Mammy twist the collar of the blouse this way and that. We hadn't got to the bottom of things yet.

'It'd be different if there was any prospect of another man coming into the house,' says she, not looking at me. There was a fluttering, like a hedgeful of sparrows, in my stomach. As it rose into my chest and throat, I felt it as feathers of fire along my insides. I didn't trust myself to speak.

'Have ye nothing to say for yourself, Daughter?' She was looking over at me now. I met her eyes but I kept my lips pressed tight. She grew that agitated, she could no longer sit still. She heaved herself up from sitting, with a difficulty I'd not noticed before. It came to me that she and the Aunt Imelda were about the same age.

'I'm away to my bed,' says she.

I nodded, still waiting for her to finish what she'd started. She paused in the doorway so I could hear but not see her.

'Ye can't spend your life married to a ghost, Nan Rose. What's going to become of ye, when I'm dead and gone?'

By the time, I heard her cross the bedroom floor above, I could barely sit still. I got up out of the chair but I was that beside myself, I didn't know what to be at. I must've faffed about for an hour, with everything churned up inside me. I did manage to scrub and halve potatoes and left them by in a pot of cold water, before steeping a bowl of barley and split peas, all for the morrow's meal.

I sat down then with the dregs of my tea and I must've fallen asleep, for the next thing I knew, I was running along the lane to Tyrella Beach. I was trying to catch up with Father, who was not far ahead of me. As the lane turned and twisted, I'd lose sight of him again. This time, when he came into view, I realised he wasn't alone. He was with Johnny. I ran even faster but I couldn't catch up with them. I started calling their names but neither of them turned. I started crying and soon I was shaking with tears. I stood in the lane, with them disappearing into the distance. Shaking… shaking…shaken. Michael's hands on my shoulders. Michael's face peering into mine. Michael's voice in my ears.

'Nan Rose, Nan Rose, waken up. You're hollerin' loud enough to rouse the dead, never mind the living.'

'There's been a fella asking after you Nan Rose.'

I was at Maggie's. I'd walked round with her after Mass with the intention of talking to her about what Mammy'd said and was working my way up to open the conversation. Without realising, she'd stopped me in my tracks.

'Is that so?' says I, keeping my eyes on Charlie heaving Rosie into a coal-man's lift.

'It is that. Asked me if I'd put in a good word for him with you.'

I looked across at her, but her head was bent over her darning.

'So, what have you to say?'

'You could do worse.'

I let out a guffaw so that the childer's ears pricked up. Charlie stopped the beginnings of his canter round the room with his sister on his back.

'Remind me never to ask you to put in a good word for me, Maggie.'

She laid down the needle and sock and gave me a long look.

'You could do a lot worse,' says she.

What was I supposed to say to that? I shrugged. Charlie started to canter past the table.

'Well, you wouldn't want me to be polishing him up like a holy statue, would you?' says Maggie.

'So, who is this fella? Do I know him?'

'Eamon McElhatton.'

'Is he one of them you know from the Irish classes, then?'

'He is. You met him Easter Sunday morning when we came out of Clonard. He was one of those two fellas that were heading down to Dublin.'

When I made no answer, she says, 'Well, clearly, you've made more of an impression on him than he made on you.'

And still, I couldn't put words to my thoughts. All I knew was that this wasn't the conversation I'd wanted to be having. At that, there was a thud and a howl from Rosie. Charlie must've tripped for he was on his knees and Rosie on her backside where she'd slid from his shoulders. Maggie was out of her chair and gathering Rosie into her arms.

'Whsst now. Whsst now.' Her voice was soft, but I caught her glance to the ceiling and the room above where Charles'd be asleep.

Rosie cried on. Maggie pressed her tighter against her chest, and shoogled from one foot to the other. The muffled cries eased. Charlie was still where he'd fallen. I could see him biting his bottom lip as he looked from them to the ceiling and back again. I called over to him.

'Do you want me to have a look at that knee, for that was a quare thud between it and the floor,' says I. He shook his head while he straightened himself up, his eyes glancing again at the ceiling. After a few minutes with still no sound from above, it was as if we all went as slack as empty bags of coal. Maggie sat back down, Rosie still in her arms and Charlie got up and fetched a knife and the piece of wood he'd been whittling into a spinning top this last week, before settling on the floor between us.

'Who wants a half of apple?' says I, rummaging in my pocket to fetch out the one I'd brought them.

'Lemme cut it Aunt Nan.' Charlie wiped the knife on his shorts. Rosie scrambled down onto the floor beside him and watched as he hewed the apple in two.

'So what am I to tell yer man?' Maggie was looking me straight in the face.

'Tell him whatever you like,' says I, not looking away.

She pursed her lips, but there was a mischief in her eyes.

'I'll tell him he might be in with a chance, but not to put any bets on the finish,' says she.

I couldn't help laughing despite myself. 'That'll have to do for now.' I stood up and gathered my shawl from the chair back. Maggie stood up. She put her hand on my shoulder and leaned her head towards mine.

'And maybe it'll keep Mammy off your back. For a while, anyway.'

I laughed, but I could as easily have cried.

'I should've known she'd have got here before me.'

'She means well.' Maggie paused. I could see she was in two minds. 'And there's a truth in what she's saying.'

I was in two minds myself, but the sound of footsteps, heavy on the floor above, decided me. I pulled my shawl tighter.

'I don't remember you saying that when you were the one on the receiving end of her advice.' My voice was sharper than I intended.

'You're right, Sister. But I'm older and a bit wiser now.' She walked me to the front door.

'And what I've learnt,' says she, her voice dropped to a whisper, 'is that it's hard for love to survive what life throws at ye. So it's maybe not worth putting a lot of store by it. Save it for your childer.'

I looked round at her and had to glance away, for I couldn't bear the flatness in her eyes.

I walked home, heavier than I'd arrived. I couldn't think who to talk to – not Bridie nor Michael for I'd put the bad look on them. And even though I could trust Bella, it didn't feel right to be talking about our family to somebody outside of it. So there wasn't anything for it, but to keep myself to myself.

The following Sunday, as Maggie and I came out of Mass, a fella greeted us in the porch. Even before he introduced himself, I knew it was yer man Eamon, for as soon as I saw him, I recalled his face. We'd barely said two words, when Maggie, who wasn't a woman for rosary beads, remembered that she'd left her pair on the pew. So there, he and I were, stringing words together while my insides did somersaults. He was a whippet of a man, with a good head of black hair and a moustache that did nothing for me. But, to give him his due, he'd soft eyes and a soft enough manner. Anyway, to cut to the chase, he asked if I was going to the ceili at St Peter's Hall on the Saturday coming. I said I was thinking about it.

'Would you save me a dance or two on the night?' He looked at me before glancing down at this hands. Well, it was as much as I could muster to say that that'd be fine by me. We strung a few more words together, before he bade me good day. I went back into the church to tell Maggie she could come back out. Before she and I parted, I made her swear that she'd not say a word to Mammy.

From that hour on, I was stewing in my own thoughts. By the Wednesday, I was like a baited bear and by Thursday, I was only fit to be tied. I finished my day's work and took myself up to Clonard to sit in the quiet of the church. It was large enough and dark enough not to be bothered by the handful of others scattered across the pews. I made my way as quiet as a mouse up the side aisle to the altar of Our Lady of Perpetual Succour and used one of my last farthings to light three candles – one for Johnny, one for Father and one for myself. I knelt for a minute or two in prayer before settling on the pew to just sit in the silent shadows.

After I don't know how long, I made my way back down the aisle and out into the remaining light of day. That's when it came to me. No wonder I didn't know what to make of yer man, Eamon. If I didn't have any choice but to find a man, any man, what difference did it make what I felt? Realising that didn't solve anything, but, in a funny way, it made me feel better. I knew where I stood in myself.

Later, in bed, with Mammy snoring beside me, I fell into a deeper night's sleep than I'd had since she'd spoken her mind about Michael and Bridie.

I'm walking along the Hannahstown Road in a big crowd of people. All of our ones are there. I can see Michael and Bridie either side of Mammy, and Maggie with Charles and the childer. I'm with them and not with them at the same time. I spot Bella and other women from the mill and wave to them across the crowd. Ahead of me I can see Mrs Pick gabbling away to another couple of the neighbours. I do a bit of twisting and turning through the crowd so as to pass them by without being noticed.

I don't know why we're here and what we're doing. For our heads are not down as if we're going to work. Nor are we chittering and laughing as you do when you're walking for pleasure. The day is not one thing or the other. It could rain and the sun might come out. I'm walking a bit faster than the rest and soon I'm up at the front with a few others that I don't recognise at all. I keep up my pace and now there's only me and this fella out ahead. He nods and smiles at me but keeps his distance. Friendly and not presuming he's God's gift to women. I smile back. I'd like to get a better look at him but his cap is pulled firmly down on his head and his face is half in shadow.

I can see the bend in the road where Bridie and I would stop and talk when we walked out this way. I walk faster for I've this notion to see round the bend. I turn to look at yer man. He's still walking but behind me. He lifts his cap at me before he's swallowed up in the crowd. So I'm by myself when I make the turn. And it's no longer the Hannahstown Road. I'm on the road to Clough and I know that once I'm up this hill I'll get a glimpse of the sea. I start running, for I realise I'm desperate to see the sky and sea stretch out in front of me.

As I reach the top, I hear Father calling. I look round and he's standing outside this cottage which is down the lane to my left. It's like Granny's cottage but it isn't. It's been freshly whitewashed so it gleams bright even in this dull day. I'm running now as if my life depended on it. And now I'm standing in front of him and I can see that it's Father. He looks the age he was when he and I drove out in the pony and cart to see Granny but he also looks like he was in the days before he died - except more peaceful and not ill.

'Come in and see this, Daughter,' says he, and I realise he's leading me into the cowshed. 'You won't credit it.'

We stand inside the doorway, with the smell and sound of the cow filling the air. He's pointing to the far corner on the other side of where she stands. I pick my way carefully across in the shadows. And there, I practically bump into not one, but two milking stools. Father's behind me. 'Would you believe it?' says he and he's laughing in delight now. 'After all these years, I find you can have more than one stool in the milking shed.' His laughter's catching.

I waken up to a thin ribbon of light framing the curtains

and the sound of Mammy's breathing. I slip out of bed, the dream and the delight still lingering in me. I pick my way down the stairs, gather my shawl from its peg and wrap it round me. I open the back door and stand there, watching the sky lighten.

I feel peaceful, the sort of peace that comes when you know deep down what you need to do. I'd take myself to the ceili and begin to get the measure of this Eamon fella for myself. I'd make up my own mind, no matter what anybody else thought. For, it's only me that can live my life.